'Emotive, atmospheric and chillingly suspenseful … one of the best thrillers I've read in a long time' A.A. Chaudhuri

'Her best, boldest work to date: a mystery both merciless and compassionate, subtly eerie yet flat-out frightening, featuring a detective as complicated as Jo Nesbø's Harry Hole. This is virtuoso suspense writing' A.J. Finn

'Chilling and addictive, with a completely unexpected twist … I loved it' Shari Lapena

'Another beautifully written novel from one of the rising stars of Nordic Noir' Victoria Selman

'A tense, twisty page-turner that you'll have serious trouble putting down' Catherine Ryan Howard

'An exciting and harrowing tale' Ragnar Jónasson

'Beautifully written, spine-tingling and disturbing … a thrilling new voice in Icelandic crime fiction' Yrsa Sigurðardóttir

'As chilling and atmospheric as an Icelandic winter' Lisa Gray

'Eva Björg Ægisdóttir is definitely a born storyteller and she skilfully surprised me with some amazing plot twists' Hilary Mortz

'A creepily compelling Icelandic mystery that had me hooked from page one. *Night Shadows* will make you want to sleep with the lights on' Heidi Amsinck

'I loved everything about this book: the characters, the setting, the storyline. An intricately woven cast – this book had me utterly gripped!' J.M. Hewitt

'A country-house mystery worthy of Agatha Christie'
The Times Crime Book of the Month

'As storms rage, people fall prey to a sinister figure. A canny synthesis of modern Nordic Noir and Golden Age mystery'
Financial Times

'Your new Nordic Noir obsession' *Vogue*

'Confirms Eva Björg Ægisdóttir as a leading light of Icelandic Noir ... a master of misdirection' *The Times*

'Elma is a fantastic heroine' *Sunday Times*

'So atmospheric' *Heat*

'The twist comes out of the blue ... enthralling'
Tap The Line Magazine

'An unsettling and exciting read with a couple of neat red herrings to throw the reader off the scent' *NB Magazine*

'Eva Björg establishes herself as not just one of the brightest names in Icelandic crime fiction, but in crime fiction full stop … An absolute must-read!' Nordic Watchlist

'Chilling and troubling … reminiscent of Jorn Lier Horst's Norwegian procedurals. This is a book that makes an impact' Crime Fiction Lover

'The setting in Iceland is fascinating, the descriptions creating a vivid picture of the reality of living in a small town … A captivating tale with plenty of tension and a plot to really get your teeth into' LoveReading

'The author writes so beautifully you get immediately immersed into the chilly surrounds … A genuinely excellent novel again from Eva. Can't wait for the next' Liz Loves Books

'The writing is skilful and the translation impeccable … I have found the Forbidden Iceland series to have a consistent quality throughout … I'm eager to read the next one' Fictionophile

'This series gets better with every instalment … Dark, chilling and tense. Another fabulous read from one of the best crime authors out there' Random Things through My Letterbox

'Cements her place as one of the most exciting current writers of character-driven, literary crime fiction … suspenseful, moving and unsettling. I loved every word and cannot recommend this exceptional novel highly enough' Hair Past a Freckle

'This series is gaining a real momentum now as, while becoming more familiar with the central characters, there is a growing confidence in Ægisdóttir's writing that could easily escalate her to the widespread recognition of fellow Icelandic crime authors Yrsa Sigurðardóttir and Ragnar Jónasson' Raven Crime Reads

'If you haven't yet read this series then you are really missing out, it's becoming one of my favourite series in crime fiction and I'm looking forward to reading the next book' Hooked from Page One

'One of the most compelling contemporary writers of crime fiction and psychological suspense' Fiction from Afar

'Another great addition to a series I have been thoroughly enjoying … an absolute must-read and a perfect addition to my bookshelves' Jen Med's Book Reviews

'Once again Eva Björg Ægisdóttir has woven an intricate tale that burns steadily throughout the pages and positively roars towards the finale … A great addition to a series I can't wait to get back to' From Belgium with Booklove

The Forbidden Iceland Series

ABOUT THE AUTHOR

Born in Akranes, Eva Björg Ægisdóttir studied for an MSc in Globalisation in Norway before returning to Iceland and deciding to write a novel – something she had wanted to do since she won a short-story competition at the age of fifteen. After nine months combining her writing with work as a flight attendant and caring for her children, Eva finished her debut novel, *The Creak on the Stairs*. Published in 2018, it became a bestseller in Iceland and went on to win the Blackbird Award, a prize set up by Yrsa Sigurðardóttir and Ragnar Jónasson to encourage new Icelandic crime writers, and the Storytel Award for Best Crime Novel of the Year.

The Creak on the Stairs was published in English by Orenda Books in 2020, and became a number-one bestseller in ebook, shortlisting for Capital Crime's Amazon Publishing Awards in two categories, and winning the CWA John Creasey New Blood Dagger; *Girls Who Lie*, *Night Shadows* and *You Can't See Me* soon followed suit, shortlisting for the CWA Crime in Translation Dagger, the Capital Crime Awards, and the Petrona Award for Best Scandinavian Crime Novel. *You Can't See Me* won the Storytel Award for Best Crime Novel of the Year in Iceland in 2023. In 2024, Eva won Iceland's prestigious Crime Fiction Award – the Blood Drop – and was shortlisted for the coveted Glass Key.

The Forbidden Iceland series has established Eva as one of Iceland's bestselling and most distinguished crime writers, and her books are published in fifteen languages with more than a million copies sold. She lives in Reykjavík with her husband and three children. Follow Eva on Instagram @evabjorg88 and on Twitter/X @evaaegisdottir.

ABOUT THE TRANSLATOR

Victoria Cribb studied and worked in Reykjavík for a number of years and has translated more than forty-five books by Icelandic authors, including Arnaldur Indriðason, Sjón and Yrsa Sigurðardóttir. Many of these works have been nominated for prizes. In 2021 her translation of Eva Björg Ægisdóttir's *The Creak on the Stairs* became the first translated book to win the UK Crime Writer's Association John Creasey (New Blood) Dagger. In 2017 she received the Orðstír honorary translation award for services to Icelandic literature.

Boys Who Hurt

Eva Björg Ægisdóttir

Translated by Victoria Cribb

**ORENDA
BOOKS**

Orenda Books
16 Carson Road
West Dulwich
London SE21 8HU
www.orendabooks.co.uk

First published in the United Kingdom by Orenda Books, 2024
First published in Iceland as *Strákar sem meiða* by Veröld Publishing, Reykjavík, 2022
Copyright © Eva Björg Ægisdóttir, 2022
English translation copyright © Victoria Cribb, 2024

A catalogue record for this book is available from the British Library.

Paperback ISBN 978-1-916788-20-6
Goldsboro Hardback ISBN 978-1-916788-42-8
eISBN 978-1-916788-21-3

The publication of this translation has been made possible through the financial support of

 ICELANDIC LITERATURE CENTER

Typeset in Minion by typesetter.org.uk
Printed and bound by CPI Group (UK) Ltd, Croydon CR0 4YY

MIX
Paper | Supporting
responsible forestry
FSC
www.fsc.org
FSC® C171272

For sales and distribution, please contact info@orendabooks.co.uk or visit www.orendabooks.co.uk.

Boys Who Hurt

PRONUNCIATION GUIDE

Icelandic has a couple of letters that don't exist in other European languages and which are not always easy to replicate. The letter ð is generally replaced with a d in English, but we have decided to use the Icelandic letter to remain closer to the original names. Its sound is closest to the voiced *th* in English, as found in *th*en and ba*th*e.

The Icelandic letter þ is reproduced as *th*, as in *Th*ór, and is equivalent to an unvoiced *th* in English, as in *th*ing or *th*ump.

The letter *r* is generally rolled hard with the tongue against the roof of the mouth.

In pronouncing Icelandic personal and place names, the emphasis is always placed on the first syllable.

Names like Adda, Andrea, Elma, Begga, Konni and Magnús, which are pronounced more or less as they would be in English, are not included on the list.

Aðalheiður – AATH-al-HAYTH-ur
Æðaroddi – EYE-thar-ODD-ee
Akrafjall – AAK-ra-fyatl
Akranes – AA-kra-ness
Akureyri – AA-koor-AY-ree
Ásta – OW-sta
Bárður – BOWR-thoor
Birta – BIRR-ta
Bjarnalaug – BYAARD-na-lohg
Borgarfjörður – BORK-ar-FYUR-thoor
Borgarnes – BORG-ar-ness
Breki – BREH-kee

Dagný – DAAK-nee
Dalurinn – DAA-loor-inn
Davíð – DAA-veeth
Eyrarvatn – AY-rar-VATN
Faxaflói – FAX-a-FLOH-ee
Freyja – FRAY-ya
Fríða – FREE-tha
Friðrik – FRITH-rik
Garpur – GAAR-poor
Gígja – GHYEE-ya
Guðrún Matthíasdóttir – GVOOTH-roon MATT-ee-yas-DOH-teer
Hafdís (Dísa) – HAAV-deess (DEE-ssa)
Hafþór – HAAV-thohr
Heiðar Kjartansson – HAY-thar KYAAR-tan-sson
Hörður – HUR-thoor
Hvalfjörður – KVAAL-fyur-thoor
Íris – EE-riss
Jón – YOEN
Jónína – YOE-nee-na
Kári – COW-ree
Kjartan – KYAAR-tan
Kristjana Dagsdóttir – KRISS-tya-na DAAKS-doh-teer
Laufskáli – LOHV-skow-lee
Líf – LEEV
Máni – MOW-nee
Matthías (Matti) – MATT-ee-yas
Mosfellsbær – MORS-fells-byre
Ólöf – OH-lerv
Ottó – OTT-toh
Presthúsabraut – PREST-hooss-a-BROHT
Reykjavík – RAY-kya-VEEK
Reynir – RAY-neer
Sævar – SYE-vaar
Sigrún – SIK-roon
Skagaver – SKAA-ga-vair
Skorradalur – SKORR-a-DAAL-oor
Snæja – SNYE-ya

Sóley – SOHL-ay
Thorgeir Reynisson – THOR-gyayr RAY-nee-sson
Torfi – TOR-vee
Vatnaskógur – VAT-na-SKOHG-oor
Viðvík – VITH-veek
Vogabraut – VOR-ga-BROHT

AKRANES 1995

They sit in the living room on the black leather sofa that's coming apart at the seams, he with the video tape in his hand, she gnawing at dry, cracked lips.

'I don't want to watch,' she whispers.

Her words have the opposite effect. He gets up and resolutely pushes the tape into the machine.

For a while there's nothing but a black-and-white snowstorm, accompanied by a piercing high-frequency whistle. Then a black line flashes across the screen and the picture appears.

The camera is pointing downwards. They see feet. Shoes. Hear whispering, then laughter as the camera moves up from the trainer-clad feet to baggy, light-blue jeans, a checked shirt and white T-shirt. Before it can reach a face, the camera is directed down again, then across a wooden floor. There are glimpses of the sock-clad feet belonging to the person holding the camera, then a closed door.

Abruptly the screen turns black. After a moment, the wooden legs of a bed appear, followed by bedclothes. The camera jerks up fast to show a figure lying in the bed, arms limply at their sides, head turned away from the camera, the light-brown, shoulder-length hair clearly visible. Although the lights are off, the grey glow coming from the window is just enough to see.

Someone pulls the duvet cautiously off the still figure, revealing a black T-shirt, white underpants and bare limbs. The arms and hands are slender, the fingers slim and delicate.

'Grab the legs,' says a voice. 'I'll take the arms.'

The person who is not holding the camera obeys, grasping a limp arm.

'Quietly,' another voice says, but it's hard to make out the words through the crackling, as if the sound is carrying over a bad phone connection.

'Turn it off,' the woman says suddenly, standing up. 'Turn it off now.'

But instead of stopping the tape, the man remains sitting on the sofa, staring fixedly at the screen as if she doesn't exist and he can't hear a word she's saying.

The woman leaves the room. He hears the front door slam but even then he doesn't react. As always, it's left to him to deal with the problem.

To make this disappear.

NOW

Twenty-five years later

Tuesday 8 December

When Elma and Hörður got out of the big police four-by-four, the snow that had fallen during the night lay white and untouched in the parking area and on the path leading to the front door, not a single footprint or tyre track marring its surface. The cabin, a wooden building with big windows and a generous sundeck, was considerably larger than Elma had been expecting. It was surrounded by birches, some taller than the house itself. Unusually for Iceland, the Skorradalur valley boasted a forest of mature trees, and the summer houses, clustered along the shores of the long, narrow lake with its backdrop of mountains, might almost have been somewhere in Scandinavia. Elma reflected that a handsome holiday property like this in a spot as popular as Skorradalur must have cost an arm and a leg, yet her neighbour in Akranes, the old woman who owned the place, had never given the impression of having any money to spare.

Ever since Elma and Sævar had moved into their new house, they'd regularly seen Kristjana walking past on her way to the supermarket, pulling a small shopping bag on wheels and wearing her inevitable headscarf, off-white coat and wellies. Kristjana was in her seventies but looked older. Although she barely acknowledged them when they met, Elma had noticed her watching them from behind her curtains.

Kristjana had last heard from her son on Friday, four days ago now.

She had notified the police yesterday, after Thorgeir's workplace called to say he hadn't turned up.

Thorgeir was forty-one, single and worked as a software engineer. Kristjana hadn't been aware that he was planning to spend the weekend at their summer house, but after she'd repeatedly called his phone without success, it had occurred to her that he might be there. The police from Borgarnes, half an hour's drive away on the west coast, had gone over to the property and confirmed that Thorgeir's car was parked in the drive but said there was no sign of the man himself. No one had answered the door when they knocked and they hadn't been able to see him when they peered through the windows, although, according to them, it looked as if someone had recently been there: through one window they had spotted plates on the table and steam was still rising from the hot tub on the deck behind the house.

It seemed likely, then, that Thorgeir was either inside the house or not far off, and that something had gone wrong or he had decided for some reason to cut himself off from the outside world. Another possibility did spring to mind, but Elma felt it was premature to fear the worst. However, as soon as she unlocked the door with the key she had obtained from Kristjana, she was greeted by a sickly-sweet odour, the unmistakable smell of decomposing flesh.

❁

Inside, the house was a fairly conventional holiday cabin, the walls and ceiling clad in yellowed pine. There was a kitchen to the right and a living area to the left. The bookcase in the living room was so crammed with volumes that the shelves sagged in the middle. There was a big, cumbersome sofa, an old TV set and a painting of a glacier. On another wall hung a picture of Jesus with a metal cross above it.

As far as Elma could tell, there were two bedrooms. Opening the door to the first, she found what she was looking for.

Thorgeir was lying in bed, his lower half covered by a duvet, which was tangled in a knot at his feet as if he had got too hot during the night. The white sheets were dark with congealed blood and once Elma got closer the cause of death was glaringly obvious.

Thorgeir had been stabbed with a sharp instrument, probably a knife. His upper half was naked and Elma counted at least five wounds in his chest and stomach, as well as two in his neck.

Elma bent down low so she could see a little of the underside of his body; pale discolouration, where the blood had settled due to gravity, indicated that he had been lying in this position since he died. Although Elma was no expert in forensic pathology, she had picked up this much after more than a decade in the police. The paleness of this *livor mortis* was probably a result of severe blood loss, judging by how much of the stuff had soaked into the sheet and mattress.

In some places, especially on the abdomen, the skin had taken on a bluish-green hue. Decomposition had caused it to swell up with gas, become puffy and start to flake off. The man's hair and finger nails looked as if they were coming loose too. A reddish-brown fluid had leaked from his nose and mouth. His eyes were half closed, and what could be seen beneath his eyelids was pale and matt, the dried-up corneas like contact lenses left out of their solution.

The body had evidently been lying there untouched for several days.

'I count seven stab wounds,' her boss Hörður said from behind her. 'That's pretty brutal.'

There was no arguing with that. In fact, it was the most violent murder scene Elma had ever witnessed. Images flashed before her eyes of the knife being raised and brought down to puncture the abdomen, not once but seven times. During her peaceful months on maternity leave with her baby daughter she had almost forgotten what an ugly place the world could be.

'The question is whether he came here with his mates,' Hörður continued.

'A party that ended badly?' Elma wondered aloud, immediately noting that there were various details that didn't seem to fit with this theory. Surely Thorgeir wouldn't have been lying in bed in that case?

And there would have been signs of a fight? She hadn't noticed any evidence of a party or a struggle.

The duvet and pillows on both sides of the double bed were crumpled. Either Thorgeir had been a restless sleeper who took up the whole bed or someone else had been lying beside him. On the bedside table was a contact-lens container. Pulling on a pair of gloves, Elma opened it. The lenses were floating in their solution like tiny jellyfish.

'He took out his contact lenses before he died,' she commented. 'What does that tell us?'

'That he'd retired for the night.'

'Hm?'

'I take out my lenses before going to sleep,' Hörður explained.

Elma glanced at his glasses, which were in their usual place on his nose. 'When do you use lenses?'

Hörður corrected himself. 'Well, I use them on the rare occasions when I can be bothered to put them in rather than wearing glasses. But Gígja wore lenses. The last thing she used to do at night was take them out.'

Hörður's wife, Gígja, had died just over a year previously after a short battle with cancer. No one who knew her had really got over the loss, least of all Hörður, whose unruly grey hair was now liberally streaked with white. Elma had managed to forget about it during her maternity leave with her daughter, who was now seven months old, but the moment she had gone back to work at West Iceland CID at the beginning of December the absence of Gígja had become achingly tangible again. Gígja had been a regular visitor at the police station in Akranes, generally bringing in gifts of food she had baked herself.

Not that Elma could contemplate eating anything, home-baked or otherwise, right now. 'OK, so Thorgeir was asleep in bed and someone took him by surprise,' she speculated aloud.

'He'd probably have woken up during the attack.'

'Or he was here at the cabin with one or more people and things ended badly.'

'Friends?'

'Hardly very good friends,' Elma said drily.

'Would a friend take him unawares like that? Wait for him to fall asleep before going in for the kill?'

'Unlikely, but not impossible. Thorgeir's big. Maybe the friend wouldn't have stood a chance otherwise.'

'Other possibilities?'

'Maybe a partner?' Elma suggested.

'Maybe.'

Elma raised her eyes to the pine panelling and examined the trail of blood that told its own story: it had been sprayed up the wall from below. Presumably, then, Thorgeir had been lying down while his killer stood or sat over him, stabbing him in the chest. The spattered stains reached almost to the ceiling.

Then she noticed that something had been written in black marker pen on the wall. Not very obviously, but in small, rather indistinct letters. She craned forwards, trying not to think about the rotting corpse below her.

'What's this?' she muttered to herself.

'Isn't it just some old writing?' Hörður asked.

'The writing on the wall...'

The words were hard to make out, the letters small and run together like bad joined-up writing, but Elma thought it was fairly clear that they had been scrawled there after the attack. They were written over Thorgeir's blood.

Take away my crimes and sins with blood, O Jesus.

BEFORE
Thorgeir

Thorgeir is putting a bag of oats in his shopping trolley when he sees her. She's standing on tiptoe, reaching for something on the top shelf – a box of muesli that's fallen over. She's wearing a khaki jacket, jeans and a short T-shirt that rides up when she stretches, revealing a slim waist. Her skin is as white as milk.

'Need a hand?' he asks.

She smiles. 'Yes, please. That would be great.'

Thorgeir reaches for the box and hands it to her, and she thanks him again, puts it in her basket and is about to move away when he stops her.

'Hey, haven't I seen you somewhere before?' The sentence sounds even lamer when he says it aloud than it had when he tried it out in his head. An obvious invention. They both know they've never seen each other before. He would remember her long hair, milk-white skin and those big eyes.

'No, I don't think so,' she says. 'I don't live in Akranes, I'm just visiting.'

'Oh, OK.' He's not in the habit of striking up conversations with strangers. Normally he goes out of his way to avoid making eye contact with people in public places, so he gropes around frantically for something else to say, but all he can do is stare at her shopping basket. He starts wondering why she's only got one banana and a packet of biscuits in it. Is she going on a mountain hike? Planning to stay over during this visit? Who is she here to see?

In the end it's her who breaks the silence. 'I'm Andrea.'

'Thorgeir,' he says, holding out his hand like some sad middle-aged bloke rather than a guy who's only just the wrong side of forty. She's considerably younger, barely thirty, he guesses, though he wouldn't bet on it. He's bad at guessing people's age.

She laughs and shakes his hand. 'Nice to meet you, Thorgeir, and thanks for getting down the muesli for me.'

'Are you going to be here long? In Akranes, I mean.' They are still holding hands but he comes to his senses and lets go, immediately missing the touch.

'I don't know,' she says. 'I'm not one for planning ahead.'

'The adventurous type?'

'Maybe.' She bites her lower lip as if to stop herself smiling too widely, and he realises that he's doing the same. Struggling to suppress a foolish smile that is doing its best to break free.

He wishes he could think of something clever to say. Something to elicit that wide smile, to make her laugh, but in the end all he comes out with is one, desperately uncool word: 'Awesome.'

She nods. Her smile fades.

'Well, thanks for the help, anyway.' Andrea starts to walk away, and he stares at the long, wavy pony-tail in that colour midway between brown and red. Then he hears himself calling after her.

'Hey,' he says, a little too loudly, a little too desperate.

Andrea turns round and waits.

'Er, if you need anything … anyone … I can always…' He sounds like he used to as a teenager, when he didn't know how to talk to girls. He feels himself growing hot; his cheeks are burning. And to think he believed he'd got over being that boy long ago. He's deliberately worked on himself, gone on courses and done exercises to learn to present himself as he wants to come across. To be the person he wants to be.

To hide his true nature.

Several, seemingly infinite, seconds pass before she replies.

'What's your number?'

He manages to say it right after one botched attempt. She taps it into her phone and he feels a vibration in his pocket.

'There,' she says. 'Now you've got mine.'

'What? Oh, right, of course.' He takes out his phone and sees her number on the screen. He wants to say something clever, like asking what she'd like to be called in his contacts list, but when he looks up again she's gone.

Only then does Thorgeir notice that the muesli he'd got down for her is also available on the bottom shelf. It's impossible to miss. Andrea hadn't actually needed his help at all.

NOW

Tuesday 8 December

While Elma and Hörður were waiting for the pathologist and forensics to arrive, they stationed themselves by the open front door, their breath forming clouds in the frosty air. Elma had been feeling a bit weird inside the cabin. It wasn't just the smell, it was the cross on the wall and that picture of Jesus, with eyes that seemed to follow her around. She'd never been exactly what you'd call a believer, not in God or the Holy Spirit, at any rate, but in here, enveloped in the choking miasma of decomposition, she felt oppressed by Christ's visage. Perhaps it was the effect of that writing on the wall.

'I gather Kristjana's very religious,' she remarked to Hörður. 'She runs the church Sunday school, or used to for many years.'

Elma was indebted to her mother for this information. After she and Sævar had moved into their new house, her mother had filled them in on all the gossip about their neighbours. Which is how Elma knew that the couple in the house behind theirs had recently shacked up together after divorcing their respective spouses. Elma sometimes caught sight of their six children, who now made up one large family. In addition, she knew that the man living in the house to the left of theirs had once been a promising student but had suffered from burnout at university and ended up working as a swimming-pool attendant. He lived alone but had a son who sometimes came to visit, though Elma hadn't spotted him yet. Also through her mother, she had learnt that Kristjana was not only extremely devout but eccentric as well. She had only the one son and had never remarried after losing her husband in an accident many years ago.

'Yes, I know who she is,' Hörður said.

'That writing on the bedroom wall doesn't seem consistent with the rest of the house,' Elma went on. 'It's all very neat and tidy, not the kind of place where you'd expect people to scribble on the walls in black marker pen.'

'What about Thorgeir?'

'You mean, would he deface the walls?'

'No, I mean, was he religious?' Hörður stuck his head outside to see if there was any sign of forensics arriving, but there was nothing but snow, dark, wintry trees and their vehicle parked at the end of the gravel track. He filled his lungs with the icy air, then looked back at Elma.

'No idea.'

'Could he have written the words on the wall in his death throes?' Hörður continued. 'Would he have had time or been capable of that?'

Elma edged closer to Hörður and the fresh air outside.

'To seek atonement?' she wondered aloud. '"Take away my crimes and sins…" Which begs the question: what crimes and sins?'

'Aren't we all sinners?'

'I suppose so.' Elma glanced over her shoulder at the painting of Jesus. There was no condemnation in his brown eyes but even so there was some indefinable quality that made her uneasy. Perhaps it was his air of perfect innocence and goodness. Nobody was perfectly innocent or good.

'Still, I don't believe either of them wrote those words,' Elma added. 'They were written on top of the blood. After the murder.'

'We'll leave that to forensics to judge,' Hörður said. 'Look, I'm going to step outside and call Reykjavík. Check how much longer they're going to be.'

Elma would have liked an excuse to go outside too but her curiosity got the better of her and she decided to use the chance before forensics arrived to examine the interior again for evidence that Thorgeir might not have been alone. In spite of her discomfort, or perhaps because of it, she found the summer house intriguing.

The silence that fell after the door closed behind Hörður was like someone holding their breath. Elma nearly jumped out of her skin when the fridge suddenly emitted a loud hum.

Now this was a crime scene, she took the precaution of donning shoe protectors as well as the latex gloves before embarking on her exploration of the property. First, she checked the entrance hall, but she couldn't see any shoes apart from those presumably belonging to Thorgeir and his mother: old boots, worn slippers and one pair of newish trainers. If anyone else had been there with Thorgeir they must have taken their shoes with them when they left. Not that there was anything unusual or suspicious about that: you'd expect people to leave in the same footwear they had arrived in.

There was a moss-green waxed jacket and a checked scarf hanging from one peg. A yellow rain hat too, and various other woolly hats and headscarves.

In the kitchen sink Elma found dishes, two water glasses and two wineglasses. On the table there was a bottle with dark dregs in the bottom.

It wasn't his mates Thorgeir had been entertaining but a woman, Elma thought. Or a man. She pictured a romantic evening. Red wine and a dip in the hot tub.

She surveyed the living area. It looked clean and tidy, and she couldn't see anything out of the ordinary. Apart, perhaps, from the rug, which was oddly placed in relation to the coffee table and TV. It lay askew across the middle of the room, out of sync with the rest of the furniture; too far away from the sofa and too far to the left of the television for symmetry. This misalignment would have driven Sævar nuts, judging by the OCD way he reacted every time Elma failed to straighten the bedspread or so much as accidentally opened a box of Cheerios at the wrong end.

The bathroom didn't yield any useful information either. The shower was typical for a summer house: a small, plastic cubicle with an inadequate shower head. Elma opened the medicine cabinet on the wall and found two toothbrushes and a tube of toothpaste inside. In addition, there was a tube of Gamla apótekið moisturiser and a bottle of contact-lens solution.

Next to the room Thorgeir was lying in, there was a second, smaller bedroom. It contained a single bed with a bare mattress, a wall lamp and a pile of books on the floor. Paperbacks mostly; a mixture of crime novels and love stories.

The underlying smell in here was even more pervasive than in the rest of the house, a combination of rot, mildew and the sulphurous odour of decay. The mattress had seen better days and it was hard to tell whether it had originally been yellow or white. Elma thought she would rather not know.

Something was bugging her. Something she had seen or perhaps something that should have been there but wasn't.

The instant her phone vibrated in her pocket she realised what it was: Thorgeir's phone. Nowadays, most people owned a smartphone that accompanied them everywhere, yet she hadn't seen any sign of Thorgeir's.

Taking out her own phone, she saw that Sævar had sent a selfie of him and Adda. Smiling to herself, she put the phone back in her pocket, then, holding her breath, opened the door to Thorgeir's room again. Ignoring the body, she concentrated on the other details. Thorgeir had put his clothes on a chair in the corner. The homely sight of the neatly folded jeans and dark-blue jumper was in jarring contrast to the gruesome vision on the bed.

Elma pictured Thorgeir folding his clothes, taking out his contact lenses and getting into bed. Had he been asleep when the first blow fell?

Most people kept their phone on the bedside table at night. Elma bent down and peered under the bed, hoping it might have fallen on the floor in all the commotion.

She spotted something black – not a phone but what appeared to be a crumpled sock.

When Elma fished out the item of clothing, she realised it wasn't a sock after all. Between two fingers she was holding a skimpy pair of knickers made of silk and lace, which almost certainly didn't belong to Kristjana.

❁

Matthías lay very still while Hafdís got quietly out of bed, pulled on her clothes and left the room. As he listened to her and their daughter getting themselves ready and having breakfast, his tears spilled over and seeped into the pillow. He was thinking that this was one of the last mornings he would ever wake up beside Hafdís, that they would ever be together as a family. Yet, instead of being out there with them, he was lying here, unable to face the new day.

Hafdís wanted a divorce.

She had broken it to him last weekend, the night of her work Christmas buffet. Since then, she had behaved as if nothing had happened, even though everything was about to change. Hafdís had said she wanted to wait until after Christmas for their daughter's sake: New Year, new life – perhaps that was how she saw it.

Once he had heard her and Ólöf leave, he dragged himself out of bed. Skipping breakfast, he took a six-pack of beer from the fridge and got in the car.

It was only a few minutes' drive from Akranes to the stables at Æðaroddi. The large complex of stable blocks and enclosures, used by a number of local horse owners, was located on the coast, not far from the foot of Mount Akrafjall, with views north over Borgarfjörður fjord. Matthías had practically grown up there, going over every day with his parents and siblings. These days they had five horses that they took it in turns to look after. His father mostly took care of the stables, since he was retired, but fortunately there was no one there now. No one but the animals.

He cracked open a can of beer and walked over to see Garpur, their oldest horse, twenty-five next spring. He'd been Matthías's seventeenth-birthday present. Although he'd never been a champion, never brought in much in prize money or stud fees, he remained Matthías's favourite horse to ride.

His phone vibrated in his pocket. Taking it out, he saw that it was Kristjana, his old mate Thorgeir's mother. He let the phone ring out as he had no wish to talk to her right now. All he wanted was to be left alone.

He stroked Garpur's muzzle, and the big brown eyes studied him intently. It had always been Garpur he turned to when something was troubling him. Gazing deep into those gentle eyes, he sensed warmth and sympathy, as if his horse, at least, understood him.

How could Hafdís dream of giving up on them now, after all they'd been through? He'd thought she was joking when, the moment they got back to their hotel room after the party, she'd announced she wanted a divorce. Thought she was punishing him for behaving like an idiot.

He could have understood that, because he knew he'd been an embarrassment to her, going up to her like that and making a scene about her talking to a colleague. Behaving as if there was far more to it than an innocent chat.

Matthías had always been the jealous type. He had a stunning wife and sometimes he simply couldn't handle the way everyone looked at her; the way she let them.

But never in his wildest dreams had he thought Hafdís might leave him. They had been together since they were sixteen, known each other more than half their lives. The last few months had put a strain on them both, however; it was undeniable. They'd invested a whole year's work and all their savings in opening a small café in the centre of Akranes, and it had initially done well before eventually accumulating so much debt that it just wasn't sustainable anymore. It had been a disaster: they'd taken out more and more loans until the repayments became so eye-wateringly high that they could no longer afford them. All their money, everything they had saved up over the years – gone from one minute to the next.

Matthías had got a job in construction in the immediate aftermath, but it had almost deprived him of the will to live. As a result, he'd jumped at Thorgeir's idea of coming in with him on the design of an app they could flog to a load of companies. They had broken their backs working on the project, received a grant from the Icelandic Innovation Fund and made countless trips to promote their concept to potential investors. It all appeared extremely promising. Thorgeir had secured the necessary capital and Matthías was confident that things were looking up at last; that he would be able to extricate himself and Hafdís from their sea of debts and they would finally be able to live the life they had always imagined for themselves.

Ice-cold sweat broke out on his back and he drained the rest of the can in one go. He pictured her again, standing at the basin in their hotel bathroom, brushing her teeth – such a mundane activity. Something they had done every evening for more than twenty years.

'This isn't working anymore,' she had said, spitting toothpaste into the sink.

'What isn't working?' he'd asked, never suspecting what was to come.

'This. Us.' Hafdís had opened a pot of face cream and started massaging it into her cheeks with firm, circular motions.

He couldn't take in what she meant, just stood there gaping at her like an idiot.

She went on: 'It hasn't been working for a long time and I don't think there's any point dragging it out anymore.'

'A long time … dragging it out anymore…' Matthías thought he sounded like one of those toys that repeat everything that is said to them.

Hafdís turned. 'I want a divorce.'

Matthías's first reaction had been to laugh. His second, to think of their daughter.

Ólöf had been going to see a therapist ever since they had discovered the cuts on her inner thighs and upper arms. By then, she hadn't been herself for a while; too silent, constantly shutting herself away in her room. Matthías hadn't taken it seriously, regarding it as normal behaviour for a fourteen-year-old. It had never occurred to him that Ólöf might be feeling bad enough to self-harm. The whole thing had come out when some of her schoolfriends had spoken to a teacher after noticing her cuts in the changing rooms before games. For the last six months, they had been going to family sessions with the therapist every two weeks in an attempt to improve their relationship and banish Ólöf's negative thoughts. To try to fix her.

Sometimes Matthías caught himself wishing that her illness was physical rather than mental – something that could be cut out with a simple operation.

'She'll cope,' Hafdís had said when he'd brought up the subject of their daughter, and continued to massage in cream, moving on to her neck now. 'We'll both still be there for her, we just won't be together. After all, it's not like she's a little kid anymore.'

Matthías had pursued Hafdís back into the bedroom where they had both sat down on the bed. 'Have you met someone else?' he had asked, thinking that if she had, they could work it out. He would take her back. He'd forgive her anything.

But Hafdís had insisted there was no one else. She had yawned while he was struggling to comprehend what was happening to him. Afterwards, he had lain there, wide awake half the night, listening to her regular breathing as she slept.

That had been three days ago, but Hafdís hadn't changed her mind, still hadn't so much as shed a tear, but talked about their divorce as matter-of-factly as if they were deciding what to have for supper.

Matthías found it so painful that his whole body ached.

'What the fuck am I supposed to do?' he whispered to Garpur, his throat choked with tears. 'What the fuck am I supposed to do now?'

❂

The pathologist, Hannes, lifted the duvet and pulled down Thorgeir's underpants to insert the thermometer into his rectum. It was the most common and accurate method of measuring body temperature at the scene.

'Just above room temperature,' Hannes said, after reading the thermometer. 'Which means we're looking at more than two days, but then I'd already guessed that from the degree of decomposition. His nails are still in place but beginning to loosen, his hair too, so I'd estimate about three to four days. Rigor mortis has passed and the body is flaccid again.'

'So, he died on Friday evening or in the early hours of Saturday morning,' Elma said.

'That would fit,' Hannes agreed. 'Yes, my guess is that he was murdered around then.'

'When did Kristjana last hear from him?' Hörður asked.

'On Friday morning.'

'Seven stab wounds,' Hannes resumed. 'As you can see. All with the same instrument, as far as I can tell. Have you found a knife?'

'Not yet,' Hörður said.

'A fairly broad blade. A kitchen knife possibly. That sort of size.'

Elma made a note to check the knives in the kitchen. They often came in a set.

'Thorgeir was lying on his back when the attack took place. His assailant would have been directly above him, possibly straddling him. I'll need to take a closer look tomorrow, but the pattern of the wounds would fit that scenario. Deeper up here by the neck, shallower lower down. With a kind of tail that formed when the knife was pulled out. The incisions look quite deep to me, which indicates considerable force. Possibly the use of both hands.'

'Would he have been asleep?' Elma asked.

'I can't see any sign of defensive injuries. No cuts on his hands or arms, so he can't have held them up to protect himself, or grabbed at the knife, as frequently happens.'

'So, if he was asleep...'

'If he was asleep, he may not have realised what was happening at first. Seven wounds – that wouldn't have taken long. No more than a few seconds.'

'How long would it have taken him to die?'

'Well, that would depend on the rate of blood loss. See this?' Hannes pointed to a wound by the dead man's neck. 'This was the main source of the bleeding. The knife may have hit the artery. If so, he would soon have lost consciousness. A quick death. The other wounds would have speeded things up too, so I reckon that, assuming he was asleep, he wouldn't have had much time to defend himself.'

Elma didn't know whether this was good or bad news. A quick death was better than a slow one. But to be lying there asleep and never get a chance to fight back seemed a cruel fate, even if it did nothing to change the final outcome.

Someone, it seemed, had been determined that Thorgeir shouldn't survive the attack.

❁

Feeling that she was getting underfoot wherever she stood, Elma went outside while forensics were at work. Although the weather was still, the freezing air immediately found its way inside her coat. She stamped her feet to keep warm, surveying the drive, which had filled up with vehicles belonging to forensics, the pathologist and the police. They couldn't all fit into the limited space by the summer house and were now lining the gravel access road, spoiling the beauty of the surroundings. The snow that had been so pristine earlier that day had now been trampled to a muddy, brown slush. The sun was beginning its descent in a sky that had turned an intense blue, the pale moon already riding high, waiting for darkness to fall before it could shine forth in all its brightness.

Several of her colleagues had driven over from Akranes, including Begga and Kári, who were now busy knocking on the doors of the neighbouring properties to find out if the occupants had noticed anything of interest. Members of the forensics team were also at work outside the cabin, walking slowly to and fro with sticks, poking at the snow in search of clues or tracks, but didn't seem to have discovered anything significant yet.

Elma, who had been there for hours, was thinking she might have to resort to eating snow soon to assuage her hunger pangs, when she heard the sound of the door opening. She looked round hopefully.

Líf came out and sucked air deep into her lungs as if emerging from a dive. She was clad in the usual white overalls worn by forensics technicians at crime scenes to avoid contaminating the evidence.

'Hot in there?'

'Uh huh.' Líf opened a bottle of water and practically emptied it in one go. She'd been working in forensics for years and Elma knew her quite well.

'We've still got plenty to do,' Líf said. 'But we've lifted fingerprints from all the main surfaces.'

'Anything interesting emerged?' Hörður asked, coming out to join them.

'Yes and no.' Líf stretched her spine with a grimace. 'We found some long hairs in the bed that will be sent off for analysis, and there were fingerprints on the wineglasses. We also found something that may be unrelated to the crime but is still rather odd.'

She beckoned Elma to follow her inside and led her to the living area, where the large, brown rug had been pulled aside to reveal a stain on the floorboards so dark it was almost black.

'This rug was placed at an odd angle for a reason,' Líf said. 'It appears to be blood. Old blood. And a lot of it. As if someone had bled dry here.'

'Can you tell that for sure from this evidence?' Elma asked.

'No, maybe not one hundred per cent, but it's clear that the person in question must have been pretty badly injured to suffer blood loss on this scale. And the blood would need to have been seeping into the floorboards for some time to produce an indelible stain like that.'

'Is there any way of telling how long the stain's been there?'

'It'll be tricky,' Líf said. 'We'll take samples, but don't bank on a very accurate result.'

'What about DNA?'

'From that? No, I doubt it, but we can try.'

It occurred to Elma that if they wanted more precise information about the origin of the stain, Kristjana was more likely to be able to enlighten them than Líf and her colleagues. The old woman had obviously been at pains to hide the unsightly patch with the oddly placed rug.

Seeing the flash of a camera behind her, Elma turned and took another glance into the bedroom.

'Are there signs of a struggle anywhere, other than in the bedroom?' she asked.

'I can't find broken objects or anything like that,' Líf said. 'And no fresh blood, apart from around the body.'

'What about the writing on the wall?'

'That was a new one on me,' Líf said. 'A murderer who leaves a message. It sounds to me like we're dealing with a sick mind.'

'Not exactly your standard murder under the influence during a bar brawl.'

Líf shrugged. 'Well, under the influence possibly, but whether of drugs, drink or some kind of religious fanaticism, I wouldn't like to say.'

'So you believe the murderer wrote it?'

'Come with me.'

Elma followed Líf back into the room where Thorgeir was lying. The stench wasn't quite as nauseating now that the windows had been open for a while. They got as close to the writing on the wall as they could without touching the body.

'See these dark streaks?' Líf asked. 'The blood hadn't yet congealed when this was written, so darker lines formed beside the letters as the blood was pushed aside by the strokes of the marker pen.'

Elma shook her head. 'What kind of person would dream of writing something like that after stabbing a man to death?'

'One who felt that Thorgeir had it coming?' Líf suggested. Then, smiling briefly, she added: 'Though I'm just here to collect evidence and record the facts. Speculating is your job.'

Elma made a hasty exit from the bedroom and went straight to the kitchen window. Outside she could see steam rising from the hot tub and a few leaves floating on the surface. The tops of the birch trees were visible above the windbreak, a few sparrows hopping among their white branches. Thanks to the mountains and forest, the valley was well sheltered from the wind that was currently battering Akranes.

She felt a sudden longing to get into the hot water. She'd scarcely had a chance to go to the swimming pool on her own since Adda was born. Perhaps she should cajole Begga into filling the hot tub on her veranda one of these evenings.

The sound of a voice calling snapped her back to the present. It seemed to be coming from outside. Elma joined the others filing out of the front door to see what was up.

'We've found something down here,' called a member of forensics whose name Elma could never remember.

He waved them to follow him through a hatch cut in the deck, which led into a dark storage space under the house so large that Elma could almost stand upright. In the torchlight, she made out a mower that looked as if it dated from the last century, various other tools, and stacks of wooden panels and sheets of black corrugated iron that were probably left over from when the summer house was built. Although the deck should have provided shelter from the elements, it was actually colder under here than outside and there was a strong smell of earth from the frozen ground.

'Here,' said the man, aiming his torch at a large kitchen knife that lay beside the wooden panels.

❁

Kristjana's weeping was a monotonous keening that died down, only to start up again, as loud and piercing as before. Elma had never heard anyone cry like that before, shedding no tears, though her eyes were red and there was snot running from her nose.

Kristjana was leaning on the shoulder of the vicar Elma had collected on the way there. His name was Bjartur and although he was mostly retired these days, his duties handed over to a younger colleague, he had agreed to come because he had known Kristjana for many years.

Neither Elma nor the vicar commented on the strong whiff of alcohol emanating from the grieving woman. This wasn't the time or place.

After they had been sitting there for a while, Elma took out her phone, found the photo of the words written above Thorgeir's bed, and read them aloud to Kristjana, wanting to avoid having to show her the wall covered in her son's blood.

'Have you heard that before somewhere?' Elma had done an online search but the results hadn't shed much light on the matter, apart from telling her that the words were from a hymn.

Kristjana narrowed her swollen eyes. 'What's that?'

'A line from a hymn. It was written on the wall above the bed at the summer house.'

'What did you say?'

Elma read the sentence out again and thought Kristjana stiffened momentarily.

'Yes, I know the hymn,' Kristjana replied after a pause. '"Take away my crimes and sins, O Jesus, and ... and create in me a clean heart."'

'Does it have any special significance for you or Thorgeir?'

'No, I don't think so.'

'Was Thorgeir religious?'

Kristjana didn't answer at first, appearing suddenly fascinated by the hem of her jumper, but when Elma repeated the question, she seemed to return to the present.

'When he was younger, yes, but not since he grew up. He wouldn't even go to church with me at Christmas.' Kristjana's mouth tightened and she threw the vicar an apologetic glance. 'But I pray for him every evening and I'm sure that deep down his faith still dwelt within him.'

'Does anyone else apart from you and Thorgeir have a key to the summer house?'

Kristjana shook her head. Elma returned her phone to her pocket. Perhaps Thorgeir had rediscovered his faith on his death bed, despite his refusal to accompany his mother to church. And yet there was little chance that Thorgeir could have written those words himself. The drastic haemorrhaging following the knife attack would have made it almost impossible, and, according to Líf, the words had been written on top of the blood. Besides, 'Take away my crimes and sins' sounded like someone seeking absolution. The most obvious conclusion was that the sin in question was the murder itself, but it could also refer to Thorgeir. He could have been the sinner.

'Do you know if something had been troubling Thorgeir recently or if he'd fallen out with someone, maybe?'

Kristjana took a while to think about this. 'No, not as far as I'm aware,' she said eventually. 'My son was a beautiful soul who never wished anyone harm.'

'When did you last see him?'

'He came round here for supper with me on Monday, just over a week ago. I cooked fish: haddock, with boiled potatoes and dripping. He loved that sort of food, did my Thorgeir. Good, old-fashioned Icelandic cooking.'

'Did you notice anything out of the ordinary then?'

Kristjana shook her head.

'Did he say anything about going to the summer house?'

'No, I…' Kristjana seemed to gather herself. Her voice suddenly harsh, she burst out: 'I can't believe anyone could have done this to my boy.'

'Can you think of anyone who might have had a grudge against him?'

'My Thorgeir?' Kristjana seemed outraged that this should even occur to Elma. 'No, of course not. Everyone liked Thorgeir. He never hurt a soul.'

Kristjana probably wasn't the best judge of that, Elma thought privately. Aloud, she asked the woman to write down a list of her son's closest friends and associates.

'Is he in contact with any other members of your family at all?' she asked.

'No, it's just the two of us. Ever since his father died, it's been just the two of us … What will happen now?'

Elma couldn't tell Kristjana what her life would be like from now on, but, taking the question at face value, she replied: 'Well, first thing tomorrow they'll do a post-mortem on Thorgeir, which should hopefully give us some leads. Forensics are currently examining the summer house and you can rest assured that we'll pull out all the stops to discover what happened.'

'I always knew he'd die young. It's … it's a feeling I've had ever since he was born. Ever since I first saw him,' Kristjana said. Then she began to recite: '"Good people pass away; the godly often die before their time. But no one seems to care or wonder why. No one seems to understand that God is protecting them from the evil to come."' After a moment, seeing that Elma didn't recognise the quotation, she added: '*Isaiah*, fifty-seven.'

Elma was silent, unsure how to reply to this.

Kristjana fiddled with the paper napkin she was holding, then looked up at Elma again. 'I want to see him.'

'I don't think that's a good idea,' Elma replied.

'But I want to,' Kristjana insisted. 'I want to see my child. You can't deny me that.' Then, her voice thick with unshed tears, she intoned: '"The Lord is close to the brokenhearted and saves those who are crushed in spirit."'

The vicar responded: '"Blessed are they that mourn: for they shall be comforted."' He laid a gentle hand on Kristjana's shoulder as the ear-piercing keening started up again with such force it seemed it would never stop.

❀

When Elma got home at eight p.m., Sævar was sitting on the floor with Adda, their seven-month-old daughter. He had already cooked and eaten supper himself, and fed and bathed Adda, while absent-mindedly humming a tune he realised later was the theme song to *SpongeBob SquarePants*, which had been on TV that morning.

'Hi, poppet.' Elma crouched down and scooped up her daughter from the floor as soon as she came in. 'Have you missed your mummy?'

Adda laid her head on Elma's chest for a moment, then tore herself free and set off at a crawl, making a beeline for the unicorn soft toy that was her current obsession. That and all the boxes stacked by the wall, waiting to be unpacked, which Adda was always trying to reach inside.

They had bought this house on Vogabraut more than a month ago. It was a street of detached properties, many of which were looking a little rundown these days but were popular with younger buyers who couldn't afford houses in the newer parts of town. Elma and Sævar were slowly getting settled in, with the emphasis on *slowly*. The floor tiles in the hall had been half pulled up, an impulsive decision that they hadn't got round to finishing, and the house was still cluttered with moving boxes. Sævar had made a start on them at the beginning of his paternity leave but was having trouble deciding where to put things without having Elma there to ask.

Although it was well into December, they hadn't got as far as putting up any Christmas decorations; there had seemed little point when they were in the middle of moving. Trying to hang fairy lights and so on while they still had test patches of paint on the walls would feel as incongruous as putting up a Christmas tree in a cowshed.

'I can't answer for Adda, but *I've* missed you.' Sævar got up off the floor, grimacing as his joints cracked. 'You must be starving.'

'I am, actually. But I don't have the energy to go and fetch something to eat.' Elma flopped onto the sofa, reaching out to pat

Birta, who was lying on the floor at her feet. Sævar's Labrador bitch was so old now that she did little but sleep these days.

'It's just as well you've got your own private butler, then,' Sævar said, and disappeared into the kitchen. He returned with a plate of pasta in cream sauce and garlic bread that he had made for supper. While Elma was tucking in, she brought him up to speed on the day's events.

'The moment you turn up at the office, things get interesting,' he said, mock ruefully. 'I'm sure I've heard that story before.'

Elma eyed him wearily. 'I was hoping for a gentle return to work.'

'You'll have it solved in no time.'

'Will I?'

'Won't you?'

'God, I hope so.' Elma smothered a yawn and pulled a blanket around herself.

'Shall I make some tea?' Sævar asked.

Elma murmured what he took to be assent, so he went back into the kitchen and put on the kettle. He selected a bag of chamomile and added a little honey to the mug. Outside, the wind was raging, whirling snow off the ground and plastering it halfway up the window.

'How did Kristjana take it?' he asked when he returned to the living room and handed Elma her tea.

'Oh, you know.' Elma sat up and took the mug in both hands. 'It's never fun. And she couldn't tell us anything. Like whether he'd been having problems, or whether he'd gone to the summer house with his mates or a girl, maybe.'

She told him about the writing scribbled on the wall above the bed and the pair of lacy knickers under it.

'So you think he was there with a girl?'

'Maybe.' Elma blew on her hot tea. 'Probably.'

'Do you reckon she could have written that on the wall?'

'I've no idea.'

'And murdered him as well?'

'I've no idea,' Elma repeated, apparently too tired to speculate.

'She could have left before it happened,' Sævar pointed out.

'Meaning that they arrived in separate cars?'

'Sure. It's possible.'

Sævar wondered if a date could really end that badly. A quarrel that got out of hand and escalated into violence. A multiple stabbing seemed a pretty drastic outcome. 'Perhaps she had a boyfriend,' he suggested.

'Who stormed round in a murderous rage and knocked on the door?' Elma shrugged. 'Who knows? I'll start looking into it properly tomorrow. By the way, we couldn't find Thorgeir's phone, and his mother didn't seem to have a clue about any girl in his life.'

'Yes, so you said,' Sævar reminded her. 'But Thorgeir was over forty, wasn't he? He may not have confided in his mother about his relationships with women. Especially if it wasn't serious.'

'No, I suppose not.' Elma took a sip of tea. 'Kristjana's very odd. I've had to go round and break news like that to quite a few families over the years, but this is the first time a mother has told me she knew her child would die young.'

'Oof, I wouldn't want to live with knowledge like that.'

'No. In any case, it's bullshit. You can't know something like that in advance.'

'Unless you're clairvoyant.'

'I'd roll my eyes if I wasn't so knackered. And cold.' She shivered.

'Want me to run you a bath?' Sævar offered.

Their new house had two bathrooms, one with a shower, the other with a tub. The only downside was that the one with the tub resembled something from a 1970s horror movie: brown tiles, avocado-green bathroom suite and cherry-wood fittings. Worst of all, the tub was so small it was more like a basin than a proper bath.

'Oh, no, thanks. I miss the bath in my old flat.' Elma sighed. 'Anyway, I think I'm too tired for one now.'

She patted the sofa beside her, and Birta jumped up and lay down, pressing against her, as if she understood that her mistress needed warming up.

Elma put down her empty mug and passed Sævar her phone with the photo of the writing on the wall above the bed. 'This is what I was talking about. It's a line from a hymn.'

Sævar furrowed his brow as he read.

'Pretty weird, huh?' Elma said.

'Could Thorgeir have been murdered by some religious nutter?' Sævar asked, looking up.

'Apparently he wasn't a believer himself,' Elma said, reaching down to pick up Adda, who was holding out her arms to her. 'Much to his mother's dismay. She seemed almost ashamed of the fact.'

'Shall I put Adda to bed?'

'No, I'll do it,' Elma said. 'I want a chance for a cuddle first. And my boobs are ready to burst.'

❁

Sævar stayed behind in the sitting room, smiling as he heard Elma talking to Adda in the bedroom. He knew mother and daughter would probably fall asleep in bed together once Adda had finished breastfeeding.

He wasn't quite ready to go up yet and was enjoying having a bit of time to himself. Opening his laptop, he typed in the text Elma had shown him.

After a short search he tracked down the source of the quotation. As Elma had said, it was taken from a hymn, identified only as 'Hymn 594' on the Church of Iceland website, originally a Swedish folk tune, with Icelandic words by Magnús Runólfsson. It turned up on various Christian sites, including the YMCA/YWCA one, where it was apparently part of the repertoire at Vatnaskógur, an outward-bound centre about half an hour's drive from Akranes, where they held Christian summer camps for children.

Sævar closed his laptop, none the wiser about the significance the line from the hymn could have had in the context of this particular murder. He examined the photo on Elma's phone again.

Take away my crimes and sins with blood, O Jesus.

Since the wall was red with blood, it didn't take a genius to spot the relevance of the quotation to the conditions at the scene, regardless of whether they applied to Thorgeir or the killer.

BEFORE
Thorgeir

Thorgeir is distracted for the rest of the day. When he gets home, he opens the fridge, then, finding he has no appetite, turns on the TV and his games console instead. He plays a FIFA game and loses, unusually for him, then flings down the controller, which bounces off the sofa and clatters onto the floor.

Thorgeir is forty-one. He has lived alone since he bought his flat seventeen years ago. If he wants to chuck his controller on the floor, he will. Yet it feels as if he's losing his grip – not just on the game but on everything.

He opens his laptop and as he does so his phone starts ringing. His mother's number flashes up on the screen. In no mood to talk to her right now, he lets it ring and turns his attention back to the computer. He types the girl's name into the search engine and calls up a host of Andreas, none of whom appear to be his Andrea. Next, he opens Facebook and looks for her there. Finding no profiles that fit the girl from the supermarket, he closes the laptop, frustrated now. Then he turns on the TV again, this time tuning into some lame comedy that he's seen a hundred times and watches until he nods off.

In bed that evening he sends her a message:

Hi, it's me. Did you enjoy the muesli?

The instant he's sent it, he's wishes he hadn't. He's totally blown his chance: the message was too contrived, like he was trying to be clever, which he was. The longer he waits without getting a reply, the worse he feels. So bad, in fact, that he hurls his phone across the room and the screen shatters. Getting out of bed, he picks up a shard of glass and turns it over between his fingers until his thumb produces a trickle of bright-red blood that tastes of iron. He can't stand blood; he starts seeing spots when he blinks and his breathing grows shallow. He's even been known to faint. During the night, the cut leaves a red smear on his sheets.

The next day, he takes his phone to the repair shop, changes his sheets and sticks a plaster over the wound.

Three long days pass.

Three days of cursing himself for his clumsy come-on, for exposing himself to hurt like this after building up his armour all these years. When he was younger, he used to become obsessed with girls and lose his head. He'd come on too strong and end up doing something regrettable. Make a fool of himself. His history with women is littered with disasters. Since then, he's been careful to stay away from them, because, if he doesn't, things have a habit of going badly wrong.

The only time he's truly fallen in love was with a classmate at school. He can't get her out of his head, despite the passing of the years. She's always there, a part of his life, whether he likes it or not. With her, he's always felt a connection, felt they're alike on some level, although he's never sure whether this sense of kinship is shared.

But now there's a ray of light. Now this girl, glimpsed only for a few brief moments in the shop, has intruded into his consciousness. He's hardly been able to think about anything else since. He has no idea how she feels, though, or whether she's thinking about him. Everything seems to point to the opposite, since his phone has remained silent as the grave.

Telling himself to stop thinking about Andrea, Thorgeir rips the plaster off his thumb and inspects the healed wound. He resolves to stop thinking about girls. He never wants to be tied down. Commitment just isn't for him.

Then, without warning, her name appears on his screen. A phone call that makes his heart miss a beat and sends all his certainties up in smoke.

NOW

Wednesday 9 December

Hörður generally cycled the long way round to work. The house he had shared with Gígja was on Grenigrund, and every day he cycled clockwise round the Grund neighbourhood, then along the shore overlooking Langisandur beach, to the police station.

The snow made no difference to him, but he could hear Gígja's voice in his head warning him about the slippery conditions: *One of these days you're going to fly over the handlebars and break your hip like an old man.*

Once, they had agreed that they would never let themselves become doddering pensioners, but later he had actively looked forward to growing old with Gígja. Looked forward to the leisure time, the travelling, the freedom from stress, the quiet life.

Now, life had lost all its meaning, he thought. In his sudden frustration he was just like his grandchild, he realised, crumpling up a picture and throwing it in the bin because she'd accidentally coloured outside the lines. Nothing had any meaning and life was unfair. The world had become a pointless, lonely place.

More than a year had passed and people had long since stopped asking him how he was coping or regarding him with eyes full of compassion. Everyone was getting on with their lives. Even his children seemed to be sailing on as if nothing had happened, while he was adrift, no land in sight, with every likelihood that he would drown.

No, he mustn't think like that. Mustn't let himself.

Hörður turned down towards Langisandur and pedalled along the pavement until he was past the Höfði Retirement Home. It was high tide, the waves breaking on the rocks at the top of the beach. The great expanse of Faxaflói bay was rough and grey, the air too thick with cloud for him to see all the way to Reykjavík in the south. He brought his attention back to where he was going, but just as he was turning onto the path that ran along the top of the beach, he skidded and went over, crashing down like the chimney of the local cement factory that had been demolished the previous year. So much for his dignity.

The thin covering of snow received him into its icy embrace. Hörður landed on his hip, scraping his palms along the tarmac. He became aware of a stabbing pain and was about to get straight up again when he heard someone calling his name.

Damn, he thought. The last thing he needed was to be found sprawled on the ground like this.

'Are you all right?' asked a woman's voice.

'Yes, I'm fine,' he said, trying to see who it was as she came towards him. When he realised it was Fríða, an old classmate of his, he was even more mortified. He felt such an idiot, lying here like a snowman knocked over by a bunch of naughty kids.

'I stopped when I saw you go down,' she said.

Hörður noticed a car parked at the side of the road with its hazard-warning lights on.

'There's nothing wrong with me,' he said, getting to his feet with an effort. 'I'm absolutely fine.'

'Are you sure?' Fríða's gaze was sympathetic. They hadn't known each other well at school, or afterwards, but he vaguely remembered her being one of the clever kids. The type who passed all her exams with flying colours and took extra subjects.

'I'm absolutely fine,' Hörður repeated, forcing a smile and trying to ignore the agony in his hip.

'I can give you a lift if you like.'

'No, thanks, there's really no need,' Hörður said and swung his leg over his bike. The pain was almost unbearable but he gave another tight smile and said goodbye.

'Are you quite sure?' he heard Fríða calling after him, but he was far enough away by then to be spared the necessity of answering.

❀

Entering the meeting room, Elma felt as though she hadn't been there for years and, simultaneously, as if she'd never left. She ran a palm over the table top, feeling a sense of well-being spreading through her body. In spite of being tired and missing Adda, it was good to be back. She had returned to work just over a week ago, doing half-days to begin with and spending most of her time getting on top of things and reading reports, her thoughts still dwelling at home with Adda and Sævar. Now, however, it felt as if she was properly back in the saddle. Had recovered her former self.

'Right,' Hörður said, the moment he appeared. 'The preliminary findings of the post-mortem have come through.'

'Already?' she exclaimed. Hannes, the pathologist, hadn't wasted any time. He must have performed the post-mortem as soon as he got back yesterday evening or first thing this morning. It was only just gone eleven now.

Hörður grimaced a little as he lowered himself into the chair at the head of the table.

'Are you OK?'

'Oh, I took a bit of a tumble on my way to work this morning.'

'From your bike?'

'Yes.' Hörður opened his laptop. 'It's nothing. I'm just a little stiff.'

Elma raised her eyebrows. It looked like more than just a little stiffness.

'Are you sure you're OK?'

Hörður ignored her question. 'The body had seven stab wounds made by a knife. The blade would have been approximately fifteen to twenty centimetres long, though it's hard to be precise. Smooth, not serrated. As Hannes said yesterday, the orientation of the wounds indicates that the attacker was standing over Thorgeir.' He angled the screen towards Elma. 'You can see better here.'

The photo showed Thorgeir's chest, neck and jaw. His body had been washed to give them a clearer view of the incisions. Seven wounds, five on his chest and two in his neck.

'The wounds in his chest are less regular, which, according to Hannes, suggests Thorgeir was moving while they were inflicted. The blade would have been jogged as it was entering the flesh, forming openings like this. In contrast, the incisions in his neck are straight, displaying no sideways displacement of the blade.'

'Meaning he was dead by then?'

'Or unconscious. At any rate, he doesn't seem to have put up much resistance.'

Elma pictured the blade of the knife entering the body. First five times, then twice. Perhaps with a brief pause in between.

'Could it have been the knife that was found under the house?'

'No. That one was smaller and serrated.'

'But there was blood on it, wasn't there?'

'We don't know that yet, but, if there was, it must have been old.'

Elma studied the photo. It seemed so unreal. As if all the victim's humanity had been removed and nothing but the simulacrum of a body remained. The husk. At least this made it easier to view it dispassionately.

'They found skin under his nails and hairs caught between his fingers. Hairs that didn't belong to him.'

'Long ones?'

'See for yourself.' Hörður called up another photo, of Thorgeir's hands this time. His swollen fingers had turned strange colours and the nails were coming loose. Between them, Elma could see hairs of an indeterminate shade and length. Another photo showed the strands beside a ruler. Fifty centimetres. Quite long, Elma thought.

'He also had defensive injuries.'

'As if he'd been defending himself?'

'No,' Hörður said. 'As if someone had been defending themself against him.'

'How do you mean?'

'Well, for example, there were scratches made by fingernails here and there on his body.'

'As if someone had been pushing him away?' Elma asked.

'Possibly. But it's hard to tell because of the decomposition.'

'There were two wineglasses at the summer house and I'm guessing those lace knickers didn't belong to Kristjana. At least, she doesn't look the type to wear a thong.'

Elma thought Hörður's mouth twitched. 'You're probably right,' he said.

'Which begs the question, did he have a date?'

'That's the question, all right.' Hörður scrolled through a series of photos showing the body from various angles as well as close-ups of the stab wounds and other injuries.

'His mother was familiar with the quotation on the wall,' Elma said. 'Though she wasn't aware that anything had been written there. It's a line from a hymn. Hymn number 594, to be precise. A Swedish folk tune with Icelandic words, sung at Christian ceremonies. According to Sævar, they sing it at Vatnaskógur.'

Elma knew of Vatnaskógur, though she had never been there herself, as the Christian summer camps there mainly catered for boys. It was located on a lake in the countryside just to the north of Hvalfjörður fjord. There were other camps for girls, at Ölver and Vindáshlíð, which had been popular when Elma was younger. She hadn't a clue whether they still enjoyed the same popularity now that church membership was on the decline in Iceland.

'Ah yes, my son went when he was a boy,' Hörður said. 'He and his mates had a whale of a time. The Christian part was a bit of an afterthought.'

'I had the feeling it might be.'

'It's still very popular,' Hörður said. 'Always booked out. Gígja used to know Magnús, who's been running the centre for years.'

'Oh, did she?' Elma felt a pang whenever Hörður mentioned Gígja. She missed seeing his wife's cheerful face in the office, and if she missed her, Hörður's sense of loss must be unbearable. He had always been the earnest type, but Gígja used to jolly him along. She had been as cheerful and animated as he was staid and serious.

'I think it's less important where the hymn came from than what it says,' Hörður continued. 'The person who wrote it obviously believed they were either washing away their own sins or Thorgeir's.'

'With blood,' Elma added.

'Quite literally.'

'So, either the killer regretted what they had done or they were taking revenge for something Thorgeir had done.'

'Exactly,' Hörður said, turning the screen back to face him. 'I think it's best we start with Thorgeir's flat, then talk to his closest family and friends. There may be a computer in his flat that we can examine. We'll need to contact his phone provider too. Even though we don't have his physical phone, we can get hold of a list of his calls.'

'Yes.' Elma watched Hörður, noticing how much it hurt him to stand up. His forehead was damp with sweat, his trousers were slightly torn at the side. 'Just one thing first,' she said, getting to her feet as well.

'What?' Hörður groaned.

'We're going to zip over to the hospital together.'

❀

Matthías collected Ólöf first. She was waiting outside the school, dyed-black hair falling over her eyes as a result of the fringe she'd cut herself that autumn. Her eyes were heavily made up with black mascara and thick eyeliner; her lips pale, almost white. When he looked at her, he had the feeling that someone had painted over a picture he used to know well, until it was almost unrecognisable. At least, this girl bore scant resemblance to the happy little daughter he used to have a few years ago.

He waved to her, smiling.

'Good day at school?' he asked as she got in the back. His cheerful tone was patently fake.

'Fine.'

'Great.' Matthías held on to his smile.

They picked up Hafdís next. She got into the car reeking of perfume, her lipstick freshly applied. Not pale like her daughter's but a pinky-brown colour. She was so gorgeous that Matthías felt his stomach constrict. Hafdís had been teaching swimming lessons until late the previous evening. He had got home before supper, having finished the entire six-pack of beer at the stables, then driven home like an idiot. But the police hardly ever stopped him and, in the unlikely case that they did, one glance at his face would be enough to make them apologise and wave him on. Sometimes it was useful having a dad who had been the local inspector for many years.

Matthías had cooked supper for himself and Ólöf, if boiling noodles could be called cooking, then gone to bed, though he tried to stay awake until Hafdís got in. He'd been planning to tell her how much he loved her but fell sound asleep before he got a chance. He hadn't heard her get up in the morning, so this was the first time he'd seen her for more than twenty-four hours.

Matthías greeted her in an upbeat tone, but Hafdís avoided his gaze and immediately began tapping at her phone with her varnished nails. Had she painted them for someone at work? For the man she'd been talking to at the work party?

Matthías had no idea and was still brooding over the question when the therapist invited them to take a seat on the sofa.

'So, how have you all been?' she asked.

'Oh, fine,' Matthías replied, smiling until his cheeks ached.

There they had sat, every other week, talking about their feelings and relationships and the importance of allowing themselves to feel hurt and about what it was like to acknowledge that you were hurting inside.

Matthías usually sat there in silence, nodding or looking serious at all the right moments, but mainly feeling completely useless.

'How are you?' the therapist asked Ólöf.

'Fine.'

'That's good to hear.' The therapist was holding a tablet and making notes with a digital pen. 'How have you been feeling this week?'

'Good.'

Fine. Good. Matthías wished he could say the same. He had to fight back the urge to hijack the session and drown the therapist in the tide of his emotions before his head burst from the pressure of trying to hold them in.

'Have the thoughts we were discussing last time been troubling you at all?' the therapist continued, in her characteristically gentle, soothing tone.

'No.' Ólöf dropped her eyes to the floor.

The therapist waited, her gaze travelling down the girl's arms as Ólöf clutched at the cuffs of her jumper, keeping her head lowered.

'Oh, what? Seriously, Ólöf? Not again.' Hafdís had guessed what was going on and was staring at Ólöf's arms as well. 'Let me see them.'

'We needn't—'

But Hafdís cut across the therapist, addressing her daughter: 'I can't believe you're still doing it.'

'Ólöf,' the therapist said. 'Would you like to talk to me in private?'

'Is that a good idea?' Hafdís snapped. 'I want to know why she's doing it. Why she feels she has to … to hurt herself. We're paying you to make her stop but she just won't. Why, Ólöf? Why do you do it?'

Ólöf remained stubbornly silent, staring at the floor.

Mother and daughter didn't get on. Hafdís had little patience with Ólöf's behaviour, regarding it as self-indulgently melodramatic. When Ólöf was born, Hafdís had no doubt been expecting another version of herself, a girl who was tough and fearless, but Ólöf was everything her mother was not. If you asked Matthías, there were advantages and disadvantages to this, though mostly, despite his love for Hafdís, he felt it was a good thing. His wife was strong, ruthless and never apologised for anything. Ólöf was clever, sensitive and had a strong sense of justice. If she could only get over the depression that had taken hold of her a year ago, Matthías was confident that she would thrive one day.

'What would you like, Ólöf?' the therapist asked calmly, ignoring Hafdís.

'Yes, sure.' Ólöf didn't raise her eyes from the floor.

'Yes, what?' Hafdís demanded.

'I want to talk. In private.'

'But—' Hafdís began.

Matthías interrupted. 'Give them some space,' he said, signalling to his wife to step outside with him.

As he was leaving the room, he saw that his daughter had raised her head. A tear ran down her cheek and the corner of her mouth quivered as she caught his eye.

Perhaps in an attempt to thank him.

❁

Hörður was still grumbling, his face like that of a recalcitrant child who doesn't want to go to school, when Elma parked in front of Akranes hospital.

'This is a total waste of time. I can hardly feel it anymore.'

Elma merely smiled and gestured at him to take a seat in the waiting area while she talked to the man on reception.

While she was queuing, she received a text from a phone company. Apparently Thorgeir's phone had last been used on 4 December, that is, on Friday five days ago. It had been picked up that evening by the mast near his summer house. After that the phone had been switched off. This gave them a fairly precise clue to the time of death, given that most people checked their phones regularly while they were awake.

A couple of minutes later, she said goodbye to Hörður, who seemed resigned now to seeing a doctor. But that didn't prevent him from giving her orders to ring him if anything came up.

Kári, one of her uniformed colleagues, rang her before she'd even had time to reverse out of the parking space.

'While I remember,' she said, before he could get a word in, 'could you put the reports from your and Begga's door-knocking among the neighbouring summer houses on my desk?'

'Already done.'

'Did you learn anything interesting?'

'Nah, not really, or I'd have told you straight away. Someone heard a car and another person saw the lights on in the cabin during the night. Even though the summer houses are close together, they're quite private. The thick trees stop people being able to spy much on their neighbours.'

Elma had got that impression, so she hadn't been pinning any great hopes on the neighbours' testimony.

'But there is one thing,' Kári said. 'I looked Thorgeir up on the database and found an old charge against him.'

'What kind of charge?'

'It was around twenty years ago, so I don't suppose it's relevant to the investigation, but he was accused of rape. The charge was dropped, but, still, it could be linked to what happened.'

'I see what you mean.'

Elma thanked Kári and finished backing out of the parking space. She found it unlikely that an old rape accusation could have any relevance to the case, but it did at least suggest that Thorgeir might not have been as blameless as his mother believed. Perhaps he'd had more enemies than anyone had realised.

BEFORE
Thorgeir

Thorgeir finds himself getting stupidly excited, more like a teenager than a grown man who has always thought of himself as a bit of a lone wolf. Not made for relationships or a conventional family life. That doesn't mean he's suddenly ready for commitment or anything like that, but he does feel a powerful desire to know more about this girl, who smiles with her entire face in a way that makes his heart beat faster.

They agree to meet at five o'clock on Saturday afternoon at a restaurant in the centre of Reykjavík. Thorgeir turns up early and secures a good table by the window. By the time she walks in, he's finished one beer and is trying to catch the waiter's eye to order another. His thoughts don't seem able to settle on anything. He keeps checking his phone, looking out of the window, searching for her face. But when she does arrive, he fails to notice her until she's standing by the table.

He starts and jumps to his feet like an idiot, not knowing whether to shake hands. He isn't usually this socially awkward, but suddenly his tongue feels big and clumsy in his mouth, and he starts worrying what she'll think about the beer. Maybe she only wanted to meet him for coffee.

He's still dithering over the handshake when she sits down opposite him.

'Sorry, am I late? I'm always late. I'm trying to turn over a new leaf but it's not going particularly well, to be honest.' She laughs and he thinks she's even more beautiful than he remembered. Whatever it is – the smile, that tiny gap between her front teeth or those big round eyes – he can't stop looking at her. Images rise into his mind, the ones his imagination has been conjuring up ever since he first met her, and he has to force himself to stop before he gets too excited.

'No, it's fine,' he says, when he can speak. 'I expect I got here too early. Would you like a coffee or…?'

'No, just a beer like you,' she says.

He manages to attract the waiter's attention at last and signals to him to bring two more beers.

'Did you drive all the way over from Akranes?' she asks.

'Yes, it's not that far.'

'No, I suppose not. Though not many people from Reykjavík bother to go there.'

'No, most people just drive straight past.'

'Right. The Ring Road misses out the town and takes you on to Borgarnes.' She smiles. 'Akranes always gets forgotten about. Nobody has a reason to go unless they know someone who lives there.'

'Do you know someone who lives there?'

'Yeah.' She doesn't elaborate and he doesn't ask.

The waiter brings the beers and puts them down on the table in front of them. The glasses are so full that foam dribbles over the sides. His gaze is drawn to the froth left behind on her upper lip when she drinks. She licks it off, sees him watching, and smiles.

'But the town's really come up in the world these days, hasn't it?' she says.

'Yes, sure. They've been building a lot of new housing.'

She nods. 'So, what do you do?'

'I'm a software engineer for a company based in Akranes.'

'Exciting,' she says, and he can't tell if she's being serious or ironic.

'What about you?' he asks.

'I do the odd shift at a restaurant and work at a library too. I studied literature at uni.' She sighs. 'I know what you're going to say: why choose a degree course purely for the money? I don't know how to answer that, except to say that I suppose earning a decent salary matters to me. I like to have enough in my pocket.' Her face is deadpan as she sips her beer.

'Oh, so studying literature pays well, does it?'

'I'm joking, of course,' she says, laughing. 'I just love books and can't imagine anything more fun than working in a library surrounded by thousands of the things. Do you read?'

'Sometimes.' He doesn't actually, not novels, anyway. He sometimes listens to audio books; reference works mainly, or non-fiction books by high-achieving men. Biographies and self-help manuals.

'I'm such a book nerd that I usually have several on the go at once,' she says.

'Really?'

'One to read in bed, one to read during breaks at work, and usually an audio book to listen to on the bus or when I go for a walk.'

'Don't you get them muddled up?' He's having difficulty keeping up with the tempo of the conversation. If it ever had a tempo. Andrea seems perfectly relaxed, whereas he's a bundle of nerves, acutely conscious of how he's sitting and where he's directing his gaze and whether he's smiling too much or too little. He raises his beer to his lips, then, realising how little he has left, tries not to take too big a mouthful. Andrea isn't even halfway down her glass.

'No, never.' She grins, revealing the little dimples in her cheeks. 'Which is pretty amazing, considering that I'm so scatterbrained. I'm always putting the milk in the dishwasher and my phone in the fridge.'

'In the fridge?' He laughs. 'Have you actually done that?'

'Yep, and that's not even the worst.'

'What's the worst?'

'If I told you that I'd have to kill you,' she says solemnly.

'I'm willing to take the risk.'

'Quite sure?' she asks.

He pulls a serious face. 'Quite sure.'

There's a moment, a few brief seconds, in which their eyes meet and he feels light-headed, though he's only had two beers. Her eyes are the colour of earth and moss, brown with hints of green around the pupils, and an image pops into his mind of her on top of him. He pictures her breathing faster and faster until she closes her eyes and emits a loud groan.

'I'll tell you later,' she says.

She finishes her beer, asks if he'd like another, and instantly catches the eye of the waiter, who goes to fetch two more. 'What about you? No bad stuff to share with me?'

'Have we reached the stage yet where I start revealing the bad stuff?' He can feel himself slipping into gear, relaxing, able to flirt at last. Or make a stab at it, anyway.

'I don't know, what do you reckon?'

'Oh, I'd say we're well on the way. Shall we see how it's going at the end of the evening?'

Their beers arrive but neither of them looks up.

'We could do,' she says. 'Though it'll take quite a few dates before I tell you the absolute worst.'

'Dates? Is this a date?'

'A half-date, I'd say.'

'A half-date?'

'It's a word,' she says. 'Anyway, we're doing this all wrong. You must be aware that it's not the custom in Iceland to go on a date and get to know each other before taking the next step in a relationship. Most people meet in a bar, sleep together, and only then start talking, get to know each other better and then maybe, just maybe, go and see a film or do something even more serious like...'

'Going out for a meal?'

'No. God, no! Out for a meal? You might as well pop the question straight away.'

'Maybe I will,' he says. 'Invite you out for a meal, I mean.'

She runs her thumb around the rim of her glass, then peeps up at him coyly from under her long lashes.

'Are you sure you want to do something that bold?' she asks. Their eyes meet again and the crotch of his trousers feels suddenly tight.

NOW

Wednesday 9 December

Sævar had overestimated how much space there was under the pram for the shopping. He crouched down, working away at the yellow supermarket bag until he could squeeze it underneath. He would just have to carry the other two bags, though that didn't seem feasible as he needed a hand free to push the pram. Through the snow, as well.

Nevertheless, he managed somehow to exit the supermarket with a bag hanging from each of his elbows. He was bound to end up with bruises but that was tough. He set off for home, pushing the pram in front of him. In spite of everything, his spirits were high, as if nothing could dampen them.

He turned onto the footpath that ran across the neighbourhood. Being on paternity leave was going to be good, he thought. He was fed up with all the reports and paperwork and the monotonously repetitive cases that landed on his desk in CID: car crashes, burglaries and drugs offences. People never seemed to learn. New generations came along to replace the old, treading the same path, making the same mistakes. The job was beginning to take more out of him than it gave, and the time had come to recharge his batteries while he was working out what he wanted to do in the future. Because that was the thing; he wasn't sure he wanted to continue in the police. And that was something he had hardly even admitted to himself yet.

The pram came to an abrupt halt, as if it had run into a wall. But the obstruction turned out to be no more than a small ridge of snow in the middle of the path. Sævar warily pushed at the pram but it wouldn't budge. As he did so, he heard a sound from inside, a low whimper that usually presaged a full-blown bawling. 'There, there.' He put down both shopping bags and pulled the pram towards him. Perhaps he would be able to go round the ridge. But before he could try it, he heard a voice.

'Been buying up half the shop, I see.'

His mother-in-law, Aðalheiður, had stopped her four-by-four next to the path and wound down her window on the passenger side.

'Are you stuck? Do you need a hand?'

'No, it's no problem,' he said, but Adda was screaming now. Clearly, she could have done with a longer rest. After a good nap, she always woke up making happy gurgling and cooing noises. Not this ear-piercing howl.

Before he knew it, Aðalheiður had got out and come over, leaving her engine running.

'Look, why don't we put your bags in the boot,' she suggested. 'Then you can hurry home with the little one.'

Sævar didn't even try to object.

His mother-in-law was waiting outside the house when he got back with the pram. She ordered him to deal with the shopping, saying she would take care of Adda, who was wide awake after all the jolting.

Sævar did as he was told, letting Aðalheiður tend to Adda while he put away the shopping in the kitchen.

'You know, seeing you've still got so much work to do on the house, why don't I borrow Adda for a while so you can get on with it?' Aðalheiður said. 'It's no problem – I've got a child seat in the car.'

So, that's my day organised for me, Sævar thought as he accepted this fait-accompli disguised as an offer.

Once his mother-in-law had left with Adda and an overflowing nappy bag, Sævar made himself coffee and wondered where to begin.

The boxes had been methodically packed, and when they moved in, he had stacked them in the appropriate rooms. There were boxes marked *SITTING ROOM* in the sitting room and others marked

KITCHEN in the kitchen. Things from his old place and Elma's old flat now combined in their new home.

It was all quite symbolic, he thought: two lives merging into one.

He opened several boxes, then stood there at a loss, undecided about where to put the lumpy candlestick or the photo of Elma with her sister Dagný. In the end he emptied one box by arranging all the contents rather haphazardly on a shelf.

When he opened the next, he discovered that it didn't contain any ornaments, and, on closer inspection, that it hadn't been labelled in capital letters with a marker pen.

It turned out to be full of schoolbooks and loose papers, and only then did Sævar realise what it was. It was the box they'd discovered in the loft shortly after moving in, left behind by the previous owners. The loft had a sloping roof and hadn't been converted into an attic room; there was bare insulation on the ceiling and the rafters were exposed underfoot. He and Elma had visualised it as a cosy space furnished with bookshelves and comfy chairs. A quiet corner. The former occupants had used it as a storage space, and to the delight (or not) of the new owners, had left plenty of junk behind. Old paint pots, offcuts of parquet flooring and tiles, and all kinds of other rubbish that Sævar and Elma had taken to the tip.

Among the junk had been this box containing papers, magazines and old homework exercises, and it had ended up being placed alongside their own boxes.

Sævar took out the sheet of paper on top. It appeared to be an algebra test. The score was 9.8 out of 10.

'Not bad,' he muttered. In the top right-hand corner was a name: *Máni*. Sævar didn't know anyone called Máni but assumed he was a boy who had once lived in the house.

Máni had clearly been better than him at maths.

Next, Sævar lifted out a bundle of pages that were stapled together. An Icelandic test. Turning them over, he saw that the score this time was 9.5. Evidently, schoolwork had presented no problems for Máni.

He replaced the bundle of papers, then noticed that there were some old magazines in there too. He took out a few issues of *Youth*, which was like a trip down memory lane. He used to read them from cover to cover back in the day. Beneath these were some copies of a magazine called *The Fountain*, published in connection with the Christian summer camps at Vatnaskógur. He flicked quickly through them without spotting hymn number 594, but saw countless pictures of boys with happy faces and wished he'd had a chance to go when he was their age.

At the bottom of the box was a spiral-bound notebook, which had presumably belonged to Máni as well. It was dark blue and green, with a picture of a clown on the cover. This wasn't an exercise book.

When Sævar opened it, he saw the word 'Vatnaskógur' written on the first page in big letters. Máni hadn't only been a good student, he'd also had elegant, grown-up handwriting. The year and date had been added underneath: 8 August 1995.

Sævar turned to the next page and read: 'I probably won't write much in this book.'

Yet it appeared that Máni had conscientiously recorded his trip, at least to begin with. Judging by the number of blank pages at the back, he hadn't kept his journal going for the entire week, though. No doubt there had been a packed programme of activities and little time to record everything that happened. Sævar had tried several times to keep a diary himself when he was younger but his attempts had never lasted long.

Closing the book, he put it back in its place, reluctant to pry into someone else's private thoughts. It would be better to track down this Máni and return the stuff to him. He would probably be pleased to recover his old belongings and relive his time at Vatnaskógur.

❂

'The trouble with blows to the hips,' said the doctor, a girl who might as well have been fresh out of school, 'is that they can displace the joints slightly, resulting in shooting pains down the thigh.'

'I see.' Hörður would have liked to tell the girl that he didn't have time for this now. An important investigation had landed on his desk and, while he didn't exactly welcome it, he was glad of the distraction.

'But it looks to me as if you've got off lightly, with no more than a bit of swelling, so I'll write you a prescription for an anti-inflammatory.' The girl carried on talking and Hörður felt foolish. Here he was, barely able to walk, and all that was wrong with him was a swollen hip. Why had he let himself be talked into coming to hospital? He should have resisted instead of listening to Elma.

He left the hospital, hobbling along as fast as his hip would allow. So fast that he didn't notice the woman coming towards him across the foyer until he collided with her.

'Sorry,' he muttered, then saw her face and did a double-take.

Not again.

His cheeks grew hot as he recognised his former classmate who had found him on the ground that morning.

'Why, Hörður!' she said. 'Are you ... were you here because of that fall earlier?'

'Er, no ... well, actually I did get someone to take a quick look at it. My colleague...' What was the matter with him? He could barely stammer out a proper sentence.

'I see. Well, it's a good idea to get these things checked out. I hope it's nothing serious.' Fríða smiled.

'No, no, it's fine.'

'Good.' Fríða smiled again, tucking a lock of hair behind her ear. She had short, dark hair. 'I, er ... actually, I was wondering if we could maybe go for coffee some time? Not because ... I just ... We've both lost our partners after difficult illnesses and it can be helpful to talk to someone who's been through the same ordeal.'

A family walked past, a couple carrying a baby car-seat and luggage. Hörður and Fríða watched them disappear into the December weather outside.

'Yes ... er, sure.' Hörður coughed. 'Though I've got rather a lot on at the moment. I'm heading an investigation – quite a major one.'

'OK.' Fríða nodded, and Hörður thought her face fell. 'Well, you can find me on Facebook if you change your mind.'

Hörður muttered a goodbye and left the building without mentioning that he wasn't even on Facebook and had no intention of changing that.

Great, he thought to himself as he got the full force of the wind in his face. Now he felt guilty, as well as embarrassed at making an unnecessary fuss about his injury. He just didn't need this.

Taking out his phone, he rang Elma.

She'd better come and pick him up right now. When all was said and done, it was her fault he'd been put in this mortifying position.

BEFORE

A Month Earlier

Thorgeir

They're both a little drunk when they leave the restaurant. Outside, it has been dark for a while and the town has undergone a transformation: families and tourists kitted out in arctic survival gear have been replaced by young people inadequately dressed for the weather. In Iceland, November brings frost, not rain, yet the revellers appear oblivious to the freezing conditions.

Neither of them is properly dressed either, but alcohol and excitement keep them warm as they walk through the centre of Reykjavík, first along Austurstræti, then up Laugavegur.

'Where are we going?' she asks eventually.

He realises he has no idea. He's been wandering aimlessly, with no goal other than to spend more time with her.

'We could go to another bar,' he suggests.

'Yes, sure,' she says. 'Somewhere with horribly cheesy music. Like some ageing has-been belting out oldies.'

They pause to take stock and their eyes alight on a bar that is blasting out guitar music and a voice singing '*Sweet Caroline, oh – oh – oh.*'

'There?' he asks.

She nods and takes his hand. There's no queue outside as it's still relatively early, but the place is heaving and they have to elbow their way through the throng to reach the bar.

Thorgeir orders two beers, then changes his mind and gets shots instead. He doesn't fancy trying to hold a beer glass among this jostling crowd and, besides, he wants his hands free, especially as hers is still resting in his.

It's so small. The fingers so delicate he's afraid they'd snap if he squeezed them too tight. In fact, everything about her is petite, pretty and fragile, her neck so slim he could encircle it with the fingers of one hand.

They down their shots at the bar, then abandon their glasses and work their way closer to the singer, not on the dancefloor itself but keeping to the wall. The people around them are singing along. On the floor, two girls are holding hands and caressing each other as they dance.

'This guy's not bad.' He has to raise his voice and lean closer to her to be heard.

'Not bad at all,' she says. 'Great voice.'

'Can you sing?'

'What?' She moves closer to him as the singer increases the volume.

'I said: can you sing? You've got such a lovely voice.'

She bursts out laughing. 'I can sing all right but not very well. Understatement.'

'I wouldn't mind hearing you.'

'You never know, I might let you hear me later.'

'So, you want to see me again?' He's like a nervous schoolboy. She's the one calling the shots. He feels he'd do anything for her.

Andrea half smiles and doesn't say anything, just nods. Her face is so close to his that he can smell the scent of her hair, the mildly perfumed shampoo she uses. A tiny crumb of mascara has fallen onto her cheek and he unthinkingly brushes it away with his finger.

'Sorry,' he says, laughing. 'You had something there.'

'Has it gone?'

'Hang on, let me see.' He leans in, examining her face; the milky skin and luscious, pale-pink lips.

'Maybe not quite,' he says, so softly he's almost whispering, and runs his finger along her lower lip. Her mouth opens a little.

She sucks in a breath and looks suddenly terribly vulnerable, as if his touch has disarmed her. Robbed her of all her defences, her self-confidence.

Thorgeir kisses her to the accompaniment of the singer. The kiss is tentative at first, as if they're reconnoitring the terrain before deciding whether to land. But in the end he lands, pushing her against the wall, tasting her, drinking her in with all his senses.

Not too eager, he warns himself, and backs off slightly. Gazes into her eyes and gently strokes her hair off her face with one finger. He must hold back, mustn't be too impulsive. Mustn't lose control.

'We must have met before,' he says. 'I feel like I know you.'

'I don't think so,' she says.

'That's a shame.'

'Is it?'

He doesn't immediately answer, just smiles. He's feeling better now, more self-confident, certain that Andrea will say yes when he offers her another drink. That she'll say yes when he leads her outside and calls a taxi. Will say *yes, yes, yes* later tonight at the hotel.

'Should we get out of here?' he asks.

And she answers, as he knew she would, with one beautiful word: 'Yes.'

NOW

Wednesday 9 December

'How did it go?' Elma asked when she got back to the hospital, watching as Hörður lowered himself with infinite care into the passenger seat.

He didn't answer until he had finished fastening his seatbelt. 'It was nothing.'

'Nothing? Are you sure?' Elma crumpled up the plastic wrapper from the sandwich she had been eating and pushed it into the compartment between the seats.

'Positive,' Hörður said, adding accusingly: 'As I said all along.'

'Well, that's a relief.'

Elma was glad Thorgeir's flat wasn't far from the hospital as the atmosphere during the drive there was distinctly tense. Hörður was clearly in pain and the doctor's verdict only seemed to have made him more irritable.

'Didn't they even give you a prescription?' Elma asked as she parked. 'We can drop by the chemist.'

'I'll be fine.'

Elma sighed inwardly. She'd never understood people who felt they had to grin and bear it. Like Sævar, for example. He would only take painkillers if he had no choice, whereas she saw no reason to suffer unnecessarily and would happily pop a pill if she felt a headache coming on.

Still, Hörður was an adult and she wasn't about to start bossing him around.

She got out of the car and read the house numbers on the two blocks of flats that stood on a piece of flat, grassy ground and were never called anything other than the Skagaver blocks. The name was taken from the building beside them that had once housed the Skagaver grocer's shop.

As a child, Elma used to skate on the meadow where the blocks now stood. Although there hadn't been a proper pond there, the ground had been so wet and marshy that it had frozen in winter. But now the modern high-rises towered above the surrounding buildings like trolls turned to stone by the coming of the dawn, and no one skated here anymore.

When they reached the top floor, Elma unlocked Thorgeir's flat with a set of keys provided by his mother.

The entrance hall was spacious and tidy. There was a bowl of keys on the chest of drawers, a shoe rack on the floor and a few jackets hanging from the coat hooks. Opening off to the right was a living room; to the left, a kitchen, and a hallway leading to the bedroom and presumably bathroom. Hörður headed for these while Elma went into the kitchen.

The fittings – dark-brown cupboards and black granite surfaces – looked fairly new. Everything was clean apart from two glasses in the sink, which, judging by the sticky residue in the bottom, appeared to have contained some fizzy drink.

Elma pulled on a pair of gloves before opening the fridge. There was no strong odour of rotting food, but, on inspection, the milk turned out to be well past its sell-by date and there was an open packet of ham that smelt a bit off. She closed the fridge and went into the living room.

There was no mess, only an oversized TV mounted on the wall and dark-brown furniture to match the kitchen. Elma was sufficiently familiar with IKEA to recognise various items.

The sun shone in through the window, lighting up a thick layer of dust on the television.

'Elma,' Hörður called.

She found him in the bathroom, gloved up like her. He had opened the medicine cabinet, which turned out to contain several brands of aftershave, a razor and miscellaneous lotions and pots of hair gel.

Hörður took out a glass bottle of aftershave marked *BOSS*. Opening it, he sniffed at the contents before replacing the bottle on the shelf.

'Good smell?'

Elma shrugged. The smell was pleasingly familiar, as if she'd come across it before, though not on Sævar.

'Fluoxetine.' Hörður read the labels on two pill bottles.

'An anti-depressant, isn't it?' Elma picked up one of the bottles and examined the pills. There were only a few left. The other bottle was empty.

'Yes, I think so.'

She put the bottle back in the cabinet and looked around.

The bathroom was small, containing no more than a shower in a smoked glass cubicle, a toilet and a tall cupboard. No sign that anyone but a single man had been living there.

Elma went into the bedroom next. The bed had been made in a hurry; the duvet was crooked under the bedspread, which was also crooked, as if it had been hastily chucked on. Not that this necessarily meant anything. She doubted many people were as fussy as Sævar when it came to making their bed, and she had simply got used to everything being at perfect right angles. She sometimes teased him that if he ever got bored of the police, he could apply for a job as a chambermaid in a hotel.

The windows offered a view of the town centre – in other words, of the short, rather nondescript street that ran past Akratorg square and the church. The white covering of snow lent the scene a certain charm that it normally lacked, and Elma felt a sudden rush of happy anticipation.

She hadn't looked forward to Christmas since she was a child, but this year the prospect of celebrating it with her family filled her with warmth. She looked forward to giving Adda the present she had chosen for her, though her daughter was still far too young to understand what all the fuss was about.

Turning away from the window, Elma contemplated the wardrobe on the other side of the room. She could hear Hörður's footsteps in the hall and the sound of his phone. The ringtone was always set at such a high volume that whenever it rang, everyone else at the police station would jump, regardless of where they were in the building.

'Hörður,' she heard him answer, before his voice moved further away, as if he'd stepped into another room.

She opened the wardrobe, not expecting to find anything useful there. Perhaps she was just being nosy. It was full of clothes, crammed in anyhow rather than neatly folded on the shelves, and she was hit by a wall of aftershave. Clearly, Thorgeir had doused himself in the stuff.

She hurriedly closed the wardrobe again.

The bedroom provided no clues as to why Thorgeir had died like that. She couldn't see his phone anywhere either – not that she had been expecting to. He must have taken it with him to the summer house, where his killer had found and removed it. Did that mean there was incriminating evidence on his phone that could lead them to his murderer?

Remembering the lacy thong she had found in the cabin, Elma bent down and peered under his bed. Sure enough, she glimpsed an item of clothing, which turned out to be a pair of black nylon tights. Not Thorgeir's, presumably, but further confirmation that he'd had a girlfriend or at least a female visitor, whatever the nature of their relationship.

Elma examined the tights. Whoever their owner was, she must have been unusually slim. Then she noticed that they were torn. When she stretched them out, she saw that they were in tatters, as if someone had deliberately ripped them off.

Her thoughts immediately went to the rape charge levelled at Thorgeir twenty years ago. She wondered if he had reverted to his old bad habits. Admittedly, the charge had been dropped. And although Elma didn't know the truth behind it, the statistics told their own story. Very few people brought rape charges without good reason, but the system was seriously flawed and few charges were upheld.

She knew she mustn't read too much into the ripped tights under the bed, but the evidence didn't look good.

❀

Kristjana apparently had no idea she was being watched. She must have got used to having an empty house next door as no one had lived there for months before Elma and Sævar moved in. Or perhaps she simply didn't care who could see her. She appeared to be lost in a world of her own as she waved two scarves in the air and swayed to the music.

At least, Sævar assumed she was listening to music. He couldn't hear any, though the window next to him was open and he leant towards it, straining his ears. He watched as she reached an arm into the air, then whipped it back in a dramatic gesture, twirling the scarf in circles.

He felt he ought to look away. As if he was watching something private.

Kristjana had lost her son, and all he could think was that she must have decided to drown her sorrows.

He only withdrew his gaze when he heard Adda growing restless on her playmat. Aðalheiður hadn't brought her home until dusk was falling. In the meantime, he had managed to unpack several more boxes and done two lots of laundry. Tiny as his daughter was, the pressure on the washing machine had increased exponentially since she came into the world.

Sævar picked her up, then went straight back into the kitchen to see if Kristjana was still at it. Yes, she was there, but she paused abruptly in her dance and wiped her eyes. Was she crying?

Sævar craned his neck sideways to get a better view.

She *was* crying. Kristjana remained standing on the same spot, her shoulders heaving as if she were having trouble breathing.

Sævar felt he should do something. Knock on her door, perhaps, and ask if she was all right or whether he could help in any way. She seemed so alone, and Sævar wondered if she had anybody to turn to; anybody who could support her through the shattering grief that must inevitably result from losing one's child.

Abruptly Kristjana raised her chin. She appeared to have stopped crying. She stood there without moving, staring into space. Time passed. Sævar put Adda down on the floor while he heated water to make porridge.

He was fetching the porridge oats from the cupboard when he saw Kristjana suddenly move fast and purposefully towards one of her kitchen cupboards. Instinctively, he dodged sideways to avoid being seen. Kristjana's kitchen faced their house and when she was standing at the window she had a good view into their place; an opportunity Sævar had seen her taking advantage of on numerous occasions.

Of course, Sævar should respect her privacy and stop spying on her like this. The trouble was that when he finally got a clear glimpse of her face at close quarters, her expression cut him to the quick. The corners of her mouth were turned down, her lips pressed together, her eyes red and bloodshot.

The poor woman.

Only now did he notice what she was holding – a bottle of pills that she shook out into her palm. For a moment or two, she stared down at her hand, then quickly raised it to her mouth. After that, she filled a glass at the sink and took a big gulp. Sævar saw her swallow several times, her eyes closed, her face haggard with suffering.

Sævar put down the packet of oats and stooped to pick up Adda. When he looked out of the window again, there was no sign of Kristjana.

Acting on an impulse, he dashed out of the house in his slippers with Adda still in his arms, and rapped loudly on their neighbour's door.

'Hello,' he called, then waited.

No one answered.

'Sh, sh, it'll be all right,' he whispered to Adda, who was mutely watching what was going on. 'There, there.'

It wasn't the child who needed reassuring.

'Hello,' he called louder.

When nothing happened, he tried the doorhandle. It was open. After a second's hesitation, he walked in.

Inside the house, music was playing, quietly but unmistakably. A Frank Sinatra song. '*Something in your eyes,*' he sang in his silky voice. The air was filled with a heavy scent of roses, tinged with an undertone of something rotten. Sævar found himself stepping softly into the hall, though a voice in his head was telling him that maybe he'd been too impulsive.

He called out Kristjana's name, then, through the door on the left, saw into her kitchen, with a clear view through the window into his own illuminated kitchen next door. A minute ago, Kristjana had been standing there, knocking back pills. There was an empty glass in the sink but he couldn't see the pill bottle anywhere.

Sævar called her name again, then advanced further into the house until he came to a closed bedroom door. He braced himself for the worst – to see the woman lying in bed or on the floor, out for the count. He'd come across people who had overdosed before, and it wasn't a pretty sight. For a moment he wavered, wondering if it was wise to take Adda in there with him, then told himself she was too young to understand what was going on. She wouldn't remember anything.

He turned the doorhandle, holding his breath, but even so he was totally unprepared for the sight that met him. Kristjana was on her feet in the middle of the room, stark naked, with one of the scarves wrapped around her neck. Sævar froze. He was so fazed that he had no idea whether to shut the door and make a hasty exit or to speak to the woman.

'Is … is everything OK?' he asked awkwardly, averting his gaze.

Kristjana's eyes were glazed and the room reeked of alcohol. She stared at him for a long moment, then the corners of her mouth lifted in a smile that was utterly vacant and devoid of mirth, the rest of her face frozen into immobility.

Then she spoke in a deep voice: 'Death is coming,' she said. 'It'll come for us all. You'll see. Mark my words. "And after death we will stand before God, the righteous judge, and be judged by him." … "For the wages of sin is death, but the gift of God is eternal life in Christ Jesus our Lord."'

❁

A gale blew up that afternoon, sweeping clouds of loose snow off the road and trees, which obscured Elma's view as she drove at a snail's pace down the street where Matthías Ottósson lived, peering out at the house numbers.

Elma knew who Matthías was from Hörður, who had mentioned that his father, Ottó, had been the inspector of police in Akranes for many years. According to Kristjana, Matthías had been a friend of Thorgeir's ever since they were kids. Elma was hoping that even if Thorgeir hadn't let on to his mother that he was seeing a woman, he might have discussed that kind of thing with his old friend.

She scurried up the path to the front door, trying to protect her face with her scarf, but couldn't keep the stinging snowflakes out of her eyes. There was no porch to shelter under. She waited a moment for Hörður, who was limping along behind her, to catch up, before pressing the doorbell.

Matthías turned out to be quite a good-looking man, a little older than her, with noticeably small teeth and a gap between the front ones. The gap wasn't unattractive, though it added a coarse note to his appearance, together with the springy, dark hair that he tried unsuccessfully to smooth down once they were sitting in the kitchen.

'I don't know what to say,' Matthías sighed. 'I've only just heard the news from his mother and I can't take it in. I feel like I'm dreaming

– that there must have been a mistake. How did you say it happened? Was he stabbed?'

Elma nodded.

'No, that's impossible. I don't believe it.' His voice was hollow and he was blinking rapidly. 'We've been mates since kindergarten.'

'I'm very sorry,' Elma said. 'Did you have much contact with each other?'

'Did we!? We were developing a program together. Or rather Toggi – Thorgeir – was working on an app.'

'What kind of app?'

'A comprehensive solution for businesses and individuals. It's supposed to be a single platform designed to coordinate information relating to every aspect of your health and well-being. A way of integrating multiple apps within a single user interface, enabling you to share your progress towards various health goals, and that sort of thing.'

This was obviously a well-rehearsed spiel.

'And was it going well?' Hörður asked.

'Very well. We've already signed contracts with several clients as well as securing sponsorship and funding.' Matthías scratched his neck. The fleeting hint of eager anticipation in his expression was abruptly extinguished. 'But I don't suppose anything will come of it now. My input wasn't actually that important when I come to think about it. Toggi was responsible for the design. I'm no good with computers. I just took care of the marketing side.'

Elma wondered if Matthías had had high hopes for this venture with Thorgeir. That might explain why he was sitting at home in his tracksuit on a Wednesday afternoon. He didn't look as if he was about to head out anywhere.

'Do you know if Thorgeir was in any kind of trouble? If anyone had it in for him? If he had any enemies?' Elma always felt a little foolish asking these questions. Unless they were superheroes in a Hollywood movie, few people had enemies. And since most murders were committed by close associates of the victim, people were far more likely to be killed by their friends than by their enemies.

'No, I can't think of anyone. That's why it's so impossible to understand. Are you sure it was him?'

Elma nodded. They had shown Kristjana a photo so she could identify the body. 'Were you aware that he was going to the summer house?'

'No.'

'Do you know who he could have gone with?'

'Well, maybe with the girl he was seeing.'

'So he was in a relationship?' Perhaps there was a harmless explanation for the ripped tights, then. Nylon tights tore easily, after all, and their owner could simply have been in a hurry to pull them off.

'I don't know if things had gone far enough yet to be able to call it a relationship.'

'But he was seeing a girl?'

'Yes,' Matthías said. 'Her name's Andrea.'

Elma made a note of this, relieved to have her suspicion confirmed.

'Have you ever met this Andrea?' Hörður asked.

'Once,' Matthías said. 'Thorgeir invited me and my wife round to supper.'

'Do you have her phone number?'

Matthías shook his head.

'Her full name?' Hörður continued.

'I'm afraid not.'

'Are you friends on Facebook or any other social-media site?' Elma tried.

'No, nothing like that.'

'All right.'

'Though I'm sure you'll find her among Thorgeir's Facebook friends,' Matthías said.

'Yes, no doubt.'

They both stood up and Matthías escorted them to the door.

'Do you know if Thorgeir had shown any signs of becoming interested in religion lately?' Elma asked.

'Religion?' Matthías snorted. 'No way.'

'"No way"? Why do you say that?' Hörður asked.

'Because Thorgeir despised religion and everything to do with it.'

'His mother's very religious,' Elma pointed out.

'Exactly.'

Elma didn't know how to interpret that 'exactly'. Had Kristjana's faith had a negative impact on Thorgeir? All she could think of was that Kristjana might have given him a strict Christian upbringing that Thorgeir had later rebelled against. But before she got a chance to ask, Matthías's phone rang and the call was apparently important because he waved them away and closed the front door behind them as quickly as he could.

❂

That evening they had spaghetti and mince for supper. Ólöf merely nibbled at her food, winding the spaghetti round her fork and letting it slide off again. Then putting a small amount in her mouth and chewing it so slowly that Matthías wanted to grab her chin and forcibly move it up and down.

Hafdís didn't eat much either and hardly so much as glanced at their daughter. She appeared to be in a bad mood following the session with the therapist. Or perhaps it was the news of Thorgeir's death that was weighing heavily on her.

Matthías couldn't work out which it was. Not that it mattered; in just a few short days his life had been turned upside down. He felt like tearing his hair out, just to see if it would hurt; if this was really happening and wasn't some kind of bad dream.

'I've got the papers. The petition for a divorce,' Hafdís announced, once Ólöf had left the table. 'All you need to do is sign.'

Matthías almost dropped his fork on the floor. 'You've got to be joking.'

'What?'

'After the news we've just had, that's all you can think about? Today of all days? Couldn't you have waited ... I don't know, at least a few more days before springing this on me?' He leapt up from the table and slammed his plate down in the sink.

Hafdís didn't move. Matthías was torn by conflicting emotions; one part of him wanted to walk out of the room, the other for Hafdís to apologise and give him a hug. It was such a long time since she – since anyone – had given him a proper hug.

He stood there irresolute for a moment, then leant back against the kitchen unit, his arms folded across his chest as though he were trying to hug himself.

'Matthías,' Hafdís said in a level voice. 'I just can't see the point of delaying. I've made an appointment with the magistrate for immediately after Christmas, but it would be best to fill out the papers in advance. Decide how we intend to share custody and divide up our assets and—'

'Don't,' Matthías broke in, and luckily Hafdís shut up. They were both silent for a while.

Matthías felt as if his ability to think rationally, his sense of self-respect and his grief were all inextricably tangled in one big mess. He wanted what he wasn't supposed to want, and when he acted, it wasn't the way he wanted to.

'Couldn't you just ... just give me a hug?' he asked at last, ashamed of how it sounded.

He could feel Hafdís staring at him but didn't dare look up for fear of what he might see in her eyes. He couldn't bear the coldness, the remoteness he had been aware of over the last few days. She was like a stranger, though they had known each other since their teens. She was his best friend. The mother of his child. His wife.

She was Hafdís. They were Dísa and Matti.

For a long moment, he thought she wasn't going to move, but in the end she came over and put her arms around him. Her embrace was loose at first but he clutched at her as though he were clinging to a rock in a bottomless, raging sea.

Thursday 10 December

'You're in bright and early.' Kári was standing by the coffee machine in the police-station kitchen, emptying yesterday's old grounds into the bin.

'Am I?' Elma looked at the clock. A quarter past seven. 'I've been up for ages.'

'Motherhood?'

'I suppose so.'

Adda had woken up so early that a year ago it would still have counted as night as far as Elma was concerned. It had been half past five when she crawled out of bed and fetched a happily gurgling Adda from her cot. Sævar hadn't even stirred, and Elma had wanted to make the most of this quality time with her daughter since she had a feeling it was going to be a hectic day at work. Yet she had been distracted as she and Adda ate breakfast. Unpacking the previous evening, she had come across a photo album of Sævar's in one of the boxes, and Sævar had reacted strangely, practically tearing it from her hands and rushing out of the room. Elma had been left sitting there, reflecting on the fact that Sævar almost never spoke about his family, about his parents who had died in a car crash when he was twenty. She didn't really know anything about them, and Sævar clearly wanted to keep it that way. She had no idea why.

'The coffee will be ready in a few minutes.' Kári smiled, his dark eyes almost disappearing into their creases. 'Then you can tank up on Mummy fuel.'

Elma returned his smile, though she found the term vaguely offensive. 'Thanks, I'll be in my office.'

On Elma's desk was a pile of papers that hadn't been there the day before. Stuck on top was a yellow Post-it note in Hörður's handwriting: *This arrived yesterday evening. Take a look.*

The first thing she picked up off the pile was a printout of an email. Elma noticed that it had been received at 22:24, which meant that Hörður had been in the office late.

She felt overwhelmed by a mixture of sadness and guilt. She knew Hörður was spending more and more time at the office, presumably to avoid going home. He was still living in the house he had shared with Gígja. Although Elma hadn't been round recently herself, when Sævar visited Hörður back in the summer, he'd reported that nothing had changed since Gígja died. Her jackets were still hanging in the hall cupboard, her shoes were on the floor, her books on the bedside table and her toothbrush in the bathroom.

At the time, it had occurred to Elma to get in touch with Hörður's children, but somehow she'd never got round to it. This was partly because she didn't know whether she ought to interfere, but in the end the truth was that she'd simply forgotten about it. Her own life was so busy with looking after a baby and a dog and moving into a new house; all the fun stuff, all the things associated with starting a new chapter in one's life – things that made her happy.

Her only real complaint was that she wasn't getting enough sleep. Meanwhile, poor Hörður was working late at the office and was probably still confronted with his dead wife's toothbrush every time he got ready for bed in the evening. He'd been in a foul mood all day yesterday too, but soldiered on as if there was nothing wrong. Hörður didn't usually take his temper out on his team like that but perhaps things had changed.

Elma released a long breath and started reading the email.

It contained everything the IT department had extracted from Thorgeir's computer. This hadn't taken long since, despite being a software engineer, Thorgeir hadn't bothered to protect his computer with a password, which was strange in itself. Unless he didn't see any point since he lived alone. There was his search history, his photos and files, his social media profiles and everything he had watched or searched for on Netflix, YouTube and the other main platforms over the last few weeks.

Which was quite a lot, judging by the stack of papers awaiting Elma's attention.

Before she could get stuck in, the door opened. She was expecting to see Kári's dark head but instead it was Begga who appeared, bearing two mugs of coffee. She and Elma had become good friends since Elma started work at the Akranes police station three years ago.

'You need a hand,' she said. It wasn't a question but a statement.

'Have a seat.' Elma waved to the chair on the other side of the desk and gratefully accepted a mug. Coffee never tasted better than in the morning after a bad night's sleep. She was more than ready for another cup.

'So, what do we have here?'

Elma put her in the picture, then set about dividing the papers into smaller piles, one for the search history, another for social media. In addition, she noticed that although they didn't have Thorgeir's phone, his text messages had been linked to his computer, which meant they were stored there as well.

Elma looked up the first number and saw Matthías's name.

'Matthías,' Begga said. 'Wasn't he a friend of Thorgeir's?'

'Yes.'

'Right.' Begga chucked a handful of toffees onto the desk, retrieved from some invisible source.

Elma unwrapped one. Judging by how warm they were, she guessed they'd been sitting in Begga's pocket.

'Do you know him?'

'No, not personally,' Begga said. 'But I heard they were working on an app together. I saw something about it in the local news.'

'That's right.'

'I heard it was going brilliantly. Something relating to health and lifestyle, wasn't it? That would enable you to link everything via a single app to produce an overall picture. I think the idea was that companies could use the app to reward their employees.'

'Reward them? What for?'

'Getting enough sleep and exercise, walking to work, etcetera.'

'Seriously? Isn't that rather intrusive? The Data Protection Authority is bound to have objections if companies use an app to track personal information like that.'

'Maybe. But they'd secured backers and a grant and everything.'

'So I hear.'

'Right.'

'How come you know so much about it? Did all this info come out in the news?'

Begga looked a little sheepish. 'A friend told me. He's pretty well informed about that kind of thing.'

'What friend?'

'Just a guy I've been chatting to.'

'I see.' Elma gave Begga a searching look. It occurred to her that, as in the case of Hörður, she hadn't been fully present recently. Begga had been round for the odd visit and cuddled and patted Adda as if she were her cat rather than a small child. In the early weeks, Elma had been constantly on edge, afraid that Begga wasn't supporting the baby's head properly. Begga could be a bit clumsy and over boisterous at times, but Adda adored her and lit up every time she saw her. Nevertheless, it was a long time since Elma and Begga had sat down together over a glass of wine. A long time since they'd last had a proper heart-to-heart.

'Is he fit?' she asked.

Begga looked up in surprise, then shrugged. 'I couldn't give a toss about looks. He's funny, Elma. You know what a soft spot I have for guys who make me laugh.'

'I do.' Elma smiled.

'And he's got a bit of a gut on him. You know what a soft spot I have for those too.'

Elma burst out laughing. She was well aware that Begga preferred her men to be on the cuddly side. 'We'll have to have a catch-up in your hot tub as soon as things have calmed down a bit.'

'We will,' Begga agreed.

'By the way,' Elma said, 'did nothing useful emerge from your interviews with the summer-house owners in Skorradalur?' Kári had told her he'd put the report on her desk but it must be buried underneath all the papers from Hörður.

'Well ... we didn't manage to get hold of everyone, but no one we talked to had seen or heard anything suspicious. The only interesting detail we learnt was that some people had noticed that Thorgeir was at the property. Oh, and one man thought it was strange that the lights had been on all night on Friday, or at least he thought so, then not at all after that.'

'Not at all?'

'No, not during the day or night. It struck him as odd because the car was still parked outside.'

'I have to agree with him,' Elma said. This information confirmed their assumption that Thorgeir had died not long after his arrival at the cabin. 'But no one noticed anyone there with him?'

'No.' Begga unwrapped another toffee. 'But someone saw a taxi there on Friday night.'

'Interesting.' Elma would have to get on to the taxi companies and find out if any had a record of driving a client to or from the summer-house area in Skorradalur.

'And there's another thing. I don't know if it's important but I spoke to Matthías's parents too, Ottó and Jónína. Ottó used to be the inspector here.'

'Yes, I was aware of that,' Elma said. According to Hörður, his old boss Ottó had a reputation for being bloody-minded and difficult to get along with.

'They own a cabin in the vicinity,' Begga continued. 'Not near enough to have seen anything, but I felt I ought to share the information with you.'

'That's exactly the kind of information you ought to share with me.' Elma leant back in her chair.

'Yes, I had a feeling it was.'

'And has anyone been at their cabin during the last couple of weeks?'

'Ottó didn't think so. He was away at the weekend,' Begga replied. 'But they said all their kids have keys and can use the summer house whenever they like.'

'Including Matthías?' Elma asked.

'Including Matthías.'

❀

Thorgeir's search history was certainly revealing, though not in the way Elma had hoped. The portrait it painted was of a man who had mainly looked at stuff connected to football, cars and porn. But the porn wasn't even steamy enough to shock Elma. Although some of the search terms were pretty hardcore and Thorgeir had apparently had a taste for fairly crude material, that wasn't uncommon. The websites were all the usual ones too, sites popular with Icelanders, none of them illegal, though no doubt some of the videos and their contents would be seen as controversial.

Thorgeir had hung out on social media too but mainly in the role of observer rather than participant. One of those people who have profiles everywhere but don't post much themselves, despite spending a lot of time online.

He had been spending less time on social media in recent weeks, though, and Elma wondered if this was due to Andrea. Some evenings his computer showed virtually no activity at all. Had those been the evenings he spent with her?

When Elma trawled through the messages linked to his phone, she saw that most of Thorgeir's interactions had been with his friend Matthías.

Sorted, said one text, accompanied by the money-with-wings emoji. Others showed that they met up frequently. Short messages such as *here* or *outside* had been sent fairly regularly on both sides. They'd exchanged a lot of phone calls too, according to the records from Thorgeir's provider, at all times of the day and night. Elma used a highlighter to mark his interactions with Matthías.

She went through all the numbers that appeared on Thorgeir's phone summary without finding a single one registered to an Andrea. Though she did find an unlisted number, presumably belonging to a burner phone.

Thorgeir's interaction with this number had begun over a month ago and although it was intermittent, there were a few messages that Elma guessed must be from Andrea. On 2 November Thorgeir had sent a text asking about muesli. Strange, but maybe Elma just didn't understand the context.

Over the next two weekends it was clear from the texts they exchanged that they had agreed to meet up at Thorgeir's place in Akranes. But the messages gave no clue as to whether they'd gone to the summer house together the weekend of Thorgeir's murder. On the other hand, they had exchanged some phone calls, including one on the Friday morning before the weekend in question.

Perhaps Thorgeir had given her a lift and they'd travelled to the summer house together. Apart from the taxi, no one had seen another car outside the property that weekend, so Elma assumed that Thorgeir's guest must have shared a car with him. In that case, she wondered, how had the guest got home?

Elma pulled up a list of all the taxi companies in Iceland. But experience told her that although the companies recorded all their jobs, going through their records was a time-consuming business. Nevertheless, if a taxi had gone all the way out to Skorradalur that weekend for a pick-up, it would soon come to light.

Elma wasn't optimistic, though. The idea that someone would butcher Thorgeir by stabbing him seven times, then coolly call themselves a cab just didn't sound plausible to her.

BEFORE
Thorgeir

She's gone by the time he wakes up. She hasn't even left a dent in the pillow beside him. Yet her scent lingers in the air. Not perfume but a hair product of some kind. He remembers burying his nose in her hair and breathing in the fragrance as she lay underneath him last night.

Snatches of yesterday evening and night come back to him; things they said and did, the way her eyes sparkled when she laughed.

The memories are still there when Thorgeir gets home later that day. This is unusual, since he rarely lets his mind dwell long on the girls he sleeps with. Not because he's arrogant enough to think that no girl is good enough for him, but for two reasons that long ago dictated his decision to remain single. The first is that no one can compare to the girl who has possessed his heart ever since his school days. There's no room for anyone else as long as that girl is still in his life.

The second reason is that he is damaged. No good. He's a flawed human being and has been ever since he was a child. He has nothing to offer; he's not like other people in that respect and can't picture himself ever having a normal family life. Perhaps the truth is that he's afraid. Afraid of recreating his own childhood. Afraid of turning into his parents.

He's experiencing an odd sensation: not hungover exactly, but his mood is simultaneously heavy yet light. Andrea's scent seems to linger in his nose and he doesn't want it to fade. He wonders why she left the way she did, vanishing like a ghost at first light.

For a moment it occurs to him that she might not have been real. There's something dreamlike about his memories of their evening and night together.

The days pass and his feelings only intensify.

He hasn't experienced anything like this since he was in his teens; the need to release the pent-up tension in his body several times a day, each time closing his eyes and giving free rein to his fantasies instead of resorting to the internet as he usually does. Visualising again those small, perfectly formed breasts and stiff nipples. Imagining her moans as he enters her, picturing her face, eyes closed, lips slightly parted.

He hopes fervently that he'll get to meet Andrea again. This is a new experience for him and he can't quite grasp what is happening.

He just hopes she doesn't search for his name online.

NOW

Thursday 10 December

'Why do people have unlisted phone numbers?' Elma asked Hörður as she walked into his office.

'Because they want to conceal their identity,' Hörður replied.

'Just what I thought.'

'But that doesn't necessarily mean they have bad intentions. Some people just don't want their name associated with a number.'

'No, I suppose not,' Elma agreed, thinking, nevertheless, that anyone who didn't want to be associated with a particular number must have something to hide.

Although Andrea's name hadn't cropped up anywhere in the text messages Thorgeir had exchanged with the unlisted number, Elma was fairly sure that it must be the girl Matthías had mentioned. She'd assumed the relationship had been fairly well established, but now it seemed they had only met recently. The first texts they'd exchanged were from around six weeks ago, at the beginning of November.

The fact that Andrea was such a shadowy presence – nowhere to be found on social media, her phone number unlisted – seemed suspicious. Did she have something to hide or was it purely coincidental?

'Any more news from forensics yet?' Elma asked, taking a seat.

'No, they're still looking into it.'

'What about the knife? Or the blood on the floor?'

Hörður removed his glasses and rubbed his eyes. He looked tired and drawn, and the impression was even more obvious without his glasses. 'We do know that the knife wasn't used to kill Thorgeir; there was no sign of fresh blood on it. The stain on the floor was old as well. Why don't we just ask Kristjana about it?'

'OK.' Elma hadn't liked to raise the subject when she went round to break it to the old woman that her son had been murdered, since there was no reason to believe it was directly linked to the case. 'It looks almost as if there had been another murder at the summer house.'

'You'd think so.' Hörður gave a wry smile. 'But there's bound to be a harmless explanation.'

'They built the cabin.'

'Hmm?'

'Kristjana and her husband built the cabin, so it's not like anyone else has ever lived there.'

'Then no doubt all will be explained when we talk to her.'

Líf from forensics had told Elma that blood loss on that scale could only have resulted from a serious accident. But the knife discovered under the house may simply have been an old kitchen one. It had been dirty and covered in rust, which made it impossible to tell whether there was blood on the blade. Perhaps it was just Elma's overactive imagination, but she found her next-door neighbour hard to work out. One moment, Kristjana seemed capable of anything; the next, she seemed like a helpless old lady. Deeply eccentric, yes, but hardly dangerous.

There was a knock at the door and Begga appeared. 'Am I interrupting?' she asked.

'No. What is it?' Hörður began rapidly drumming the desk with two fingers. It was a habit that set Elma's teeth on edge and ratcheted up her stress levels.

'I've been sifting through the evidence relating to the case and I came across the girl who brought a charge against Thorgeir.'

'Yes, right. Sól—…' Elma said.

'Sóley.' Begga came right into the room and pushed the door to behind her. 'I looked her up online, and guess what?'

Elma and Hörður didn't even try, just waited for Begga to continue.

'She posted a status update. Just before the weekend.'

'And…'

'About Thorgeir,' Begga said. 'I mean, she doesn't come right out and name him, but, reading between the lines, it's clear what she's talking about.'

'The rape charge that was dropped?'

'That's it,' Begga said. 'She's one of the women who are sharing their stories.'

The debate had been raging on social media ever since the #MeToo movement had gathered pace. People found a release for their heated emotions through their keyboards. Elma was sceptical that this could have anything to do with the murder, though. Maybe if the case had been recent, still fresh in the victim's memory, but it was twenty years since Sóley had brought the accusation.

'She gives quite a detailed account of what happened,' Begga continued. 'I compared her story to the report on file. They were at a party with mutual friends and knew each other vaguely. He was twenty, she was seventeen. They got chatting and were both drinking. She claims she got drunk and can hardly remember anything until she was lying in bed with Thorgeir on top of her. Her friends had gone home but there were still some boys in the other room. They all gave witness statements saying that Thorgeir and Sóley had been getting physical with each other during the evening and had started kissing before they disappeared into one of the bedrooms. None of them heard her protesting or calling for help, and Thorgeir insisted that the sex had been consensual.'

In other words, Elma thought, it was one of those cases that weren't straightforwardly black and white, which made it difficult for the victim to press charges. The main problem was that it was impossible to prove that the alleged rapist had intended to commit a crime. At least, many men claimed that it had never occurred to them they were doing anything wrong, and there was rarely a third party present to testify against them.

'So she didn't mention Thorgeir by name?' Elma asked.

'Not directly,' Begga replied. 'But she said the man lived in Akranes and she mentioned his workplace. It would have been pretty easy to discover his identity from those details. Akranes is a small town.'

'Yes, that wouldn't present any problems,' Hörður agreed, suddenly rapping the desk with all his fingers at once, loud enough to make them both start.

❂

At eleven o'clock it was finally time for Adda's first sleep. Sævar, feeling as if he'd been up for twenty-four hours already, wouldn't have minded taking a nap too, preferably in a pram designed for grown-ups, seeing how cosy his daughter looked in her little sleeping bag.

But that line from the hymn kept running through his head. What kind of person would stab a man to death, then write that on the wall? 'Take away my crimes and sins with blood.' It had to have some special significance, beyond the obvious context. The murderer had evidently felt compelled to leave a message for the people who found Thorgeir.

Sævar searched for the text on his phone and got the same results as before. Since the hymn was sung on a variety of Christian occasions, this could conceivably point to someone who had attended an event of this kind with Thorgeir. His mother must have seen to it that he had a Christian education, given that she had run the Sunday school for many years, but the hymn seemed an odd choice for children.

Nevertheless, it did seem to have a connection to the YMCA, more specifically to the centre at Vatnaskógur, and Sævar wondered if Thorgeir had attended summer camps there, like Máni, the owner of the diary he'd found. Could the boys have been neighbours? Friends even? Could they have gone to Vatnaskógur together?

He picked up Máni's diary and saw again that the date he'd written at the front was 1995, which meant it was twenty-five years old.

In 1995 Sævar himself had been thirteen and living a carefree life up north in Akureyri, messing around with his friends. Hanging out together in the evenings and playing games that had mainly consisted of dares, like ringing people's doorbells and running away, or kissing girls.

Sævar opened his laptop and typed the year and 'Vatnaskógur' into the search engine. Various results appeared, and after scrolling through them for a while he came across an article from an old issue of *The Fountain*, the magazine produced by the YMCA centre at Vatnaskógur. It included adverts for the courses held there in 1995. After a spot of mental arithmetic, which required an embarrassing amount of effort on his part, Sævar worked out that Thorgeir would have been sixteen at the time.

Which meant that he could well have gone to Vatnaskógur that summer.

According to Sævar's mother-in-law, Aðalheiður, Thorgeir and his mother had lived in the house next door for many years, so Thorgeir must therefore have been Máni's neighbour. Sævar didn't know how old Máni was but guessed from his handwriting and the sort of thing he had written that he would have been a teenager in 1995. There had only been one week open to teenagers that summer: 8 to 16 August. Eight days. And the group had been mixed, with both girls and boys, which would no doubt have been even more of a draw. Thorgeir and Máni could easily have been at the camp together that summer.

Sævar was born in 1982; he was two years short of forty. When he reached that age it would be twenty years since his parents had died, and he would have lived as long without them as with them. It was a disconcerting thought.

He would have been too young for the teenage group that summer, even if he had been living in Akranes at the time, but some of the older guys he knew from school might have gone to Vatnaskógur. Perhaps they had known Máni and would be able to put him in touch, so he could hand over the box of belongings.

The hymn, the line on the wall, might also make more sense to his friends than it did to him and Elma. Maybe you had to have attended the camps to understand what it meant, assuming it had any significance beyond the obvious one of taking away sins with blood.

Sævar played dads' football with some of these guys every Thursday evening and it just so happened that today was Thursday. He hadn't necessarily been intending to go along but now he logged onto Facebook and let the group know he was planning to attend.

❂

Sóley worked as a CrossFit trainer and had just finished a class when Elma turned up. Her hair was drawn back into such a severe pony-tail that despite her sweaty face she had scarcely a single hair out of place. She was wearing a tight orange vest and black trousers that were covered in a white powder that looked like flour. Her skin glowed with endorphins as she flashed Elma a brilliantly white smile.

But the instant Elma explained why she was there, the smile was switched off.

'I was seventeen when it happened,' Sóley said. 'I'd only just started drinking. Really, I was no more than a child. I had no idea what I was doing or how risky it was. Me and my friends went to the party together. There were some older boys there and my friend had a crush on one of them.'

Elma had read both the account on Sóley's Twitter feed and the police report, so she knew how the story continued, but she decided to let Sóley tell it her own way.

'Thorgeir was all over me that evening. He wouldn't leave me alone, kept touching me. Stroking my stomach, my bum. He was three years older than me and I found it uncomfortable, but I didn't dare say anything. I suppose it was because me and my friends were much younger than the kids holding the party and I was afraid we'd be thrown out.' Sóley's face suddenly split in a wide smile, her eyes focusing on something beyond Elma. 'Thanks for coming,' she called to a couple who waved to her and thanked her in return.

Elma expected Sóley to continue with her tale once the couple had gone, but instead she lapsed into silence, her gaze resting on the closed door.

'Did you have any contact with Thorgeir after that?' Elma asked.

'No, God help me. No way.'

Elma wondered whether this mention of God had any deeper significance. Could Sóley be religious; the type to leave behind a quotation about sins and blood? Thorgeir appeared to have sinned, in her eyes at least.

Before Elma could ask, Sóley added: 'You know, I didn't go to the police until several days later. And all that time he kept pestering me with emails, asking me to meet up with him. Like he didn't think anything had happened. Like he couldn't see what he'd done.'

'What sort of things did he say to you?'

'Oh, the usual – asking how I was and what I was up to that evening. I didn't answer, but that didn't stop him. He even emailed my friend to find out why I wasn't replying.' Sóley took a swig from her water bottle. 'One evening, when I went to pull the curtains, I saw a car parked by the kerb near our house. The lights were on and there was somebody in the front seat.'

'Was it him?'

Sóley nodded. 'I was so scared I lay awake all night, listening for noises outside. I jumped every time I heard a door slam or the trees rustling in the garden. Next day I told my dad what had happened.'

'Did he stop harassing you after you went to the police?' Elma asked. She doubted Thorgeir would have seen his behaviour as harassment at the time, and she had no idea whether he had subsequently changed his behaviour towards women.

'He sent me a long email that was half apology, half accusing me of being a liar. "Sorry that you misunderstood me like that" was the basic message.' Sóley gave an exasperated sigh. 'Anyway, I blocked him and changed my phone number, and after that we went abroad – me and my family. We were away for a month. When I got back, he didn't try to contact me again. Either that or he never managed to get hold of my new number. As for the bloody rape charge, it just lay there on somebody's desk at the police station until it was eventually filed away in a drawer.'

The bitterness in Sóley's voice was unmistakeable. She had good reason to want Thorgeir dead, even though a long time had elapsed since the alleged rape.

'Where were you last weekend?' Elma asked.

Sóley didn't turn a hair at the question. 'On Friday I was at home with my partner. I led a training session on Saturday morning and another on Sunday afternoon. On Saturday evening I met up with my sewing circle and at Sunday lunchtime I attended a children's birthday party.'

'OK, great.' Elma asked for the phone numbers of Sóley's partner and her friends from the sewing circle to confirm her alibi.

'Wow, how ironic,' Sóley said, unsmiling. 'It never occurred to me that I'd one day be asked for an alibi in connection with a crime involving Thorgeir. I mean, it's not like my case was ever properly followed up. The police went and had a word with Thorgeir, but they chose to believe him, not me.'

'I'm sorry,' Elma said and meant it. She often felt frustrated by her own powerlessness in cases like these. Wished she could do more to fight the system, wished the cases themselves weren't so complicated.

Sóley shrugged. As far as she was concerned, the fact that Elma was sorry was neither here nor there.

'To be honest, I couldn't care less what happened to Thorgeir,' she said. 'He was murdered, wasn't he?'

Elma nodded.

'Perhaps it was another girl like me,' Sóley said pensively. 'Only she did what I should have done at the time instead of just lying there, not even daring to cry.'

The computer emitted a loud bleep to notify Hörður that he'd received an email. He jumped, then hammered on the button to turn down the volume.

Who the hell had set it that high? No need to announce to the whole station that he'd got a message.

He clenched his fists, closed his eyes and inhaled deeply.

His foul temper wasn't achieving anything. He barely recognised himself anymore. Soon he'd be as bad as his old boss, forever muttering under his breath or barking out orders left and right. Hörður had loathed the man but put up with him because he'd liked his job.

When he took over the position himself, he'd made a deliberate decision not to emulate his predecessor but to be a completely different kind of boss. There was no question that, as a result, the atmosphere at the station was far better today than it had been twenty years ago. Treating colleagues as equals rather than enforcing a reign of terror quite simply worked better. Hörður had once seen a TV programme about how a fear-based workplace culture increased the risk of serious accidents, particularly in cases where there was an obvious hierarchy: in hospitals, for example, where nurses were afraid to question doctors' decisions, or on aeroplanes where the flight attendants didn't dare criticise the pilot.

Similarly, Hörður was convinced that a number of cases could have been solved more speedily if the atmosphere at the station in Akranes had been less toxic when he started working there.

He sensed that the painkillers were beginning to kick in – presumably the pills he'd taken an hour ago rather than the ones he'd just this minute knocked back. A pleasant numbness spread through his body and he could feel his tension easing. The pain didn't disappear altogether but it became more bearable. Then suddenly he found he was having trouble swallowing, his heartbeat became erratic and it felt as if there was a lead weight on his chest. He tried to massage it away with his fist before turning back to his computer.

The email turned out to contain Thorgeir's bank statement, which

Hörður had requested the day before. It showed all Thorgeir's transactions over the last few months. Hörður's attention was immediately drawn to one entry, and, after mulling it over for a minute or two, he went and knocked on Elma's door.

'There's something I'd like you to come and take a look at,' he said.

Elma followed him into his office where the air was filled with the smell of hot paper and freshly printed ink.

'This is Thorgeir's bank statement,' Hörður said, pulling a sheet of paper out of the printer.

Elma's eyes widened when she saw the sums involved. There were ninety-two million krónur in Thorgeir's account. That was more than six hundred and fifty thousand US dollars. A hundred million had been transferred to him by a company called RxB.

'It's not an Icelandic company,' Hörður said. 'It's registered in Switzerland, so it's going to be tricky getting our hands on any information about the owners.'

The simple fact that the firm was registered in Switzerland was enough to rouse suspicion. Thanks to the country's low-tax regime, people from all over the world chose to register companies there. The purpose was obvious: to avoid paying high taxes in their homelands.

Elma noticed something else. Ten million krónur had been transferred from Thorgeir's account a week ago, just a day or two before he was murdered. The most interesting part wasn't the amount, though, but the identity of the recipient.

❂

Hafdís could hardly wait to get out of the house. The atmosphere was so oppressive that she looked forward to every minute she could spend away from her soon-to-be ex-husband. Maybe she was a bad person but she could hardly stand to look Matthías in the face anymore.

The more he tried to cling to her, the more desperately she longed to tear herself free. He was suffocating her and all she wanted was to get away so she could breathe again.

She couldn't believe she had stuck it out this long. Married for eleven years, together for twenty-five. Far too large a part of her life wasted on something she had never been a hundred-per-cent sure about and now couldn't take any longer. As far as she was concerned, Matthías was history. She'd had enough.

Hafdís scraped her hair back in a bun, fastened the band over her ears, then pulled on her swimming shoes and gloves, and emerged from the changing rooms into the icy air. She didn't bother with a robe or wrap a towel around herself since it was only a few steps down to the beach and from there to the water. As she descended the concrete steps and crossed the wet sand, she looked straight ahead, over the black sea to the lights of Reykjavík twinkling in the distance.

She was perfectly aware that swimming alone in the sea in the cold and dark wasn't recommended, but it didn't worry her. She just assumed that this advice was aimed at other people – like the elderly or those who didn't enjoy her level of health and fitness.

The moon gleamed on the waves and her senses were filled with the smell and sound of the sea.

She needed to purge her thoughts. Ever since Thorgeir died, she had been waiting for the police to contact her. She knew it was inevitable, but not when it would happen. She'd rather get it over with as soon as possible. She had even decided exactly what she was going to say.

The shock of the cold temporarily froze her limbs. Then the sensation went full circle and became its opposite, burning her like fire. Used to the effects, Hafdís walked steadily forwards until the water came up to her waist.

It was a head game. A question of willpower. How far was she prepared to push her boundaries? What was she capable of?

She'd always had an unshakeable belief in herself and acted without stopping to think. Reckless? Maybe. But at least she was a woman who achieved things rather than watching and waiting. She just dealt with the consequences later. If there was something she couldn't stand it was passivity and fear.

Hafdís filled her lungs, then crouched down until the water was up to her neck. Mentally she counted – *one, two, three* – focusing on her breathing, trying to slow her thunderous heartbeat and move her arms. She swam a few strokes, her limbs sluggish, almost paralysed by the cold.

In temperatures as low as this it took only a few brief minutes for the effects to be felt. She closed her eyes, forcing herself to stay submerged a few seconds longer.

Something brushed against her foot, making her gasp. Only seaweed, she thought, but she couldn't ward off the idea that it might be something else.

Someone else.

At times she was seized by a conviction that there was something on the seabed tugging at her, trying to drag her down. For years she'd had recurrent dreams about drowning; not of sinking to the bottom so much as being pulled inexorably under the surface while she thrashed in vain to escape.

Strong-minded as she was, she hadn't been able to prevent these dreams and she hated the fact. Hated not being perfectly in control of her circumstances and her own mind.

Hafdís kicked her leg to free it from the weed, then glanced back at the shore. There was a figure silhouetted against the distant street lights, standing on the beach beside the rocks, head turned in her direction. She peered through the gloom, trying to see if it was someone she knew, but she couldn't even tell if it was a man or a woman.

The cold suddenly became so overpowering that Hafdís had to get out, and she waded back to the beach so fast that she stumbled and almost lost her footing. Once she was back on dry land, the icy wind felt like a warm breeze as it flowed over her blotchy red skin, which was now on fire from the cold.

Hafdís watched the distant figure disappear in the direction of the retirement home. Just someone taking an evening stroll, she supposed. Langisandur beach and its surroundings were one of the town's chief beauty spots and, as such, a popular area with walkers.

Feeling energised after her sea swim, she walked unhurriedly up the steps towards the changing cabins.

'Hafdís?'

Hafdís realised immediately who it was. She knew Hörður, the head of police in Akranes, by sight, and she'd also seen the female officer with him before, though she couldn't remember her name.

'Could we have a very quick word?' It was the woman who spoke.

'Can I get dressed first?' Hafdís asked, smiling. In spite of her gloves and shoes, she was starting to feel the cold.

'Of course,' the woman said.

Hafdís took her time about getting dressed, her body moving slowly after her immersion in the freezing water. Meanwhile, she mentally rehearsed her answers to the questions she knew the police were waiting to ask her. Where had the money come from and what was the nature of her relationship with Thorgeir? She had the answers down pat and by the time she emerged from the changing rooms, she was prepared for anything they might throw at her.

BEFORE
Thorgeir

Two weeks pass and they meet several times. He drives to see her in Reykjavík and she comes to visit him. Everything is going well. Better than well: Thorgeir is on cloud nine.

He decides to invite her for dinner with Matthías and Hafdís. It's something he's always dreamt of doing. He's been the third wheel all these years, but no longer – he's got Andrea now. So Thorgeir turns down an invitation to go to his mother's house for fish on Friday evening, then, feeling guilty, promises to drop by the bakery in the morning. His mother has lived alone and drunk too much ever since his father died, when Thorgeir was in his teens. They both pretend it's not a problem. Some things can't be changed.

From the moment Thorgeir gets home from work on Friday until Andrea arrives, he rushes around, tidying up and cleaning. He just has time to jump in the shower and change into a white T-shirt and light-grey trousers. Opening the bathroom cabinet, he selects his most expensive aftershave.

By the time the doorbell rings, the flat is almost embarrassingly immaculate. The whole place reeks of cleaning products and he wishes he'd made do with a tidy-up. It gives the impression he's trying too hard and it's so … obvious.

When he sees her, though, she's the one who is being obvious, fiddling with her hair, constantly winding a strand round her finger and tugging at it.

'Feeling stressed?' he asks, finally breaking off his kiss.

'No,' she says. 'Not at all.'

He knows her well enough by now to tell when she's lying.

'It'll be fun,' he says, taking her hand and leading her into the living room, where he's already opened a bottle of fizz, her favourite kind. He wants to spoil her, to give her everything in his power. He genuinely wants her to be happy. This desire to go out of his way to please a girl is a new experience for him, but it feels good. Very good. He has even started letting his thoughts stray further, much further than he would like to admit. He's starting to wonder if she'd be willing to move into his flat, whether she could get a job in Akranes and whether she'd actually want to live here.

'What are your friends' names again?' she asks.

'It's only my best friend, Matthías, or Matti, and his wife Hafdís. They're great,' he reassures her. 'I've known them both since we were kids. You're going to like them.'

'I'm sure I will.'

'You only have to smile and everyone will love you,' he adds.

Andrea nods, sucking on her lower lip, and it comes home to Thorgeir that he loves her. The realisation hits him like a shock wave: he loves her.

They clink glasses, and Andrea practically empties hers in one go. She's cute when she's stressed like this. Thorgeir wants to tell her at once that he loves her. He wants to announce it to the world, shout it from the rooftops. Without pausing to think, he goes ahead and says it, the words spilling out of him like a glass overflowing.

'I love you,' he says, and the three words hang in the air between them as the seconds tick by and his heart begins to beat uncomfortably fast.

Andrea is very still for a moment, then she opens her mouth, but before she can speak the doorbell rings. Never in his life has he hated a sound so much. He wishes he could tell the bell to fuck off. Instead, he smiles and gets to his feet.

Because he *can* control his temper. Even when he's drinking.

'Come in,' he says, holding the door open for Hafdís and Matthías.

Andrea hangs back, a shy smile on her lips. She's wearing a short, wide dress with thin straps, revealing slender shoulders, and sheer tights above high boots with thick heels.

Andrea is young and beside his friends she looks even younger. Like their daughter, almost. But they don't show what they're thinking as they greet her; Hafdís gives her a hug.

After dinner, they migrate to the sofa and Matthías opens a bottle of champagne: Veuve Clicquot 2012. 'So, where did you two meet?' he asks.

Andrea catches Thorgeir's eye and he answers vaguely: 'In town.'

Hafdís, misunderstanding, sighs. 'Those were the days. How long is it since we went out on the town, Matti?'

'We go out together,' he replies, slightly defensively.

'Yes, but not in Reykjavík.'

'No, that's true. We used to go clubbing when we were kids in our teens and twenties.' Matthías glances at Andrea and makes a face. 'Sorry – not kids. I didn't mean it like that.'

Andrea smiles. 'No worries, I didn't take it that way,' she says and tries to sip from her glass without realising that it's empty. Thorgeir gives her a refill.

A brief silence falls, then Hafdís says, as if to herself: 'God, I miss it.'

'What?' Matthías asks.

'Being young and not having to think about anything except where you're going to start the weekend. No worries about mortgages or being a taxi service for your kids day in, day out.'

'Oh, sorry, I didn't realise your life was so tough,' Matthías teases, but there's an edge to his voice. A hurt note.

'You know I don't mean it like that,' Hafdís says.

'Why don't we mix ourselves some whiskey sours?' Thorgeir says to Matthías, trying to head off a marital tiff. 'I've bought everything we need.'

'Sure, now you're talking.'

Thorgeir rises to his feet, reluctant to leave Andrea there on her own. But he's reassured to see that she's started chatting to Hafdís, smiling as she tells her something.

'You've done well there,' Matthías says in an undertone once they're in the kitchen. 'I mean…' He snatches a glance back into the living room, puffs air into his cheeks, then slowly releases it. 'She's young, but you seem well suited.'

'Yes. I know.' Thorgeir can feel his chest swelling with pride.

'How did you manage …? Where…?' Matthías laughs ruefully and shakes his head. 'Nah, it doesn't matter. I'm just glad you've found someone. I don't think I ever remember you introducing us to a girl before.'

'No,' Thorgeir says, thinking privately that there's a reason for that.

'Doesn't the age difference bother you?'

'No, I don't really give it a thought,' Thorgeir replies.

'Seriously?' Matthías shoots another glance in the direction of the living room. 'Sometimes I wish I could turn the clock back and be twenty again. Relive that time with Hafdís – the early years.'

Thorgeir's mouth twitches down in a half-smile but he doesn't reply. The truth is, he doesn't miss being twenty. It was great until suddenly it wasn't. Until, without warning, everybody turned against him. He tries not to dwell on the fact that when he needed his friends most, his phone never rang. Underneath he's still hurt and angry that Matthías didn't stand by him when that girl accused him of rape, but he buries his resentment deep inside. He can't afford to lose any more friends. They've only ever referred to the incident once, not long after it happened. They were drinking at the time and Matthías whispered a single sentence to him:

'Sorry, man, I just didn't know what to believe.'

A single sentence that was supposed to wipe out the memory of all the weeks when Matthías had turned his back on him. Despite everything they'd been through together.

At the time, Thorgeir had been so beaten down and exhausted that he'd pretended it didn't matter. Said it was OK. But it did matter and nothing had been OK.

Thorgeir closes his eyes briefly and wrenches his mind back to the present. He's not going to let the bitter memory destroy this evening. Then he notices that Matthías is sunk in thought too.

'Are things all right between you and Hafdís?' he asks.

'What? Yeah, sure. Everything's peachy.' Matthías smiles but he's not fooling anyone, least of all Thorgeir, who has known him since they were little kids playing Teenage Mutant Ninja Turtles.

'Cheers,' Matthías adds, raising a glass of fizzing white liquid topped with a shaving of orange peel. 'To love!'

'To love,' Thorgeir replies, feeling his whole body aching with tenderness. Because, without meaning to, he's fallen head over heels.

❁

The instant the door closes behind Hafdís and Matthías, Thorgeir's self-control snaps. He's so drunk he can't see straight anymore. He seizes Andrea in his arms and starts kissing her hungrily, ignoring the warning bells, allowing himself to touch her body the way he's been longing to.

And she lets him. She doesn't utter a word of protest as he strips off her dress, breaking one of the straps. As he tears off her tights.

Afterwards, as he's sinking into sleep, she whispers the words he's been waiting to hear:

'I love you too.'

His heart melts and he kisses her hair, breathing in her scent.

'Do you have any secrets?' she asks, after a little silence.

'What do you mean?' He's so drowsy, he's drifting off.

Andrea is lying on her side, stroking his chest with one finger. 'I mean big secrets – the kind you've never dared tell anyone?'

'No,' he lies. 'Why do you ask?'

'No reason,' she says, nestling against him.

'Have you got secrets?' he asks.

She chuckles. 'A few. I might even tell you about them one day.'

He holds her tight in his arms until mercifully sleep claims him.

The last thing he wants to do now is start raking up memories he's done his best to forget, though there's a part of him that longs to unburden itself and tell her everything. But he's afraid that if he does, she'll have a change of heart and stop loving him.

During the night Thorgeir wakes up to find himself alone in bed. He listens and hears Andrea in the other room. Hears the squeaking as a cupboard door is opened, then closed again.

What the hell is she doing?

He hears footsteps, the parquet creaking, as though she's walking around the flat. She moves something and there's a rustle of paper. It sounds as though she's searching for something.

He sits up, as noiselessly as he can, places a wary foot on the floor, then tiptoes into the hall, only for the parquet to emit a loud squeak. He freezes and strains his ears.

There's a deathly hush in the flat, then Andrea calls out: 'Thorgeir?'

'What are you doing?' he says, quickly moving towards her voice and finding her standing in the middle of the living room.

'Oh, I was just so hungry.'

'And you thought you'd find something to eat in the living room?' He laughs.

'No,' she says, laughing too. 'I was looking for my phone. Sorry, I didn't mean to wake you.'

'That's all right.'

He takes her head in his hands, tilts it back and kisses her gently.

'I think I'm still a bit drunk,' she says.

'Nothing wrong with that, is there?' He lifts her off her feet and carries her back to bed. 'I'll give you something to eat,' he whispers in her ear. 'Just not quite yet.'

NOW

Thursday 10 December

Elma stamped her feet, hunched her shoulders and buried her hands even deeper in her pockets. She was chilly from hanging around waiting for Hafdís, who was taking her time in the changing rooms.

'How did you know I was here?' Hafdís sounded oddly cheerful when she finally emerged, wearing black yoga pants and a long, red PrimaLoft down jacket. Her dark, curly hair was still pulled back in a bun, and she was carrying a large bag that looked too smart to be used for swimming gear.

'We went round to your house,' Elma replied, 'and your daughter told us where you were.'

'I see,' Hafdís said. 'It must be important if you came down here to find me.'

Elma found this an odd comment in the circumstances. Her husband's best friend had been murdered, so Hafdís must know what this was about. She could hardly have failed to notice the transfer to her bank account.

When Elma explained what they wanted, Hafdís smiled, apparently unsurprised by the question. 'I had a feeling you were going to ask me about the money.'

'Did you?'

'Yes, or at least I suspected you would,' Hafdís said. 'It was a big sum and it might look odd to you that he paid it into my account, but, you see, Thorgeir and I were good mates. Our friendship was quite independent of Matthías.'

'I see,' Elma said, though she didn't actually. She had some good friends herself but wouldn't expect them to transfer millions of krónur into her bank account out of the blue. 'Was there some reason for the payment? Were you involved in the app they were designing?'

'God, no. That app.' Hafdís groaned as though bored of the whole subject. 'No, it was a loan.'

'A loan? Just to you, or to you and your husband, or…?' Up to now, Hörður had been listening to the conversation in silence, and, from the way Hafdís started when he spoke, she appeared to have forgotten he was there.

'To me.' Hafdís hastily scanned their surroundings, then lowered her voice. 'Matthías and I are getting divorced. The last couple of years have been difficult for us, not least financially. We set up a business, a small café, but it did badly and we ended up heavily in debt and … Anyway, long story short, I needed the loan so I could apply for a divorce. You see, when Matthías and I got married, his parents gave us the house we live in but specified in the pre-nup that if the marriage ever ended, Matthías would keep the house.'

'Ottó's doing?' Hörður said.

'Yes, Ottó.' Hafdís smiled briefly. 'I was faced with the prospect of leaving my marriage with nothing to my name. Or nothing but debts, anyway. I knew Matthías and Thorgeir had been given a hefty sum to work on their project, and Thorgeir sympathised with my situation and agreed to lend me the money. I reckoned the amount would be enough to allow me to move out and get myself settled somewhere else.'

'When did you meet to discuss this?' Elma asked.

'When?' Hafdís repeated, as if stalling for time.

'The transfer is dated last Thursday. Did you see Thorgeir then?'

'Yes, I think so,' Hafdís said, appearing to search her memory.

'And he agreed just like that to lend you the money to divorce his best friend?' The story struck Elma as pretty implausible. No way did she buy the idea that Hafdís couldn't remember exactly when she'd met Thorgeir, especially in light of what had happened to him afterwards.

'Like I said, Thorgeir and I were good friends, independently of Matthías. Sure, they were mates, but Thorgeir found the situation as unfair as I did. He understood my predicament and wanted to help.'

'Do you know where the money came from?' Hörður asked. 'Who their investors were?'

'No, I don't. From what I understood, they were family connections of Thorgeir's.' Hafdís shrugged. 'To be honest, I got the impression from Matthías that the investment was a bit dodgy.'

'Oh?'

'Because it wasn't a direct investment. An investment is non-refundable, isn't it? But there were conditions attached to this money. It was part loan, part investment.'

'What, so you think the investors might have wanted some of their money back?' Elma asked.

'I do, yes.'

This story sounded distinctly dodgy to Elma. She didn't understand the deal with the money, but it seemed an improbably generous investment in a single venture – not that she had a clue what was normal in the start-up world. No doubt it varied a lot.

'Did Thorgeir say anything to give you that impression when you saw him on Thursday?'

'No, he didn't, actually.'

'Was there anything out of the ordinary about his behaviour? Anything that struck you as unusual?'

'No, not that I noticed.'

'What do you think happened?' Elma asked.

Hafdís hesitated. 'I think Thorgeir borrowed money from the wrong people, but of course I don't know that for sure. Have … have you discovered anything? Any clues?'

'Not yet,' Elma said.

'Do you think it could have been them?' Hafdís threw a hasty glance around. 'Am *I* in danger now?'

Elma picked up on the fact that she said 'I' not 'we'. It would have been more natural to be concerned about her husband, Matthías, who had been working on the app with Thorgeir. Surely no one would be aware that she had any of the money in her account, least of all the shadowy investors?

'If it's linked to the money, there's no reason why you should be at risk,' Elma pointed out. 'After all, the bulk of it is still sitting in Thorgeir's bank account, apart from the ten million he transferred to you. Unless someone else knows you have it?'

'No, nobody knows.' Hafdís zipped her coat up tighter. 'I want to give the money back, but I don't know how. I don't want to put myself in any danger.'

'No, I can understand that,' Elma said.

There was a brief silence, punctuated by the boom and hiss of the waves. The tide was coming in and the sea was approaching the rocks, filling the air with icy spray. Elma felt her breasts becoming engorged as the milk flowed in, and realised that, in the normal course of things, Adda would be having her last feed now before bedtime.

'Thorgeir had recently met a girl,' she said, suddenly impatient to wind up the conversation. 'Her name's Andrea. Your husband said you'd both met her, but we can't find any record of her. Do you have any idea what her second name was or where she lives?'

Hafdís's features hardened slightly. 'I only met her that one time and we didn't talk much. Thorgeir was never the type for … well, relationships. So I wasn't expecting to see her again.'

'Could you describe her for us?'

Hafdís sighed heavily. 'Young. Long, reddish hair. Very slim. She was shy and didn't really talk about herself.'

'Do you know how long Thorgeir had been seeing her?'

'Not long. A few weeks maybe.'

Elma felt suddenly disheartened. Clearly it wasn't going to be easy to track Andrea down and the conviction was growing inside her that this was no coincidence: Andrea didn't want to be found.

'One last thing,' Elma said, and pulled her phone from her pocket. She found the image she wanted and turned the phone round to show

Hafdís; it was a photo of the writing on the wall above Thorgeir's bed. 'Does this mean anything to you?'

Hafdís narrowed her eyes and bent her head closer. 'No. What is it?'

'It's a line from a hymn. The words were written on the wall above the bed where Thorgeir's body was found. Can you think of any possible significance those words could have?'

Hafdís straightened up, her face completely blank as she answered: 'No, I haven't a clue.'

Elma and Hörður thanked her for her time and watched her walk away with her bag slung over her shoulder.

Elma didn't believe everything Hafdís had said, in particular her claim not to recognise the quotation. She could swear that Hafdís had got a shock when she showed her the photo. Her face had been wiped clean of expression for several seconds, as if frozen. As if temporarily struck dumb. Something about those words had Hafdís badly rattled, but Elma had no idea why.

❁

'You're crowning. I can see a dark head.' Dagný smiled at the exhausted young woman in the bed. 'Your little girl's got a good head of hair.'

The mother's smile quickly changed into a rictus as her body cramped with yet another contraction.

Dagný received the head as it gradually slid out. 'There you are,' she said. 'Gently now, so you don't tear anything.'

A few moments later she was holding a large baby girl, who was wailing at the top of her lungs. Dagný placed the child directly on the breast of her mother, who was crying and laughing all at once. The father wore a fixed smile on his lips and there were tears in his eyes as he stroked a finger down one tiny arm.

'She's so small,' he breathed.

'Not that small,' Dagný replied. 'She must be at least eight pounds seven ounces.'

'Well, I've never seen anything so tiny,' the young man insisted.

Dagný just smiled. She'd seen a lot of babies far smaller than this bouncing girl.

'Diddi, don't forget to take a photo,' the mother said.

Diddi came to his senses and, taking out a Canon camera, snapped a few pictures of mother and baby. They were a young couple, barely out of their teens, and this was their first child.

'Why doesn't Sólveig take a picture of the three of you?' Dagný suggested, and the student who had been assisting at the birth took over the camera.

Dagný was bathed in a warm glow as she watched this big moment in the life of the little family. When everything went well, there was nothing to beat the experience of being involved in bringing a new life into the world. It was the reason Dagný had become a midwife.

On the flip side, there were few things worse than being there when something went wrong. Life and death were two sides of the same coin, as became all too clear at times like this.

'Did it go well?' Ásta asked when Dagný went into the kitchen.

'Yes, very well.' Dagný's thoughts had turned longingly to coffee once she had finished weighing the baby, but when her cup was only half full, the pump on the thermos spluttered and dried up.

'I'll make some more,' Ásta offered.

'Thanks.'

The evening shift had got off to a lively start – Dagný had arrived just in time to take over the birth she'd just overseen. It had already been well under way. The change of shift had initially upset the mother-to-be but Dagný had met her several times during her antenatal care and she soon became reconciled to the idea that Dagný would deliver her baby.

Ásta handed Dagný an open packet of biscuits and she accepted it gratefully. If there was ever a moment to allow oneself sugary snacks it was during these evening shifts. Come to think of it, though, she'd put away so many treats since the beginning of December that if she went on like this she felt she'd soon be leaking syrup from every orifice.

'How's your sister doing?' Ásta asked.

'Elma? Well, I think.'

Ásta responded with what sounded like 'hmm'. She was one of the oldest midwives on the ward, with only a year left until she retired. When Dagný was younger, Ásta had been the school nurse, responsible for the annual weighing and measuring of the children. They had all been a little in awe of her. Ásta was a big woman with coarse features and permanently pursed lips. She had the air of someone who would tolerate no nonsense and sharp eyes that never missed a trick.

'That's a hell of a business,' Ásta said now. 'It's hard to believe.'

'Yes, it is unbelievable.' As the adrenaline associated with delivering a child began to ebb, Dagný became conscious of a growing fatigue.

'A murder. In Akranes.'

'Well, Skorradalur.'

'Yes, but still.' Ásta clearly felt it amounted to the same thing. 'I remember Thorgeir well.'

'Do you?' Dagný had been trying to summon up her own memories of him. Apart from his face, she could recall little, though they had only been three years apart in age. 'He must have been at the other school because I don't really remember him.'

'Yes, he was at Brekkubær.'

'Right, I thought so.' Dagný smiled. 'Do you remember *all* the kids you weighed and measured? Like, what I weighed when I was ten, for example?'

'You were a wee little thing.'

'A wee little thing?' Dagný laughed. 'I wasn't exactly short. You must be thinking of Elma.'

'You were so skinny, I mean. No flesh on your bones.'

'You could be right.' Dagný recalled her mother's anxious attempts to get her to eat in those days. Dagný hadn't cared about her weight, she'd just been a fussy eater. She wouldn't touch butter or vegetables or any meat apart from chicken, to the despair of her mother.

'But I remember Thorgeir well,' Ásta said again. 'He was such a big lad. Much taller than the rest of his age group. Heavier too. And he was just … He always gave the impression he was suffering somehow.'

'Oh?'

Ásta picked at her teeth with a finger nail. 'Yes, I never really got to the bottom of it, but it bothered me a lot at the time. I used to lie awake at night, wondering what was wrong.'

'Hang on, what do you mean? Was he ill or something?'

'No, not ill, but I suspected that things at home weren't … weren't OK.'

'Really?'

Ásta took the coffee jug from the machine and reached out for Dagný's mug. 'Of course, I shouldn't really talk about it, but I don't suppose it can do any harm now. He had a lot of unexplained injuries. His parents claimed to know nothing about it but … I always got a bad feeling about them. His mother was taken up with working for the church, and his father was the kind of bloke who's always up to something but no one knew exactly what. I don't have any proof, just a hunch, but Thorgeir was one of the kids I kept an especially close eye on.'

'What kind of injuries?' Dagný asked, taking the mug Ásta handed her.

'On his back mainly. I…' Ásta frowned and puckered her lips. 'They looked to me like the kind of welts you'd get from being hit with some long, narrow object. I wrote a report for the Child Protection Agency. Apparently they followed it up but didn't find anything. He did a lot of sport and they concluded that the injuries could be related to that, but … it just didn't fit. What kind of sport results in welts like that on your back?'

'Riding?' Dagný couldn't think of anything else.

'Yes, maybe, if you were a horse that was being broken in,' Ásta scoffed.

'Was he bullied at all?'

'No.' Ásta shook her head. 'If anything, it was the other way round.

Mind you, I sometimes heard the other kids calling him names, like they were trying to goad him.'

'So he was the violent one?'

'Yes. The other kids were afraid of him, and not just because of his size.'

'Oh?'

'No.' Ásta sighed. 'Look, I'd never talk about good or bad children, but … let's just say Thorgeir wasn't a happy kid.'

❊

Kristjana couldn't concentrate on the book that was lying open in her lap. But her headache had receded at least, since she'd added a splash of brandy to her tea, and now she was feeling a little brighter. Her memories of yesterday evening were fragmentary, no more than disjointed images that appeared from time to time behind her eyelids, only to vanish as soon as she opened her eyes.

She gave up trying to piece them together. Had no wish to recall anything uncomfortable or unpleasant. The terrible weight constricting her chest wasn't caused solely by her grief for Thorgeir but by her shame about yesterday's drunken episode, which she was now doing her best to forget.

She sat in the armchair, staring at her book, but the letters kept blurring together, the pages dissolving into mist, and her thoughts were miles away from the two lovers in the story. In part to defend herself against memories of yesterday evening, she had started brooding on unhappy episodes in the distant past – thoughts about Thorgeir's father, Reynir, and their life together.

Thorgeir had been fifteen when his father died. Fifteen but already going his own way, listening to neither her nor his dad.

Her mind drifted even further back.

'I can't take it,' Reynir used to say, making himself scarce when Thorgeir was having a tantrum as a baby.

He'd said it as if they actually had a choice about whether to take it or not. To stay or go. She'd never understood that. To her mind, there had only been one way, one path, and she had no choice about whether she took it or not.

Kristjana put down her book, got to her feet and went over to the kitchen window.

She had undone the ties that held the curtains back, but through the gap she still had a sightline into the kitchen of the young couple next door. The police officers. Darkness had fallen and she could see them standing in the illuminated kitchen, playing with their little girl. What was her name again? Little Adda, that was it, or Aðalheiður, like her grandmother. And the parents were called Sævar and Elma. Sævar had thick dark hair and a matt of black fuzz on his arms. He was holding a beaker, making it fly around all over the place before the spout ended up in the baby's mouth. Some things never changed. She had played the same game with Thorgeir when he was young, turning the spoonful of food into a car, a train, an aeroplane.

Thorgeir had always been a good eater and had quickly grown into a tall, strapping lad. She'd been so pleased about that. So proud whenever he was praised for his appetite. But later his size had got him into trouble. People never understood that although Thorgeir was big for his age, he was no more mature than any of the other kids in his year. His appearance said nothing about his character, but many parents felt it was unfair that he should be allowed to play sport with his own age group when physically he seemed so much older.

The volcanic rage that always seemed to be simmering away beneath the surface had done nothing to help either. And his compulsion to bully the other kids. Smaller kids. But what people didn't understand was that Thorgeir had himself been the child everyone pointed at, laughed at and talked about. He'd only wanted to turn the tables on them, she believed. In a kind of self-defence. The only alternatives were to be the aggressor or the victim.

The world of children could be so cruel, and Thorgeir hadn't been the same person in the playground as he was at home.

'Discipline is good for children,' his teacher had said. 'Thorgeir needs strict ground rules. Needs to know that he can't just get away with things.'

Oh, she had thought. *So that's what you think, is it? You think he's allowed to get away with anything at home?* Nothing had been further from the truth. But she hadn't said anything aloud. In those days she had rarely spoken up, and that was usually the best policy. Caused the fewest problems.

In the kitchen next door, Sævar abandoned the attempt to give the little girl her beaker and her mother took over. The young police woman with the mousy-blond hair and friendly face. She struck Kristjana as a bit naïve.

Kristjana thought about the children who used to live next door. The little girl and the two boys. They had been much older than this baby and their house had been full of life. She used to hear their voices carrying from their kitchen window over to hers. Voices that only drew attention to the silence that reigned in her own home.

She used to see them out in the garden, especially in summer. On sunny days their father would start up the sprinkler and the children would race round in circles in their swimming costumes. A happy family. And they really had been happy – for many years.

And while their happiness was a constant reminder of what she herself lacked, she had never found it actively upsetting to watch them. On the contrary, she had taken pleasure in their joy, as she did in the books she read or the music she listened to. She chose to escape into another world, allowing herself to find happiness there, however intangible.

She often wondered what the children who used to live there were doing now – the two who were still alive, that is. Were they still happy?

She saw Elma lift up the baby, burying her face in her tummy, and the little girl laughing.

Now another happy family had moved into the house next door. Another family to watch from afar, hidden behind her blue floral curtains; alone now that she had no family of her own left. But she had only herself to blame for that; at the end of the day, it was all her fault.

She poured more brandy into her cup and drank it neat this time.

❁

'How's paternity leave agreeing with you, Sævar?' Konni handed him an ice-cold Tuborg.

Dads' football was twice a week, often late in the evening, as that was the only time when the sports hall was free. On Thursdays they had beers in the changing rooms afterwards, taking it in turns to provide them. This time it was Konni's turn and he'd done them proud by bringing a large cooler along.

'Being on leave is the sweet life,' Sævar said.

'Yes, so long as you've only got the one,' Konni replied. He was father to four strong-minded daughters and had zero say in his household. He was always up for a beer on Thursday evenings and would stay on for as long as anyone was willing to sit with him. Yet Sævar knew that, despite these little Thursday breaks, Konni lived for his girls.

'Do you think there'll be more coming along soon?' Torfi asked. He had two children, a seven-year-old son and a daughter who was three. He worked as a lawyer but didn't look like one. In fact, he was about as far from the stereotypical lawyer as you could imagine. He never wore a suit, left it far too long between haircuts and only shaved when his stubble was beginning to irritate him.

'I haven't thought that far.' Sævar laughed. He was feeling good after the exercise and hot shower. And he felt even better once the beer had induced a pleasant numbness in his body.

'Two's a good number,' Torfi said. 'With two, it's man-to-man. With a third child, you've got to switch to zone defence. That's the big difference.'

'Four's too many.' Konni shook his head. 'Four's just crazy.'

Gradually the others left until it was only the three of them remaining for beer number two. Sævar stuck at one but enjoyed sitting on for a while. It dawned on him that he'd not yet used the opportunity to ask the questions he had for his friends.

'By the way, did you two know Thorgeir, the man whose body they found?'

Konni cracked open a third can. 'Yes, a little. He used to be a real bully in the old days. Everyone was shit-scared of him, remember?'

'Yeah, he used to hold the whole school hostage at one time,' Torfi said. 'When he appeared in the playground it was like seeing a shark blundering into a shoal of fish. Everyone started swimming for their lives in the opposite direction.'

'But he calmed down later, didn't he?' Konni asked.

'Well, I don't remember him much from college,' Torfi admitted. 'What was he – three or four years older than us?'

'Two,' Konni said. 'And yes, I expect he mellowed a bit over the years.'

'Did he actually hurt anyone?' Sævar asked. 'This was before my time. I have no memory of him at all.'

'I don't remember anything serious,' Konni said. 'Just the usual – grabbing people by the scruff of the neck and threatening them. I think it was mainly that he was such a big, strong bastard. And not exactly friendly either.'

'Then there was that business with the girl, of course,' Torfi added.

'Yeah, but that was much later,' Konni replied. 'Wasn't he in his twenties by then?'

'The girl?' Sævar prompted.

'I heard that some girl had accused him of rape, but I think the charges were dropped,' Torfi explained.

'Oh yes, that's right,' Konni said.

A silence fell after this. It was Sævar who broke it: 'Anyway, changing the subject. Did either of you go to Vatnaskógur in around ninety-five?'

'Vatnaskógur? What kind of questions are these? Is this an interrogation or something?' Konni laughed at his own feeble joke. 'Why do you want to know?'

'Oh, it's just that I found some junk in the loft and it included material from Vatnaskógur dating back to that time.'

'What year did you say?' Torfi asked.

'Nineteen ninety-five.'

'Yes, that would fit,' Torfi said. 'I went in ninety-three, ninety-four and ninety-five. Oh, and ninety-six too. So did you, Konni. Remember?'

'I've totally forgotten,' Konni said. 'My memory gets worse with every child. These days, I'm lucky if I remember to get dressed in the mornings.'

'Nineteen ninety-five. Wasn't that the year that…?' Torfi and Konni exchanged a glance, and Sævar thought he saw a light come on in Konni's eyes.

'Yes, of course, the year that kid died.'

'What kid?'

'There was an accident at Vatnaskógur,' said Torfi. 'A boy died at the camp. But he'd been ill beforehand, apparently. It was an accident, but it was still terrible.'

'Yes, the memory's coming back now,' Konni said. 'But I have to admit I've forgotten his name. He'd only recently moved here.'

'What exactly happened?' Sævar asked.

'He wandered out in the middle of the night and was found later in the lake. I have a feeling he went out in a boat, and either it was an accident or…'

'Or it wasn't,' Torfi finished.

'Why, do you remember it better?' Konni asked.

'No, not really. Just that they found him in the lake a day or two later. We'd gone home by then.'

'Seriously?' Sævar said. 'Was there no investigation?' He'd never heard of the case, but, then, it had happened before he moved to Akranes.

'Ask your colleagues,' Konni said. 'I'm sure the police looked into it at the time but I don't think there was any reason to believe it was … a crime or anything.'

'All pretty tragic.' Torfi stared into space, then gave a slightly twisted smile. 'After that there was always a certain mystery attached to the room where he'd spent his last night. Us boys used to want to stay in it but at the same time we didn't want to, if that makes sense. It was all very exciting – until it got dark, that is.'

'What happened then?' Sævar asked.

Torfi was silent for a moment before answering. 'I don't know,' he said eventually. 'But God, if anywhere was haunted it was room number four in the Laufskáli hut.'

'You're full of crap,' Konni said.

Torfi just shrugged.

'We used to draw lots as to who should sleep in his bed,' Konni added, in a lighter tone.

'Draw lots?' Sævar raised his eyebrows enquiringly.

'Pieces of grass.' Torfi stood up. 'Whoever drew the short straw had to take his bunk. I don't know if it was actually the same bed but everyone used to pretend they'd heard something during the night. Like a knocking on the window or the floorboards creaking.'

'Some boys got so scared they'd start crying and saying they wanted to go home.'

'Didn't they build new huts, though?' said Torfi. 'Weren't the old ones torn down?'

'Yes, the Laufskáli hut was torn down not long afterwards. Which was probably just as well.' Konni reached for his fourth beer and raised it in a toast. 'One for each girl. What can you do?'

'You went to Vatnaskógur that often, did you?' Sævar asked, intent on sticking to the subject.

'I suppose I must have gone two or three times,' Konni replied.

'I went those four times,' Torfi said. 'I still know all the Bible songs. I get them on the brain now and then, like some bloody record playing in my head.'

'"B-I-B-L-E,"' Konni began to sing, '"*is the book of books.*"'

'Right, that's it. I'm off.' Torfi slung his rucksack over his shoulder and made the sign of the cross over his friends. 'God bless you, my boys. Amen.'

BEFORE
Thorgeir

Their first trip together.

Thorgeir had wanted to do something special, like going away on a short break. He was desperate to spend more time with Andrea. A whole weekend to themselves, uninterrupted, with no one else around to disturb them.

Andrea had a disconcerting habit of vanishing without warning. She would get a phone message and suddenly say that she had to hurry home or go to work. It wasn't that he didn't trust her, but he found these abrupt departures strange and unsettling. When he pressed her, the answers she gave were unconvincingly vague. To love was to know fear. He was constantly terrified of losing her and the new feelings she had awoken in his breast. But if they were at the summer house, it occurred to him, she wouldn't be able to go anywhere. They would arrive and leave together.

'Should we maybe go away for the weekend?' he had asked earlier that week when they were chatting on the phone. 'Just the two of us?'

'Away? Where to?' She was frying supper for herself and her flatmate and he could hear the fat sizzling in the pan.

'I thought we could go to my summer house.' He'd told Andrea about the cabin his father had built when he was a child. A summer house in the valley of Skorradalur, nestled in among the birch woods on the shores of the lake, where you could take out a boat or fish. It was a beautiful spot in summer, carpeted with lupins, an idyllic location for family holidays. And equally scenic now, in winter, with the mountains capped in white. From the way he waxed lyrical about holidays there,

Andrea probably assumed that Thorgeir's family had been one of those lucky, happy ones, but the truth was more complicated.

Andrea had reacted enthusiastically to his suggestion, but now, as they drive along the last stretch of tree-lined track towards the cabin, Thorgeir experiences a twinge of regret at having suggested Skorradalur for their break. A creeping sense of anxiety makes it hard to breathe. It's the same stifling feeling he used to have as a boy in the back seat of his parents' car as they bumped along the track. The cabin has a strong association with his father; the old man's presence feels inescapable here, which might explain why neither Thorgeir nor his mother use it much.

'Nice house,' Andrea says as she gets out of the car. 'I'd been picturing a little shack.'

'Ah, no,' Thorgeir said, opening the boot. 'This is the real deal. A hot tub and everything – assuming it still works. It's a while since I was last here.'

Andrea smiles. When she tries to take her case, he intervenes and takes it himself. He still has this compulsion to do everything for her, to spoil her. She's his princess. He wants to show her what it could be like if they were a proper couple.

The wind is starting to gust and although it isn't snowing yet, the air is bitterly cold outside. Nearly minus five. They hurry over to the front door.

Thorgeir inserts the key in the lock and has a bit of a struggle to turn it before the door finally opens and they go inside. He starts apologising for the stale smell and the dated furniture. 'Like I say, Mum and I don't spend much time here nowadays.'

'It's great,' Andrea says, looking around. She goes over to the window. 'You can't see any neighbours. How far is it to the next cabin?'

'Far enough for us to be left in peace,' Thorgeir says.

'Perfect.' Andrea's smile makes him melt inside, as always.

Putting down their luggage, Thorgeir joins her in the middle of the room and puts his arms around her. As he kisses her, he tries not to think about the stain under the rug they're standing on.

NOW

'Could you tell us about your relationship with Thorgeir?'

Elma was sitting with Hörður, face to face with Matthías in his kitchen, on some rather cold, hard plastic chairs. Elma was acutely aware of them since she and Sævar were currently on the lookout for kitchen chairs and still hadn't found any comfortable ones that didn't cost an arm and a leg. Not that price was any guarantee of comfort, as was probably the case with the chairs they were sitting on now. She remembered seeing a similar model in a furniture shop that mainly sold Scandinavian designer goods.

'As I've already told you, we'd known each other since we were small.'

'And you'd stayed in touch?'

Matthías nodded.

'How did your collaboration on the app work in practice?' Elma asked. 'You told me something about it but could you explain in more detail?'

'Yes, it's basically like a start-up. We launched it about a year ago, but didn't begin working on it properly until last spring, when I quit my job.'

'You gave up your job to work full time on the start-up?' Hörður asked, his voice tinged with disapproval.

Elma tried to mitigate the effect by giving Matthías a conciliatory smile.

'Well … yes, you could say that.' Matthías seemed barely awake.

His hair was tousled and the bags under his eyes looked as if they were sliding down his cheeks.

'Could you take us through what it involves?' Hörður asked.

'It's an app we're developing. Or rather that Thorgeir was developing.' Matthías described how the app worked, more or less echoing what Begga had said.

'And what's your role again?' Hörður asked.

'I communicate with potential clients. Promoting the product and so on. We've already been taken on by two businesses that want to give it a trial run.'

'And you found investors,' Elma remarked.

'Yes,' Matthías replied. 'But Thorgeir took care of that side of things.'

'Investors acquire shares in the company, if I've understood right,' Elma said. 'They put money into the venture and acquire shares in return. Was that how it worked in your case?' Before Matthías could answer, she added: 'Because I got the impression from your wife that this was a different kind of arrangement.'

Matthías shrugged. 'Like I said, Thorgeir took care of all that sort of thing.'

'Can you tell us why he would have transferred some of the money to Hafdís's bank account?'

A shadow crossed Matthías's face, though he didn't seem thrown by the question. Hafdís must have broken the news to him after they had spoken to her yesterday evening.

'I gather she needed a loan,' Matthías said.

'Were she and Thorgeir that close?'

'What are you implying?' His tone was sharp.

Elma waited, not saying anything.

'We're getting divorced,' Matthías continued after a moment. 'She doesn't confide in me anymore. So I don't have a proper idea of what went on between them, but I don't believe Thorgeir would have done it unless she…'

'She…?'

'Did something to convince him. But I still don't understand it. I feel like they've made a fool of me.'

'Do you think perhaps their relationship was closer than it ought to have been?'

'No, I—' Matthías broke off, as if suddenly unsure. 'I don't know. They always got on well, but Thorgeir would never…'

Elma found it interesting that it was Thorgeir Matthías mentioned in this context rather than Hafdís. Had he trusted his friend more than his wife? It wouldn't be the first time a murder had been precipitated by an extra-marital affair. On the other hand, the police had confirmed that both Matthías and Hafdís had been at a Christmas party in Reykjavík on the Saturday, which gave them an alibi for that day. Then again, it was always possible that Thorgeir had died on the Friday night, for which the couple had a weaker alibi. They claimed they'd both been at home at the time; that Hafdís had gone to bed early, while Matthías had stayed up late watching a film.

'You haven't come here just to ask about that, have you?' Matthías said after a lengthy silence. 'What's happening with the investigation? Is there any news?'

'We're working on it,' Elma said, keeping her answer deliberately vague. 'Do you have any ideas yourself about what might have happened?'

'Me?' Matthías wrinkled his brow in apparent consideration. 'I'm still trying to get my head around it. I feel like I'm in a movie or something – that this can't be real. I'm still waiting for someone to tell me it's a joke or that there's a hidden camera somewhere.'

He leant forwards on the table, rubbing his forehead with his palms. As he did so, he crushed a wet Cheerio ring under his elbow, but didn't seem to notice.

'Can you think of anyone who might have had it in for Thorgeir?' Elma asked. She had put the same question to Matthías before, but since then he'd had time to reflect.

Matthías looked up, obviously making a determined effort to keep his features under control.

'No, no one comes to mind.'

'Your wife seemed to think the investment might have been a bit dodgy. That the people behind it might have been dangerous.'

'No.' Matthías shook his head emphatically. 'No way.'

'So you do know where the money came from?'

Silence.

Elma glanced at Hörður, who was no doubt wondering the same as her: what was it that Matthías didn't want to tell them?

'It's nothing you need worry about,' Matthías said.

'Oh?' Hörður started drumming a finger on the table, which seemed to fray Matthías's nerves as badly as it did Elma's.

'No.'

'So, go on, where did the investment come from?' Hörður persisted. 'It's important for us to know.'

Matthías coughed. 'It came ... it came from his mother.'

'From whose mother?'

'Thorgeir's.'

'Kristjana?' Elma was flabbergasted at the suggestion that the old woman who lived next door to her, in a house that was in dire need of renovation; the woman who drove around in an ancient jeep that was falling to bits, could have had a hundred million krónur spare to invest in an app that her son was developing.

But Matthías nodded firmly. 'Yes, from Kristjana.'

❂

By the time Adda went for her nap at eleven, Sævar felt worn out. His single beer the previous evening had been enough to disturb his sleep.

The house looked like a tornado had hit it. There were children's toys, food and dishes all over the floor. The rosy glow through which he had viewed the beginning of his paternity leave was beginning to fade, but he was too tired to think about that now and kept yawning as he wiped splats of porridge off the kitchen wall.

As he straightened up and arched his back after kneeling on the floor with the cloth, his gaze fell on the window and he caught a stealthy movement in the house next door.

Kristjana.

Sævar wondered what on earth she was up to. Perhaps she was just naturally nosy, the type who liked to keep an eye on her neighbours. Come to think of it, she may have spied on Máni and his family as well.

Sævar had been able to think about little else but Vatnaskógur since the previous evening. It was most unlike him to leave a mess untidied, but instead of picking up the toys from the floor, he ensconced himself on the sofa with a cup of coffee and his laptop. Next thing he knew, he was aware of a wet patch on his thigh. He must have nodded off and tipped over his coffee cup, spilling it onto the sofa.

After he had finished scrubbing the stain off the pale fabric, he decided to have another go at digging around for information. He'd meant to see if he could find anything online about the accident. There was still plenty of time; he'd only conked out for ten minutes and Adda would sleep outside in her pram, well wrapped up against the freezing air in true Icelandic fashion, for the next hour at least.

The coffee in the jug was still hot, so he refilled his cup and tried again.

The YMCA centre at Vatnaskógur in the Svínadalur valley, just north of Hvalfjörður fjord, had been set up almost a hundred years ago, according to the brief article on Wikipedia, and was still going strong. If their homepage was to be believed, the popularity of the residential camps there had in no way waned, despite the fact that the Christian faith was up against it in Iceland these days.

When Sævar first arrived in Akranes at fifteen, he'd been forced to listen to endless stories from his friends about their experiences at Vatnaskógur. He used to feel rather left out during these reminiscences and wished he'd moved to the town earlier and been able to share in these summer adventures. But in time, of course, new adventures had come along to replace the old, and he had been a full participant in those.

Scrolling down the homepage, he saw that the centre offered a variety of watercraft, including rowing boats, pedalos and canoes; held all kinds of sports competitions, and organised entertainments every evening. In addition to this, there were art workshops, camping trips and hot tubs.

Sævar tried entering 'Vatnaskógur' and the year 1995 in the search engine, as he had done yesterday, but nothing of interest came up apart from an item about construction beginning on a new dormitory hut that year. When he tried typing the same information into the Icelandic newspaper archives, however, he hit upon a short news article from August 1995.

'A teenage boy was killed in an accident at the YMCA summer camp in Vatnaskógur on Thursday night.'

A week later there was an update, including a name and a photograph of the boy.

'The teenage boy who was killed in an accident at Vatnaskógur last week has been named as Heiðar Kjartansson of Presthúsabraut, Akranes.'

Heiðar looked much younger than Sævar would have expected. Boys his age tended to resemble either overgrown children or miniature adults. They were often lanky and out of proportion, as if their nose and feet had grown faster than the rest of their body. Few were at their most attractive, since, in addition to wonky proportions, they usually had acne, wispy facial hair and voices that wavered between bass one minute and falsetto the next.

Laying aside his laptop, Sævar decided to take out Máni's box again. After rummaging around in it for a while, he found the diary and began to read the first page, which was entitled 'Vatnaskógur', with the date '8 August 1995' on the line below.

❂

'Dagný. What are you doing here?' Elma was surprised to find her sister waiting for her in her office at the police station when she got back from visiting Matthías.

'Oh, I just happened to be passing.'

'You sound like Mum.'

'Do I?' Dagný sat down, placing her bag on her lap.

'We both know you weren't just passing,' Elma said teasingly. 'Come on, out with it. What's up?'

'I just felt … I just wanted … I don't know…'

It was a novel experience for Elma to see the usually confident Dagný struggling for words. She sat back and waited, giving her sister time.

'I know you're investigating the Thorgeir case.'

'Right.'

'It's just … I was working last night and got talking to Ásta. You remember Ásta, don't you? The school nurse.'

'Yes, of course.' Elma immediately pictured Ásta's hulking figure and brusque manner, and was flooded by uncomfortable feelings that she hadn't experienced since she was at school. Feelings associated with visits to the nurse; being weighed and measured, and the way everyone went around comparing their statistics afterwards. She'd loathed the whole thing.

'She let slip something interesting about Thorgeir.' Dagný proceeded to tell Elma about the old school nurse's concerns about Thorgeir's injuries, which she'd suspected had something to do with his home situation. 'She had no proof of that, but I thought I ought to let you know anyway.'

'Thanks for telling me, but…' Elma hesitated. 'I find it hard to see how that's relevant to his death.'

'No, I expect you're right,' Dagný said ruefully. 'It's just that I found it so sad. I mean, what can have happened to him? Ásta said it wasn't just the once but almost every time she examined him over the years.'

'Really? That's awful.' Elma's thoughts strayed to Kristjana, and she wondered if the woman could have been violent towards her son. It seemed scarcely credible, but then you couldn't tell these things from appearances. And who knew what kind of father Thorgeir had had? He'd died when Thorgeir was in his teens. Perhaps his death had come as a relief to the boy. And to his mother as well.

'I know. I'll never understand how any parent could deliberately hurt their children,' Dagný said, her face a picture of dismay at the very idea. She had always been the maternal type. As a child she'd lost no opportunity to mother her dolls; later, she'd actively sought out babysitting jobs, and of course she'd ended up as a midwife.

'No, it's incomprehensible.'

'Anyway, I'm off home to put my feet up. I only got two hours' sleep after my shift because I went to my CrossFit class.'

'You're crazy.' Elma sometimes got the impression that Dagný and her husband, Viðar, had joined a cult when they started CrossFit training. These days their life seemed to revolve around the sport as much as it did around their sons.

'I'm still waiting to see you there.' Dagný winked at her on her way out, but missed Elma's muttered comment that that would be the day hell froze over.

❂

The pain in his hip had intensified into a grinding agony, but there was no way Hörður was going back to the hospital. He read the instructions on the pill bottle, which stipulated four hours between doses, and snorted derisively, though there was no one to hear but him. He shook out a pill into his palm and swallowed it with a gulp of water.

Scorning the instructions felt like a minor victory of sorts. The doctor had said there was nothing wrong with him, yet he had barely got a wink of sleep last night for the pains that kept shooting down his thigh and up his spine to his head.

The doctor was clueless and he wasn't setting foot in that hospital again. He would simply grit his teeth and wait until the pain wore off on its own. If nothing else, it distracted his attention from his mental suffering, which couldn't be alleviated by pills.

Sleepless nights had become the norm rather than the exception, and last night had been particularly bad. Perhaps because, towards morning, he had been lying in a doze halfway between sleeping and waking – the result of the drugs maybe – when he became convinced that Gígja was beside him. He'd been woken by his own voice asking her to turn off the alarm clock, momentarily forgetting that there would be no reply. There was no one to turn off the alarm but him.

He was in such an evil temper by the time he turned up to work that if he'd been a cartoon character there would have been smoke coming out of his ears. On his way into his office, he came face to face with Elma's sister, Dagný.

'Oh dear, look at the state of you!' she exclaimed, putting a concerned hand on his shoulder. 'You're limping.'

'No,' he said. 'I'm fine.'

'What happened?'

'He fell off his bike,' Elma said, coming out of her office.

'I'm all right.'

'He's refusing to go back to the hospital for another check-up.'

'I've already been there once.'

'And I say you need to go back.' Dagný smiled kindly.

'I'm fine,' Hörður repeated, forcing his features into an answering smile. 'But thanks very much for your concern.'

Leaving the sisters in the corridor, he took refuge in his office, catching the glance of weary sympathy they exchanged before he closed his door.

He couldn't stand weary, sympathetic glances.

Fortunately, just then the phone rang. It was a man from forensics to tell him they'd finished analysing the blood found at the summer house. 'The blood we found by Thorgeir's body was definitely his, but the stain in the living room is much older. We can't be more precise than that because it's more than two years old.'

'In other words, it could have been there a lot longer than two years?' Hörður said.

'It could.' The man hesitated. 'I'd check when the cabin was built. Then at least you'd have some sort of time frame, even if it's a broad one.'

After a pause, he continued: 'We've got the results of the fingerprint check as well. There were two sets on the wineglasses, one a match for the victim, the other unknown.'

Hörður thanked him and hung up. He stared at his computer for a while, pondering this latest news. The information about the fingerprints merely confirmed what they already knew: that Thorgeir had been at the summer house with his girlfriend, the mysterious Andrea, and that she didn't have a criminal record. But the old bloodstain gave him pause for thought. He'd long known who Kristjana was; she was a familiar figure to most people in Akranes due to her role as a Sunday-school teacher. In addition, she had run the town's dry cleaner's for many years.

An idea began to take shape in his mind. Although far-fetched, it might explain a thing or two. After a bit of a search, he found the information he needed.

Kristjana's husband, Reynir, had been thirty-five at the time of his death. In September 1994 he had taken his boat out on Lake Skorradalur and fallen overboard. His body was never found, despite attempts to drag the lake, since the water was up to sixty metres deep in places. If Hörður remembered right, the boat had been found adrift, with several bottles of alcohol stashed inside. He couldn't remember whether Reynir had been alone at the summer house at the time or whether his family had been there too.

Father and son had both met untimely ends, twenty-six years apart, and Kristjana had been a presence in their lives in both cases. Was it possible that the investigation had been barking up completely the wrong tree at the time? That someone had deliberately pushed the boat out onto the lake in order to mislead the police?

Hörður leant back in his chair. It was a long shot, and he didn't feel he had any reason to suspect Kristjana of lying. But, when it came down to it, what did he actually know about the woman?

She had always been part of the Akranes landscape, as much of a fixture as the beach or the mountain. Hörður regularly saw her around, either at the shops or out and about in the town. She had a reputation for being eccentric.

Gígja used to take their clothes to Kristjana and Reynir's dry cleaner's; as Hörður was now guiltily aware, he had generally left all such chores to her.

Reynir had been a notorious local drunk and Hörður had crossed paths with him on more than one occasion in the early nineties, either for brawling or for drunk and disorderly behaviour.

Kristjana had carried on running the dry cleaner's after her husband's death. But when she retired, no one else had replaced her, and somehow Hörður couldn't imagine that she would have made much money from the business.

A hundred million was the sum she had supposedly invested in her son's start-up. The dry cleaner's turnover couldn't have been that high, surely, though what did he know about it? Still, it sounded like an awful lot of money to Hörður, though to some people he supposed it might not seem that steep. It could have been an inheritance or savings that Reynir had left behind. Perhaps there was nothing odd about sitting on the equivalent of over seven hundred thousand US dollars in your old age.

Nevertheless, something smelt wrong to Hörður. Motivated by curiosity, he picked up the phone to the tax office and requested the tax returns for the last few years that Reynir's Dry Cleaning had been in business.

❂

Kristjana felt that familiar tightness in her chest as she made coffee that Friday lunchtime. It used to be Thorgeir's day for coming round to eat supper with her, but all that was in the past now, like so much else.

Time passed – that was the great, inexorable truth. Yet many people seemed to believe that they could somehow evade its remorseless progress.

When Kristjana had finished her cup, she put on her coat and boots and went out. A chilly wind cut into her cheeks as she trudged over to the library, the bag digging into her shoulder. She had gone there every day this week. She preferred to go often and only take out a few books at a time.

It flashed through her mind that she would soon be one of those lonely old pensioners who spent their days wandering between shops and institutions in search of company, making a nuisance of themselves and getting under everyone's feet.

The elderly were an uncomfortable reminder of the fate that awaits most, if not all of us, and she had never meant to be like them. Not after growing up in her grandparents' place, where everything was old and rotten, and where their smell had clung to her clothes: a combination of tobacco, cloying perfume and boiled fish. Everything they ate was boiled and the steam had impregnated the very structure of the house so that it was never entirely free of the odour.

No, she would die before she got that old and decrepit herself.

Not that there was anything to prevent her from dying these days. Now that Thorgeir had gone, she was alone in the world, and if she were to drop dead at home she didn't suppose anyone would notice for a long time. Recently she'd read about the case of a woman in her eighties in France who had died at home and not been discovered until four years later. Four years!

The woman had kept a diary describing her lonely existence.

Kristjana had read another article about a woman who died, but in that case she'd had a cat and by the time they found her the cat had eaten part of her face.

Kristjana shuddered. She had no intention of keeping either a diary or a cat.

'Back again, Kristjana?' The librarian sounded cheerful. 'Already finished the two you borrowed yesterday?'

Kristjana slammed the books down on the desk in front of the woman. She refused to engage with the self-service system that had recently been imposed on visitors to the library. Having to scan your own books in and out, as if there weren't any staff working there.

'I don't have much else to do these days,' she sighed.

The woman's face immediately softened in sympathy, showing that Kristjana's words had had the intended effect. 'If there's anything I can do to help…' the librarian began.

'No, thanks,' Kristjana replied, taking care to include a tragic catch in her voice. Then she stood up straighter and smiled wanly. 'I've managed by myself up to now and I mean to go on doing the same.'

The librarian's smile contained pity and, yes, a touch of admiration too.

Kristjana turned and walked slowly towards the bookshelves, aware that she was being watched. She had always been invisible: at home with her grandparents, as a child and adolescent at school, and later on in her own home as long as her husband was alive. But no more. Now everyone could see her for what she was – a woman who refused to break down, no matter what life flung at her. And for that she had earned their respect.

❁

Hörður put on his hazard warning lights, parked on the side of the road and rolled down his right-hand window.

'Can I give you a lift home?'

He'd been on his way to pay Kristjana a visit when he spotted her coming towards him along the road.

'I can walk,' she said – with little conviction, though. She appeared to be buckling under the weight of the cloth bag full of books that hung from her shoulder.

'As a matter of fact, I was on my way round to see you,' Hörður told her. 'So you'd be doing me a favour.'

'Oh. Well, then.'

Hörður got out of the car and relieved Kristjana of her bag. 'Go on, get in,' he said.

She obeyed, climbing into the front seat after scanning their surroundings, as if to make sure no one was watching.

The roads were busy in the run-up to Christmas, and they were receiving some dirty looks from the drivers whose way Hörður was blocking. He waved an apology and drove off smartly.

'Is it about Thorgeir?' Kristjana asked. 'Have you found out who did this to him?'

'No, not yet,' Hörður said. 'But the investigation is in full swing and we hope to have some answers for you soon.'

After a moment's silence he added: 'How are you holding up?'

'As you'd expect, I suppose,' Kristjana said with a heavy sigh. 'I won't deny that it's tough.'

'No, that's understandable.'

Kristjana gave him a look as if he'd meant something more by this. 'Yes, of course you'd know all about loss yourself,' she said. 'But no one should have to outlive their children. It's unspeakably cruel. Though I have to believe that God has taken my Thorgeir for a reason. "The Lord gave and the Lord has taken away." I believe that Thorgeir has gone to a better place and that we will soon be reunited in heaven.'

'Still, no one should have to go through losing a child,' Hörður said as he drew up outside Kristjana's house.

When Kristjana inserted her key in the lock of her front door, he saw that her hand was shaking.

'Shall we sit in the kitchen?' she said, gesturing to him to put the bag of books on the floor.

She lowered herself into her chair as if in pain, then rested her clasped hands in her lap, seeming almost to shrink before his eyes. She was such a pathetic figure that Hörður found it hard to launch into the difficult questions he needed to ask her.

But there was no getting around it.

He began by sharing with her what little information he could divulge about the investigation. Kristjana already knew how her son had died and there wasn't much to add to that, as yet.

'Forensics have examined the cabin,' Hörður continued, 'and they found a pretty sizeable bloodstain on the living-room floor. Could you tell me how it got there?'

Kristjana took her time considering this. The pause lasted so long that Hörður had opened his mouth to repeat the question when she finally spoke.

'It was an accident,' she said. 'I … I cut myself on a knife.'

'In the living room?'

Kristjana glared at him. 'Thorgeir had taken it. He was only a child at the time. I was in such a hurry to snatch it off him that I stupidly cut my hand on the blade.'

'We found a knife in the crawl space under the deck. Do you know what it was doing there?'

'Yes, like I said.'

'You didn't actually say anything about that.'

'Well, that's where I put it.'

'I see.' Hörður looked her up and down. It occurred to him that Kristjana might not be as frail as she appeared at first sight. He remembered hearing rumours that she could be a tricky customer. He'd heard stories about her son too. Having a son of his own the same age, he knew that Thorgeir had been no angel as a boy. He'd inspired terror in the school playground.

'It was a great deal of blood,' Hörður said levelly. 'Are you sure you cut your hand?'

'Of course I am,' Kristjana said.

'Did you get it looked at by a doctor?'

'No, I didn't.'

Hörður was fairly sure that she was lying, though he doubted he'd be able to prove it. According to forensics, for a stain that large, the person in question would have had to lose so much blood that they'd almost certainly have needed a transfusion to survive.

'Fine,' Hörður said, unwilling to subject Kristjana to a grilling in the circumstances. 'Your husband died many years ago, didn't he?'

'Yes, what of it?'

'I wondered if you were with him at the summer house the day he went out on the lake?'

'I was there, yes.'

'So you witnessed him taking the boat out?'

'No, actually.' Kristjana sighed. 'Does it matter?'

Hörður thought for a moment, then said: 'Your husband and your son both died in the same place in suspicious circumstances. I don't know if that's a coincidence but…'

Kristjana gave him a long, enigmatic look before answering: 'That morning I'd gone to the supermarket in Borgarnes. Thorgeir stayed behind and saw his father take the boat out. Reynir was … he was a heavy drinker. He'd been at it all night, so I don't think anyone would call his accident suspicious.'

'No, maybe not,' Hörður conceded. 'But one final thing: we spoke to Thorgeir's friend, Matthías. They'd been working together on a smartphone app and they'd received a pretty substantial investment to get it off the ground. Do you have any idea where it came from?'

'Me?' Kristjana laughed. 'No, I haven't the foggiest.'

'Really?' Hörður asked in feigned surprise. 'You see, Matthías was under the impression that you had invested in the project.'

'An old woman like me?' Kristjana looked as if she'd never heard anything so absurd. 'I don't know where he got that idea from.'

'You ran a successful business for many years, didn't you?' Hörður asked. 'We thought maybe Thorgeir had turned to you for advice.'

'Me? What would I have had to tell him? All I did was run a dry cleaner's. Thorgeir's work was very different, from what I understand.'

Hörður nodded and got to his feet. 'Well, I won't take up any more of your time.'

Outside in the car, he wondered if Matthías could have misunderstood his friend. Perhaps Thorgeir had had funds of his own in a foreign bank account, acquired via an inheritance or something similar. At any rate, Hörður just couldn't picture Kristjana as a secret millionaire. The very idea was ridiculous.

✷

Vatnaskógur
8 August 1995
Day 1
We got a lift here with Dad. My brother Breki wanted to come with us so badly that he threw a fit. Mum says he can go when he's older. She gave me this book to record what happens at the camp. I don't suppose I'll get round to it, though it would be good practice for the book I intend to write one day.

Anyway, I've arrived in Vatnaskógur and should be asleep by now. Some of the others came up by coach from Reykjavík and I made a note of the lads who looked like they'd be good at football. It's vital to get a strong team together so we can win the camp tournament. Last year we came second, but this year I'm determined we're going to come top.

It was kind of weird seeing all the girls arrive. This is the first time I've been in the mixed-sex youth group. I reckon it's made the atmosphere a bit different from previous years. The reek of aftershave is definitely way stronger!

We started off by choosing our dorms, and me and my mates went for the same room in the Laufskáli hut as last year. There aren't as many rooms in Laufskáli as there are in the Old Hut and we made sure we bagged the one furthest away from the leaders. I'm sharing with Matti, Thorgeir and Heiðar. Heiðar's the new guy in our class. He only started in the spring. I really like him. He reads a lot and he's seriously clever. I know because I sat next to him one week and caught a glimpse of his marks. He came top in everything and he let me copy his answers when we had a test in Icelandic.

Sævar wondered if this could be the same Heiðar as the one who had died in Vatnaskógur that year. He checked the date in the news story and compared it to the date Máni had written at the front of his diary. It was the same week. So it had to be the same boy.

After that we went to the canteen, where we chose table seven and were officially welcomed and fed sandwiches and hot chocolate. Our table leader is a lad called Doddi. After that we went out in the boats and rowed into the middle of the lake, where Thorgeir rocked the boat so violently that Matti fell overboard. We laughed so hard we nearly wet ourselves.

Day 2
I've talked to several of the guys from Reykjavík, who are great, and just now we played football and some of them turned out to be seriously good. At home I spend most of my time with Matti and Thorgeir, but I'm getting a bit tired of them, to be honest – Thorgeir especially. He always has to talk the loudest and does stupid things for laughs. Lots of the other kids at school are scared of him because he's so big and can go completely mental when he gets wound up. Not that I've ever been scared of him. He's always been gentle and easy-going around me, and he'd do anything for me too. This can get quite tiring, though. Sometimes when he comes round I get Mum to say I'm busy, but it's difficult because he lives next door, and I reckon he watches to see when I come home. He often turns up the moment I walk through the door.

I'm looking forward to going to college as then I won't have to be in the same class as Thorgeir anymore.

The weather's fantastic and we all took our shirts off while we were playing football. Tomorrow we're going to start building our soap-box cars ready for the rally, and if the weather carries on being this good, the plan is to climb Mount Skarðsheiði.

During the evening entertainment we sang 'Fair Forest Grove' so loudly they could probably hear us all the way back in Akranes. I'm totally knackered now, though, so more tomorrow.

Turning the page, Sævar saw that Máni's prediction that he probably wouldn't get round to writing much in his diary had been borne out. There were no entries for the next two days but on the fourth day he had picked up his pen again.

Day 4
There's been loads going on.
I'm on table seven with Matti, Thorgeir, Heiðar and Júlíus. We came second in the shot-put and third in the football tournament, which sucks. For yesterday's evening entertainment we were supposed to come up with a sketch, so we recreated a scene from Forrest Gump, *the one where he runs away and gets chased by some boys. Dísa played Jenny and Matti played Forrest, and it was quite funny. Everyone laughed, though it wasn't really that good. Heiðar's got a video camera with him and tomorrow we're going to shoot a short film that Magnús, the camp director, has agreed to show. The girls put on a gymnastics performance. It was nothing special but Dísa was involved, so of course Matti and Thorgeir were competing over who could clap loudest.*

Anyway, it's late and we've got to wake up early tomorrow to salute the flag.

Day 5
Today we shot a film and it was awesome. It's like a kind of thriller, and Matti plays the lead with Dísa. The funniest part was how pissed off Thorgeir got. Heiðar was director and responsible for allocating the parts, or at least that's what Matti and I have agreed to say.

At first Thorgeir stormed off, but when he came back later he seemed to have got over it.

The worst part is that ever since then he's been really mean to Heiðar, though Heiðar hasn't done anything and it was me and Matti who allocated the roles. For example, Thorgeir deliberately tripped Heiðar up when we were going to the evening entertainment and Heiðar fell quite hard. But Thorgeir just laughed and so did Dísa.

Really, they're made for each other.

Dísa has smuggled in some landi *and whispered to us that this evening a group of them are going to sneak into the woods to drink it. I've got to stop writing now because someone's tapping on my window.*

He hadn't written any more that day but Sævar was itching to know what happened. Had Máni gone out with the other kids? Had they got away with it?

Landi – illegally distilled spirits – could be dangerously strong. Sævar knew that the drinking of alcohol was strictly forbidden at Vatnaskógur. Even during the August bank holiday festival they held there, which was open to the public, no alcohol was permitted on the site. At least, not when the organisers were looking. If the teenagers had been caught drinking, he assumed they would have been sent straight home to their parents.

But since Máni had written a few more pages, he obviously hadn't gone home in disgrace.

Day 6
Thorgeir's an idiot. He came home in the early hours after drinking all night and threw up in the toilet. Now the whole room stinks of vomit. I can't believe none of the leaders have noticed.

Still, I can't be bothered to waste time thinking about him. Me and Heiðar are planning to make another film. I'm going to write the screenplay and Heiðar's going to shoot it. He showed me all kinds of clips he's filmed and they're really cool. I'm seriously excited about this.

Matti's going to take part too, but I don't want Thorgeir to be involved because he'll only wreck everything as usual.

I realise I've been saying a lot of negative stuff about Thorgeir and maybe I shouldn't. He's been having a hard time. His dad died in an accident last year, and now he's left alone with his mum, who's weird. I know I should be kinder to him.'

Day 7
This is our last evening and I can't wait to go home and start working
on the film with Heiðar. I've made it up with Thorgeir and he says he's
got something fun planned for later. He was actually nice to Heiðar
today too, so I hope things are going to be OK from now on. Heiðar's
such a cool guy. I think we're going to be good mates after this trip.

Not a bad group to start college with.

Speaking of which, Thorgeir said we should welcome Heiðar properly
into the gang. Not that we're really a gang, but I'm sure it'll be a laugh.
It's some kind of initiation ceremony, apparently.

To be honest, I've been dreading the initiation rites at college. I've
heard about new kids being dunked in a tub full of cod-liver oil. I just
hope Thorgeir hasn't got anything like that in mind.

We'll soon find out.

The rest of the diary was blank. Sævar opened his laptop again and
called up the photo of Heiðar. Light-brown, shoulder-length hair,
dark eyebrows and a good-looking face – a face spared the usual
unfortunate proportions and hormonal acne of the adolescent –
smiling shyly at the camera.

Initiation ceremony.

Sævar had vivid memories of his own initiation when he'd started
college. He and the other new kids had been forced to walk along in
a line while being pelted with all kinds of muck: milk, cod-liver oil
and something else, though what he'd rather not know. It had been
fun but stressful. His heart had been racing fit to burst.

One of the boys had been tied to a pillar in the canteen until a
teacher came and released him. Sævar knew that these days the
initiation rites were much more innocuous than they used to be, but
in 1995 a blind eye had been turned to various things that wouldn't
be tolerated today.

Yet this hadn't been an initiation into college but into a group of
friends – Máni hadn't wanted to call them a gang.

Sævar dreaded to think what kind of ideas Thorgeir might have got into his head; what kind of initiation he'd had in mind for Heiðar, the new kid his friends were so dazzled by. The kid Máni was so dazzled by – Máni, who Thorgeir was obviously desperate to hang out with, forever turning up on his doorstep to ask if he was home.

Had he seen Heiðar as a potential threat to his own position within the group? Had he been jealous that Máni obviously liked Heiðar so much?

Sævar recognised the friendship dynamic Máni had described in his diary. He himself had been part of a large, troublesome gang of boys at school in Akureyri. Gangs of boys differed from girls' friendship groups in that they were often larger and more tolerant, at least in his experience. Sævar had been mates with boys he had nothing in common with, boys he couldn't actually stand, just because they were part of the same group.

It was fairly obvious from the diary that Heiðar had got on Thorgeir's nerves. More than that, he suspected that the so-called initiation ceremony had ended in disaster.

He closed his laptop, wondering what to do and whether this information could have any possible bearing on the investigation into Thorgeir's death.

The phone was lying on the table in front of him but he was in two minds about whether to ring Elma. It might be better to see what else he could find out himself first, because what did he actually have to say? That he suspected that the death of a teenage boy in 1995 had not in fact been an accident as was reported at the time? He had no evidence for that apart from this diary. Stuck here at home, there was very little he could do but speculate.

Getting his hands on the official police report from the time would mean going into the station, and he didn't know how his colleagues would react to that. By colleagues, he mainly meant Elma, of course.

❂

The company that had paid the large sum of money into Thorgeir's bank account several months before his murder was registered in Switzerland, but the police still hadn't managed to obtain any details about the owners. This came as no surprise to Hörður, since information always took much longer to arrive from abroad than when they were dealing with local banks or institutions. In fact, they would be lucky if it turned up at all; it wasn't unknown for such information to be withheld at source by the foreign bank.

Those who chose to register their companies in Switzerland were well aware of this, of course, as their entire purpose was to avoid paying tax at home in Iceland. There were all kinds of legal loopholes that could be exploited. Some Icelandic companies were technically owned by offshore entities – firms that Icelanders had set up in places like Switzerland. These firms would then issue loans to the operations in Iceland – so essentially the companies were lending money to themselves. These loans would then accrue a huge amount of interest that was in turn paid to the offshore company. In this way the owners profited from the fact that their money was diverted out of Iceland to a country with lower taxes. The arrangement was legal, but a grey area, and above all unethical. Yet in the business world this never seemed to be regarded as a problem.

Hörður, recalling Kristjana's laughter when he asked whether she had lent her son the money, wasn't sure what to believe. There could well be more to the old woman – as she'd called herself – than met the eye, but to the tune of a hundred million ...? Surely a sum that substantial couldn't have originated with her?

In Hörður's view, Thorgeir and Matthías's app concept sounded like a non-starter: he simply couldn't imagine any employer buying it for their staff, let alone their staff agreeing to allow their employer to keep tabs on their health like that.

Was it even remotely plausible that somebody would have transferred a large sum of money to Thorgeir because the person in question genuinely had faith in the app?

Hörður reached for the blister pack of painkillers and took

another. His damned hip was playing up worse than ever and he couldn't afford to be distracted by it now.

He tried to focus on the matter at hand. It was possible, he supposed, that Kristjana had acquired a small fortune from something other than the dry-cleaning business: from a legacy, say, or through the sale of land she'd inherited. Hörður could think of examples where people had made serious money from that kind of deal. But this wasn't his area of expertise, so when the tax office sent him the tax summary for the dry cleaner's, he'd done no more than flick through it, before forwarding it to the economic-crimes team in Reykjavík.

The whole idea that Kristjana was behind the money sounded pretty ludicrous to him. In fact, the more he thought about it, the more absurd it seemed. Individuals capable of lending a cool hundred million like that would almost certainly be sitting on even larger reserves, whereas Kristjana drove around in a battered jeep, and nothing about her house or her appearance betrayed the slightest hint that she was well off. Matthías must have been mistaken.

Nevertheless, Hörður decided to follow up the email he'd sent the economic-crimes team with a phone call.

'Could you do me a favour?' he asked the member of the team who picked up.

'What's that?'

'I've just sent over some files. Could you take a look into a business that operated here in Akranes for many years? A dry cleaner registered in the name of Kristjana Dagsdóttir?'

'Sure. What is it you want me to check?'

'Whether you can see any signs of irregularities in the bookkeeping.'

❁

The first thing Elma noticed when she came upstairs was a familiar-looking pram. Then she saw that the coffee room was unusually crowded. The sound of a high-pitched babbling that she knew better than her own voice removed all doubt of who was there.

'Hello, hello,' she said, walking into the coffee room, where she saw her daughter in Begga's arms. Kári was standing beside her, pulling funny faces.

Adda seemed pleased with the attention but the moment she spotted Elma she made a disgruntled noise and stretched out her arms to her mother.

'Where's Sævar?' Elma asked, taking her daughter from Begga.

'In his office,' Begga replied. 'At least, the last I knew.'

'When was that?'

'Half an hour, forty minutes ago.'

'You've got to be joking.' Elma kissed her daughter on the cheek and Adda's eyelids drooped. She was plainly worn out. When Elma laid her in the pram, the little girl protested briefly, before burying her nose in her teddy-bear blanket and closing her eyes.

Sævar was glued to his computer screen when Elma opened the door to his office.

'Back at work, are we?' she asked, leaning against the doorframe. 'Should I go home then, or what?'

'Is …? Where's Adda?' Sævar glanced at his watch and made a dismayed grimace. 'Is it really that late? I completely forgot to—'

'Relax, she's asleep,' Elma said. 'She flaked out the instant I put her down in her pram. Far too late for her normal nap time, though, which means we won't be able to get her to sleep this evening.'

'Sorry. There was just one thing I needed to check.'

Elma took the chair facing him, suddenly aware how much she had missed Sævar's presence at work. They had first met when Elma moved home from Reykjavík. Thinking back to that time now, it was as if a completely different person had turned up to work at Akranes police station that autumn morning in 2017. So much had changed in three years.

'What was it you were checking?' she asked.

'Remember that box we found in the loft?'

'Yes?'

'Well, I started digging around in the contents and found something rather interesting.'

'Oh? I thought it was just old schoolwork,' Elma said. 'Which reminds me: I meant to try and track down the previous owners and give it back.'

'Most of it belonged to a boy called Máni,' Sævar said. 'He was a friend of Thorgeir's. They were neighbours as kids and, it just so happens, they both attended the Vatnaskógur summer camp in 1995. While they were there, a boy called Heiðar was killed in an accident, but I reckon there's reason to believe it wasn't an accident at all.'

'OK,' Elma said cautiously, unsure where this was going.

'Have a look at this.' Sævar handed her the diary, and she began to read.

At first sight, Máni's diary entries appeared perfectly innocent, but in light of later events, they took on a new significance. Plainly, there had been tensions between Heiðar and Thorgeir, and Thorgeir's sudden change of heart and decision to initiate the new boy into the gang struck her as strange and unconvincing. It sounded as if his real motivation had been quite different.

When Elma put down the diary, Sævar showed her the news article with the photo of Heiðar.

'This is the boy who died at Vatnaskógur. In an accident, it states here.'

'How did he die?'

'He drowned.' Sævar clicked the mouse and a familiar form appeared. Or rather, Elma recognised the layout, having filled in any number of similar police reports over the years. 'It's not very informative, but it appears that on the morning of Friday, the sixteenth of August 1995 one of the instructors at Vatnaskógur discovered that Heiðar wasn't in his bed. They searched the area and noticed that a boat had been untied from the jetty and could be seen adrift on Lake Eyrarvatn. Heiðar's body was found in the water the following day.'

'And you think that Thorgeir and his friends had something to do with that? Matti and Dísa – that must be Matthías and Hafdís, mustn't it? Do you think we should ask them about it?'

'I don't know,' Sævar said. 'But, I mean, what was Heiðar doing in a boat on the lake in the middle of the night? He was barefoot and only wearing the clothes he slept in. I don't believe he went there of his own accord.'

Elma agreed that it did sound unlikely.

'This diary suggests that something quite different happened,' Sævar persisted.

'Yes, but what?'

'I don't know,' Sævar said again. 'But I believe we can still find out. I'd like to see the post-mortem report to be sure, but I can't seem to track it down.'

'Strange. There must have been one.' Post-mortems were the rule in the case of sudden death in uncertain circumstances.

'Yes, you'd have thought so. I just need to find out where it is.'

'Oh, you do, do you?' Elma said with a grin. 'I'm busy with another case right now, in case you hadn't noticed. Oh, and by the way, aren't you the guy who couldn't wait to go on paternity leave and have a break from policework? Maybe we should just call the nursery and ask if we can register Adda at seven months. Do they take infants, do you know?'

Sævar ignored Elma's teasing. 'Don't you think there's a chance the two cases are linked?'

Elma considered this. She certainly didn't think the idea should be dismissed out of hand. It would be easy to hop on board with Sævar and take a closer look. On the other hand, although the murder inquiry had only just got off the ground, they had already identified a number of other murky areas in Thorgeir's life: an old rape accusation, a dodgy investment, and now a relationship with a girl who seemed to have gone out of her way to cover up her trail. Taking all this into account, Elma doubted the case had its roots in something that had happened a quarter of a century ago.

She shook her head. 'No, it sounds pretty tenuous to me.'

Sævar's shoulders sagged and he nodded. 'You're right. But I still get the feeling the boy's death wasn't properly investigated at the time.'

'That's quite possible,' Elma said. Once Thorgeir's case was closed, she would look into Heiðar's. There might well be sufficient grounds to reopen the old inquiry in light of this new information.

She said goodbye to Sævar and Adda, hoping to see them again shortly, but a few minutes later Begga walked into her office without knocking.

'What's up?' Elma asked, stifling a yawn.

'I've found her,' Begga announced.

'Who?'

'Andrea.' Begga thumped down in the chair facing Elma. 'I decided to take a closer look at the bits of Thorgeir's internet history I was going through and came across an interesting search on Google Maps. Thorgeir had looked up directions to an address during a recent trip to Reykjavík. When I checked out the address, it turned out to be a block of flats. I went through all the owners and occupants and – ta-da!'

'Ta-da?'

'Andrea Friðriksdóttir.'

'Brilliant,' Elma said, finally feeling they were getting somewhere, while simultaneously warning herself not to get her hopes up too much. Given how difficult it had been to trace Andrea, the chances were that she had something to hide. The fact they were now in possession of her address didn't automatically mean they had found the girl herself. But at least it was a start.

BEFORE
Thorgeir

He manages to get the hot tub working, and, right on demand, the blustery breeze drops and the clouds part to reveal a star-studded night sky. He adjusts the controls to ensure a constant flow so the water in the tub won't get cold.

'This is fantastic,' Andrea says, leaning back and gazing up at the sky. Her breath forms clouds of steam that float up into the darkness.

'Like another?' Thorgeir asks, reaching for a couple more beers.

Andrea takes one but he notices that she barely takes a sip.

She's been rather quiet all evening. He barbecued lamb for supper and served it with red wine, after which they listened to music and chatted, but her gaze kept straying to the window as if she'd seen something outside.

Even now she starts every time there's a rustle of old leaves or a twig snaps in the birch forest.

'Are you scared of the dark?' he asks.

'What? Why do you ask?'

'Because I can tell from looking at you.'

She laughs. 'Is it that obvious?'

He smiles and moves closer to her, putting down his beer to free up his hands.

'It's terribly dark out here,' she whispers.

'Good.'

He kisses her, a deep, intimate kiss, feeling as if his heart could burst with love for her. He loves every single thing about her.

She jumps again at the sound of a car driving along the gravel road in the distance. He smiles and brushes a strand of hair from her face. 'It's only a car,' he says. 'Not a ghost.'

'No, I know,' she says. 'I just thought…'

'You needn't be afraid,' he says. 'I'll look after you.'

'Will you?'

'Of course. I love you. I'd do anything for you.'

In the moonlight he can see Andrea smiling faintly, with a look in her eyes that tells him no one's ever taken proper care of her before. She hasn't been very forthcoming about her family. All he knows is that she doesn't have much contact with them.

He releases her and, shifting back a little, takes a sip of beer.

'I never thought I'd feel like this,' he says. He must be rather drunk because he keeps talking, telling her things he never thought he'd hear himself saying. 'But it's like I've found something special with you. I've got this sudden urge to start a family, to move in with you, have children … the whole package.'

Andrea is staring at him, her expression unreadable.

The silence compels him to keep talking. 'Since Dad died it's only been the two of us, just me and my mum, and there's always been something missing. It feels like everyone I know is surrounded by family and I'm on my own. Mum and me … we don't always get on. But it's not like Dad and I got on either.'

'When did he die?'

'When I was fifteen. I miss him sometimes, but still…' Thorgeir lowers his gaze to the water, to the stars and moon reflected in its surface. He hasn't spoken this openly since … No, he's never spoken this openly before. But suddenly he wants to. For her. He wants to know everything about her and for her to know him inside out. Well, perhaps not quite inside out. He's done various things he's not proud of, but he'd rather not think about them. He'd rather bury the past, because he's not the same person anymore. He hasn't been that person for a long time.

'It's so complicated. Maybe I just miss the idea of having a dad,' he continues. 'I hoped for so long that … that things would get better.'

Only now is it dawning on him. For years he's been mourning a father he never had. He doesn't miss his actual father, the man who used to come home and call him in that chilling, hissing tone. Sometimes he still hears that voice, whispering his name in the rustling of leaves in autumn or the crunch of snow in winter. Thorgeir doesn't miss that constant sense of dread. He glances over at Andrea, who appears to be sunk in thought too, and tries to shake off the unsettling memories. 'Have you ever lost anyone?' he asks.

'Yes.' She nods and starts fiddling with her hair. 'My brother.'

NOW

Friday 11 December

Unable to face going home after work, Hafdís went to the shops instead and looked at clothes for nearly an hour. In the end she bought a pair of jeans and a thin, semi-transparent patterned shirt, without trying them on.

She returned to the car that she had left on Mánabraut, chucked the bag in the back and started the engine. But instead of heading home, she drove down to the sea, then along the coast road to the docks. A car overtook her, the driver glaring at her through the window, no doubt irritated by her slowness.

She didn't care. She'd never been a people-pleaser. And, anyway, she was too distracted to concentrate on her driving. In fact, she had hardly been able to concentrate on anything all day, or for the last few days, for that matter.

It wasn't thoughts of Thorgeir she was preoccupied with – not directly, anyway. Rather, her mind kept harking back in time, dwelling on events from long ago; on the days when she had first moved to Akranes and met Matthías, and the years immediately after that. Good years. Full of promise and hope for the future.

Well, she'd done a great job of wrecking that.

Hafdís couldn't work out exactly how it had happened or what she had done to deserve it, but she couldn't conceal from herself that everything around her had a habit of ending in disaster and that she played some part in that.

As a child she used to become totally absorbed in manipulating people, deriving too much pleasure from winning their attention and admiration.

That hadn't lasted long.

Almost without her noticing, other things had begun to take centre stage – important things, like education and work. Like husbands, children and looking after a home. But she was no good at those things. She was a bad mother, because she quite simply didn't like her daughter. That was the truth. They'd never got on; they were just too different. She'd loved her when she was first placed in her arms as a baby, but over time it had become increasingly apparent that this love was limited to the basic parental role. She wasn't capable of feeling a love that went beyond the basics, and the older Ólöf got, the more watered down the emotion became. It was a truth that couldn't be spoken of, although such feelings were common enough in the animal kingdom, where mothers abandoned their young as soon as they were able to fend for themselves. It was a law of nature. Once the mothers had fulfilled their role, they could revert to focusing on their own interests.

The sensation of emerging from the torpor that had characterised her life for more than a decade had intensified over the last few months. Hafdís had almost forgotten who she was. But now that was changing. Finally, she had the courage to take charge of her own life, which also meant facing up to the past and everything she had done.

Take away my crimes and sins with blood…

Perhaps it was the only way, now that she came to think about it.

The light was failing as she drew up outside her house. The illuminated windows indicated that somebody was home. Just a few more days, then she could leave this place for good.

As she retrieved her bag from the passenger seat, she heard the bleeping of an incoming phone message. It gave her an excuse to linger in the car a few moments longer, though she thought she had seen Matthías appear briefly at the window. Poor Matthías. He was so weak that Hafdís was sure he would soon break down completely.

She couldn't stand his vulnerability. Men who were afraid of losing everything were capable of anything. They did crazy, unpredictable things.

She looked out of the car window again. Although she couldn't see Matthías, she could sense his suffocating presence.

He might look innocent, but she'd seen with her own eyes how he could react when he was backed into a corner.

Hafdís checked the message she'd received on Instagram. It was from an unknown sender and had gone into her message requests. Not a text but a video.

When she pressed play, the image that appeared was of a computer screen on which another video was playing. A video of a video. Hafdís brought the phone closer to her face.

She saw a floor, followed by a bunk bed. Heard familiar laughter and saw an even more familiar arm. Before she could see any more, she deleted the video, blocked the sender and switched off her phone. It was all she could do not to fling it away from her.

❂

'It's here,' Elma exclaimed, unnecessarily loudly.

Flustered by the tension in her voice, Hörður slammed on the brakes.

'No spaces,' he muttered, peering around. 'Never anywhere to park in this town.'

If there was one thing Hörður couldn't stand it was Reykjavík. Elma had lost count of the times she had heard him moaning about the congestion, the noise, the overcrowding and the shortage of parking spaces. It was a subject on which Hörður and her mother were in complete agreement.

In the end, they left the car at the end of the street and walked the short distance through the rain. The snow had vanished for the time being but would no doubt be back with a vengeance in a day or two. Already the rain was turning to sleet, the heavy, icy droplets soaking their hair and dripping down their necks. This chopping and changing between freeze and thaw was typical Reykjavík weather. The city streets never remained a pristine white for long but were quickly reduced to a sea of black slush, before refreezing into treacherous lumps and mounds of ice.

'Can't the weather ever make up its mind?' Elma grumbled, trying to make a hood out of her scarf.

For once, Hörður wasn't wearing his Russian fur hat but seemed determined to brave the elements, walking with his head held defiantly high, making no attempt to shield his face.

Elma halted outside the correct address. Each of the buildings in this terrace on Holtsgata was differentiated from its neighbours by its colour; this one was blue, those flanking it yellow and red. She realised glumly that they wouldn't be able to shelter in the hallway unless someone in one of the flats let them in.

'There are four flats,' Hörður said, checking the doorbells.

Elma peered at the names but couldn't see Andrea's.

'There's no name on the top bell, so let's try giving that a ring,' she suggested.

The seconds crept by as they waited for an answer, shivering in the icy rain. Then there was a crackle of static from the intercom, followed by an enquiring: 'Yes?'

'We're looking for Andrea, does she live here?' Elma held her breath and felt a rush of disappointment when the 'no' came. She sighed. As if to rub salt in the wound, the sleet found a gap in her scarf-hood and sent a sudden icy trickle down her neck.

There was another crackle of static, then the same voice said: 'Andrea lives in the flat opposite. I'll let you in.'

Before they could respond there was a low buzzing, then a click and Hörður pushed the front door open. 'After you.'

They entered an entrance hall of drab raw concrete. A metal banister ran up the stairs to the top floor, where Andrea lived.

They knocked and the door opened to reveal a youngish woman with short-cropped hair, dyed silvery white, and rather coarse features: thick lips, a broad nose and a square jaw.

'We're looking for Andrea,' Elma said, after introducing herself and Hörður. 'Are you…?'

The woman shook her head. 'No, I'm not Andrea. We live together but I haven't seen her for several days.'

'Do you know where she is?'

'No,' the woman said. 'Why, has something happened?'

'We're trying to get hold of her in connection with a murder inquiry,' Elma explained. 'Could we possibly ask you a few questions?'

'Yes, of course,' the woman said, looking visibly shaken. She stepped aside. 'Would you like to come in?'

They took seats on the sofa in a fairly tidy but unconventional sitting room, characterised by brightly clashing colours. In addition to the blue sofa, there was a green armchair and a yellow, glass-doored cabinet in which a framed photo of a dog took pride of place.

'May I ask how you know Andrea?' Elma began. Then smiled and added: 'Sorry, what was your name again?'

'Freyja. We share a flat but we don't actually know each other apart from that.'

'Surely if you live together, you must know each other fairly well?'

Freyja shrugged. 'We've only lived together for about six months.'

'And you didn't know each other before that?'

'No, not at all. I responded to an advert for a flatmate that Andrea posted on Facebook. We met up in a café and hit it off so well that we walked straight over here afterwards and sealed the deal with a handshake. That's it.'

A white cat with black and brown patches jumped onto Freyja's lap and made itself comfortable.

'I see,' Elma said. She threw a sideways glance at Hörður, who was sitting beside her, not saying a word. Presumably he thought Elma would do a better job of talking to this woman. 'When did you last see Andrea?'

'Last…' Freyja looked at her phone and appeared to be counting in her head. 'It must have been before the weekend. Last Friday, I think. She told me she was going out of town and didn't know when she'd be back.'

'And you haven't heard from her since?'

'No, not a word. I was beginning to wonder if I'd misunderstood. That she meant she was going abroad, not just out of town. Because I tried to call her but she didn't get back to me, so I thought maybe she was abroad with no phone connection.'

This struck Elma as unlikely. You were bound to have a phone connection unless you were on another continent. As long as you were in Europe, there shouldn't be any problems with the phone or internet.

'You don't have any idea where she was going or who she was with?'

'I know she was seeing some guy but I don't know his name. We didn't really talk about personal stuff.'

'You don't remember any name at all?'

Freyja shook her head, and Elma sighed inwardly.

'Do you think something's happened to Andrea?' Freyja asked, pre-empting their next question. 'Or that she's gone missing or something?'

'You've probably seen the recent news reports about the man who was found dead in Skorradalur?'

'Yes.'

'Well, we have reason to believe that he was the man Andrea was seeing.'

'Oh.' Freyja seemed finally to twig. 'Oh, so you think … Was he … Was Andrea with him?'

'We can't find Andrea but we believe she may have been with him when it happened.' Elma refrained from adding that, in the circumstances, she suspected Andrea might have murdered Thorgeir then gone on the run. There were too many question marks over her behaviour. Normally it wasn't a problem to find people in Iceland, unless they didn't want to be found and had done a deliberate disappearing act. 'What do you know about Andrea?' Elma asked.

'Like I said, we don't know each other that well,' Freyja repeated apologetically.

'Do you know anything about her family?'

'Only that her patronymic is Friðriksdóttir...' Freyja replied. 'Her mother's dead but I think she has a brother. I'm afraid that's all I can tell you.'

'All right. But do you know where she works?' Elma persisted.

'She's got a part-time job at a library and sometimes works evening shifts at a restaurant in the city centre. Dalurinn, it's called.'

Elma jotted down the names of the library and restaurant, glad to have something concrete, at least. 'Have you tried to get in touch with Andrea by some other means apart from the phone? Via social media, for instance?'

Freyja laughed, though Elma couldn't see what was so funny about the question.

'Andrea doesn't really do social media,' Freyja explained. 'She doesn't believe in it; thinks it's superficial. Fake. That's something we have in common.'

This came as no surprise to Elma, since all Andrea and Thorgeir's exchanges had taken place via their phones – through calls or text messages – which was unusual these days.

'Does Andrea own a car?'

'No,' Freyja said. 'We live so close to everything here, there's no need for a car.'

'Do you know how long she'd been seeing this man?'

'Like I already said, we don't discuss things like that,' Freyja replied. 'We're not friends who share a flat and swap secrets in the evenings. We're just ... flatmates. She does her thing and I do mine. We don't often run into each other, despite living together. She works evenings, I work nights.'

'Is that her room?' Elma asked, pointing down the hall.

'Yes. The one at the end. You can take a look if ... Mind you, is that actually legal, if she's not here?'

Elma caught Hörður's eye. Searching a premises without the

permission of the owner or the courts was straying into a very grey area. Hörður seemed to be thinking along the same lines but shrugged.

'We won't touch anything,' Elma assured Freyja, rising to her feet.

'OK,' Freyja said, but stayed where she was.

They were met by a heavy, sweet smell when they entered Andrea's room, a combination of perfume and bedclothes. A smell that carried Elma back to the days when she used to sneak into her teenage sister's room when Dagný was out.

Not that Andrea was a teenager. Yet her room – the whole flat, in fact – gave the impression of being home to people who had no responsibilities in life for anyone but themselves. A dressing table cluttered with countless eye-shadow palettes; dresses and jackets hanging from a clothes rail; shelves crammed with books and ornaments. Elma paused by the bookcase and studied a photo of an adolescent boy and a girl of around five years old. A photo of Andrea with her brother?

Elma assumed Andrea must have other family members – a father perhaps? – who would be wondering what had happened to her if she didn't make contact soon.

'Nothing here.' Hörður had his hands in his jacket pockets as he wandered round the room, not touching anything.

'No, nothing here,' Elma agreed. She looked out of the window at the street below. While they were inside, the sleet had turned to snow and was well on its way to coating the grey tarmac in glittering white. Wherever Andrea was hiding, it seemed they weren't going to find any clues in her room.

Before leaving, they took Freyja's phone number. She seemed to have belatedly grasped the gravity of the situation and began pestering them with questions they wouldn't or couldn't answer, like how Thorgeir had died and whether Andrea had been present when it happened. Her anxiety manifested itself in a deep furrow between her eyebrows, but there was nothing they could do to relieve it.

Elma got into the car feeling discouraged. Of course, she shouldn't have kidded herself that it would be that easy to track Andrea down. And at least they had a few more details to go on now.

As she mulled over the few scraps of information they'd obtained from Freyja, it crossed her mind that if Andrea didn't own a car, she must have got a lift to the summer house with Thorgeir. And, in that case, she wouldn't have had many escape routes from Skorradalur, except with somebody else who had a car.

The question was, who had given her a lift and had she gone with them voluntarily?

❂

The Smáralind mall was heaving. The bags were beginning to cut into Friðrik's hands and his face was itching after hours of relentless Christmas shopping. His sixty-five-year-old body wasn't designed for such retail marathons, but that was the price he had to pay for getting hitched to a younger woman. Dís, twenty years younger than him, seemed indefatigable, despite her high-heeled boots.

'LEGO Friends or a doll?' Dís asked, holding up two boxes, both bright pink.

'Does she play with dolls, Dís?'

Friðrik had mainly seen Indíana play with her brother's superhero toys. She displayed little interest in the girly stuff Dís bought her, let alone in the pink dresses. Young though she was, Indíana had strong opinions, and Friðrik knew that their daughter-in-law, Kristný, was fed up with Dís giving Indíana presents that demonstrated her complete lack of knowledge of her granddaughter.

Indíana was Friðrik's stepson Daníel's daughter. As Daníel had been eight when Friðrik and Dís met, he had never referred to Friðrik as Dad, but so far as Indíana was concerned, he was her grandfather. Somewhere out there were his real grandchildren, but Friðrik rarely got to see them, or indeed his own children, Andrea and Breki.

'Indíana wanted a Spiderman toy the last time I asked her,' Friðrik reminded Dís.

'Oh, Friðrik, she's only four.' Dís returned the doll to the shelf. 'She'll want whatever she's given.'

'OK, fine, then let's take the LEGO Friends.' Friðrik took the big box over to the till, studying the picture on the front as he did so. It showed a shopping mall with LEGO girl figures in a variety of dresses. Indíana had been adamant the previous day when she whispered to him what she wanted for Christmas.

'A Spiderman who can do this with his arm.' She had gestured to show him how Spiderman cast out his web. Her other main interest was in spiders and creepy-crawlies of all kinds.

On his way to the till, Friðrik passed a table stacked with superhero toys. He stole a glance over his shoulder and, seeing Dís busy talking on her phone, he grabbed a Spiderman and headed purposefully towards the till.

Friðrik was in the act of parting with an eye-watering amount of money when his gaze fell on a man standing at the self-service checkout. His face was so familiar that Friðrik momentarily forgot what he was doing. The man seemed similarly nonplussed. He stood there, holding a book but apparently forgetting to scan it in. They both stared at each other for a long, frozen moment.

'Excuse me. Hello.' The girl at the till was regarding him wearily. 'Did you want a receipt?'

'Er, no.' Friðrik shoved the card in his pocket and took the bag. When he looked back at the self-service checkouts, the man was walking away.

'Friðrik, wasn't that—?' Dís had finished her phone call and come over to join him.

'Yes,' he interrupted her hastily, as if he couldn't bear to acknowledge aloud that it had indeed been him – his son.

Every time he encountered Breki or Andrea it was like picking at a festering wound. An uncomfortable reminder of the past, of another life and a different man. In the daily bustle of his life with Dís he managed to forget and to behave as if nothing had happened, but from time to time it came back to haunt him. All that agonising about what he should have done differently and how his life might have turned out. All those ifs. Some nights as he lay awake, staring into the darkness, the past felt almost palpable. The memories were so vivid in the gloom.

'Your phone, Friðrik.' Dís was giving him a strange look. 'Can't you hear it?'

As she spoke, Friðrik became aware of a loud ringing from his pocket. He took out his phone and although he didn't recognise the number on screen, for some reason his heart began to pound.

When he answered, the woman at the other end, a stranger, introduced herself as Elma.

❂

According to Íslendingabók, the database of Icelandic genealogical records, Andrea had been born in 1990 to parents called Friðrik and Jóhanna. Her mother's name was followed not only by a date of birth but by a date of death as well, so Freyja had been right about that, and it would only be possible to speak to her father, Friðrik Ingi. He answered after several rings and told Elma he'd be home in a quarter of an hour.

Conveniently for them, Friðrik lived in a newish suburb of Mosfellsbær, the small town that lay on their route home from Reykjavík to Akranes. Elma and Hörður drove north out of the city through the falling snow, before turning off to the west. Elma, following the detailed directions she'd got from Friðrik, soon found the address, a single-storey house in a concrete terrace. Hörður rang the bell and they waited a while, the snow softly settling on their heads and shoulders, before the door was answered.

Friðrik looked young for a man in his sixties, though there were touches of grey in his dark hair, particularly his beard. He gave the impression that he'd once been very fit but had recently let himself go and was growing a bit soft and flabby.

'Come in,' he said, and, after they had gone through the usual palaver of removing their coats and shoes, and brushing the snow out of their hair, they followed him through to the sitting room. There was a floor lamp by the windows, which made it impossible to see out, but Elma caught her own reflection in the glass, a pale woman with messy hair. She and Hörður sat down on a sofa upholstered in bottle-green corduroy, and Friðrik took the leather armchair facing them. It was so quiet in the house, no noise of a distant TV or radio, that Elma assumed Friðrik must live alone until she spotted a photo on a shelf, showing him embracing a woman in a white dress.

'Well,' Friðrik said. His face was grave, his eyes pale blue and his skin unusually smooth, as if his expressions were never pronounced enough to create deep lines. This blankness made him difficult to read.

Hörður got straight to the point before Elma could say a word.

'We're investigating the murder of a man by the name of Thorgeir Reynisson. He was recently found dead in his summer house in Skorradalur, and we have reason to believe that your daughter was there with him, but we're unable to get hold of her.'

'I see. What reason do you have to believe that?'

'Thorgeir's friend thought they might have gone there together,' Elma said. 'They'd been seeing each other for some time.'

'I see,' Friðrik said again, in a voice that was as toneless as his face was impassive. He was silent for a while before continuing: 'Andrea and I haven't spoken for years. We completely lost contact after her mother and I divorced when she was young.'

'What about her brother?'

'Breki? I don't know if they have any contact.'

'So you're not in touch with him either?'

'No.'

Elma glanced at Hörður and saw that he was thinking the same as her: this visit was a waste of time; they wouldn't find Andrea at her father's house.

'Do you know if Andrea is in touch with any other member of your family?' she asked.

'No, but I assume she must be.' Friðrik dropped his gaze to his hands. 'It's many years since I was part of my children's lives. I did think about contacting them after their mother died but…'

But he hadn't got round to it, Elma silently completed the sentence. The right time had never come. 'How old were they when she died?' she asked.

'It was only a few years ago – five, maybe. Andrea would have been twenty-five, Breki thirty-two.'

In other words, they had both been adults and hadn't needed Friðrik to look after them, despite the loss of their mother. 'Right, well,' Elma said, 'maybe you'd let us know if she gets in touch.' She prepared to stand up.

Friðrik nodded.

But Hörður didn't seem ready to leave quite yet. 'When did you last hear from your daughter?'

'I simply don't remember,' Friðrik replied. 'Look, I didn't deal with things very well in those days. I should have … should have behaved better. But their mother was so angry that I felt it was better to stay away to avoid a scene. I was in a bad place myself too and didn't want it to have a negative effect on them. I was drinking too much and for some reason I thought that by going away, I might be able to prevent my kids from turning out like me. From going down the same path … That boy Thorgeir – he was murdered, wasn't he?'

'Yes.'

'Do you think Andrea could be in danger? Has something happened to her?'

The thought had occurred to Elma. Andrea could have got in the way, been in the wrong place at the wrong time. While Elma hoped this wasn't the case, she couldn't say anything for sure.

'We have no reason to believe that,' Hörður replied.

'I've lost one child already. A son. I don't know if I could bear to lose another.'

Elma bit back the urge to say that it looked as if he had already lost both his children a long time ago, by his own choice. That wasn't to say that she had no compassion for him on account of his son, but she had little sympathy for those who abandoned their children just because their marriages fell apart. In her opinion, leaving your partner didn't justify you leaving your children as well.

'That's sad to hear,' Hörður said.

'Yes.' Friðrik got to his feet: 'Very sad.'

❈

Matthías had been made to look like a fool. How could he have been so stupid? So blind?

He didn't know who he was angrier with, Hafdís or himself. It was humiliating to think that while he had believed himself to be happily married, Hafdís had been planning how to leave him. Only last weekend at her Christmas work party, he had felt himself swelling with pride whenever he looked across the dinner table at her: his wife was the most beautiful woman in the room and he loved everything about her.

What Hafdís didn't understand was that he loved her as much for her faults as for her good points. He loved the fact that she was difficult, that she was determined. Loved the way people sensed that steely determination without her having to say a word, and went out of their way to try to oblige her. Were even a little intimidated by her. She was the type who sent her food back to the kitchen when it failed to meet her standards, who wasn't afraid to give teachers and sports instructors a piece of her mind. Who ticked off the children she took for swimming lessons if they didn't make an effort, and turned a deaf ear to any parents who complained.

The only person Hafdís couldn't control was their daughter. As she grew older, Ólöf had become increasingly immune to her mother's influence. At first, this had driven Hafdís berserk, but that had actually been preferable to the indifference with which she now treated their daughter. Hafdís appeared to have given up on Ólöf, not to care a damn anymore what happened to her, and for the first time in all the years they had lived together, Matthías had looked at his wife and felt that her charms had faded; the embers of his affection had suddenly cooled.

'I haven't a clue,' she answered carelessly that suppertime when Matthías asked where Ólöf was. Neither of them had given any thought to cooking this week, either foraging for whatever they could find in the fridge or ordering separate takeaways. It was Matthías who had seen to it that Ólöf got something to eat.

'She's not answering her phone.'

'No.' Hafdís, who was painting her nails, didn't look up.

'Have you heard from her since she got out of school?'

Hafdís shook her head.

Matthías breathed slowly through his nose. His daughter hadn't come home from school or got in touch to say where she was, and it was now past suppertime. He had been preoccupied with his own affairs and so, clearly, had Hafdís. He felt a stab of guilt.

'I'm going to ring round her friends,' he said. 'Have you got the number of that dark-haired girl she's always hanging out with?'

'Snæja.'

'Yes, her. What's her number?'

'You'll find her on the school intranet.'

Matthías duly tracked down the girl's parents' number. After they had explained to him that his daughter wasn't round at their house, they passed the phone to Snæja.

'Hello, Snæja,' Matthías said, 'this is Ólöf's dad. She didn't come home today after school. Do you have any idea where she might be?'

'No, I don't know where she is.'

'She was at school today, though, wasn't she?'

'Yes, we both had home economics in our last period.'

'Did you see her walking home?'

'I … I saw her start walking, but then, like, this car stopped and she got in.'

Matthías's heart missed a beat. Whose car had his daughter got into? He'd impressed upon her ever since she was small that she must never accept lifts from strangers. She must always run away, regardless of what the driver said.

'Do you remember what the car looked like? Did you see who was driving it?'

'Uhhh…' Snæja must be chewing gum because her words were punctuated by smacking noises. 'It was white. Like, quite small.'

'Did you see who was driving it?'

'No.'

Matthías wasn't sure whether to believe Snæja. Her 'no' had sounded hesitant to him. He mentally ran through their acquaintance, trying to think of anyone who owned a small white car, but drew a blank. The fact was that adults who earned a proper wage didn't drive around in cheap vehicles like that: it was much more likely to be a teenager, a kid from the sixth-form college.

The thought of Ólöf with an older boy made his heart sink but didn't surprise him. That summer he had collected her from a party held at the home of some kids from the local college, so he was already aware that she socialised with sixth-formers.

'She'll come home in her own time,' Hafdís said. 'Calm down.'

Matthías didn't understand how she could be so unconcerned, how she could tell him to calm down like that. It was getting late and their fifteen-year-old daughter hadn't come home from school or got in touch to tell them where she was, and she wasn't answering her phone. When had Hafdís become so cold-bloodedly indifferent to their daughter?

When she was a newborn, they had both flown into a panic if she so much as coughed oddly or took too big a mouthful of food. They had cut everything up into tiny chunks for fear she might choke. But now, when there was a chance she was out with older boys or had even got into a car with a stranger, Hafdís seemed more concerned with her own nails.

He studied her as she sat there at the kitchen table, applying another coat of varnish, something she did at least every other day, and the realisation hit him that he didn't know her. Perhaps he never had.

'She's just taking some time out,' Hafdís continued unconcernedly, blowing on her nails.

Matthías suddenly had a vision of himself grabbing those slender fingers and viciously twisting them back. He sprang up and filled a glass at the tap, trying to push these thoughts away. He'd persuaded himself for so long that he wasn't a violent man; that although he hadn't always done the right thing, he wasn't like his father.

'I think we ought to call the police,' he said, making an effort to control his voice.

Hafdís glanced up quickly. 'That would be incredibly stupid.'

From her tone Matthías was sure she wanted to add that it would be typical of him; after all, he was stupid enough already.

Hafdís never tired of telling him that. Not in so many words, but it was the subtext to all those superior smirks and withering looks. To those brief, cryptic remarks and contemptuous snorts. It had never got to him before, he'd just ignored her snarky comments, perhaps because he was inured to them. He'd grown up hearing exactly the same kind of remarks from his father.

Matthías snatched up the car keys from the table.

'Where are you going?' Hafdís called after him.

'Out,' he said. 'To look for Ólöf.'

❂

'What do you want in it?'

'Strawberries, liquorice shavings and…' Over the phone Elma could hear Sævar sucking in air between his teeth. 'And chocolate caramel.'

Elma repeated the list to the young man serving in the kiosk, and ordered a strawberry shake for herself. Her gaze fell on a group of school-age boys who were sitting at one of the tables, talking loudly over their fizzy drinks and crisps. They looked so young to her, no more than children, though it seemed like only yesterday she had been sitting there herself with her friends, discussing exams or what video they were planning to rent that evening.

While she was waiting for the ice cream, she opened her unread emails. Several turned out to be from taxi companies she had contacted, none of which had any record of a callout to Skorradalur the previous weekend. Though one company explained that, since their drivers used their own vehicles, it was possible that one could have been working privately on the side.

'Here you go,' the young man said, putting the ice cream on the counter.

Elma's phone rang. She recognised the number because she had just been trying to call it, and decided to step outside to answer. On the drive back from Reykjavík, she had tried to get hold of Andrea's brother, Breki, but got no answer. She had looked him up on social media while queuing for the ice cream and the image that appeared was of a man of about her own age, posed as if it had been taken for an election campaign: grey suit, light-blue shirt and a neatly trimmed beard.

'Could you keep this for me?' she asked the young man behind the counter. 'I'll be back in a sec.'

He pulled a face, then shrugged and put the ice cream on the table behind him.

Apparently Breki had been for a swim and was returning Elma's call on his walk home. From time to time the wind blew into the receiver, making a crackling noise. Only now did it occur to Elma what a bad idea it had been to step outside to take this call. It was freezing and her moist breath was condensing into clouds of steam in the light outside the kiosk. She hoped Breki would be able to hear her brief explanation of what this was about. There was a long silence on the other end. So long that Elma thought the connection had been lost.

'I'm still here,' Breki said eventually. He seemed to have got into shelter because his voice was no longer breaking up. 'I'm just … I'm having trouble getting my head around this.'

'Do you have much contact with Andrea?'

'We don't see each other that often but we speak regularly. I tried to call her the other day but she didn't pick up. It's just the two of us left, really. Mum's dead and our father, Friðrik … I haven't talked to him since I was in my teens. But, like I said, I just can't get my head around this.'

'Why is that?'

'Because, I mean, I know who Thorgeir is.'

Elma waited for him to explain.

'He used to live next door to us when I was a kid.'

Elma leant against the wall in an attempt to shelter from the biting wind. 'Next door. I don't understand…'

'No. I don't understand either. You see, we used to live in Akranes when we were young. I don't remember the name of the street. Vigur—, no Vog—…'

'Vogabraut.' Elma should know the name since she lived there herself.

'That's the one,' Breki said. 'We used to live on Vogabraut, next door to Thorgeir and his parents. He and my brother were good mates. They always hung out together, right through school, along with some other boys a few years older than me.'

'So Andrea would have known Thorgeir too?' It dawned on Elma that neither she nor Hörður had thought to ask Friðrik where the family had lived when his children were young. It simply hadn't crossed her mind that Andrea could have known Thorgeir from before. There had been nothing in the messages they'd exchanged to suggest that.

'Not at the time. She was only five or six when we moved away, so she wouldn't have recognised him, unless…'

'Unless what?'

'No, I don't know,' Breki said.

'What was your brother's name?' Elma asked.

'Máni. He was called Máni.'

'Máni…' Elma recognised the name and knew where she'd come

across it. Máni was the owner of the box of belongings that had been left at their house. The schoolwork and books. 'Where is he now?'

'Máni? He's with Mum.'

'Dead?'

'Yes. An overdose.' Breki cleared his throat. 'It … it had been a long time coming.'

Friðrik's words echoed in Elma's head. The claim that he'd left his family in an attempt to prevent his children from going down the same road as him. It wasn't really a reason but an excuse. A story he told himself to assuage his conscience. But the path he'd chosen didn't seem to have helped anyone.

'When did Máni die?' she asked.

'About eight months ago. An overdose. Whether deliberate or not, I don't know. He'd been struggling with addiction for years. Just like Dad.'

'You said earlier that Andrea wouldn't have known Thorgeir at the time. What did you mean by that? Does she know him now? Were you aware that they'd been seeing each other?'

'Seeing each other…'

Elma thought Breki snorted in disbelief but wasn't sure. The wind kept distorting the connection, making it hard to hear him properly. She wished now that they'd gone to meet him in person.

'No way was Andrea seeing Thorgeir,' Breki went on.

'Why do you say that?'

'Because she knew who he was and what he'd done.'

'What had he done?'

'Thorgeir and his mates started a rumour. A rumour that most people believed, including our dad. Mum too maybe, but she chose to stick by her son instead of deserting him like Dad did. Dad treated him like he was … a pariah.'

'What was the rumour?'

'I don't remember exactly what happened when, but it all began when a friend of Máni's died at the summer camp in Vatnaskógur. He drowned. It was an accident, but afterwards all these stories started circulating. Rumours that Máni had been involved somehow.'

'But he drowned, so there can hardly have been any basis for the stories.'

'I wouldn't know. Was it an accident or was there more to it? The way I heard it, the boy who died had been new at the school, and various people claimed that my brother and his mates had been giving him a hard time. I don't know if there's any truth in that; whether his death was an accident or suicide or what. Maybe people thought Máni had bullied him into taking the boat out and throwing himself overboard.'

'What do you think?'

'I think it's rubbish. Máni just wasn't like that. He was nice to everyone, especially to underdogs.'

'What was Thorgeir's part in all this?'

'Thorgeir took sides against Máni. They'd been friends but he turned his back on him after the rumours started. So did his best mate, Matti – Matthías, that is. His dad was a cop, if I remember right. Máni became increasingly isolated and it changed him. He dropped out of school in the end. Mind you, I don't really know what was to blame for that. Whether it was Dad leaving us, the death of that boy, or being shunned by his mates. It was probably a combination of all those things.'

'Did you ever ask Máni what happened?' Elma asked, thinking privately that she needed to have another word with Matthías. Something had happened at Vatnaskógur, and he was one of the few witnesses still alive to tell the tale.

'Sure. He said he hadn't done a thing to that boy, but he didn't want to talk about it.'

'And Andrea was aware of all this?' Elma asked.

'Ye-es … part of the story, anyway. She was so young when it happened. Andrea was always a real daddy's girl and she worshipped Máni too. They were very close, much closer than she was to me, despite the age gap. She would never believe that Máni had done anything wrong. After he died, she kept harping on about that old business, for some reason. Blaming Máni's ex-friends for everything that had gone wrong with our family. For Dad leaving, Máni getting into drugs and Mum falling ill. Of course, it was an oversimplification, but I could understand why she needed to find a scapegoat. Somebody to blame. It's easier that way, isn't it?'

'Can you think of any reason why she might have been meeting up with Thorgeir?'

'No, unless … unless she thought she could get him to apologise or something like that. Or she was looking for answers. I haven't a clue, but, for my own part, I've always wondered what really happened in Vatnaskógur. I'm just not obsessed by it like Andrea.'

'Is she obsessed with it?'

'Well, she's been talking about it an awful lot recently.'

'About what aspect of it?'

'Oh, just wanting me to tell her my memories of what happened. I think she was desperate to get to the bottom of it.'

'How much older than you was Máni?'

'Three years.'

'Meaning you were twelve at the time?' Elma had been a constant nuisance to her fifteen-year-old sister when she was twelve. Always wanting to hang out with Dagný and her friends, though the feeling wasn't mutual. 'Did you know Thorgeir yourself?'

'Only through Máni. He was a sad case, to be honest. His dad was a bastard, incredibly controlling. I actually felt sorry for Thorgeir.'

'Did you?'

'Yes, I did,' Breki said. 'It's always bugged me that I witnessed his parents doing stuff to him but never let on. At the time, I was afraid it would be embarrassing for Thorgeir. I thought I was helping him by keeping quiet.'

'What did you witness?'

'Once, they beat him on the back with a stick. I saw through the window. He was sitting on a stool in the kitchen and they hit him three times. Afterwards, he just sat there, without moving. But that wasn't the worst. The worst part was the mental abuse. I didn't understand what was happening when I was a kid, but it often comes back to me now. All the horrible things his dad used to say to him, the way he humiliated Thorgeir in front of his friends. He used to call him "Porker" or something like that. So, yes, I felt sorry for him, but I don't think Andrea did.'

BEFORE
Andrea

Andrea clocks him standing in front of a shelf of goods, examining the packets of porridge, before he notices her.

She recognises him instantly, having looked him up on social media from time to time over the years. She doesn't know why she has this habit, unless it's because she wants to see what a man like him looks like. Whenever she's depressed, she does a search for his name and studies the photos that come up. Scrutinises every detail of his features, and all the clues about his life: the photos of his friends, his posts and who comments on them.

This is the first time she has met him in the flesh, and although she has often imagined such an encounter, planning how she would react, the things she would say, the reality is quite different. When it comes to the point, she doesn't say anything, just stands there gaping at him, aware of the turmoil inside her. A tumult of feelings she can't pin down.

She edges closer without him noticing and pretends to be deciding what to buy. Then tries to reach up to the top shelf in the hope that he'll offer to help.

He takes the bait. Of course he does.

'Haven't I seen you somewhere before?' he asks, after passing her the packet of muesli. Her heart is racing. She thinks: is it possible? Does he recognise her? But she was so young at the time that there's no way he could know who she was.

She realises almost immediately that he doesn't and breathes a silent sigh of relief. It's just a line, a chat-up line he uses on girls he fancies. Girls he wants.

What he doesn't know is that there are various things *she* wants from him. And to get what she wants, she will have to give him something in return. Give him what he wants. Temporarily, at least.

So Andrea plays the game, chatting and smiling and flirting with her eyes. She's good at games like this and he doesn't notice anything amiss. Can't tear his gaze from her.

When she turns away after thanking him for his help, she's confident that he'll call after her.

And, of course, he does. Thorgeir is *so* predictable.

He stammers out the words, suddenly awkward. She decides to stop torturing the poor guy and save him the effort. Smiling at him, she says: 'What's your number?'

NOW

Friday 11 December

When Matthías got home, Hafdís was curled up in the armchair by the sitting-room window, holding a glass of wine. She had a woollen blanket draped over her shoulders and had changed into her nightclothes.

Matthías dropped onto the sofa in front of the blank TV. Hafdís smiled at him but he couldn't bring himself to smile back.

'Aren't you even going to ask if I found her?' he said, after a tense silence.

He'd been out for what felt like hours. After ringing round all Ólöf's friends, he'd finally winkled out the information from one girl that Ólöf had been seeing a boy. A boy who was eighteen and owned a white car.

Matthías had knocked on the door of the boy's parents' house and tracked his daughter down to their garage conversion, led there by the reek of grass that had carried all the way out into the street. It had proved impossible to get any sense out of Ólöf.

When they got home, she had gone straight to her room.

'Did you find her?' Hafdís asked obligingly.

'Yes.'

'Great.'

'You think so?'

'Of course I do,' Hafdís said. 'But then I always knew she'd come home in the end. She's just going through a rebellious phase. She wants us to chase after her and rescue her. It's just a cry for attention.'

Matthías didn't say anything. For some reason his mind flew back to their wedding day. Ólöf had been four at the time. It was in September and the forecast had been for good weather, but by the time the ceremony began at two p.m., it had started to rain. Not that this had mattered. To him, the weather had been of minor importance.

Hafdís had been late and there had been an agonising delay as he stood there at the altar, waiting and wondering: *What if she doesn't come?* The idea had filled him with terror. He'd thought he would die if Hafdís didn't turn up.

But then the doors had swung open and the organ had struck up and Hafdís had looked so beautiful. So bloody beautiful as she walked up the aisle in her white dress, her dark hair in wavy locks, wearing that smile.

That smile.

Being with Hafdís had filled Matthías with pride, especially when they were out in company and he knew that he was the envy of all the men present. Especially Thorgeir. Thorgeir had always had a massive crush on Hafdís, and Matthías had derived a guilty pleasure from rubbing his friend's nose in the fact that she was his wife.

But then, as Hafdís walked up the aisle, he'd noticed that Ólöf wasn't behind her. For weeks his little daughter had told everyone who would listen that she was going to hold the rings for Mummy and Daddy. She'd taken the role very seriously and even tried to insist on taking care of the rings in the run-up to the big day. She had promised to keep them safe in her anorak pocket while she was at nursery.

'Where's Ólöf?' he'd whispered to Hafdís when she reached his side.

'Chocolate milk,' Hafdís had hissed back. 'You've your mother to thank for that.'

Matthías had looked round and spotted their daughter on her grandmother's lap at the back of the church. Her magnolia-coloured dress had a brown stain down the front, her cheeks were red and swollen from weeping and her chest was rising and falling with her sobs.

The incident had left him churning with such rage that he hadn't been able to concentrate on the rest of the ceremony. Not rage that a four-year-old child had spilt her drink on herself but that her mother had robbed her of her big moment, forbidden her to walk up the aisle carrying the bloody rings just because she had a stain on her dress. As if that mattered?

Matthías didn't know why this memory should have come back to him now, but he experienced the same furious resentment towards Hafdís as he had then. The same bad taste in his mouth, as if he'd eaten something rancid.

'You don't give a shit.' His voice was thick with fury.

Hafdís gave him an icy look, swirling the dregs of wine in her glass. 'Stop being so melodramatic, Matti,' she said, then added, with a mocking smile: 'Don't give a shit about what?'

'About this. About us. About Ólöf. Just what are you planning to do with all that money?'

'Well, since no one's likely to claim it now, how about a trip to Bali?'

Although Matthías knew she was joking, he suddenly lost the last shreds of his self-control. He leapt to his feet and struck the wineglass from her hands, sending it flying to the floor with a smash.

Hafdís's only reaction was to raise her eyebrows. He suspected that she was enjoying the scene. His wife had always thrived on drama. She sought it out. Provoked it.

'There's something wrong with you, Hafdís,' he hissed between clenched teeth. 'There's always been something wrong with you.'

'Is that a fact?' she asked sarcastically. 'And what about you, Matthías? What's your excuse?'

Elma would have given anything to be able to lounge around in her pyjamas all morning but instead she forced herself to head into the office bright and early. They'd put out a request for information about Andrea, after talking to her father and brother, and the story was now on the front pages of all the main news outlets:

> 'West Iceland police are requesting information about the whereabouts of Andrea Friðriksdóttir in connection with an ongoing investigation.'

The deliberately vague wording would no doubt stir up a great deal of interest and speculation among the public. But then the murder had already done that.

'Any leads?' Elma asked Begga, who was sitting at her desk when she arrived.

'A few. But none that have produced any results.'

They couldn't even establish exactly where Andrea had last been seen, let alone what she'd been wearing. When contacted, the staff at Dalurinn, the restaurant where Andrea worked, said she hadn't been due to work the weekend she went to the summer house, and that they hadn't seen her since. There was no help to be had from the library either, since they hadn't been expecting her to go in until the following week.

'Well, let me know if anything interesting comes up.'

'*Will do*,' Begga replied in English, with an American twang straight out of the Deep South.

In the meantime, Elma decided to take a closer look at the file on Andrea's brother, Máni. A post-mortem had been performed, as was the custom in these types of cases, though it had been low priority as his death wasn't regarded as suspicious. There was a pathologist's report accompanying the police one, dated several weeks after the event.

Elma skimmed through it, then compared the two reports.

Máni had been discovered dead at home after a colleague had gone round to see what was wrong when he didn't turn up to work. He had been sitting in the middle of his sofa and there were no signs of a struggle or evidence that anyone else had been present. There was a half-empty bottle of vodka on the coffee table, a half-smoked joint and a Visa card that had been used to cut lines of cocaine. Máni had been wearing underpants and a T-shirt, and was partly covered by a blanket, as if he'd sunk back on the sofa and fallen asleep.

The post-mortem report indicated that Máni had died from an overdose of Fentanyl, a drug related to morphine. The scene was becoming a depressingly familiar one to the police, resembling numerous other deaths they were seeing every year.

On closer inspection, however, there were various details that didn't fit, and Elma found it odd that the police hadn't taken more trouble over the case. Presumably they had regarded further investigations as a waste of time, since Máni had a history of drug abuse and, on the face of it, there had been nothing unusual about his demise. The drug was dangerous; overdoses were common and frequently fatal.

Yet, although Máni had died of an overdose of Fentanyl, no trace of the drug had been found at the scene. Instead, a small quantity of cocaine had been found wrapped in clingfilm. He'd also had some drugs in pill form, such as sleeping pills and sedatives. All of them in small doses, for personal use.

Máni's family had reportedly told the police that he had been engaged in a long struggle with drugs, and no one had said a word about his death being unexpected or requested that the case should be investigated in more detail.

Elma opened the photos that had been taken at the scene, showing Máni slumped on the sofa. He didn't look as though he was sleeping; he looked dead. The colour of his skin and the angle of his body both appeared unnatural. His head was tipped back as if he were contemplating the ceiling, and his arms were spread out, his palms facing upwards. Strange, but perhaps no stranger than any other position in the circumstances.

The sofa he was sitting on was upholstered in cheap dark-grey fabric and, as Elma scrolled through the photos, more of the poorly furnished flat was revealed. The only decorative items were a statue of a horse and another of a dove, placed either side of the sofa. Ornaments that Elma guessed he was more likely to have inherited from his mother than bought for himself.

She thought of all the schoolwork with top marks that they'd found in his box of possessions left in their loft, and the elegant handwriting in his diary. The boy who wrote it had had big dreams for the future. Máni had intended to write a book. A sad, squalid early death hadn't featured in those dreams, but when did it ever?

People didn't plan to become addicts.

Elma closed the file of photos. Had Máni's fate driven Andrea to resort to desperate measures? No doubt you could find a culprit to blame for anything if you searched long and hard enough. But Elma didn't buy the idea that Thorgeir had been the culprit Andrea was so desperate to find.

❁

Hafdís's hand shook as she raised the coffee cup to her lips. Much to her relief, Matthías had gone out somewhere. When she looked into the sitting room, she saw the red-wine stains on the floor and shivered.

What would he do next?

Hafdís might give the illusion of being tough but inside she was scared. Most people were scared of something, they just weren't all as good at hiding it as she was.

Hafdís was the youngest of five children. She'd never had to fight for attention because she'd always been the favourite, the pretty little girl, the baby of the family. But she'd had to fight for her siblings' respect. To be recognised as the best, not just the youngest and smallest. All the children had taken swimming lessons, but only Hafdís had taken every extra lesson on offer, and by the time they were in their teens, she thirteen, her oldest brother seventeen, she had been regarded as promising. A year later she had been the best.

She had discovered while still young that how you regarded yourself had a direct impact on how others saw you. As a result, she had made sure that other people noticed how pleased she was with herself. A sufficiently well-honed arrogance could get you a long way in life.

But today she was scared.

It wasn't only the video that had been sent to her phone but Matthías's reaction last night. When he struck the wineglass from her hand, the expression in his eyes had reminded her of his father, Ottó.

Admittedly, she had reason to be grateful to Ottó, who had gone out of his way to help them over the years. But she was conscious that she had only enjoyed her father-in-law's favour and protection because of Matthías. It dawned on her that now she wanted a divorce, Ottó would have no reason to help her anymore.

Hafdís stood up, her eyes on the door of Ólöf's room, where the girl was still asleep. She wondered if she would be prepared to stick her neck out as far for her daughter as Ottó had for his son, but she had no answer to that.

Hafdís finished her coffee and went into her bedroom.

Thorgeir was dead. He'd been murdered and the words written on the wall above his bed kept running, singing, through her head. She knew those words, knew the whole hymn, and, as far as she was concerned, they could refer to only one thing. The video she'd been sent had been further confirmation of what this was about.

She opened the wardrobe, which was crammed full of clothes she would soon have to part with. She could fit only a tiny selection of them into one suitcase. Closing the wardrobe again, she went out to the garage, where she found her suitcase and was just dragging it into the house when she noticed a car in the street. There was nothing out of the ordinary about that – plenty of people parked there during the day – but she didn't recognise this particular vehicle, and she could have sworn there was someone sitting in the driver's seat, head turned in her direction.

She paused for an instant, trying to see inside the car, but the late-winter dawn hadn't yet broken and the streetlights were too dim to provide enough light. Yet Hafdís could make out a shadowy figure. She locked the front door securely behind her.

No doubt she was just being paranoid and the person in the car had nothing to do with her. But she felt a sudden pressure to hurry, the prickling in her skin telling her that she was no longer safe here.

❂

'Shall Granny give you a pancake, my poppet?'

Aðalheiður had already started frying pancakes on a griddle pan that wouldn't have looked out of place in a traditional turf farmhouse a century ago.

'She's still only on porridge and purées, Mum.'

It must have been the three-hundredth time Elma had pointed this out to her mother, but Aðalheiður merely smiled as if ignoring the chatter of a child.

'People get so worked up over nothing nowadays. When you and Dagný were little, you ate what we were eating.'

'Presumably that was after our teeth had come through,' Elma retorted dryly.

'Adda's already got teeth,' remarked Elma's father, Jón, who was sitting at the kitchen table, turning the pages of the weekend paper. 'You can only just see them.'

A week ago, they had noticed white patches on Adda's gums either side of where her front teeth would eventually appear. Sævar had joked that Adda would look like a vampire with only her eye-teeth.

'Old people lose their teeth but that doesn't stop them eating.'

Elma refrained from pointing out to her father that this wasn't exactly comparable to a seven-month-old baby, and helped herself to a freshly made pancake instead. It was delicious with whipped cream and strawberry jam. She let Adda have a few tiny pieces, though she knew her sister would have a fit if she found out.

'I've been thinking,' Aðalheiður said, once she'd finally sat down. Jón had vanished into the sitting room with his book of Sudoku puzzles, and Elma, like any Icelandic mother, had wrapped Adda up warmly and put her in her pram outside the open kitchen window, where she was now sleeping peacefully.

'What have you been thinking?' Elma prompted, wondering whether to have another pancake.

'I think you should come here for Christmas. Then I can take care of the cooking and cleaning, and you two can concentrate on relaxing and enjoying yourselves. I know you've both had a lot on your plate, what with work and getting settled into the new house.'

'Well…' Elma had to admit that she hadn't even got round to thinking about Christmas yet. She supposed she'd pictured a quiet evening at home, with Sævar taking care of the food. Knowing him, he'd probably already started planning something delicious. 'I'll ask Sævar,' she said.

'I can make that parfait you love so much,' Aðalheiður said. 'And the apple salad.'

'I'll ask Sævar,' Elma repeated. She smiled to soften the effect when she realised how brusquely she'd replied to her mother's generous offer, and added: 'It sounds great and I'm sure we'll be happy to accept your invitation. Things have been very hectic.'

Aðalheiður smiled with satisfaction. 'By the way, what are you two planning to do in Vatnaskógur?'

Elma hadn't come round to her parents' house for pancakes but to ask them to babysit.

'We thought we'd treat ourselves to a Christian experience in the run-up to Christmas.'

'You're quite the joker today.' Aðalheiður didn't smile.

'Like every day,' Elma said, sprinkling sugar on a second pancake, then rolling it up. 'We're looking into an old case. Do you remember when a teenage boy from Akranes died at Vatnaskógur?'

'Of course I do.'

'I can't explain how it's relevant to Thorgeir's murder, only that I think there could be a link. And the original investigation appears to have left something to be desired.'

'He drowned, didn't he?'

'Yes.'

'His poor parents,' Aðalheiður said.

'Yes, it must have been terrible,' Elma agreed.

Everything about the case seemed terrible to her, yet simultaneously intriguing and perplexing. She couldn't get a proper handle on the people connected to Thorgeir, whether it was Andrea or the couple, Matthías and Hafdís. She would have to talk to them first thing on Monday morning, as it was obvious that they knew more than they were letting on.

The conversation with Andrea's brother had raised a number of questions. Elma simply couldn't believe that Andrea would have murdered Thorgeir in revenge for the destruction of her family. She could hardly have blamed the whole thing on him. When she was eight or nine, perhaps, but not today. Not when she was thirty and must have realised by now that her family's problems had been far from straightforward. But Elma was still puzzled as to what Andrea could have had in mind when she started seeing Thorgeir. Had she been genuinely attracted to him or had she been plotting to harm him in some way?

Elma swallowed the last mouthful of pancake and said goodbye to her parents.

Since the investigation into Thorgeir's murder was moving at such a glacial pace, Elma had decided it was worth using the time to dig a little deeper into Heiðar's death, and that would involve a trip over to Vatnaskógur to talk to the director of the YMCA centre. He was the same man as had been in the post in 1995, so there was a chance he might be able to help them decide whether there were any grounds to reopen Heiðar's case.

❀

The plants were dying a slow death in Hörður's sunroom now that Gígja was no longer there to look after them. He tried his best and things had gone well for the first year, but this winter he had clearly done something wrong because most of the leaves had developed brown tips and the plants were wilting, as if they wanted nothing more than to lie down on the tiles and die.

Hörður cradled his teacup, allowing the sun to warm his face. After yet another sleepless night, he needed its heat and brightness.

His phone rang before he could take a first sip of tea.

'Listen, I've spent hours combing through the tax returns for Reynir's Dry Cleaning,' said the expert from the economic-crimes team in Reykjavík, without preamble. 'I can't actually see anything questionable about the business, apart from the fact that it was so successful – the turnover increased significantly from 1990 to 2000, although the population of Akranes only grew by around a hundred people during that period. That in itself is curious.'

'Is it possible that the company had arrangements with other businesses or something like that?' Hörður asked.

'No, I considered that but couldn't find any evidence of it.'

'Could—?'

'What's more, and excuse me for interrupting, they relied primarily on payments in cash. Of course, that was more common at the time, but where it gets suspicious is that I can't see any move towards card transactions between 1990 and 2000, which just isn't plausible.'

'How do you interpret that?' Hörður asked.

'I think it's pretty standard behaviour for a company that's involved in money laundering, which begs the question, whose money were they laundering?'

'That can't be right.' Hörður couldn't for a moment picture Kristjana being involved in a shady activity like that. The very idea that she should be acquainted with the type of person who would have a reason to launder money, let alone collude with them, was absurd. Where on earth was she supposed to have come into contact with them?

'The most unlikely people do it,' the man from economic crimes assured him. 'People who aren't involved in anything dodgy themselves but agree to launder money for other parties, and are naturally well rewarded for their pains.'

'Yes, right.' Hörður wasn't born yesterday. He knew this, of course, and was aware that economic crime was on the rise in Iceland. Money laundering was practised in the most unlikely places. But Kristjana … a woman he'd known well enough to pass the time of day with for most of his life.

'This is what things are coming to,' the man continued. 'I've lost track of the number of cases we've dealt with in recent years.'

'But then presumably she – or she and her husband – must have passed the proceeds back,' Hörður observed. 'Is there no way of finding out who the beneficiary was?'

'Yes, there is.' The man paused, then added: 'I've already checked the company's payroll and saw only one employee listed.'

'Oh?'

'From 1993 to 2003.' He read out a name. 'Do you know her?'

Hörður certainly did. More than that, he knew for a fact that she had never worked for Reynir's Dry Cleaning.

❁

While Sævar drove, Elma read the police report on Heiðar's death. It was so short that it took no time at all.

'This says so little,' she complained. 'They don't even seem to have spoken to the boys who shared his room, or, if they did, there's no mention of the fact here. And was it really that easy to take a boat from the jetty and row it out onto the lake? Wouldn't the oars have been kept locked up in the boathouse or something?'

'I haven't the foggiest,' Sævar said, attempting to brush chocolate crumbs from his chest without taking his eyes off the road. They had stopped at a kiosk on the way out of town and Sævar had bought a bar of chocolate and a can of fizzy drink. He took another bite of the bar, then asked with his mouth full: 'Who compiled the report?'

'Ottó Matthíasson. Hörður's predecessor and Matthías's father. There must have been a post-mortem but I can't find any record of it.'

'No. What did I tell you?' Sævar grinned.

He was right. He'd pointed out that the post-mortem report was missing when he came to the police station to look into the matter himself.

'You could check if the person who conducted the post-mortem still has a copy,' Sævar went on. 'As it was 1995, they would presumably have had to get someone in from abroad. There weren't any pathologists based in Iceland back then.'

'Quite.'

Elma had rung ahead and learnt that Magnús, the director of the YMCA centre, was at Vatnaskógur over the weekend to organise an Advent activity group for ten- to twelve-year-old boys. He had said they were welcome to come, but hadn't asked what their visit was about.

The road to Vatnaskógur turned off the main route round Hvalfjörður fjord, and wound up and down through the mountains until the tarmac ran out and the road was surfaced with gravel. The weather was mild and the snow was largely untouched by human or motor traffic. Birches and tall firs provided shelter from the wind and in the distance white mountains rose against a brilliantly blue sky.

They parked in a space marked for visitors and got out of the car. They still couldn't see any buildings but, hearing shouts and calls, they set off in the direction of the sound. When they got closer, they saw a group of boys running around, throwing snowballs. Several older boys, probably in the role of leaders, were also involved in the game. One of them, a young man of about twenty, noticed them and came over, ruddy cheeked and smiling, and told them where to find Magnús.

On the way there they passed a boathouse beside a wooden jetty that jutted out into the lake with a few boats moored to it. There were a couple more boats out on the water, the boys in them clearly visible in their orange life-vests.

Lake Eyrarvatn presented a scene of tranquil beauty now, with the gleaming white fells reflected in its still waters, but its association with Heiðar's death cast a chill over it in Elma's mind. This is where he'd been found. This is where his body had lain for more than twenty-four hours before being dragged out.

The young helper must have rung Magnús, because the director now came strolling to greet them. He had greying hair, a dark goatee and overlong sideburns. As they made the introductions, he produced a genial, practised smile.

'Ah, yes, we spoke on the phone,' he said.

'That's correct,' Elma replied.

Some boys raced past, yelling in excitement.

'Would you like to come in?' Magnús clearly understood that what they had to say required privacy.

Once they'd taken a seat in his office, Sævar explained why they were there. 'We're looking into the case of Heiðar Kjartansson who died at a summer camp here in 1995. You were the director at the time, weren't you?'

Magnús's easy smile vanished as quickly as it had appeared, but his amiable tone didn't desert him. 'Yes, that would have been my second year in the job. I remember that terrible accident like it was yesterday. Remember Heiðar too. What aspect of the case are you looking into? Have you reopened the investigation? I wouldn't have thought there was anything else to go over. After all, it was twenty-five years ago.'

'As it happens, I'm on paternity leave,' Sævar replied, perhaps hoping this would make Magnús relax his guard. Because, in spite of the director's friendly tone, Elma had noted the way he'd tensed up as soon as Sævar explained why they were there.

She spoke up now. 'We're investigating a murder. The victim attended a summer camp here at the time of the accident and ... well, to cut a long story short, I came across this incident in the course of my enquiries. We're wondering if there was something the police who handled the case at the time might have overlooked.'

She kept the details about Thorgeir's death deliberately vague, as that didn't concern Magnús.

'Hmm, I see.' Magnús regarded them both through narrowed eyes. 'I doubt the police would have overlooked anything.'

'Nevertheless, would you mind taking us through what happened the evening before Heiðar was found, and the next morning – and also the day after that, when he was discovered?'

'Oh, my memory's a bit hazy, I'm afraid.'

Elma bit back the urge to point out to him that a moment ago he'd said he remembered it like it was yesterday. 'If you could cast your mind back, anyway...'

'Yes, of course, I can try.' Magnús sat up in his chair, resting his elbows on the desk. 'It was in August, the last week of summer, a mixed-sex group of teenagers. The week had gone very smoothly. I don't recall exactly what we did the day before but we used to organise entertainments in the evenings, so there would have been a programme of activities. We weren't aware of any disturbances during the night. Naturally, we always have a bit of trouble persuading the kids to go to bed at the appropriate time, but I don't remember it being a particular problem that evening, And I certainly don't recall that I or any of the leaders were woken by any disturbances during the night. But then, in the morning, the boy's bunk was empty.'

'How did you find out?'

'It was one of the leaders assigned to their hut who noticed. You see, there are leaders, or instructors – whatever you like to call them – who are responsible for particular tables and rooms. When the leader went to wake the boys in the morning, he saw that Heiðar was missing.'

'How many were there in the room?'

'Only the four of them. This was in the old Laufskáli dormitory. It was a hut we acquired from the Búrfell power station as a stopgap when we were short of sleeping spaces.'

'And none of the other boys had seen or heard him leaving the room?' This struck Elma as unlikely. Three other boys in the room and none of them had stirred when Heiðar crept out, or noticed that he wasn't in his bed when they woke up.

'Well, as far as I can remember it was the leader who discovered that his bunk was empty. Maybe the other boys reported the fact to him, but I've forgotten the details now.'

'Would it have been easy for him to slip out?'

'Er … the walls were pretty thin, so I'd have thought sound would have carried from the corridor, but anything's possible, I suppose. And he could have climbed out of the window without anyone hearing. They searched for him everywhere, first in the huts, then … then in the surrounding area.'

'Who found him?'

'We didn't find him. We just saw the boat on the lake and…' Magnús lowered his eyes. 'He was found the following day, in the water.'

'Would it have been easy to take a boat out?' Elma asked. 'I mean, aren't they secured to the jetty and the oars kept locked in the boathouse or something?'

'Oh, no. The boats are normally just moored to the jetty with the oars inside them. Nothing's locked up.'

'I see,' Elma said. Then, changing tack: 'Can you remember if there had been any issues involving Heiðar before that?'

'There's always something. Kids falling out or quarrelling, often in connection with the sports competitions.' Magnús smiled. 'It's only natural, since boys that age tend to be extremely competitive. The teenage groups are a bit different too in that they're mixed. The presence of girls in the group definitely creates a different atmosphere. But I can't recall any issues involving Heiðar.'

'Was there anything unusual about that particular group?'

Magnús drew a deep breath and stared into the middle distance. 'Well, I do remember thinking they seemed quite old for their age. That was when we'd only just started hosting teenage groups. We'd realised these older kids were drinking, though of course the consumption of alcohol is strictly forbidden at the camp and in the surrounding area. Even during the August Bank Holiday weekend festival, when a large number of people congregate at the camp site, there's a total ban on drink and drugs. But come to think of it … Yes, I have a feeling it was someone from that group who smuggled in alcohol. We discovered a bottle in one of the bushes but never managed to catch the guilty party. I gave them a serious talking-to during the lunch hour and invited the person who had brought in the bottle to come forward, but no one ever did.'

'But that had nothing to do with Heiðar, did it?' Elma asked, deciding to keep to herself the knowledge that it had been Hafdís who smuggled in *landi*, according to Máni's diary.

'No, we never found out who was guilty.'

'How did Heiðar fit in with the group?'

'He was the quiet type. Not one of the attention-seekers, though he did seem to have some friends. He was always carrying a video camera around, so we added a film group to the options one day.'

'The options?'

'Yes, they had the option to choose from a variety of activities – boating, fishing, football, hiking and so on. As Heiðar had brought his camera, we decided to set up a film group. Several of the boys got together and made a short film.'

This wasn't news to Elma as she'd read about it in Máni's diary. 'What do *you* think happened that night?'

'If you ask me, I think he may have walked in his sleep.'

'Really?' Elma said sceptically.

Magnús didn't respond, even after Elma left a long pause, so she decided to try something different and see if she couldn't shake him up a bit. She pulled out her phone, found the photo of the text written on the wall at Thorgeir's summer house and turned the screen towards him.

'Do you recognise these words?'

'Of course I recognise them. They're from a hymn we sometimes sing here. Hymn number 594. "Take away my crimes and sins with blood, O Jesus, and create in me a clean heart and your holy will." It's based on Psalm Number Fifty-One. As it happens, we've got a quotation from the same psalm inscribed above the altar in our chapel: "Create in me a clean heart, O God, and renew a steadfast spirit within me." Why do you ask?'

This time it was Sævar who replied: 'Because the sentence was found at the scene of the murder my colleague is investigating.'

Magnús turned a little pale. 'Surely not.'

'Can you think what it might mean?' Elma asked.

'No, I can't imagine.'

'You mentioned a chapel?'

'Yes. A very small one.'

'Could we see it?'

'Well,' Magnús said apologetically. 'I really do need to get back to work.'

But in the face of Elma and Sævar's silence, he gave way.

'Oh, if it's really necessary, then…' Magnús cleared his throat. 'Come with me.'

❁

Guðrún Matthíasdóttir was married to a man called Bárður, who Hörður knew only too well. Bárður had been captain of the trawler *Viðvík*, which had been based in Akranes for many years. According to the latest information Hörður had, the trawler had moved some years ago and now operated out of Reykjavík. Bárður had retired but still lived in Akranes, not far from Hörður's own place.

Guðrún also just happened to be the sister of Ottó, Hörður's former boss. Hörður had worked with him from when he joined the police, aged twenty-eight, in 1985, until Ottó retired. He could still remember encountering Ottó on his first day in the job. He had been sitting at a desk and was unsure how to behave when Ottó entered the room. After dithering for a moment, Hörður had decided he'd better stand up and introduce himself.

By an unlucky chance, just as he did so, another officer came in to speak to Ottó. Hörður had stepped aside, too embarrassed to sit down again but reluctant to interrupt their conversation. He'd hovered there, feeling more and more foolish with every passing second until eventually Ottó had rounded on him, glaring, and asked in an icy tone what on earth he wanted.

'I just wanted to introduce myself,' Hörður had said, nervously holding out his hand. Then, seeing the expression on Ottó's face, he had awkwardly added his name.

After the most uncomfortable silence Hörður had ever experienced, Ottó had given his hand the briefest of shakes, then asked whether there was anything else he wanted to bother them with or could they get back to their conversation now? Since there wasn't, Hörður had sunk into his chair in a state of sweating, humiliated consternation.

Ottó had been the type of boss, aloof and forbidding, that Hörður had been determined never to become himself.

Guðrún also had rather an aloof manner, though she was much more pleasant than her brother. She had been a housewife while the children were young and Bárður was at sea, but in the years leading up to her retirement she had worked at a local shop, called Bjarg, that sold cosmetics, clothes and also, at one time, furniture.

Hörður was positive that she had never been an employee of Reynir's Dry Cleaning, despite having been on their payroll for a decade.

Guðrún was alone at home when Hörður rang the bell.

'Well, hello, Hörður,' she said, a polite smile hastily replacing a disconcerted look.

'Hello,' Hörður said. 'Sorry to disturb you, but I've got a few questions. I'll only take up a minute of your time.'

'Oh?' Guðrún replied, making no move to invite him in.

'Maybe it would be better if…'

'Oh, right, yes, come in.' She beckoned to him to follow her inside.

The home she shared with Bárður was attractively furnished in a modern style. Hörður got an impression of dark wood, leather and grey walls. All very tasteful, nothing excessive.

'Can I offer you something?' she asked.

'No, thank you.' He wasn't intending to stay long.

They settled themselves in the sitting room, and Hörður became aware of a sweet floral scent emanating from some invisible source. He had been racking his brain about how to broach the subject of her employment. He didn't want to sound too accusatory, nor did he want to prompt a lot of questions about why he was asking.

'Have you given up work?' he asked eventually.

'Yes, about a year ago now,' Guðrún replied.

'You used to work at Bjarg, didn't you?'

'Yes, I did.'

'Had you been working anywhere else in recent years?'

'I worked at the shop and—' Guðrún broke off and smiled. 'Surely you haven't come here to ask about my jobs, Hörður? What's this all about?'

'We've been taking a look at a business. More specifically, a dry cleaner's that was based in Akranes for many years – Reynir's Dry Cleaning. According to their payroll records, you were an employee there for ten years, from 1993 to 2003.'

Guðrún sat up a little. 'That's right.'

'What did you do there?'

'I stepped in whenever they needed someone.'

'I see. I wasn't aware of that.' Hörður had been asking around and it seemed that no one else had been aware that Guðrún had ever worked at the dry cleaner's. Indeed, the very idea was absurd, and Hörður had a feeling they both knew it.

'Well, you can't be expected to know everything that goes on in this town.'

'No.' Hörður would never claim that, but he did know a thing or two. Such as the fact that Guðrún's pay had been well above the average wage, not to mention the kind of pay you might expect for the casual work she claimed to have been doing. 'You were on a pretty good salary,' he remarked.

Guðrún raised her eyebrows superciliously. 'I wasn't aware that it was anybody else's business what I got paid.'

'No, as you say.'

'If there's nothing else I can help you with, Hörður…' Guðrún stood up.

He rose to his feet as well. 'No, that was all.'

She escorted him to the door where he took his time putting on his boots with the aid of the shoehorn.

'One more thing,' he said, pausing with a hand on the doorknob. 'You stopped working there in 2003. The same year as Bárður left the trawler.'

Guðrún was silent.

'I was just wondering why that was. Because the dry-cleaning business remained open until 2005, and, with a good salary like yours and not yet having reached retirement age…'

'I had other things on my plate.'

'Ah, of course, you worked at the shop too.' Hörður smiled. 'Doing two jobs must have been tiring.'

Guðrún's only answer was an enigmatic smile, but her manner as she said goodbye was a good deal frostier than when she had greeted him.

❂

The chapel was located in a small clearing not far from the Old Hut and the boathouse. It turned out to be a tiny, pale-green building with a cross on the protruding gable at the front and windows and pillars picked out in dark green. Enclosing it was a white picket fence so low as to be purely for decorative purposes. The arched door was of dark wood and there was a small sign next to it, saying *Chapel*.

Inside, they were greeted by a smell of wood and a silence that felt almost palpable. Something about the size and shape reminded Elma of being in a tent.

A red carpet ran up the aisle and the pews on either side were only large enough to seat two to three adults. On the altar was a white statue of Christ, flanked on either side by silver candlesticks.

'Here we are – this is our little chapel,' Magnús said. 'We're very pleased with it. Although it was originally built in 1949, it's undergone a lot of renovation since then. Most recently the roof and foundations.'

Elma found herself staring at the quotations inscribed in arched recesses in the wooden panelling either side of the altar. One said: *Create in me a clean heart, O God*, and the other: *And renew a steadfast spirit within me*. Beneath each stood a tall floor candelabra.

Was it conceivable that the person who murdered Thorgeir had been trying to recreate this tableau from the chapel? It was probably an absurd idea, as the two settings were in no way comparable, and yet – those words written on the cabin wall, taken from the hymn based on the psalm quoted here. Could it be symbolic?

'What do you use the chapel for?' Sævar asked.

'Well, we hold prayer time here in the evenings, when the boys – or girls – can come here for a period of peaceful reflection. But the chapel's usually left open all day, so they can come here and pray whenever they like.'

'What about the group Heiðar was in?' Elma asked. 'Did you hold prayers in the chapel for them?'

'I'm afraid I can't remember,' Magnús replied. 'But I expect so. As I said, all our guests are welcome to use the chapel for prayers.'

'And there were no incidents, nothing that happened here in the chapel during that camp?'

'No, not that I can recall,' Magnús said. Elma noticed how his gaze slid away from hers after he'd answered.

He picked up a book, presumably a New Testament or Bible, from a pile on a small table beside the altar and started flicking through it.

'So you can't think of any significance the quotation at the murder scene might have had?'

'No, as I've already explained.'

Magnús kept his eyes fixed on the book as if deliberately avoiding Elma's gaze.

✷

Matthías had ordered a pizza for him and Ólöf, most of which he had ended up eating himself. Hafdís was teaching a swimming lesson at the Bjarnalaug pool and wouldn't be home until later that evening.

Over supper, he and Ólöf had a talk and she confided in him that the boy she had been with the previous evening was called Birnir and that they'd been seeing each other for a while.

Though Matthías wasn't wild about the idea, he had to remind himself that he and Hafdís had been around the same age when they got together. But the three-year age gap between his daughter and this boy seemed a lot to him, though Ólöf told him not to worry about it. In truth, he was probably more bothered by the fact they'd been smoking weed. Ólöf insisted that it was Birnir's brother who'd been smoking weed in the garage, and that neither she nor Birnir ever touched the stuff themselves. Matthías didn't know what to believe, especially when he recalled all the half-truths and downright lies he had told his own parents at her age. But he decided to give Ólöf the benefit of the doubt this time.

'Don't tell Mum,' Ólöf said, after sharing her secret with him.

'Why not?'

'Because she'll only give me a hard time about it.'

'I'm sure she won't.'

'Yes, she will. You don't know what she's like.'

'What do you mean?'

Ólöf merely shrugged.

'Does she give you a hard time about a lot of things, then?'

'Well, maybe not exactly, but…'

'But?'

'It's the way she looks at me, like I'm…' Ólöf paused for what felt like a long time, searching for the right word and when she did, it hurt Matthías to the core. 'Like I'm nothing.'

The worst part was that he already knew this. He'd seen that expression in Hafdís's eyes. The way she sometimes looked right through the two of them as if they were nothing but obstacles in her path.

The more he thought about it, the more clearly he saw that it was Hafdís who bore a large part of the blame for the state Ólöf was in. It was Hafdís's fault that Ólöf was driven to self-harm. Hafdís was the reason why Ólöf needed therapy.

Anger welled up inside him as he sat there, his eyes resting unseeingly on the TV, mentally reviewing various little incidents over the years. How could he have been so blind to Hafdís's true character?

The scales should have fallen from his eyes a long time ago, while they were still young. She had always been sharp-tongued and unfeeling, but these had seemed like attractive qualities to him at the time. They'd come across as self-confidence. He'd convinced himself that her heartlessness was only because she demanded high standards of people. But now he found himself wondering if he had been wrong about Hafdís all along. He'd kidded himself that underneath that hard exterior was a beautiful soul, when really there had been nothing there.

Ólöf said she wasn't that hungry and went up to her room, leaving most of her pizza. As he sat on the sofa, working his way through the rest in front of the news, Matthías looked up and caught sight of Hafdís's laptop, which lay open on the dining table, its screen black.

When the news was over, he got to his feet and put a finger on the computer touchpad. A password request popped up on screen. He knew her password; he'd memorised it years ago and Hafdís had never changed it.

Matthías opened the internet browser and wondered what he should look at. He asked himself what was he hoping to find. The reason why Hafdís had suddenly decided she wanted a divorce? Because he suspected she wasn't being entirely straight with him about that. He wanted to find out if there had been anything going on between her and Thorgeir, his best mate. Just the thought of it caused him physical pain.

After a moment's hesitation, he opened her search history and saw that she had been spending a lot of time recently on property sites. Was she looking to move out already?

Holding his breath, he clicked on her inbox. Part of him was reluctant to do this, afraid of what he might find. But there didn't seem to be anything incriminating at first sight. He scrolled down and was just giving way to relief when he spotted an email from an airline. Hafdís had bought a ticket to Spain. One way.

The shock of it was like a punch in the guts. How could Hafdís do this to him? To Ólöf?

When he saw the date, his pain only intensified. Hafdís had bought the ticket on the Friday, the day before her work Christmas party, *before* she'd told him she wanted a divorce. Then it came home to him what this meant: Hafdís had booked the ticket just before his best friend was murdered.

BEFORE
Andrea

Thorgeir is staring at her as if he would like to eat her up. Andrea has a vision of herself reaching across the table and wiping drool from the corner of his mouth with her napkin.

During their conversation, she has learnt that he plays computer games and loves *Star Wars*, cars and sport, especially football, though she can't picture him being that nifty on the pitch himself.

He's tanned like it's 2007, obviously banishes his grey hairs by going for a regular touch-up, and is clean-shaven. She guesses it's not just his head that is clean-shaven and wonders idly whether he uses the same razor for both places.

'I work in IT,' he says, and she fakes an interest.

Andrea is good at making other people feel interesting. She throws herself whole-heartedly into the role, becoming the person they want her to be. Losing herself in the moment, experiencing their conversational exchanges, eye-meets and hesitant smiles as if they've been lifted straight out of a romantic novel or film. She is Sally meeting Harry, or Rose meeting Jack just before the ship goes down.

When they kiss later that evening, she feels a flutter in her stomach and imagines that she could be that girl. The girl who meets a boy and falls in love.

Because the fact is that, against all the odds, she finds Thorgeir attractive, though not in the way he might think. No doubt he believes his attraction lies in the care he takes of his appearance, the price tags on his clothes, but she can see past all that to the vulnerability in his eyes. An anxiety that intrigues her. He probably thinks she can't see through the arrogant front, but she can. She can see him.

By the time they enter the hotel and he pays for a room, everything else has retreated before her desire. All she can think about is touching him as they ascend in the lift, then walk along the corridor in search of the number on their room key.

Her favourite memory, the memory she dwells on pleasurably for a long time afterwards, is the moment when he sweeps her off her feet as the door slams behind them. Hands gripping her under the thighs, he holds her against him as they kiss, moving slowly towards the bed, where he lays her down without once breaking off their kiss.

Afterwards, Andrea waits for him to fall asleep before cautiously sitting up. It doesn't take long. He's drunk, satisfied, and sinks almost immediately into a heavy slumber. But, to be on the safe side, she waits until his breathing has deepened. Then she studies him in as much detail as she can in the gloom. Lying there, peacefully asleep, Thorgeir gives the impression of being harmless, but she knows better.

Andrea activates the torch on her phone and shines it over the floor, illuminating the pile of their hastily shed clothes at the foot of the bed. She eases herself out of bed and, picking up Thorgeir's jeans, goes through the pockets, which turn out to be empty.

Thorgeir rolls over in bed.

She's not worried; if he wakes up, she'll pretend she needed a pee. But she must hurry up and find his jacket, where he presumably keeps his wallet and keys. She flashes her torch beam around the room until she spots his jacket on the back of a chair, then tiptoes over to it and fumbles in the pockets. The manmade fabric crackles as her fingers detect the shape of the keys. Next moment, they emit a bleep and she freezes.

Thorgeir has his back to her but she senses that his breathing is no longer as deep. As if he's lying there, listening.

Her heart speeds up and suddenly she can't get enough air. But then he releases a long breath and from the quiet snore that accompanies it, she guesses that he is sound asleep.

Andrea slips back into bed as stealthily as she can. She feels sick, still a little drunk, and the world spins when she closes her eyes. Perhaps she drops off at some point, but she doubts it, because it feels as if no time at all has passed when she gets up. It's still pitch-dark outside.

She finds her clothes and gets dressed in the bathroom without switching on the light. Then tiptoes out of the room, closing the door softly behind her.

NOW

Saturday 12 December

Hafdís had put the suitcase back in the garage before Matthías got home, having convinced herself that there was nothing to be afraid of, she'd just been imagining things. Recent events had made her paranoid.

She sometimes had a skin-crawling sensation of being watched, especially during the long winter nights, the dark mornings and early dusks, but when the light returned, so did her courage and she was able to shake off her unease.

Now, as she stood on the side of the Bjarnalaug pool, watching her class swimming up and down, normal life seemed to have been restored. It was hard to feel afraid in these bright, familiar surroundings. Nothing bad could happen to her here.

'How many more lengths?' asked a girl who never did a stroke more than required and preferred to do less whenever she could get away with it.

'Until I say stop,' Hafdís replied briskly.

The girl opened her mouth to complain, but thought better of it when she saw Hafdís's uncompromising expression, and carried on swimming.

Hafdís had occasionally spoken to Thorgeir about what had happened that time at Vatnaskógur. They had always got on well together, though their friendship had relied mainly on his attraction to her. She had always liked having admirers but sensed how much more she needed their admiration now, as the years passed by and she got older. It had been different when she was young. In those days, she had only to go out clubbing to refill the tank of egocentricity that seemed to exist at her core. Back then, life had still been an unwritten page, full of possibilities. Now, all that had changed.

'And … good,' she called over the pool, and the kids instantly stopped swimming. Not one of them put in an ounce more effort than required. 'You can have a bit of free time before you get out. Five minutes.'

Without waiting to be told twice, the kids began shouting and laughing, and chucking around their water-wings and floats. Hafdís went into the reception cubicle that divided the foyer from the pool and took a slug from her water bottle.

Although she still had plenty of time left, she was aware that she'd run through a major part of her life. She'd got married, had a child and wasted far too long in a job that she would never have guessed she'd be stuck in for twenty years. Her life hadn't turned out the way she'd imagined.

When these thoughts became too depressing, it was good to have a friend like Thorgeir who still saw the beautiful girl in her. That was why she had encouraged his crush, flirting with him just often enough over the years to keep it alive. Allowed their hugs to last a few seconds longer than could be regarded as normal between friends. So when she'd seen Thorgeir with that girl and sensed that all his attention was fixed on her, Hafdís had felt worthless, more invisible than ever before.

That had been the lightbulb moment, when she'd realised she had to leave Matthías.

She went back into the pool area and shouted to her class: 'Out you get, kids. Playtime is over.'

Hafdís had no patience with children who wanted to linger in the water once the lesson was finished. She was eager to get off home as soon as possible, even if home wasn't exactly an alluring prospect right now.

She was desperate to get away, and the money Thorgeir had given her would help. Her divorce from Matthías would leave her with nothing but debts. All she wanted was to escape and see if there was a better life waiting for her somewhere else. She'd booked a one-way ticket and couldn't wait to live in a place where there was no such thing as predictability, where she didn't have the crushing sense that her life had been laid out for her in a straight line from cradle to grave.

'Hurry up,' she called to the last few children who were still messing around in the deep end.

A girl and boy seemed to be caught up in a game of chase, though Hafdís had trouble working out the rules. Those two were always up to something. They couldn't leave each other alone, though the girl was worse. She pursued the boy like a mad hyena, while he gave her just enough attention to encourage her. Hafdís had to raise her voice before they obeyed.

While she was waiting for the class to emerge from the showers, she did a circuit of the pool, collecting up the pieces of equipment left lying on the side. Unusually for Iceland, where most of the pools were in the open air, Bjarnalaug was an old-fashioned indoor bath, familiar to almost everyone in Akranes. It was where Hafdís had learnt to swim herself, like so many of her contemporaries.

A wave of shame rolled over her as she recalled her last encounter with Thorgeir. She'd told Matthías that she was going for a swim in the sea but instead she'd driven round to Thorgeir's place. She was well aware that there was something dodgy about the money Thorgeir had acquired via his mother and suspected that Thorgeir was stressed about the fact too, but that hadn't put her off.

He had invited her in and, when he offered her a drink, she'd accepted a beer. But when he'd sat down beside her on the sofa and she'd laid a hand on his thigh, he had gone rigid. She had been open to anything he might want, but Thorgeir had rejected her.

'Look, I'm actually in a relationship now, so I can't…' he had stammered, avoiding her eye.

Hafdís would rather he had hit her. She had certainly wanted to hit him. Not just hit him; at that moment she could cheerfully have killed him. She'd pictured herself smashing the bottom off the bottle and driving the sharp edge into his neck.

Instead, she had asked him for money. A small sum to fund her escape. In the last eighteen months all her money had gone towards paying off the sea of debts Matthías had got them into, and now she just wanted out. A fresh start. At home, Hafdís felt like a spare part. A piece that didn't fit into the jigsaw.

Once she'd finished tidying up the poolside area, Hafdís sat down and began to scroll through her phone.

The kids always took forever to get dressed and emerge from the changing rooms. They would chatter away for hours if you didn't chivvy them along. When the front door finally closed behind the last of them, silence settled over the building and all at once she was overwhelmed by a profound sense of loneliness. So profound that she wanted to cry. How could everything have gone so terribly awry?

Hafdís wiped away her tears, gave a loud sigh, and rose to her feet. Everything would be better soon. It had to be.

She called into both changing rooms to make sure everyone had gone and received no answer. But as she went to fetch her own belongings, she thought she heard a noise, perhaps a door shutting somewhere inside the building.

'Hello?' she called out wearily. She was in no mood to deal with naughty children who didn't have the sense to get themselves off home. 'Is there somebody there?'

No answer.

She checked the changing rooms again, went into the showers and opened the toilet stalls, but there was nobody there. Everyone had gone and she was alone in the building. All there was left to do now was lock up and head home.

When she returned to the pool area she spotted something floating in the water that she'd somehow failed to notice earlier. She craned forwards to see what it was. It appeared to be an item of clothing, like a woolly hat, but she wasn't sure.

Just as she made up her mind to go and fetch a net, a blow caught her on the back of her skull, so hard that it knocked all the wind out of her and sent her toppling forwards.

She came to her senses when she touched the bottom of the pool. She started flailing around frantically. For a few seconds she was completely disorientated, then, seeing a light above her, she launched herself upwards.

Through the ripples on the surface she could see a figure standing on the side of the pool, looking down. At first, she thought it was one of the kids, but next moment she realised that couldn't be right. This person was too tall. She blinked, her nose and throat burning from the chlorine, her lungs screaming out for oxygen. But before she could break the surface, the figure knelt down and she saw that it was holding something in its hand.

Then the second blow struck.

Andrea's brother, Breki, had rung twice the previous day to ask for news and Elma had begun to dread his calls, wishing she had more to offer than *I'm sorry*.

'I reckon it wouldn't be such a bad idea to talk to Heiðar's parents,' Sævar remarked, taking a T-shirt out of the wardrobe. 'See what they thought of the investigation at the time.'

'Yes, I suppose that would be sensible but…'

'But you don't want to risk upsetting them if this turns out not to be linked to your case,' Sævar finished for her.

Elma nodded. It was twenty-five years since Heiðar had died and she didn't want to be responsible for reopening his parents' old wounds.

'I think our top priority should be locating Andrea,' Elma said. 'We haven't had a single usable lead on her whereabouts.'

'The way I see it, there are two alternatives,' Sævar said thoughtfully. 'Either she was murdered at the same time as Thorgeir and we're looking for her body…'

'Or?'

'Or she killed Thorgeir and has gone into hiding.'

'But where?' Elma asked.

The police had already checked whether Andrea's family owned any other properties or had relatives she might have taken refuge with, but the answer was no. Elma was inclined to believe that sooner or later Andrea's body would turn up under the snow in Skorradalur.

It was perfectly possible that the case had nothing to do with Vatnaskógur but was connected to some trouble Thorgeir had got mixed up in more recently. There were big question marks over the origin of the money in his bank account, and Elma also had her suspicions about the nature of his relationship with Hafdís, which would turn the spotlight on Matthías, or even Hafdís herself. Perhaps something had happened there that wouldn't bear the light of day.

Even supposing that Andrea had engineered a meeting with Thorgeir with a secret agenda of her own, such as exposing his lies or avenging her family, she could still have been an innocent victim – the wrong person in the wrong place. She could have witnessed a murder or got in the way, and therefore had to be silenced.

Elma had traced all the calls to and from Thorgeir's phone without finding any evidence to suggest that he'd spoken to anyone after arriving at the summer house. Needless to say, though, the police didn't have access to all his social-media accounts, so he could, unbeknownst to them, have communicated with someone that way.

Not everyone in his inner circle had a watertight alibi, either. Matthías and Hafdís had been at a Christmas party in Reykjavík on the Saturday and claimed to have been at home on the Friday, but a couple providing each other with an alibi couldn't be considered particularly reliable.

Kristjana had also been alone at home but, despite her lack of an alibi, Elma found it impossible to believe that she would have harmed her son or Andrea. While Elma suspected Kristjana of being less than squeaky clean, the old woman simply didn't have the physical strength the killer would have required.

All these possibilities whirled round in Elma's head until she felt that the only way she'd win any respite from them was to put them down on paper.

'The writing on the wall has to be a declaration of some kind,' said Sævar, who was clearly wrestling with the same problem. '"Take away my crimes and sins with blood, O Jesus." Surely that's saying that there are sins that have to be taken away with blood, isn't it?'

'Or just a clue that there's a link to the little chapel at Vatnaskógur.'

'Who's the clue intended for?'

Elma considered this for a moment. 'For those involved?'

'You think so?'

Elma sighed. She didn't know what to think. The fact was that they had no idea who had written the text or what it referred to.

'If it is a clue pointing to Vatnaskógur, we would have to rule out Andrea as the killer, wouldn't we?' She stuffed Adda's swimming costume into a bag, along with a waterproof nappy. 'Andrea wasn't seeing Thorgeir because of Heiðar but because of her brother and her family. Besides, she was so young when Heiðar died that she couldn't possibly have any inside knowledge about what happened at the camp. She wouldn't have left a message like that.'

'No, you're right. It has to be someone connected to Heiðar.'

'In which case it can't be Matthías or Hafdís either. I doubt they'd go looking to avenge Heiðar's death. But who else is there?'

'Search me,' Sævar said. 'But I'm convinced Matthías and Hafdís know more about Vatnaskógur than they're letting on, so they may have some answers.'

Elma nodded. She had already spoken to the couple individually and neither had brought up the subject of Vatnaskógur, despite the clue in the quotation on the wall. Somehow she doubted they would reveal any more unless they were forced to. Perhaps it would be better to build up a clearer picture of events first, then approach the couple again, armed with information that would really put them on the spot.

❈

Elma was in two minds about whether she was doing the right thing as she drove over to see Heiðar's parents. She didn't want to sow any seeds of doubt in their minds, suggesting there was more to their son's death than they thought, as that would be a terrible blow: knowing that their loved one had died at the hands of another human being was bound to evoke very different emotions from losing a loved one in an accident, even if the end result was the same. So, although she was finding Sævar's suspicions increasingly compelling, she had no intention of sharing them at this stage with Heiðar's closest family.

Still debating with herself, Elma parked in front of the address on Presthúsabraut, a small, green house that was as pretty as a picture in the freshly fallen snow.

She hadn't called in advance, just come on an impulse, hoping perhaps to have a quick word with the couple before taking Adda swimming. But now, unable to see any sign of life inside, it occurred to her that it was only just gone nine on a Sunday morning and she might have come too early in the day. Her internal clock was hopelessly messed up at the moment, thanks to a combination of the winter darkness and lack of sleep. Heiðar's parents were in their seventies, presumably both retired, and while their generation were often early risers, she thought it would probably be better to come back later.

She started the car again, then caught sight in her wing mirror of two people walking along the road. A man in a down jacket with arrestingly large gloves and a woman in a long, brown coat and a white knitted hat.

Elma switched off the engine again and opened the door.

'Good morning,' she said. 'Are you by any chance Kjartan and Sigrún?'

'Guilty as charged,' Sigrún replied.

Elma introduced herself and asked if she could have a brief chat with them in connection with Thorgeir's murder.

'With us?' Sigrún asked. 'I don't see how we can help. We didn't know him.'

'That's the murder in the news, isn't it?' Kjartan said. 'The body found in Skorradalur?'

'Yes, that's the one.' Elma's heart started beating a little faster as she added: 'As it happens, he attended the summer camp at Vatnaskógur with your son the year he died and we found a clue at the scene that suggests a possible link.' She felt she was expressing herself very badly but didn't know how else to explain without spelling it out.

They were both gaping at her now as though she'd told them the earth was flat or that snow was hot.

'Linked to Heiðar, you mean?' Kjartan said eventually.

'Look, why don't we go indoors?' Sigrún said, gently taking her husband's arm. 'We can't stand about discussing it out here in the cold. Let's have a hot drink inside.'

Elma smiled and followed them into their green, picture-postcard house.

❋

The kitchen table was covered with a flower-patterned plastic cloth. All the fittings and furniture appeared to date from the beginning of the twentieth century, which is when the house itself had been built, as Sigrún informed Elma while she was making coffee.

'I'm so stuck in my ways,' Sigrún said, taking out a Christmas cake and putting it on a plate. 'I always bake the same recipe for Christmas – a raisin sponge.'

'I'm in luck, having a treat like this on a Sunday morning.' Elma smiled and transferred a slice to her blue-patterned cake plate.

'What were you saying about Heiðar?' Kjartan asked, once they were seated round the table.

'Well…' Realising she would have to provide some sort of explanation, Elma conveyed the gist of the quotation found on the wall at Thorgeir's summer house, carefully omitting any reference to the suspicion that Heiðar's death might have been a criminal matter.

'Afterwards, one of my colleagues started looking into Heiðar's death and discovered that various aspects of the investigation could have been better handled at the time.'

'Like what?' Kjartan asked. Clearly he wasn't going to let her off lightly on this. Which was understandable, she supposed.

'Like the fact that the report is quite short and not very thorough,' Elma said. 'And it appears that there were no interviews conducted with potential witnesses or members of staff at the camp. A couple of other pieces of information that I'm not at liberty to reveal have also come to light, which may have a connection to Heiðar's death.' She had decided not to mention Máni or his diary as there were still too many unanswered questions around that. 'I'm not saying it would have changed anything, only that a number of things could have been done better. For example, I can't find a post-mortem report. Do you know if they conducted one?'

'A post-mortem? No, I don't think so,' Kjartan said.

Elma watched as the couple exchanged meaningful glances across the table. When Sigrún next spoke, the humorous gleam in her eyes had vanished and her expression was bleak.

'There was quite a lot about the case that struck us as strange at the time, but we trusted the police to do their job properly. Are you saying that something has come to light that casts doubt on that?' Sigrún looked from Elma to Kjartan and back again. 'I don't understand what you're implying.'

Elma, still keen not to distress the couple, tried to do her best to limit the damage of her revelations. 'I'm just trying to get a clearer picture of what happened at Vatnaskógur,' she said, her manner deliberately relaxed. 'It may sound odd, but I'm afraid I can't explain in any more detail at this stage.'

'Can't you talk to your colleagues who were responsible for the investigation at the time?' Kjartan asked. 'Surely they ought to know more than we do?'

Elma had been thinking of doing exactly that but suspected there would be a conflict of interests. After all, Ottó, the inspector in charge of the original inquiry, was Matthías's father, and she had a nasty feeling that this might have influenced the investigation into Heiðar's death. But of course she didn't voice these thoughts aloud.

'Most of the officers who were involved at the time have only a hazy memory of the events,' Elma said. 'I've spoken to Magnús, the director of the centre at Vatnaskógur both then and now, but I'm afraid he wasn't able to add much.'

'Then the case must be clear,' Kjartan snapped.

Sigrún laid a hand on his arm. 'To be honest, they kept us out of the investigation, rather. We tried to get more detailed information because there were a lot of things that struck us as a bit strange. We sent our son to the summer camp in good faith, taking it for granted that he would be safe there, but then this happened. I realise it was a large group of teenagers and you can never prevent every accident, but why wasn't anyone checking that the kids didn't go out at night?'

'Was your son in the habit of sleepwalking?' Elma asked, mindful of what Magnús had said.

'No, he wasn't, but…' Sigrún hesitated and glanced at Kjartan, who narrowed his eyes, shaking his head faintly. 'No, not Heiðar.'

Elma couldn't interpret this silent communication between the couple. Was it possible that Heiðar had at some point walked in his sleep but that they had their own reasons for wanting to conceal the fact?

'What was Heiðar like?' she asked, deciding to move on. The big question in her mind was whether he could have been depressed. It was often difficult to gauge when someone close to you was suffering, but in hindsight you might be able to recognise certain hints. Elma's thoughts flew to her former partner, Davíð. Afterwards, she had looked back and seen all kinds of warning signs, and blamed herself for not having intervened and encouraged him to seek help. The problem was that when you weren't looking for signs, it was easy to miss them or interpret them as something quite different. No one expected the worst. Could there have been similar clues in Heiðar's behaviour to indicate that he might have taken his own life?

'Heiðar was clever. Intelligent and level-headed.' Sigrún spoke slowly, her eyes lowered to the table. 'He was mature for his age. Such a kind-hearted boy, who…' There was a catch in her voice but she coughed and persevered: 'Who only wanted the best for everyone.'

'Did he have a sunny temperament? Was he happy?' Elma smiled, but Sigrún didn't notice.

'Heiðar was … he was quiet and not very sociable, I suppose. But he always seemed contented, in spite of that.'

Elma glanced at Kjartan while Sigrún was talking. He seemed to tense up and his jaw tightened. He looked as if he'd like to put a stop to this conversation, as if it was distressing him. She couldn't blame him. Who would want to be forced to rake up the worst experience of their life?

'Had there been any recent changes in his life before he went to Vatnaskógur?' Elma asked. 'Did you feel he was himself?'

Sigrún shot a look at Kjartan before she answered. 'He was absolutely his usual self.'

'So there were no incidents shortly beforehand? You'd only recently moved to Akranes, hadn't you?'

'We moved here in the spring of that year,' Sigrún said. 'But no, I don't remember any incidents. It had been a good summer. Heiðar was doing well at school and had a job mowing lawns. It was his own idea to put up advertisements around town.'

'I see.'

Kjartan scraped his chair back from the table and announced gruffly that, if that was all, he was going upstairs to listen to the radio. Elma realised that she had been sitting there long enough and made to stand up as well, but Sigrún stopped her.

'Wait a minute,' she said once Kjartan had left the room. 'Let me show you something.'

Sigrún went out and came back with a framed photo. 'Here's Heiðar with our dog. It was taken just before he died.'

The picture showed a teenage boy with his arms around the neck of what appeared to be a black Labrador.

'He was a nice-looking boy,' Elma said.

'He was.' Sigrún smiled, but her eyes were sad. And her smile vanished as she put down the photo and continued: 'They said we could see him after they pulled him out of the water. Kjartan didn't want to, but I went. I wanted to see my boy because I was afraid that, if I didn't, it would never be real to me. They led me into a room with the lights dimmed, as though they were trying to shield me from the worst. But there was no need. I had already experienced the worst that could happen, and when I saw him there I didn't feel bad. More as if I was being given a chance to say goodbye to him. He was lying on a table with his eyes closed and his face colourless. Not like he was asleep but like he was no longer there, and I found that a comfort, strange though it might sound. But what I noticed most was the wounds on his face. The doctor said he looked like that because he'd been in the water, but still … I found it hard to believe.'

'How do you mean?'

'They looked like cuts and bruises to me. His lips were swollen and there was a gash on his forehead. I wanted to believe the doctor when he said it was only because Heiðar had been battered about in the water, but all the same … it could have been caused by something else.'

'Do you think someone could have hit him?'

'I wouldn't like to say.' Sigrún's gaze returned to the photo, then she turned it face down, as though she couldn't bring herself to talk about it with Heiðar looking up at them.

'Did he ever have run-ins with other kids his age?' Elma asked.

'No, never.'

'Had he made any friends here in Akranes?'

'I don't know.' Sigrún shrugged. 'He never brought any home with him.'

Elma waited for her to elaborate but she didn't.

Upstairs the radio was suddenly turned up loud and they heard the announcer giving the time. Elma realised she would miss the baby-swimming lesson if she didn't get a move on. But there was one more question she needed to ask.

'Was there a video camera among Heiðar's possessions when they were returned to you from Vatnaskógur?' She had been thinking about the description in Máni's diary of the short film he and Heiðar had made together.

'Yes, Heiðar had a video camera,' Sigrún said. 'He carried it with him everywhere. But it wasn't among his belongings when we got them back from the police. Perhaps he'd taken it out on the lake with him.'

Elma's suspicions were immediately roused. Was it possible that somebody had deliberately disposed of the camera for fear of the evidence it might contain?

❂

'Were they up that early?' Sævar asked as he fastened the child seat in the back of the car. They had been taking Adda to baby-swimming lessons every Sunday morning at ten since the autumn.

'I met them coming home from a walk,' Elma said, and gave him a brief summary of their conversation. 'I'm going to have to have a word with our ex-inspector – Matthías's father,' she added. 'It's looking increasingly unavoidable…'

'Ottó?'

'That's the one.'

'What I can't understand,' Sævar said, 'is why no one seems to have questioned the idea that Heiðar woke up in the middle of the night, took a boat out on the lake and fell overboard. I mean, who would do something like that?'

'People do a lot of strange things,' Elma pointed out. 'Like Thorgeir's father, for instance. The boat he allegedly took out was also found adrift on a lake. And although his body was never found, the police concluded that he'd fallen overboard.'

'Accident or suicide?'

'Haven't a clue,' Elma replied. 'Apparently, he was drunk at the time … Mind you, we still haven't received a satisfactory explanation for that blood stain at the summer house.'

'The old patch in the living room?' Sævar asked. 'You don't think it came from Thorgeir's father?'

'Who knows?' Elma parked in the only empty space by the swimming pool. 'But if you ask me, there's more to Kristjana than meets the eye.'

'But you've seen her – she's so small and fragile. You don't seriously believe she'd have been capable of overpowering her husband?'

'All I know is that he vanished and his body was never found, and we've seen before that size isn't everything. Small women can be killers too. And don't forget that Thorgeir was a big lad for his age. For all we know, it could have been two against one…'

'I think you're getting a bit ahead of yourself now.' Sævar undid his seatbelt.

'I'm only saying that I find it an extraordinary coincidence. Two accidents in two years, both involving people going out on a lake in a boat and apparently falling overboard. And Thorgeir was staying in the same place as the victim on both occasions. Is it possible that Thorgeir began by getting rid of his father? We know the school nurse repeatedly witnessed injuries on Thorgeir's body that he wouldn't explain. And Máni's brother, Breki, said he'd seen Thorgeir's parents beating him on the back with a stick. Supposing his father was the worst offender, and when Thorgeir was old enough, he hit back. And hit hard. God knows whether Kristjana was involved too, but I'm guessing she must have helped him dispose of the body.'

'But surely Kristjana couldn't have lugged the body to the boat and rowed it out onto the lake without being spotted?' Sævar undid the car seat and lifted Adda out.

'Who says she did?' Elma locked the car. 'There's no evidence that the body's actually in the lake. She could have dumped it somewhere else then cast the boat adrift from its moorings, after chucking a few bottles of booze in it to make it look like an accident.'

'Then Thorgeir takes it into his head to do the same thing a year later in Vatnaskógur … But why?'

'Search me.' Elma sighed. 'Why are teenagers capable of being violent and sometimes downright savage? That's the million-dollar question.'

'Well, it's a theory,' Sævar said, as they stepped into the warmth and powerful smell of chlorine in the pool reception area.

'If you ask me, it's quite a good theo—' Elma began, then broke off, belatedly registering that there was some sort of commotion going on.

Several parents were standing there with their babies, but none appeared to be heading into the changing rooms. Instead, they were staring, transfixed, through the glass partition into the pool area. On the other side, the young woman who taught the babies' session was pacing back and forth, talking into her phone. She was in tears and appeared to be speaking in great distress, though they couldn't hear the words.

'What's happened?' Elma whispered, then saw the problem for herself.

A woman was lying on the side of the pool, a puddle forming around her from her sodden clothes. Since she was face up, Elma could see that her skin was an unnaturally pale blue and oddly puffy. She had seen similar sights before and knew what it meant. The woman must have been in the water for a considerable time and there was no possibility that she was alive.

❄

Elma had turned away all the other parents and babies, as clearly there would be no swimming lesson on this occasion. Sævar had taken Adda home and, shortly after Elma had rung him, Hörður arrived at the scene. Elma pretended not to notice the way he hobbled into the building, his face drawn as if he hadn't slept all night.

Hafdís was still lying beside the pool. Elma hadn't touched her, but forensics and the pathologist should be arriving soon. They would not be happy to receive a callout on a Sunday morning.

Hörður limped over to the body and studied it in silence.

'There are injuries to her head,' Elma said after he'd had time to take in the situation.

'I can see that.'

'She could have fallen,' Elma suggested, though she didn't believe it for a minute. Hörður didn't reply. When Elma felt the silence had gone on long enough, she added: 'This has to be connected to the other murder.'

Hörður made an indistinct noise, perhaps of agreement. 'Though

I don't think we should jump the gun,' he said, making his way with difficulty to a folding chair by the wall and lowering himself into it.

He was obviously in agony but, once again, Elma decided there was no point commenting on the fact. She couldn't force him to pay another visit to the hospital if he didn't want to.

She sighed inwardly and surveyed the surroundings. She knew the pool well from having swimming lessons here herself as a girl, and more recently the weekly baby sessions with Adda.

'She must have had a bag with her,' Elma mused aloud, and walked over to the reception desk, which was in a small cubicle with windows dividing it from the pool and foyer.

Presumably Hafdís had been here to coach, yesterday evening most probably, given the state of her skin. Elma hadn't had a chance yet to question the young woman who had found her.

She scanned the reception cubicle and spotted a backpack on the floor by the wall.

Elma pulled on a pair of gloves, picked up the backpack and unzipped it. Inside was a towel and, after rooting around, she discovered a phone as well. It was locked, of course, but the screen lit up to show an unanswered call from Matthías.

He had rung at 21:23 the previous evening, which suggested that Hafdís could have been murdered before that time, in which case her body would have been here all night, as Elma suspected. On the other hand, if she hadn't come home after her swimming lesson, it seemed odd that Matthías had rung only once to check up on her. True, they were getting a divorce, but even so Elma found it suspicious that Matthías hadn't made any further attempts to contact his wife when she hadn't come home.

❂

The swimming instructor responsible for the baby lessons was a woman in her late twenties called Anna Gréta. Elma had asked her to hang on while she carried out a brief examination of the scene. A few minutes later, she went to see her in the women's changing room, where Anna Gréta was sitting on a wooden bench, her clothes dripping, staring vacantly at the floor.

'Do you think you're up to answering a few questions?' Elma asked, sitting down on the bench opposite her.

Anna Gréta nodded. Her eyes were red and she was clutching a paper tissue.

'What time did you arrive this morning?'

'Just before the lesson. I was running a bit late because my son was being a pain in the neck. I always give him a lift to my parents' house before I teach. It was about…' She glanced at her smart watch. 'About ten to ten.'

'Did you notice anything unusual when you arrived?'

'The door was unlocked. I just assumed someone had forgotten to lock up last night, but I called inside anyway, in case someone had got in before me. But there was no one here. Anyway, I'm usually the first person in on a Sunday morning. There were a few parents already hanging about so I told them to go on into the changing rooms. Then I went inside myself to fetch the equipment for my session and get everything ready, and that's when I saw her in the pool and I…' She gave a gasping sob and her eyes filled with tears. 'I can't believe this is happening.'

'Was she floating in the pool when you went in?'

'Yes.' Anna Gréta wiped away her tears with the scrunched-up tissue. 'I jumped in and pulled her out. I would have tried to perform CPR but I could see that … that it was too late.'

'Did you know her well?'

Anna Gréta nodded. 'We know each other through swimming. She used to coach me when I was younger and we'd sometimes see each other here. She was supposed to be teaching the class after the baby session. Oh God, we'll have to let people know. What time is it? They might come and catch sight of … The kids…'

'Don't worry, we'll take care of that,' Elma reassured her. 'Do you know what time Hafdís was teaching?'

'It must have been yesterday. Yes, there are swimming lessons on Saturday afternoons.'

'And there was no class earlier this morning?'

'No, like I said, I'm the first one in on Sundays.'

'I see.' Confirmation that Hafdís had been missing all night, yet Matthías had only bothered to check up on her once.

'Was she … Did someone do this to her?' Anna Gréta fixed anxious eyes on Elma, as if afraid of the answer. 'I saw her head. It was bleeding.'

'We'll get the pathologist to examine her and give us his opinion on that.'

'She must have fallen. It must have been an accident.' Anna Gréta sounded as though she was trying to persuade herself.

Elma didn't comment but asked instead: 'Do you have any reason to think someone might have done this to her deliberately?'

'What? No. I don't know…' Anna Gréta bit her lower lip, then added: 'I mean, she's never been that well liked, but I can't imagine anyone going this far.'

'No, one never can,' Elma said drily.

❁

'I'll need to conduct a post-mortem to establish whether we're looking at a drowning but I think it's fairly safe to assume we are. She's got wounds on her head and there are injuries to the back of her neck too, indicating that her head was forcibly held under water. These are pressure marks, here at the back.' The pathologist lifted Hafdís's dark hair and pointed to the patches of discolouration. 'She also received a heavy blow to the back of her skull. Did you notice an implement of any kind on the poolside?'

'Only the pole the instructors use to direct the swimming lessons,' Elma told him.

'Ah, that's a possibility,' the pathologist said. 'Right, I'm going to measure her body temperature and that should give us a rough time of death.'

'She was lying in the water until about an hour ago,' Elma said. 'The woman who came in this morning pulled her out.'

'Could you find out what time that was, and also the temperature of the pool?'

Elma glanced at the clock. 'She told me she got here at ten to ten. Just before the lesson was due to begin.'

The pathologist made a note of this, then got back to work.

Elma longed for some fresh air. The suffocating smell of chlorine and the humidity were getting to her. Nevertheless, she lingered, studying the scene. Memories of school swimming lessons came crowding into her mind. She could almost hear the teacher's hoarse voice as he barked – 'Bend, point, apart, together.' She had loathed the wooden pole he used to poke at the soles of their feet if they weren't pointed enough.

Another time, she had gone to a birthday party at the pool, with multi-coloured disco lights and music, probably by Britney Spears or the Backstreet Boys.

The pool still looked almost exactly the same: the blue cover, the steps on the right-hand side where either she or Sævar would sit while the other supported Adda in the water, the unusually narrow poolside area, and the windows at the far end, four of them, each with six panes, and a clock between the middle two. The white walls hadn't been painted for a while, and, on closer inspection, Elma noticed that something had been written on the wall in marker pen. Not words this time but a number – the number four.

Elma heard the door to the entrance slam and, hurrying out, was just in time to prevent Anna Gréta from leaving.

'Could you take a quick look at something for me?' she asked.

Anna Gréta reluctantly came back inside, removing her woolly hat.

Elma led her into the pool area and past the body. Elma noticed the young woman averting her eyes; they were still red and swollen from weeping and she must have blown her nose repeatedly because it was bright red too.

Elma pointed at the number on the wall. 'Has that always been there?'

Anna Gréta furrowed her brow. 'No, I've never seen it before.'

'Do you have any idea what it might mean?'

'No,' she said. 'I mean, it's just a number.'

'So people wouldn't usually write numbers on boards or on the walls in connection with swimming lessons?'

'Definitely not. I can't imagine any member of staff doing that.'

'No, I thought not,' Elma said. She thanked Anna Gréta, who put her hat back on and headed for the exit.

However, just before she reached the door, she turned. 'But … it's unlucky, isn't it?'

'Unlucky?'

'Yes, I mean the number four is considered unlucky in China. You know, like the number thirteen here and in lots of other countries.' Anna Gréta blushed slightly, as if afraid what she was saying sounded foolish. 'Anyway, it just occurred to me when you asked what the number might mean.'

BEFORE
Andrea

'How was it?' It's the first question she hears when she gets home.

'Fantastic. Like shagging Brad Pitt,' Andrea says, tugging off her boots. She pads barefoot into the sitting room, where Freyja is busy rolling a joint.

They'd met when Andrea was looking for a flatmate. She'd sold her brother's flat and bought another one with the money, but there was no chance she could live alone and afford to pay off the mortgage, so renting out a room had been a convenient solution. Freyja had answered the ad Andrea posted online and despite the age gap – Freyja was quite a bit older – they had hit it off instantly.

'That good, was he?' Freyja asks, licking the Rizla.

'Nah, I've had better. Too old and out of shape.' Andrea flops down on the sofa and tucks her legs underneath her.

'That's how most of them end up.'

'True.' Andrea watches Freyja suck in smoke before passing over the joint. Andrea inhales deeply, holds the smoke in her lungs for a long beat, then slowly releases it. 'Maybe if Brad Pitt was still like he was in that film – oh, you know, the one where he's always fighting.'

'*Fight Club.*'

'That's it,' Andrea says. 'Then maybe it would have been better.'

'You think so?' Freyja grins.

'I know so.' Andrea is longing for a shower. She feels dirty and is conscious of an unfamiliar smell clinging to her body.

Freyja seems to sense how she's feeling because she puts a hand on her shoulder and smiles. 'Well done. You're doing the right thing,' she says. 'Brad Pitt's rolling in it. Stick with him and you'll be rich.'

Andrea laughs, but her laughter is hollow and insincere.

Once the joint is finished, Freyja announces that she's off to bed, but Andrea fetches her computer and stays in the sitting room. She types Thorgeir's name into the search engine and studies a photo of him sitting with a big glass of beer on a beach somewhere.

He's a good-looking guy. It's so unfair; if there was any justice in the world, he would be as ugly on the outside as he is on the inside.

She has often thought how much simpler the world would be if everything was transparently obvious, like in an old Disney film, where, as a rule, the bad guy is ugly, though of course there are always exceptions. In reality, there is no correlation between someone's outer appearance and their character, and that makes the world a complicated, confusing place.

Evil can lurk behind the most attractive of smiles.

NOW

Sunday 13 December

Begga had spoken to three of the twelve kids who'd attended Hafdís's swimming lesson on Saturday. She was tempted to ask them how they felt about having to attend extra coaching sessions on a Saturday afternoon but stopped herself.

Two told the same story: the class had been in no way different from usual. They had done some exercises and at the end of the period they'd been given free time to play. At six, Hafdís had ordered them out of the pool and they'd gone home about a quarter of an hour later.

One of the girls Begga talked to told her that two kids by the names of Aron and Ína had been the last to get out. And now Begga was sitting opposite Aron, a dark-haired boy with a sprinkling of reddish freckles across his nose even though it was December and the sun was in hiding almost round the clock.

'Hi there,' Begga said cheerily, hoping she could get the boy to relax a little. He was as tightly wound as if he were being interrogated. Which, technically speaking, she supposed he was.

'Hi,' he replied in a low voice.

'So, what's up? How are you doing?'

He shrugged.

Begga sighed. 'Look, I'll be super quick, but the police need to know what happened, so I'm afraid we have to ask a few questions.'

'All right.'

'Great. Are you a good swimmer?'

'Sure.'

'Intending to go professional?' Begga scratched her head. 'Do they have professional swimmers?'

'Yes.' Aron nodded eagerly. 'Like, it's possible, but I don't think it's for me. I expect I'll do some other job.'

'Oh, really?' Begga smiled. 'Is it normal to have swimming lessons late on a Saturday afternoon, like yesterday? If so, you have my sympathy.'

'Er, yeah, they're every Saturday. It sucks, actually.'

'You were the last person to leave yesterday, weren't you? Were you the last out of the changing rooms too?'

'Yes – out of the boys' changing room, anyway.'

'Was Hafdís still there when you left?'

'Yes, she was inside, on her phone.'

'In reception?'

Aron nodded.

'Was she talking on her phone?'

Aron shook his head and said she'd just been looking at it.

'Did you speak to her?'

'I said bye, and she said bye back.'

'OK, good to know. Great.' Begga smiled at the boy, who had relaxed a little now and no longer looked as if he'd been lined up against a wall with a gun to his head. 'Did you leave the building with anyone else?'

'No, they'd all gone. I was the last.'

'Did someone collect you?'

'No, I live nearby. My street's Víðigerði.'

'Víðigerði. That's very near here. Convenient,' Begga said, and the boy nodded. 'Tell me, Aron, did you see anyone as you were leaving? Outside, perhaps, or…'

'Yes.' Aron seemed suddenly excited to have something to tell. 'I noticed someone outside but, like, I don't know who it was or anything.'

'No, OK, but could you describe them?'

'It was an old man with white hair and he was patting a cat.'

An old man patting a cat. Begga sighed under her breath but kept her expression carefully neutral. 'Where was this old man standing?'

'Just outside,' Aron said. 'I didn't see his face or anything, but I looked back as I started walking home and he was just standing there, staring at the building.'

'Where was he standing?'

'In front of the entrance.'

'Did you see him go in?'

Aron shook his head. 'No, but … but I think he meant to go in.'

'What makes you think that?'

'Because when I looked round again, after walking a bit further, he'd disappeared.'

❂

'I tried to ring her yesterday.' Matthías looked lost sitting there, almost swallowed up by the big sofa.

Elma and Hörður had gone round to break the news of Hafdís's death. Their daughter was out and Matthías, alone at home, was behaving as if he had departed from his body, leaving it behind on the sofa. Even his voice had changed and become oddly toneless.

'I thought she was with somebody else. She wanted a divorce and I felt I didn't … I didn't want to…' Matthías gulped. 'I felt it wasn't my business anymore to ask where she was.'

'And that's why you didn't try calling her again?' Elma asked.

Matthías's head drooped, which Elma took as a yes.

She asked a few more questions about the sort of relationship Hafdís had had with Thorgeir and what Matthías had felt about Thorgeir transferring money to her bank account, but Matthías seemed indifferent. He said he didn't care about the money and that he didn't believe there had been anything going on between them.

'They'd always got on well, but I'd have known if there'd been any more to it.'

Elma was sceptical about that but decided to leave it for now.

'Where were you yesterday evening?' she asked instead.

'Here.'

'Can anyone confirm that?'

'Yes.' His lips trembled. 'Ólöf.'

'Your daughter?'

'Yes.'

Elma had been intending to ask him about the events in Vatnaskógur, but Matthías was plainly in shock and barely capable of producing words of more than one syllable. When, a few moments later, they were interrupted by the front door opening and his daughter, Ólöf, appeared in the room, Elma decided to postpone the conversation.

The sight of his daughter appeared to rouse Matthías from his stupor. 'Sweetheart,' he whispered and, getting up, went over to her. 'I'm so sorry…'

❂

'What did you say was written on the wall?' Sævar asked, holding Adda's hands out of the way while Elma was changing her nappy. Elma was back home after a long day and had picked up a takeaway pizza for supper. The box lay open on the coffee table.

'The number four,' Elma replied. 'I have no idea if it's linked to the murder. Theoretically, anyone could have written it on the wall, and it could mean anything from "four kids here" to "four minutes" or "four lengths of the pool". Who knows? Maybe someone completely different wrote it. But Anna Gréta pointed out that it's an unlucky number in China.'

'Unlucky?'

'I looked it up and she was right. The number four is regarded as unlucky in China because it resembles the Chinese word for death. They often leave out the fourth floor or room number four in buildings, jumping straight from three to five.'

'Apparently, some buildings miss out the thirteenth floor.'

'God, people are superstitious.' Elma made a face at Adda. 'There's no hope for the human race.'

'Four,' Sævar muttered. 'Wasn't that…?'

'Hm?'

'Hang on.' He got up and disappeared into the kitchen.

'Sævar?' Elma, who was in the middle of fastening the nappy, couldn't follow him. She turned instead to Adda. 'What's your dad on about now?'

He returned after a brief interval, brandishing his phone.

'Room four,' he exclaimed. 'Heiðar was in room four at Vatnaskógur.'

'How do you know that?'

'My mates from football were talking about it the other day. They used to draw lots to decide who slept in the bed that was supposed to have been Heiðar's. It was rumoured to be haunted after Heiðar died.'

'Haunted?'

'I'm not claiming there was anything to it,' Sævar said. 'It was just a story that went around, which meant that nobody wanted to sleep in that room. The management must have been relieved when the huts were demolished.'

'Room four,' Elma mused aloud.

She had no way of knowing if the number on the wall of the pool was really a reference to Heiðar's room or just the unlucky number four, but it still seemed an incredible coincidence.

If it wasn't a coincidence, it appeared that the murderer had chosen to leave a trail. And whatever reason the murderer had for leaving a trail, Elma was sure that it must contain clues. Perhaps the killer wanted the world to know their motive.

Monday 14 December

'Could Matthías have wanted to get his revenge on Thorgeir and Hafdís?' Hörður suggested.

'That's the most obvious conclusion,' Elma said absently, jotting something down in her notebook.

The two of them were sitting in the meeting room, going over the progress of the investigation and the jobs that still needed doing. The post-mortem on Hafdís was scheduled for later that day and Hörður was thinking of attending.

'We know that Hafdís wanted a divorce and Matthías seemed anything but happy about it.'

'It's a possibility.' Without realising it, Elma had scribbled the number four in her notebook. It was likely that Thorgeir had been murdered on 4 December. There had been four boys in room four at Vatnaskógur. Elma had lain awake last night, unable to switch off, the number spinning in her head.

Perhaps the Chinese were onto something.

'Matthías doesn't have a watertight alibi for the evening Hafdís died,' Hörður continued. 'He claims he was at home with his daughter, but, as she was in her room most of the time, she couldn't confirm that her father had been there all evening.'

'What was his motive, though?'

'Well, I can think of several,' Hörður said. 'The divorce, adultery, money.'

'But Thorgeir was at the summer house with another girl, so it seems unlikely he was having an affair with Hafdís,' Elma pointed out. Andrea kept veering, in her imagination, between killer and victim. The more she thought about it, the more convinced she became that the case was related somehow to the long-ago events in Vatnaskógur.

'Matthías had a connection to both victims. He had a motive to murder both of them.' Hörður kept clicking his pen on and off with his thumb.

'There are other aspects that we need to bear in mind,' Elma said, restraining an urge to snatch the pen away from him. 'Maybe the case isn't connected to adultery or divorce but to the boy who died in Vatnaskógur in 1995. There were clues left at the scene of both murders that point to that.'

Elma now produced Máni's diary and laid it on the table.

'This diary hints that something untoward may have happened at the summer camp, which resulted in Heiðar's death. He was a new boy at the school, and he and Máni obviously hit it off, but Thorgeir clearly wasn't too happy about the fact. You can read about it here.'

Hörður pulled the diary towards him as Elma continued:

'According to the final entry, Thorgeir was organising some kind of initiation ceremony to "welcome" Heiðar into the gang.' Elma made air quotes around the world 'welcome' to indicate that Heiðar had been anything but, at least in Thorgeir's eyes.

'An initiation ceremony?'

'They were all about to start sixth-form college in the autumn, so maybe they got the idea from that.'

'And you think this initiation could have led to Heiðar's death?' Hörður asked.

'I do, yes.'

'What, that they deliberately cast him adrift in the boat and he fell overboard?'

'Maybe…' Elma paused to think about it. If that is what happened, it must presumably have been an accident, however reprehensible and dangerous the boys' behaviour had been. 'I don't know what exactly went on that night but I do believe it resulted in Heiðar's death, and there are various details that fit that theory.'

'You mean that the two recent murders were a form of revenge?'

'Think about it. In both cases, the writing on the wall connects the murders to Heiðar.'

'That number four at the pool?' Hörður frowned. 'Are we quite sure that it wasn't one of the staff or kids?'

'No, but Heiðar was in room four at Vatnaskógur.' Elma told Hörður about the stories that used to circulate among the boys about room four being haunted. 'I just don't believe it's a coincidence. There are plenty of examples of murderers leaving clues at the scene, either to mislead the police or to claim responsibility for the crime. If I'm right, and the quotation at the summer house and the number on the swimming-pool wall were both the work of the murderer, it suggests that he wants us to understand why these two people were killed. That he believes they deserved to die and wants other people to know why. Maybe the killer feels he's the victim of injustice.'

'*He*?'

'Or she.'

'OK, let's say you're right.' Hörður closed the diary. 'Let's say the two murders are in revenge for what happened. Then who's the culprit? Who wants vengeance?'

Elma had been racking her brain about this without coming to any conclusion.

Hörður answered his own question: 'Possibly Andrea, but we still haven't managed to find her. She would hardly have murdered Thorgeir and Hafdís now, all these years later, though. What reason would she have had?'

'Well, when I spoke to her brother, he alleged that Thorgeir and his mates had blamed Máni for what happened at the camp. They'd spread rumours that he'd done something to Heiðar. Then there's the fact that the original investigation seems to have left a lot to be desired, as if somebody wanted to hush the matter up.'

'Ottó?'

'Yes … of course, Ottó was inspector at the time.'

'Meaning that they kept quiet about the fact that the boys may have forced Heiðar onto that boat? Let it appear that he'd gone out of his own accord?' Hörður scratched the back of his head. 'Well, I can't imagine Ottó wanting it to come out in public if his son had been involved in an affair like that. But, on the other hand, I'd be very surprised if he'd concealed evidence to protect his own interests. That would be an incredibly serious matter.' He cleared his throat. 'It's certainly a theory, but, to be honest, I find it a bit of a stretch. You see, I believe the writing on the wall could be interpreted differently in both cases. After all, the number four, on its own, doesn't necessarily tell us anything. And all the quotation on the wall above Thorgeir's bed tells us is that the killer may be some kind of religious maniac who feels burdened by sin or some such madness. We must be careful not to become fixated on a single theory.'

'I know,' Elma said.

'By the way, I spoke to the economic-crimes team and asked them to run some checks on the company Kristjana owned with her husband, Reynir. It turns out that they only had one employee on their payroll – Guðrún Matthíasdóttir, who's married to Bárður. But I think I can state with some confidence that she never worked for their dry-cleaning business.'

'Bárður?' Elma was bad at remembering names and couldn't put a face to this one, though it sounded vaguely familiar.

'Bárður was captain of the trawler Viðvík for many years. And it gets better: Guðrún is the sister of none other than Ottó.'

'Meaning what?'

Hörður shrugged. 'That the dry cleaner's was laundering money, possibly. The first thing that springs to mind is that the trawler may have been smuggling in goods to be sold on the black market here and that the illegal profits needed to be laundered somehow.'

'Drugs?'

'Maybe. Or something else, like tobacco or ... who knows?' Hörður shrugged. 'Registering Guðrún as an employee would have given them a legal channel through which to pay the money back to the couple. It's a well-known scam.'

Elma rubbed her temples. 'So that's another connection between them. Isn't that typical Akranes?'

'It has nothing to do with Akranes,' retorted Hörður, who got on the defensive whenever he felt his town was being impugned. 'You can find black sheep anywhere.'

Elma grinned. 'Anyhow, to recap: we've got Matthías, Hafdís and Thorgeir, all linked by pretty strong bonds. Matthías and Hafdís got together in their teens, and now you're telling me that Thorgeir's parents ran a business that played an important role for Ottó's sister, Guðrún, and her husband, Bárður. Ottó may even have known about the scam and covered up for his sister and brother-in-law. So that's three prominent families who may have decided to close ranks.'

'And throw the others overboard?'

'Maybe not literally but, yes, in a way.'

Elma was reasonably sure by now that the murders were connected to Heiðar's death, but what was still missing from the puzzle was the identity of the killer. She was none the wiser about a possible candidate, although this was the most vital piece of the jigsaw.

'Anyway, to return to your original point,' Elma continued, 'we still don't have anyone with a sufficiently strong motive to kill both Hafdís and Thorgeir. All we have are theories, no proof. I spoke to Heiðar's parents and we can safely rule them out. They weren't aware of any shortcomings in the investigation into Heiðar's death – though, mind you, when his mother viewed his body, she noticed some odd cuts and bruises on his face. The doctors told her this was the result of him being knocked about in the water, but who knows? At any rate, I think it's safe to assume that these murders were premeditated. Not committed in the heat of the moment but planned in advance.'

'But murders in Iceland aren't like that.' Hörður grabbed the diary again and opened it. 'Icelandic murders are sordid, amateurish affairs. Committed under the influence of alcohol or drugs or in domestic situations.'

'Granted, we don't often see that kind of murder here,' Elma admitted. After a moment's reflection, she added: 'There is one man who could shed some light on the matter, but somehow I doubt he'll be willing to talk.'

Elma had already looked him up and made a note of his address. If she was right, he was guilty of covering up for his son and his son's friends, but she reckoned the chances of getting him to admit the fact were close to zero.

'Yes, well, I'll let you take care of talking to Ottó,' Hörður said. 'I don't think it would be appropriate for me to do it as Ottó and I know each other far too well.'

'OK, I'll get on to it,' Elma said, rising to her feet.

'Just approach him warily – he's liable to bite.'

'I'm not scared of him.'

'You should be.' Although Hörður's tone was jokey, there was an underlying seriousness there. Elma had heard plenty of stories about Ottó, few of them good.

'I can't find any information about whether they did a post-mortem on Heiðar at the time,' she went on. 'I'd have thought it would have been standard procedure, given that his body was found in the lake in suspicious circumstances.'

'Yes, that's true. When was this again?' Hörður asked.

'Nineteen ninety-five.'

'Ah, yes. There must have been a post-mortem.' Hörður tapped his finger several times on the table. 'But there were no pathologists based in Iceland at the time, as you know. I seem to remember that they used to bring a woman over from Germany when required. The reports often took forever to turn up. Not like now, when they're delivered pretty much the same day.' Hörður stood up as well, visibly wincing at the pain in his hip. 'I'll dig out the names of the pathologists we used at the time and email them to you. They may still have the original reports.'

'Fingers crossed.'

BEFORE
Andrea

Andrea wakes with a jerk in the middle of the night, her mouth so dry that she has trouble swallowing. She has no memory of how the evening ended. Thorgeir invited his friends round, and she can remember Hafdís dancing and Matthías mixing drinks, but not when they left or how she got to bed herself. Once she's quite sure that Thorgeir is asleep, she slips out from under the duvet.

The table is still covered with bottles and glasses, and there's a cloying smell of alcohol in the air, like in a bar after closing time. Thanks to the dim glow from the streetlights outside, she can manage without the torch on her phone.

Andrea works quickly. She's searched Thorgeir's place before; once, when he popped out to buy something to drink, she went through his bedroom wardrobe, checking behind all his clothes and riffling through his drawers, but drew a blank. Another time she went through the kitchen cupboards while he was in the shower.

The only place left is the sitting-room cupboards. She'd started going through them the day she searched his wardrobe, but heard the sound of Thorgeir inserting his key in the lock before she could finish the job. Now she crouches down and opens the cupboard she didn't manage to check last time. It contains two baskets full of assorted items. She pulls them out and goes through them: tealights, lighters and postcards. Thinking she hears a noise from the bedroom she pauses, listening intently.

Nothing. Only the wind whistling in the gaps around the sitting-room window. Stealthily, she eases open the door of the next cupboard.

On the top shelf are DVDs of old films, mainly action movies, that she doubts Thorgeir watches anymore. The bottom shelf appears to contain nothing but a tangle of electric cords. She fumbles towards the back of the cupboard, just to make sure, and her hand encounters a hard object. When she takes it out, she sees that it's a camera. An old video camera.

She tries switching it on but nothing happens. Either there are no batteries in it or it stopped working a long time ago. Andrea inspects it, trying to guess how old it is. It's a silver Philips model, heavy and clunky in her hands. Just as her fingers find and click open the small compartment in the side, she hears a squeak from the parquet in the hallway.

Her heart is pounding and she can feel her pulse throbbing in her fingertips as she puts the camera back, overwhelmed with disappointment. This is hopeless. She'll never be able to find out what happened. What she's looking for was probably destroyed long ago. It's the only logical conclusion and it was absurd ever to think this would work. She's close to tears when her gaze falls on a small tape at the back of the cupboard that looks like a miniature version of a VHS cassette. Hastily, fingers trembling, she tucks it inside the T-shirt that is all she's wearing.

The parquet squeaks again and, closing the cupboard, she calls out: 'Thorgeir?'

'What are you doing?' he asks, appearing in the doorway. He's wearing nothing but his underpants; the elastic with the Calvin Klein logo is twisted on one side.

'Oh, I was just so hungry.'

He takes her head in his hands, tilts it back and kisses her gently. His breath is sour, mingled with booze. But she returns his kiss, closing her eyes and feeling her head swim.

He picks her up and carries her back into the bedroom, and she's fairly sure that he doesn't suspect anything, but her heartbeat doesn't slow until the little cassette she managed to tuck into her T-shirt is hidden in a safe place.

NOW

Monday 14 December

Ottó Matthíasson had served as the police inspector in Akranes from 1985 until 2002. These days, he lived in a house on Sandabraut. Although many of the properties on the street looked rather shabby and rundown, Ottó's place appeared well maintained and was surrounded by a large garden. When Elma drew up outside, she saw a man shovelling snow off the pavement in front of the house. He was tall but his dark-blue down jacket seemed to hang off his big frame.

'Hello, Ottó?' she said, once she was within hailing distance.

The man turned, leaning on the handle of his shovel as he squinted into the sun. He allowed a few moments to pass before answering in the affirmative.

'My name's Elma,' she said.

'I know who you are.'

As far as she could remember, this was the first time Elma had met Ottó, but she guessed he must still keep tabs on his old workplace.

'I take it you want to talk to me?' he said, before she could respond. 'Come in, then. The street is no place for conversations of that sort.'

Elma followed him into the house, where she encountered a small woman, dressed rather dowdily in a dress and tights, her limp hair trailing halfway down her back.

'This is my wife, Jónína.'

Elma introduced herself and shook hands with the woman, who gave a quick smile, then snatched back her hand after the briefest of contact. She made herself scarce before Elma could say another word.

Ottó gestured to her to take a seat at the oak table in the kitchen. There was a basket of blackened bananas on it that were beginning to smell. Flies were circling above them.

'I'm terribly sorry that this should have happened to your daughter-in-law,' Elma began. 'I'll try to be quick. I can't imagine what you and your family are going through.'

'Oh, I'm sure you can,' Ottó said, dumping a mug of coffee in front of her without asking if she wanted any.

His answer disconcerted Elma. She had lost her partner Davíð three years earlier, when he'd taken his own life. That was one of the reasons for her moving home to Akranes after more than a decade in the city – something she had thought would never happen, which turned out to be the only thing she could do while the wounds were still fresh. Could Ottó be alluding to Davíð's death?

'I've known Hafdís since she started school here in Akranes when she was twelve, or thereabouts,' Ottó said. 'Matthías and her, they were childhood sweethearts. That's rare nowadays.'

'Yes, I suppose so.'

'But that's life. We never know when death's going to strike, though we all know it's going to happen sooner or later, however much we may pretend not to.'

Elma nodded. She hadn't come to see Ottó to talk about death, at least not like this. But Ottó had the air of a man who was used to dominating any situation he found himself in.

'Have you got any leads?' he asked. 'What does the post-mortem report say?'

'We're still waiting for the final results, but we do know that Hafdís died by drowning.'

'Oh, come off it. Tell me something I don't know. A good swimmer like Hafdís wouldn't have drowned just like that. What injuries did they find on her body?'

'She had injuries on her head and neck,' Elma replied, adding, before Ottó could interrupt: 'We're investigating Hafdís's death in connection with Thorgeir's murder, and some interesting facts have emerged in the course of our enquiries. Particularly in relation to an old case that I'd like more information about.'

'An old case? What are you talking about?'

Elma took a folded sheet of paper from her bag and smoothed it out on the table. 'In nineteen ninety-five a teenage boy died at the summer camp in Vatnaskógur. His name was Heiðar Kjartansson.'

Ottó looked suddenly rattled. He glared at the paper with distaste, then took a mouthful of his coffee. 'You're supposed to be finding out what happened to my daughter-in-law, not wasting your time on some cold case. What are you playing at?'

'We have reason to believe they're connected.'

'Connected how? An accident that happened twenty-five years ago and Hafdís's death? You're not fit to be in charge of the inquiry if you think that. I've half a mind to give Reykjavík a call and tell them what kind of amateurs they've got working here in Akranes.'

Elma felt her cheeks growing hot. 'We have our reasons, like I said.'

Ottó snorted.

Elma went on doggedly: 'The accident report is unsatisfactorily brief, as if part of it is missing. It's extremely short and pretty sketchy on the details. For example, I can't find any indication that interviews were conducted with the staff at the camp or the boys who shared a room with Heiðar. I'd have thought there was every reason to establish exactly what happened to Heiðar, given the seriousness of the situation.'

'"Exactly what happened to Heiðar", Ottó mimicked her. 'Listen, dear, I think you'd better concentrate on the here and now rather than getting distracted by events that were long before your time. You were hardly even born then, were you?'

'I'd been born a good while,' Elma objected.

'Yes, well. You'll just have to put your faith in the fact that your predecessors – yours and your otherwise excellent boss Hörður's – performed their job competently. I can assure you that everything was thoroughly investigated at the time.'

'Heiðar's mother thought she saw cuts and bruises on his body.'

'Bruises? Boys that age are always covered in bruises. If I remember correctly, they'd held a football tournament there the day before, and you can bet your life they weren't playing girls' games.'

'Girls' games?'

'Oh, don't start that equality bullshit with me. Boys – at least the boys I've known – play quite differently from girls.'

'In other words, they were just sports injuries resulting from a football match the day before? I've spoken to Heiðar's parents and, according to them, he didn't even like sport.'

'Well, no doubt that's why he was covered in bruises afterwards,' Ottó said. 'Didn't think of that, did you?'

Elma held her breath and silently counted to ten. 'Fine,' she said. 'Nevertheless, it looks as though the investigators jumped to the conclusion that it was an accident. I can't find a single piece of paperwork to suggest that the police spoke to anyone else at the scene, whether staff or kids – like your own son, for example.'

'*My son.*' Ottó spat out the words, spraying Elma with saliva. 'Are you insinuating that that had an influence on the investigation? On my working methods? On my professional judgement as a police inspector?'

'I'm not insinuating anything at all.' Elma had to fight to hold on to her temper, but decided that keeping her cool was a better policy. 'Please don't take it the wrong way, but there were indications at the two recent crime scenes – indications that I can't discuss – which suggest a link between Thorgeir's and Hafdís's deaths and the earlier incident in Vatnaskógur. That's why I wanted to know if you'd noticed anything untoward at the time.'

'*Untoward,*' Ottó muttered, appearing to have calmed down a little.

Elma continued, picking her words with care: 'Whether, on reflection, there were any circumstances that suggested it might not have been an accident after all.'

Ottó leant back until his chair creaked and gave an exasperated sigh to show how ridiculous he found her question.

'Could you just go over the facts with me?' Elma asked. 'The details you remember.'

'It was a long time ago.'

'I know.' Elma sipped her coffee, trying not to grimace at the taste. 'But cases like that tend to stay with you.' Deaths of children always did, she thought. And not just deaths but any instances involving violence towards or neglect of children. Most other memories faded in time, but many of the cases involving minors that Elma had worked on were still so vivid in her mind that she doubted she would ever be free of them.

'Magnús rang me on the Friday, just before noon, to report that one of the boys had gone missing in the night. He wasn't in his bed that morning. They'd already searched the area and seen that one of the boats had gone from the jetty and was out on the lake. So it was pretty obvious from the first what had happened.'

'And what was that?'

'Take an educated guess.'

'I'm terrible at guessing.' Elma smiled blandly.

Ottó regarded her with weary impatience. 'Then I'll spell it out for you. The boy sneaked out in the night, took the boat and either threw himself overboard or fell in. It happens. People do stupid things. Don't ask me why, but after forty years in the police I've learnt that you can't hope to understand everything and that in most cases things are exactly what they appear to be. You'll discover that for yourself when you've done the job as long as I have.'

Although Elma was unused to being talked down to like this, she had no intention of letting him knock her off her stride. 'Did you interview his friends and the staff at the camp?' she persisted.

'Of course we did.'

'I can't find any paperwork.'

'Then perhaps you need to look harder.'

Elma didn't respond to this and her silence had the desired effect.

'Everyone we talked to said the boy had been weird,' Ottó was eventually goaded into replying. 'A loner with hardly any friends. No one knew why he had done it, but it didn't really take anyone by surprise.'

'Except his parents,' Elma remarked.

'What?'

'It came as a surprise to his parents. They said it was completely out of character for Heiðar.'

Ottó gave her a patronising smile. 'That's what they all say. A man shoots himself in the head after a long history of problems and everybody's still astonished and claims it's "out of character".'

Elma felt sick to her stomach but tried not to let his condescending tone get to her. She just hoped for Ottó's sake that this wasn't a deliberate reference to her ex, Davíð. If it was, it would be a breathtakingly crass thing to say. In spite of her resolve, her voice trembled a little as she replied: 'So there was nothing to suggest that it had been anything other than an accident?'

'Well, accident … I wouldn't like to say. But there was nothing to indicate that anyone else was involved. No one was to blame for what happened to that boy.' Abruptly, Ottó rose to his feet with a loud screech of his chair across the tiles. 'Anyway, I reckon we're done here.'

Elma was itching to grill him for more details. She was positive now that he was hiding something. The way he avoided her gaze and spoke to her with such arrogant contempt to get out of answering any difficult questions. The way he avoided mentioning Heiðar by name, only referring to him dismissively as 'that boy'.

But she knew this was as much information as she could hope to get out of Ottó for the time being. She would have to continue her search elsewhere.

She rose to her feet too, leaving her coffee almost untouched.

'Thanks for the chat,' she said in a level voice. 'And once again, please accept my condolences. I'll do my best to keep you and your family informed.'

Ottó snorted as if he put no faith in her words.

Elma drew a deep breath, suddenly desperate to get out of this house into the cold, fresh air, away from this overbearing man. Seldom had she been more grateful to have Hörður as her boss.

She gave Ottó an insincere parting smile and turned to leave, but before she could take a step, her arm was seized in a vicious grip. Flinching, she looked round into Ottó's glowering face.

'Your boyfriend,' Ottó said. 'He's that Sævar, isn't he?'

'Yes.' Elma was momentarily thrown, confused about what relevance this had to the investigation.

'Then I recommend you leave well alone.' Ottó gave her a twisted smile. 'It would be best for your sake. For both your sakes.'

Elma opened her mouth to retort, but before she knew what was happening, Ottó had bundled her out onto the step.

The door closed behind her with a deafening slam.

BEFORE
Andrea

Thorgeir drives her home the next day. As they linger for a parting kiss in the car outside the building where she lives, it feels as if he's never going to let her go. He keeps pulling her in for one more kiss, a few minutes more.

She walks into the flat to find it reeking of pot and cat litter that badly needs changing. Freyja's door is shut. Since it's not yet one p.m., she's probably still asleep.

Andrea hurries to her room and sits on the bed for a moment, trying to catch her breath. Then takes out the cassette and examines it, wondering how she can watch it. She's panting as if she'd just come home from a session at the gym, though of course she hasn't; she's not into exercise. She lies back, trying to slow her breathing, and yawns. She's so tired. Tired of the pretence, tired of the memories that come back to haunt her so vividly whenever she visits Akranes.

The town is just as she remembered it. Despite a lot of superficial changes, the essentials are the same. More houses have sprung up, new shops have opened, yet all the things she remembers so well are still there: the mountain, the church, the potholed streets, the statue of the fisherman in the square.

She once broke her arm trying to climb that statue. Her brother Máni gave her a leg up, but she couldn't get any purchase and fell off, landing on the hard pavement. No one saw them, and Máni gave her some sweets to stop her crying. Andrea can still see his face as he told her to stick her hand in her anorak pocket and pretend nothing had happened.

Try and lift up your shoulder so your arm doesn't dangle like that. Or stick your hand in your pocket.

She sits up again and reaches for her laptop. After a brief search she finds a company that will transfer the contents of the cassette onto a USB stick, and calls them then and there.

❀

Three days later she has the USB in her hand.

It's a peculiar sensation, watching the videos appear as files on her computer screen. Now Andrea is only a couple of short clicks away from the truth. At long last, the time has come.

NOW

Monday 14 December

True to his word, Hörður had contacted the pathologist's office in Germany to ascertain whether they still had Heiðar Kjartansson's original post-mortem report in their database. Elma returned to the office to find an email waiting in her inbox with the report attached. Before opening it, she sat in front of her computer for a minute or two, trying to process what had just happened to her.

Ottó was a thug.

Her upper arm was aching where he had gripped it, but that was of minor importance compared to the way he had treated her. Being grabbed and thrown out of his house like that had left her too shocked to say a word. She had simply driven away, but now she was furious with herself.

Ottó's action had only strengthened her conviction that she was right; that the man had something to hide. Well, if he thought he could scare her off taking a closer look at the case, his plan had seriously backfired.

Elma freed her pony-tail from its elastic band and massaged her scalp. Her hair felt stiff with grease. She badly needed a good long shower, to wash her hair and at the same time wash away the memory of Ottó's manhandling.

The post-mortem report, which was in English, was dated more than a week after Heiðar's death. Elma pored over it, resorting several times to a translation program to grasp the finer points. As she read, she jotted down what appeared to be the most significant findings.

By the time she finished reading, she'd made quite an extensive list of notes and sat back to review them.

There had been water in Heiðar's lungs when he was found in the lake, but, in spite of this, the cause of death was not thought to be drowning. His body had been covered in injuries and the description made for harrowing reading. The most recent, those on the outsides of his arms and legs, had looked like the result of blows inflicted by a blunt object. A beating, in other words. And the cause of death was a brain haemorrhage, almost certainly from a blow to the head.

The older injuries were different. These consisted of long scars on many parts of his body, possibly also caused by blows. There were other scars that appeared to be old burns.

The report was accompanied by photos of pale skin marred by raised welts. And an old bone fracture that had gone untreated, with the result that it had healed out of alignment.

Elma found she was having trouble breathing. She had seen a thing or two in her time in the police, but Heiðar had been only fifteen when he died. According to the pathologist's report, some of the injuries could have been inflicted many years previously.

An image of Sigrún and Kjartan rose before Elma's eyes; her kindly smile, his harsh features. To think that she had accepted the offer of Christmas cake at their house. Had pitied them and wanted to spare them any worry.

The anger that had been smouldering inside her before she even started reading the report had now assumed the proportions of a raging inferno, and it was no longer directed solely against Ottó.

❂

After work, Elma was battling, head down, against the wind to cover the few metres from the police station to her car when she heard a voice calling her name over the noise of the gale.

Raising her head, she saw a man standing by a brown Mitsubishi that was parked nearby. She didn't immediately recognise him as, unlike her, he was dressed for the weather, with a hat pulled down over his forehead and ears.

Only when he came over and greeted her did she realise that it was Magnús, the director of the centre at Vatnaskógur.

'Could we maybe have a word?' he said, so quietly that she could hardly catch the words over the storm. 'Or is this a bad…?'

'No, not at all. Come in.' Elma waved at him to follow her back inside the station.

Once they were sitting in her office, Magnús took off his hat and laid it in his lap.

'Look, it's not really that big a deal,' he began. 'But I felt I needed … I ought to get this off my chest.'

Elma waited, watching Magnús stroking his hat as if it was a furry animal.

'Maybe I should have … should have mentioned it the other day. Not that I was lying exactly, you understand. It's just that it had nothing to do with the case – it was a completely unrelated incident, but … but I've sometimes wondered if it shouldn't have come out at the time.'

Magnús adjusted his glasses and ran a finger over his brow, where beads of sweat were glittering in the overhead light.

'Anyway, the thing is, I went into the chapel after that particular group of kids had left, and discovered some empty bottles in there and…' Magnús broke off for a moment, then continued: 'Ottó told me not to say anything about it, but I assume he must have taken it into account.'

'Had kids been drinking in there? Kids from that group?'

'Well … it appeared that someone had been drinking in there, like I said. There were bottles.'

'And this was just after Heiðar's group had left the camp?'

'Yes, that's right.' Magnús coughed. 'And it also looked as if there had been a fight.'

'How do you mean?'

'A piece had been broken off one of the pews and … and there was blood on the statue.'

'On the statue of Jesus?' Elma recalled the white statue that took pride of place on the altar. Could it have been used as a weapon? Her mind jumped back to the pathologist's report she had just read: Heiðar had died from a brain haemorrhage, caused by a blow to the head.

Magnús nodded.

'Was it never looked into?'

'No, like I said, it was unrelated to the other business, and the kids had all gone home. There was nothing I could do.'

'Did it never occur to anyone that it could be linked to Heiðar's death?'

Magnús's knuckles whitened around his hat. 'Heiðar drowned, so I assumed it had nothing to do with that.'

Elma leant forwards over her desk. 'What would have happened if the news had got out that Heiðar had been murdered while in your care? Would it have had an impact on attendance at your summer camps?'

'Murdered? But Heiðar drowned – all the evidence pointed to that. And you couldn't be more wrong if you think concerns about attendance at the camps had the slightest influence on my decision-making. The camps aren't run for profit, you know; they're run for the boys – the youngsters – who go there. To create happy memories while at the same time teaching them something about religion.'

'Then I'm afraid I'm at a loss to understand why you didn't report this,' Elma said, more sharply than intended. It would be unwise to lose her temper with the director of the centre, but suddenly she couldn't restrain herself any longer. 'Please help me to understand. Heiðar's body was dragged out of the lake, covered in cuts and bruises, and you found signs of a violent struggle in the chapel, but for some reason that escapes me, no one thought to look into the matter. His death was merely recorded as an accident. A drowning. How is that possible? Why didn't it occur to anyone that the incidents could be related?'

'Are you saying the boy had injuries?' Magnús asked in a horrified tone.

Elma realised she had revealed too much. After all, her gripe wasn't with Magnús but with Ottó. He was the one who had sat on the information that connected the two incidents.

'Yes,' she said curtly.

Suddenly, Magnús was angry too. 'You can't blame me – it was the police's fault. I told Ottó, but he didn't believe the incidents were related. He told me not to worry but to keep it to myself. What else was I supposed to do? Go to the papers? Tell the boy's parents or sister? I trusted the police to take care of it. Trusted that they'd done a good job.'

'Hang on, what did you just say?'

'I'm sure the police did a thorough, professional job. But I can't explain why they neglected to look into a possible link. After all, it was none of my business whether—'

Elma cut him off mid-flow. 'Just a minute, you mentioned a sister. Did Heiðar have a sister?'

Magnús leant back in his chair, clasping his hands across his stomach as if trying to contain his indignation and fear. 'Yes, he had a sister who attended camp with him. It was the last weekend of the summer so we had a mixed-sex group of teenagers. I seem to remember that she was a bit younger than him.'

'Are you absolutely sure Heiðar had a sister?' Elma asked. If that were true, surely Heiðar's parents would have mentioned her? And Elma hadn't come across any information in the files to suggest that Heiðar had had a sister.

'Yes, I'm quite sure. What was her name again? Anna, or … or Ína.' Magnús furrowed his brow as he searched his memory, then a light seemed to come on. 'Íris. That's right, her name was Íris. A clever girl – artistic too. She painted a beautiful picture in one of the classes.'

'Do you have any information about her? You must have a record of the names somewhere.'

'I can check,' Magnús said. 'But I imagine it would be quicker to talk to her parents.'

Elma nodded. She would have thought so too. The trouble was, she had already spoken to Heiðar's parents, and they hadn't breathed a word about any daughter.

BEFORE
Andrea

Andrea agrees to the summer-house trip.

'My parents built it when I was a kid,' Thorgeir says, as they take the turning for Skorradalur. Through the thick forest of fir and birch they catch a glimpse of holiday cabins and, beyond that, the grey waters of the lake. 'It's one of the bigger cabins in the area but we rarely use it. Has your family got a summer house? … Andrea?'

Andrea tears her eyes away from the road ahead. 'What?'

'You seem a bit distracted today.' Thorgeir places a hand on her thigh and she covers it with her own hand. Holds it, feeling trapped.

'Do I?'

'Yes, you seem so lost in thought.'

'Oh, I slept badly.' It's no lie. She has barely slept a wink since the day she saw what was on the video.

'OK.' He pinches her thigh gently. 'I don't actually know anything about your family. Where are they from?'

Andrea opens her mouth and for a moment it feels as though no words are going to come out. Then she coughs and manages to say: 'We used to live in Reykjavík – in Grafarvogur – when I was younger. Dad worked for a car salesroom and Mum was a developmental therapist.'

'Oh, really?'

They turn onto a narrow gravel track that vanishes among the birches, and not long afterwards Thorgeir pulls up in a clearing. They both get out and Thorgeir opens the boot. The sky is overcast, the wind roaring ominously in the trees, and Andrea is acutely aware that they are alone here. The forest is so thick that no one can see or hear them. She senses that it's arrived – the moment that will change everything.

'It's been a while since I was last here,' Thorgeir remarks.

'Let me take my bag,' she offers, but Thorgeir won't hear of it and carries all their luggage to the cabin. Then puts it down and starts searching his pockets for the key. 'Aha, here it is,' he says, producing a single key, which he inserts in the lock.

Andrea walks inside the house, which turns out to be larger than expected and light, despite the heavy, dark furnishings; the rugs, curtains and woollen throws on the sofa.

Thorgeir throws open the window by the kitchen sink to let in some fresh air.

'This is great,' Andrea says. It's cold inside and she shoves her hands in her coat pockets. The hard shape of the phone in her inside pocket is a reassuring reminder of its presence. It gives her a faint sense of security.

But only very faint.

NOW

Monday 14 December

Elma had intended to go straight home but ended up staying on at the office after Magnús had left. She could hear her colleagues chatting out front but was in no mood to join them.

When she laid all the facts of the case on the table, so much seemed to fit. Heiðar had gone to Vatnaskógur, where he had fallen victim to an act of horrific violence that had led to his death.

As if that wasn't bad enough, it was almost certain that Heiðar had previously been the victim of violence, though it wasn't clear whether this had been at home or elsewhere. Sigrún and Kjartan might have moved to Akranes to take him out of a school where he had been bullied. Then again, their move might have been dictated by the need to avoid the eyes of nosy neighbours and interfering local authorities.

Whatever the truth, it appeared that on his last day at Vatnaskógur, Heiðar had been subjected to a brutal beating that had led to his death, but that the police, under Ottó's command, had hushed it up because Ottó's son and his friends had been involved.

As the gravity of the situation sank in, Elma felt increasingly daunted. What on earth would happen when this was exposed? How would Ottó react? She would have to proceed with extreme caution, avoiding any missteps. Cases like this were complicated, and it would be easy to antagonise the wrong people if the evidence she produced wasn't watertight. There must be absolutely no leaks from the station until she had got to the bottom of this. Her best bet would be to call Magnús back in to make a formal statement, but she suspected this would be easier said than done. He was obviously frightened of Ottó and, after her own experience that day, Elma didn't blame him.

It was pitch-dark outside and the streets were quiet as it was getting on for seven o'clock. Most people would be at home in the bosom of their families by now.

Elma wasn't ready to go home yet herself but she remained undecided about her next move.

She and Hörður had spent a lot of time and energy trying to work out who could have wanted to avenge Heiðar's death, and now at last they had an individual in their sights. Heiðar had had a sister. And although the most obvious course would be to go and see the parents to ask where she was, Elma wanted more time to prepare before her next meeting with them.

She stood there for a while, her mind racing, staring out of the window at the Christmas lights dancing crazily in the wind. December was her favourite month. She preferred the darkness to the remorseless light of summer. What did that say about her?

And then it occurred to her: there was one person who might be able to tell her about the brother and sister, Heiðar and Íris, and the sort of upbringing they had had. One person who seemed to have known most of the children in Akranes in those days.

❂

'I was just going out for a walk, but come round anyway,' Ásta said when Elma rang. 'I'll hang on for a few minutes.'

Elma had got the old school nurse's telephone number from her sister, Dagný, who'd been in the middle of her Christmas baking – something Elma hadn't even thought about doing herself.

The door opened the instant Elma parked in front of the house. Ásta was wearing a long, brown coat, a woollen hat and walking boots.

'Hello, Dagný's sister,' she said in piercing tones. 'Elma, isn't it? Oh, yes, I remember you all right.'

Ásta greeted Elma with a vigorous handshake. Her manner was much warmer and friendlier than Elma had remembered. As the school nurse, Ásta had been a strict and rather forbidding figure; a woman who could make children behave merely by the force of her personality. But now she seemed quite different, her hardness softened and mellowed by the passing years. Perhaps her stern manner at school had only ever been a front.

'Let's walk along the shore,' Ásta said, setting off so briskly that Elma was soon out of breath. She had been far from conscientious about taking exercise during her maternity leave, apart from gentle walks, leaning on the pram, and Akranes was a flat town with no steep hills to keep you fit.

'I was a school nurse for thirty years. Imagine that! I spent most of my working life in the job, though that had never been the plan.' Ásta wasn't even panting. 'Towards the end, I found myself dealing with the children of kids I'd examined when I first started work. That's two generations I weighed and measured and wrote reports about.'

'I gather you're employed as a midwife at the hospital these days?'

'Oh, yes, I felt it was time to try something new, but, to be honest, I rather regret it. I always did have one foot in the hospital, but now I find I miss the schools. Miss seeing the little brats in my clinic.' Ásta grinned. 'Like you, for example.'

'I don't suppose I made much of an impression.' Elma had been a shy, retiring child. As self-effacing as a grey cloud on a rainy day.

'Nothing wrong with that, is there?' Ásta paused to look both ways before crossing the road.

'No, I suppose not. At least I wasn't a troublemaker.'

'I haven't forgotten you, though. You were such a sharp little thing. Always so alert. Your eyes darting everywhere, watching everything, drinking it in like a sponge.'

'Yes, I expect you're right.' Elma laughed. 'Since you obviously remember us all so well, I wanted to ask you about a couple of other children you'd have seen.'

'Thorgeir?'

'Yes, him,' Elma said. 'And some others too. A pair of siblings: Íris and Heiðar.'

'Íris and Heiðar.' Ásta clicked her tongue. 'Yes, I remember them. Heiðar's the one who died, isn't he?'

Elma nodded.

'A very polite, well-behaved lad. His sister was more of a handful. She flatly refused to be weighed and got away with it because no one could be bothered to argue with her. Perhaps we felt sorry for her too because of her background, and, besides, she looked pretty fit and healthy.'

'Was there anything special about them that you noticed at the time?'

Ásta stopped. They had reached the sports hall, from which they could hear shouts and the thud of balls being kicked.

'Not that I can think of,' Ásta said. 'But I do remember that they were unusually close. It was always just the two of them – they didn't have much to do with the other kids. I don't know when I've ever seen such a loving relationship between a brother and sister.'

❁

Little Gígja waddled over to Hörður on unsteady legs the moment he came through the front door of his daughter, Katrín's, house. Gígja had celebrated her first birthday earlier that autumn but had been rather slow to learn to walk, much to her parents' concern.

Hörður wasn't worried. The little girl simply wasn't in any hurry.

As well as bearing her grandmother's name, Gígja seemed to have inherited her temperament. Serene, self-possessed, her face always split by a smile. She was a little bundle of joy, and greatly attached to her grandfather. Her first word had been 'Ganpa'. It had melted Hörður's heart, but then he was turning into a real softy with age.

'Snorri's busy with the barbecue. Have a seat. By the way, you're walking a bit oddly – are you limping?' Katrín was standing at the kitchen counter, chopping vegetables for a salad. The kitchen was brand-new, like the rest of the fittings in the house. They had torn everything out and done the whole place up when they moved in. Hörður's son-in-law, who was very good with his hands, had done most of the work himself.

Hörður merely grunted and sat down.

'Yes, you are. You're limping. What happened?'

'Oh, the bike.'

'Did you fall off on the ice? Dad! You need to get yourself checked out.'

'Yes, yes,' he replied with a dismissive gesture.

Katrín sighed. She knew how stubborn he could be. 'Want a beer?'

Hörður declined the beer, then belatedly asked: 'Hang on? Is Snorri barbecuing in the middle of winter?'

'Snorri barbecues in all weathers.'

'True.' Hörður took the ball Gígja was holding out to him and threw it carefully back to her. She failed to catch it but clapped her hands together and beamed, her tiny white teeth shining.

After supper, they settled down in the sitting room to watch the news over coffee. Gígja climbed onto her grandfather's lap and fell asleep in his arms.

❂

When Hörður got back in his car, he sat there for a while in the dark without moving. He couldn't stop himself comparing his life now with what might have been. Kept picturing how different this evening's supper would have been with Gígja at his side. How she would have adored her little namesake and filled the house with her affectionate laughter and cosy chatter.

His grief was so vast, the pain so bad that he wasn't sure he could bear it.

To distract himself, he unlocked his phone and saw that he had an unread email from the Reykjavík police. The economic-crimes team had been looking into RxB, the Swiss company behind the large bank transfer to Thorgeir's account, the ownership of which Hörður had assumed would remain opaque.

But it seemed their luck was in, because the trail hadn't been obfuscated by the usual smokescreens, such as layers of shell companies. On the contrary, the Swiss-registered business turned out to be Icelandic and its owners could be identified by the simple expedient of looking up their tax records. It dawned on Hörður that RxB must stand for Reynir and Bárður, the names of the original partners, not the current owner.

Hörður stared at the name of the latter with some incredulity. Of course, he'd suspected as much but he still found it hard to take in. A hundred million krónur. A dry-cleaning business and a Swiss bank account – both registered in Kristjana's name.

❁

Íris Kjartansdóttir was nowhere to be found. Elma had searched for her in all the places she could think of, but the woman remained as elusive as Andrea. Before Elma left the office that evening, she asked Kári to dig up anything he could on Íris and contact her the moment he had something to report.

All the information Elma had learnt that day swirled around in her head as she breastfed Adda then gently lowered her into her cot.

Íris and Andrea. Both had brothers who had been at Vatnaskógur together. The only difference was that one brother had been murdered, the other might conceivably have taken part in that murder.

Elma still had no idea how the two young women were involved in the case, whether they knew each other and where they were. Though, come to think of it, no one had yet confirmed that Andrea actually was who she said she was. All the police knew for certain at this stage was that no one had managed to contact her and the appeal in the media for information about her had yielded no results.

Elma and Sævar waited until Adda was asleep before having supper, to enjoy a little time together. Recently they had got used to eating as late as eight p.m., especially when Sævar made a special effort with the cooking, as he had this evening.

Lobster pasta with white wine, parsley and all kinds of other subtle flavours that Elma couldn't put a name to, which made her feel as though she were dining in a smart restaurant in Italy.

'I'd marry you just for your expertise in the kitchen,' Elma remarked, when she had finished. 'Seriously, I wouldn't care about anything else if I could eat like this every day for the rest of my life.'

Sævar smiled and got up to clear the table.

'Having said that, I'd probably end up bedbound, so huge I couldn't move, but that would be fine so long as you carried on feeding me. We could start a YouTube channel.'

'There's an idea,' Sævar said, switching on the dishwasher.

The kitchen was spotless, Sævar had clearly been busy with Adda, and he had almost finished unpacking the moving boxes as well. Elma had been so immersed in the case since she went back after her maternity leave that she had only come home to eat and sleep.

'You've put in such a lot of hard work,' she said. 'I feel guilty.'

'You've got enough on your plate,' Sævar replied, sitting down again.

He poured himself more wine, his gaze resting on the window. He seemed preoccupied. The lights were on in Kristjana's house but they couldn't see her moving about.

'Is everything OK?' Elma asked.

'Yeah, sure.' Sævar's smile didn't reach his eyes.

Come to think of it, he'd been behaving oddly ever since Elma got home and told him about the events of that day. What Ottó had said. And how he had mentioned Sævar by name. She still felt exhausted and angry when she thought back to their meeting. Saw the ex-inspector glowering at her from under his heavy brows, felt the wince-making grip on her arm. She'd heard enough stories about how implacable and cantankerous he could be but only now did she have personal experience of it.

'Let's hope this investigation will be over soon,' she said, unsure whether it was herself or Sævar she was trying to comfort.

This wasn't how she'd pictured their December. She'd been hoping they could settle into their new house and enjoy a quiet, uneventful Christmas. But here they were, in the middle of December already, and she felt as if she'd barely slept since returning to work.

❂

A pall seemed to hang over Akranes, despite the colourful lights and festive decorations flapping in the wind. Even late in the evening, the town was busy, yet all anyone could talk about was the two shocking deaths. Sævar had overheard the conversations when he went out to buy Elma a book for Christmas. People conversing in low voices, whispering, exchanging grave looks. The mood seemed sombre, but perhaps that was just Sævar's imagination.

He'd had to get out of the house after supper. He'd been incapable of keeping up a conversation and didn't want Elma to start asking questions. She always saw at once when something was wrong.

Since he couldn't shut out the memories, the only solution was to go into town and distract himself with shopping. By the time he got home, with any luck Elma would be asleep.

Sævar would never forget Ottó. The inspector had come to see him the morning after the accident in which Sævar's parents had been killed. They had taken a seat in the sitting room. No vicar – he had come later. Ottó had regarded Sævar from under those heavy, dark brows and things unsaid had hung in the air between them.

Yet neither had put them into words.

For the first few years afterwards, Sævar had been grateful that nothing was said, but with the passing of time, the burden had become ever heavier and harder to bear. Today, he wished he had come clean right from the beginning. It was too late now, though. He would just have to live with the crushing weight of it on his conscience.

There were facts about him that no one else knew, or at least no one now living. He loved his life here in Akranes. Not just because of Elma and Adda, though they were the most important part, but also because of his brother, who had always looked up to and trusted him.

And, of course, he had a reputation to protect. People didn't realise how vital that was until it had been lost. Once your honour had gone, there wasn't much left, as increasing numbers of people were learning after being put through the mincing machine of social media.

Sævar didn't kid himself that he would get off lightly if he was found out. There would be no route back into the police, that much was certain.

There were times when he wished he could unburden himself and tell the whole story, but he knew there was too much at stake. The world would collapse around his ears if the truth emerged, and he wasn't prepared to lose Elma or Adda. Wasn't prepared to meet the eyes of the brother who had trusted him.

But now he would have to brace himself for the fact that it could happen. Because he had immediately understood the threat Ottó had issued to Elma. Knew that it was directed at him.

BEFORE
Andrea

'Does it get any better than this?' Thorgeir asks, sniffing his wineglass appreciatively.

Andrea takes a mouthful of wine without tasting anything. Then another. She's nervous and he has noticed; he keeps asking if everything's all right and what's bothering her.

I'm better than this, she thinks to herself. She's hardly ever been this nervous before. The video keeps preying on her mind. The boy's voice on the verge of tears: 'Please. Don't.' The hoarse breathing, becoming more laboured every moment.

But the laughter was the worst. That hateful laughter and the voice telling the boy to be quiet. To shut his gob.

It was horrible to hear people react with laughter when someone was begging for mercy. To witness another person's desperation and not be able to do anything to help. To see others standing by and doing nothing.

'I've filled the hot tub,' Thorgeir says, breaking into her thoughts. 'It should be ready in about half an hour.'

'Great.' Andrea looks at him, trying to smile.

Her feelings are in turmoil because, in spite of everything, she has allowed herself to forget with Thorgeir. Some part of her has enjoyed being with him. As if her body, heart and head weren't on the same wavelength, didn't belong to the same person. Part of her was drawn to him, and she has let herself forget her purpose and the past.

The trouble is that when she looks at Thorgeir now, she doesn't see the boy in the video. She doesn't even see the boy she has brooded about for years with thoughts of vengeance. She just sees Thorgeir. The man who would do anything for her; the man who is gentle and kind and loves her.

At one time she had set out to prove to her father that she'd been right about Máni. Prove to the world that her brother wasn't a monster. Now it all sounds so childish. The world isn't like a film in which justice wins out in the end. There's no such thing as someone getting their just deserts. The very idea of justice is relative.

Everything is so horribly complicated, and her thoughts and emotions are in a tangled mess.

Andrea drinks more red wine, they chat, they get into the hot tub, and everything is just like normal. She asks herself what she's doing. Why doesn't she just leave? She's already got the answers she was after. What more does she want? A plea for forgiveness? A confession?

Andrea had always looked up to her big brother. Because of the age difference, Máni had been both brother and father figure to her. When the rumours had started circulating about him being involved in that boy's death, when their home had turned into a minefield, she had been the only one to believe in his innocence.

Yet it seemed she had been wrong.

Máni had been guilty, though not to the same degree as Thorgeir. Máni had stood by while Thorgeir killed the boy. Both were crimes.

Andrea doesn't know what happened after the video ended, but she does know that the boy's death was ruled to have been an accident. Not that this did anything to stop the rumours circulating about Máni. His friends stopped talking to him, people shunned him at school, and in the end he dropped out of education.

And at home. At home everything changed.

Even supposing she could persuade Thorgeir to talk now, to tell her what happened, it wouldn't change anything. Wouldn't undo her childhood. Máni wouldn't come back to life. All it meant was that she would be alone again.

Alone again. As if she hasn't been alone all along.

They get into bed but Andrea doesn't try to get Thorgeir to talk.

He says he loves her and while they are kissing, tears trickle from her eyes into the pillow, where no one can see them. They've both drunk too much and in the end he falls asleep. Andrea lies there for a while without moving.

The thought of exposing Thorgeir, of showing him the video and extracting a confession, no longer gives her any pleasure. For the first time in years she feels at peace. As if the fire inside her has burned out.

Andrea must have dropped off but when she opens her eyes it doesn't feel as if any time has passed. She turns onto her side, gazing at Thorgeir in the gloom and smiling to herself. Perhaps, just perhaps, everything will be all right. Something must have woken her, she thinks, though she can't immediately work out what it was. Then she hears the floorboards creak in the hall and, getting up cautiously, she tiptoes out of the room. She sees at once that something is wrong. The living room is cold and there's an icy draught blowing, as if a window or door is wide open. Then, in the moonlight from the windows, she sees a dark figure standing in the hall.

'You, here … Why are you here?' Andrea whispers, snatching a nervous glance over her shoulder. Thorgeir is asleep. She hopes he won't wake up.

'Where is he?'

'Asleep. But—'

'Which room?'

'What are you doing? This isn't what we agreed. How did you know where I was?'

'Change of plan.'

Andrea watches as the figure heads straight for the bedroom, where Thorgeir is lying on his back, his head turned away from the door, breathing deeply. After a moment, she follows.

'You did a good job,' the figure adds. Andrea shudders at the smile that follows this praise. The other person is no longer whispering. Thorgeir stirs and only then does Andrea spot the gleam of a knife.

NOW

Tuesday 15 December

Heiðar's mother, Sigrún, smiled when she saw Elma at the door. Yet Elma had the impression that she'd caught her at a bad moment. Maybe it was simply because Sigrún was still in her dressing gown though it was getting on for ten in the morning.

'Come in,' Sigrún said, nevertheless, and ushered her to take a seat in the small kitchen. 'I can make some coffee if you'd like.'

'No, thanks, this won't take a long,' Elma replied.

'Oh, right.' Sigrún tied her dressing gown cord more tightly. 'Do you want me to fetch Kjartan? He's upstairs, still asleep.'

'No, there's no need,' Elma said. She was keen to get straight to the point as she had no desire to linger. 'I didn't realise you had another child. A daughter.'

'It didn't come up.'

'Do you know where Íris is now?'

'No, we haven't seen her since she moved out, in 1997.'

'How old was she then?' Elma asked.

'Sixteen and perfectly capable of looking after herself.'

Elma didn't know how to react to this cold statement. Sigrún had seemed so affectionate when she talked about Heiðar.

'And you haven't heard from her since?' Elma asked. 'How come?'

'Íris wasn't our daughter,' Sigrún said quickly, then went on in a rather milder tone: 'Not in that sense, anyway. We adopted both her and Heiðar. I couldn't have children.'

'Were they brother and sister?'

'Yes, they were. Their mother was Kjartan's sister. She couldn't look after them. She was mentally ill.'

'How old were they when they came to you?' Elma asked.

'Íris was five and Heiðar six.'

'And you haven't heard from her for more than twenty years?'

'No, not a word. Except through the lawyers who informed us that Íris wanted the adoption revoked. We didn't put up any objections.'

'But she was your daughter for more than a decade,' Elma blurted out. 'It can't have been easy to break the bond like that. Something must have happened.'

Sigrún tightened her lips. 'After Heiðar died our family was broken. I suppose we weren't there for her in her grief.'

Elma couldn't believe that Sigrún and Kjartan would have let their daughter go that easily after losing their son. They must have wanted to hold on to the only child they had left. But it seemed they had effectively lost both children.

'We did our best,' Sigrún went on. It sounded like an excuse. 'Íris was just … She didn't want to stay with us after Heiðar died. She felt we weren't enough.'

'Are you saying she left you, her parents, and the only home she had, because she felt it wasn't enough?' Elma asked incredulously. 'Where did she go?'

Sigrún shrugged. 'I'm not sure.'

Elma watched as the woman shifted in her chair, her eyes evasive, as if she couldn't wait for this conversation to be over. Was she ashamed of having failed her daughter or was there something more behind her discomfort?

'So nothing happened; there weren't any run-ins?' Elma persevered. 'Íris simply decided to walk away and you haven't heard from her since? I'm having a bit of trouble understanding how that could happen, to be honest. I mean, she was your daughter.' It was hard not to sound accusatory.

Sigrún flinched as if she'd been struck. 'It's different when they're not your own children,' she said. 'I don't care what all the books and experts say. Sometimes you just get children that … don't suit you.'

Don't suit you. Elma was at a loss as to how to respond. She felt a profound sadness.

After a moment, she said: 'But she and Heiðar got on well, didn't they?'

'Oh, yes.'

'So the tensions were between you and your husband and Íris?'

'Not exactly tensions, more … a failure to connect.'

'A failure to connect?'

'I tried.' Sigrún clutched at the neck of her dressing gown, gripping it tightly. 'I tried to love her. God knows, I tried.'

Elma felt her stomach constricting at these words. Íris had been only five years old when she came to them, but even so she must have sensed that she wasn't wanted.

Sigrún stared down at her hands as she added: 'We both tried, but she wouldn't let us get close.'

Neither Heiðar nor Íris had been their biological offspring, but the couple had adopted them. Been their parents since they were young children. How could Sigrún have loved one of them but rejected the other like that?

'You don't happen to have a photo of her?'

'I don't have many pictures of Íris,' Sigrún said. 'But let me see if I can find one.'

When she returned, she was holding a photo that had clearly been taken during the same session as the picture Elma had seen earlier of Heiðar. Heiðar was probably about eight in the photo, Íris a year younger. Between them was a dog that reminded her of Birta, but black where she was gold.

'Here they are together.' Sigrún sighed.

'Is that a Labrador?' Elma asked. 'We've got one of those.'

'Yes, that's my Freyja,' Sigrún replied. 'She was hardly more than a puppy then but she died five years ago. She lived to sixteen, quite a ripe old age in dog years.'

'That is pretty good going for a Labrador.' Elma couldn't help noticing the happier note that entered Sigrún's voice when she spoke about the dog. She put the picture down. 'By the way, I finally managed to get hold of Heiðar's post-mortem report.'

'Oh?'

'He had injuries when he was found. Both old and new.' Elma watched Sigrún's expression closely, but the woman didn't show any signs of surprise.

Sigrún didn't seem to have anything to say in response, so Elma continued: 'Can you think how he could have come by the older injuries? It looked as if Heiðar had been subjected to violence over a long period.'

Sigrún stared unblinkingly at Elma. But Elma thought her eyes glistened as if wet. The silence between them was broken by a cough upstairs and they both glanced up at the ceiling.

'You need to go,' Sigrún whispered. Elma was about to protest but Sigrún rose to her feet, her face so determined that in the end Elma gave in.

❂

After the conversation with Sigrún, Elma sat in the car for a while without going anywhere. She needed time to calm down.

She'd started out feeling sorry for the couple but now she found it hard to pin down her feelings. What in God's name had they done to Heiðar, the son they had at least pretended to love after he'd died?

She was also struggling to understand how they could have permitted themselves to take that attitude towards their daughter. She was aware that adoption wasn't easy. It could take time to develop a connection with a child, especially if they weren't babies when they came to you. But she would still have expected parents to recognise the responsibility that an adoption brought with it. Children weren't commodities you could swap or return. You didn't get to choose their personalities. But you were still supposed to love them, unconditionally and without expectations. It wasn't a choice or a feeling that either developed or didn't; it was your duty.

Íris had lost her brother, probably the only person she regarded as family, and after that there had been nobody there for her.

Elma was filled with pity at the thought, yet at the same time she was aware that a traumatic experience like that might well have resulted in a broken person. A person who had every reason to want to take revenge on those who had ruined her life.

But why now? After all these years?

Elma couldn't begin to comprehend Sigrún and Kjartan's indifference to Íris's fate. If they had really let their daughter walk away when she was sixteen and taken no further interest in her, they weren't merely guilty of neglect; they were reprehensible human beings.

Perhaps Elma was judging them unnecessarily harshly, but the fact was she couldn't imagine abandoning her daughter like that, irrespective of the circumstances or what she had done.

There must have been some sort of crisis that provoked Íris into walking out and applying to reverse the adoption. No one would do something that drastic just because her parents 'weren't enough' or because a death in the family had resulted in a broken home.

Glimpsing a movement in the window of the house, Elma realised that Sigrún was probably watching her. She stared at the window for a few moments without seeing any sign of the woman, before eventually starting the car and driving away.

❁

Kristjana put three heaped spoonfuls in the coffee machine, one for herself, another for a guest and a third for the machine. That's how she had always made coffee, though she usually had to pour half of it away; visitors were a rare sight in her house.

She had woken up and finished the book she had started the day before. A book about a forbidden love affair between a detective and the wife of a murder victim. She'd got so hot under the collar while reading it that her cheeks were flushed and she was floating around in a dreamlike state, caught somewhere between imagination and reality.

She almost expected the good-looking detective to knock on her door.

Kristjana closed her eyes while the coffee was percolating, imagining herself as the young woman with the voluptuous breasts. And men getting hard merely from looking at her.

She had never been beautiful, but as a girl she had believed that she would become pretty when she was older, as long as she had the right clothes and accessories.

Talk about self-deception.

No amount of cosmetics could make her face pretty, no treatment could lift her limp hair. She was what she was, and her grandmother had never tired of telling her how lucky she was that Reynir had proposed to her.

'Charm is deceptive, and beauty is fleeting; but a woman who fears the Lord is to be praised – Proverbs,' she reminded herself.

The doorbell rang and Kristjana felt a flutter in her stomach when she saw the policeman outside. Hörður wasn't unattractive, and she knew he had lost his wife a little over a year ago. Was it just her or were his visits becoming unusually frequent?

Smiling to herself, she opened the door.

'Hello, Kristjana, could I have a word?'

'Of course.' Turning away, she patted her hair. She was still in her nightie but had wrapped a long cardigan around herself, belted at the waist.

'Can I offer you anything?' she asked. 'Coffee? Tea?'

'No, thank you. I won't keep you.'

'I see.' She sat down at the table and, seeing Hörður's eyes resting on her, frowning and devoid of any lust, she felt herself being dragged back to cold reality. To the world where her son was dead – murdered – and she was alone. Abandoned. Old and grey.

'It was your money,' Hörður said without preamble. 'You paid that money into Thorgeir's account, didn't you?'

'Me? No, I'm a poor woman, as you can see.' She waved her hand to indicate her humble home, where everything was the way it had always been. The sofa with the scuffed, brown leather covers where Reynir had slept more often than not when he got home late.

From which she had more than once cleaned up his vomit.

Admittedly, there was the television she had bought ten years ago. A fifteen-inch flatscreen, as far as she could remember, which Thorgeir had chosen with her. But the curtains with the blue rose pattern were old, and the pictures on the walls had been there so long that if anyone were to take them down, they'd leave pale rectangles on the yellowing paint. One of the pictures still had a crack in the glass from the time it had fallen off the wall during one of Reynir's violent rages.

'You're not a poor woman, are you?' Hörður was scrutinising her with an interest that she relished. 'You made a killing from the business you ran alone for years.'

Kristjana sat up a little straighter but didn't say a word.

'You were raking it in. You had a big turnover and the profits were sky high. That's why you were able to lend your son a cool hundred million to work on that program with his friend.'

'No, I—'

'We've traced the money to you, Kristjana. The company that transferred the money to Thorgeir's bank account is registered under your ID number.'

Kristjana was silent. She had been expecting this visit for many years but it had never materialised. As long as Ottó was police inspector she hadn't been too worried, as Guðrún had promised her that he would make sure no one suspected anything.

'That made me curious,' Hörður continued. 'So much so that I took a look at the dry-cleaning business's tax returns for the last few years and spotted the large turnover. Unbelievably large turnover, in fact. Tell me, how do you know Guðrún Matthíasdóttir?'

Kristjana smiled. 'Guðrún knew my husband. Or, rather, our husbands were friends.'

'I see. And she worked for you too, did she?'

'From time to time. When we needed someone to fill in.'

'I see, yes. I noticed that she was employed by you for a whole decade. Funny that, because I've asked around and nobody ever remembers seeing her there.'

'She didn't come in that often.'

'Yet she was on a good salary?'

Kristjana smiled again. The arrangement had been simple enough: just enter the numbers and put the cash in the till. Simple and lucrative. She'd been paid her share for the inconvenience and Guðrún her salary.

'Your husbands were good friends, you say?'

'Childhood friends.' Drinking buddies, she wanted to add. Whenever Bárður was on shore leave she knew there would be weeks when the climate in their home would be as unpredictable as the Akranes weather.

'But after he died, you managed the business entirely on your own?'

'I did, yes.' Kristjana felt the pride spreading through her body. It would have been so easy to give up. In the immediate aftermath of Reynir's death that's what Bárður had assumed she would do, but she had persuaded him that she could make it work. And it had worked, like a dream.

'And when you closed down the business some years ago, your financial situation was extraordinarily good,' Hörður went on. 'But you'll know all about that.'

Kristjana sipped her coffee. When Reynir originally started the business, she'd had no idea what he had in mind. He and Bárður were forever plotting and scheming, but Reynir never told her anything. She and Thorgeir were nothing but an irritation to him. She used to try to be as self-effacing as possible around him, especially when he was drinking. Not that she had really cared about herself, but

Thorgeir had been a sensitive boy. He'd found the punishments his father inflicted on him hard to bear.

After she had been silent for a while, Hörður tried again. 'You not only ran it yourself all those years but you were able to help out your son with a sizeable investment. To tell the truth, I'm impressed. It's quite something.'

The blood flooded into her cheeks. People always mistook her for stupid, but she had her wits about her. She had always known how to look after herself and, deep down, she was quite proud, in retrospect.

'I only did what was necessary.' Kristjana sipped her coffee again, without taking her eyes off Hörður. The look of grudging admiration he was giving her was so unlike what she was used to. As a rule, people regarded her dismissively, as unworthy of their respect.

Hörður smiled. 'Maybe I will accept that coffee after all.'

❂

Once he'd finished his coffee, Hörður said goodbye to Kristjana. While they were drinking it, he'd thought she had looked rather pleased with herself, as if delighted that he knew.

A strange woman. But hardly dangerous. Though he was fairly sure that the dry cleaner's had been a cover for some illicit goings-on.

Hörður had read about this kind of case. Businesses that practised money laundering often had employees on the payroll who never set foot on the premises. Generally these were the spouses of the people who were laundering the money. Hörður had also looked into Bárður's career. He had been captain of the Viðvík until 2003. Although Hörður didn't have any proof yet, he knew that it wasn't uncommon for illegal goods to be smuggled on boats like that: alcohol, drugs, steroids, medicines. Even meat or electrical goods. All of which would later be sold on the black market.

The question was what he should do about it. It was seventeen years since Bárður had retired from the trawler, and investigating the case so long after the event would be tricky.

The fact that Hörður's old boss, Ottó, was Bárður's brother-in-law, hadn't escaped him. Had Ottó been aware of their illegal activities?

Knowing Ottó, Hörður thought it wasn't unlikely.

❀

On the one hand, Elma had no solid evidence to link Íris to the murders and no idea where she was living. On the other, at least they had a possible motive for the killings now and a clear lead to suggest that they were related to those long-ago events at Vatnaskógur.

But it wasn't enough.

Various questions remained unanswered and there was still no sign of either Andrea or Íris. The wild idea had occurred to Elma that Íris and Andrea might be the same person. That would explain a lot. And yet, on second thoughts, it wouldn't stand up. Both Matthías and Hafdís had met Andrea with Thorgeir, and Matthías hadn't commented on the photo of her that had been circulated in the press – the one the police had got from Breki, Andrea's brother.

Elma massaged her temples as she tried to work out their next steps. What she really wanted to do now was revisit Andrea's flat in Reykjavík and see if she had overlooked anything.

She found the number of Andrea's flatmate, Freyja, and rang it. Freyja picked up immediately.

'I just wanted to know if you'd heard anything from Andrea,' Elma said.

'No, I'd call you at once if I did,' Freyja replied.

'Yes, of course.' Elma hesitated. 'Um, did she ever talk to you about someone called Íris?'

'Íris.' There was a brief silence at the other end while Freyja thought. 'No, I'm afraid not. Not that I can remember.'

Elma had known it was a long shot. She was about to ring off, but before she had a chance, Freyja spoke again.

'By the way,' she said. 'I haven't actually been at the flat since you came round. I found it so uncomfortable because of the murder and

… Oh, it's probably just me being stupid but I've always been afraid of the dark and hate living alone. I should probably have told you.'

'So, for all you know Andrea might have come home?'

'Yes. I haven't been there for the last few days. I'm staying with a friend.'

Elma thanked her and hung up. She felt overwhelmed with tiredness at the realisation that she would have to drive all the way to Reykjavík to check whether Andrea had been back to the flat. Whether anything had been touched. That meant she wouldn't be home until late this evening.

'OK, think logically,' she muttered to herself, and began leafing back through the files that lay scattered over her desk.

There were Begga's reports of her interviews with the kids who had attended Hafdís's last swimming lesson. She reread them, word for word, in the hope of spotting something she had missed.

One boy said he'd seen an old man outside the pool that evening. She pictured Kjartan, Heiðar's father, who was in his seventies. Elma tapped his name into the search engine and brought up a photo of him linked to a news item on a local site. She printed it out and noted down the boy's details.

Shortly afterwards she was standing outside a block of flats, hunting for the names of the boy's parents on the bells. A man's voice answered and buzzed Elma in. She reached the top floor, puffing a little and embarrassed by her own lack of fitness. Perhaps she should start going to CrossFit with her sister after all.

A young man, probably in his mid-twenties, was standing at one of the doors with a boy who looked too old to be his son.

'Sorry to bother you like this,' Elma said, trying not to pant too obviously.

'No problem,' said the man, who had a dishcloth over one shoulder. From inside the flat came a smell of freshly baked biscuits, and Elma's stomach rumbled. 'Would you like to come in or…?'

'No, thanks. I've just got one more question for Aron, if that's OK?' she said, smiling at the boy, whose black T-shirt was covered in flour.

'That's fine, isn't it, Aron?'

'Sure,' Aron said.

Elma held out the printout of the photo. 'The man you saw outside the swimming pool after your lesson on Saturday, could it have been him?'

Aron studied the picture for a while, then shook his head. 'No.'

'Absolutely sure?' the man asked.

'Yes, Dad, I'm sure,' Aron said. 'The man I saw had white hair.'

'This man has grey hair,' Elma pointed out.

'No, I mean white. Like, totally white – and short.'

'White and short.' Elma nodded. 'Did you notice anything else striking about this man? Was he tall or short? Thin or broad-shouldered?'

'He wasn't big or fat or anything.' Aron glanced at his father, who nodded in encouragement. 'But I didn't get a very good look. I only saw him from behind.'

'I see,' Elma said. 'Never mind. Thanks for the help, anyway, Aron. And, again, sorry to disturb.'

'No problem,' repeated the boy's father. 'Would you like a cookie to take away with you?'

'No, thanks, I…' Before Elma could decline the offer, Aron had darted back inside the flat. He returned almost immediately with a freshly baked, still-warm cookie, which he handed to Elma, who had no choice but to accept. She thanked them both profusely and was about to leave when she thought of something.

'One more thing, Aron,' she said. 'Are you sure it was a man? Could it have been a woman?'

'I don't know…' Aron hesitated. 'I didn't get a clear enough look at them but I suppose it could have been.'

Elma said goodbye to father and son. As she ate the sweet cookie she remembered that Sigrún had grey hair too. And her hair had been quite a bit whiter than Kjartan's.

❈

'Where are you?' Elma asked when Hörður answered his phone.

Hörður put the phone down on the passenger seat, sweat beading his forehead. As he had been walking along the pavement after visiting Kristjana, he had skidded on the ice, wrenching his hip, and now the pain was excruciating. Ten times worse.

'I've just been for a quick visit. I'll fill you in later.'

'Is everything all right?'

'Yes, fine.'

'OK.'

There was a long silence at the other end, broken by a smothered moan of pain from Hörður as he fastened his seatbelt.

'Look, I'm on my way to Reykjavík, to Andrea's flat. Do you want me to pick you up?'

Hörður would gladly have gone along if he could have faced moving. But the sweat was pouring off his face now and his eyes were watering.

'Oh?'

'Freyja, Andrea's flatmate, hasn't been home for the last few days and I wanted to check if Andrea had been there. Shall I come and collect you?'

'No, I…' Hörður sucked in air between his teeth, then coughed. 'I can't come right now.'

'Oh, right.' Another silence. 'Are you sure everything's OK?'

'Yes.' He'd have liked to do a better job of convincing her but the words wouldn't come.

He was relieved when Elma rang off and there was no longer any need to bite back his moans of pain. With an effort he pressed the accelerator and set off, not stopping until he came to a halt in front of the big white building that housed the West Iceland Health Centre.

Having made his way painfully into the hospital lobby he spoke to the woman on reception, who told him there were no free appointments just then.

'But I can see if a nurse could take a look at you,' she said, after studying him for a while. 'Wait a minute.'

Hörður waited. There was nothing else for it. All he wanted to do now was collapse on the floor and have himself carried in on a stretcher. Preferably with a shot of morphine on the way.

'Hörður.'

He recognised the voice and glanced up, but when he saw who had addressed him, he wished the floor would swallow him whole.

'Fríða. Hello.'

'Are you … How are you doing?' Fríða was wearing a light-coloured shirt and trousers made of some soft white fabric. She didn't appear to be ill, yet it was the second time Hörður had bumped into her here at the hospital.

'Oh, just a bit of bother with my hip.'

'As a result of your fall?'

'Well…'

'Have you got an appointment?'

'No, but she was going to check if anything could be done.' Hörður jerked his head towards reception, where the woman was talking on the phone.

'Listen,' Fríða said. 'Just come with me. I'll take a look at it.'

'You? But what … why?'

'Hörður, I'm…' Fríða frowned. 'I assumed you knew I was a doctor. I work here at the hospital. I've actually finished my shift for today, but that doesn't matter. There's nowhere I have to be.'

Hörður raised his eyebrows. He'd had no idea she was a doctor.

'Oh, right, if it wouldn't be a nuisance.'

'Not at all.' Fríða smiled, said something to the woman on reception and beckoned him to follow her.

Hörður hobbled along in her wake.

⊗

The gale buffeted the car, making it judder, as Elma drove around the Kjalarnes peninsula. To her right the sea was an angry grey, flecked with white. If things had worked out differently and there had been less to do, she would have enjoyed being at home right now, cuddled up under the covers with Sævar and Adda.

Instead she was here, fighting to keep the car on the road as she headed into Reykjavík on a journey that was bound to be a waste of time.

Elma let her mind wander as the snowy slopes of Mount Esja gave way to the lower, volcanic hills on the approach to Reykjavík, picturing the people involved in the case one after the other: Andrea, Sigrún, Kjartan and Matthías. And Íris, wherever she might be.

Like last time, there were no free parking spaces to be had in front of the block of flats, which meant Elma had a bit of a walk from the car to the front door. This wouldn't have been a problem in mild, sunny weather, but now, beating against the wind, it was like a marathon. At the door, her fingers were so numb that she dropped the set of keys Freyja had left at the Reykjavík police station for her and only managed to open it at the second attempt.

Once she reached the top floor, she used the second key to open the door to Andrea and Freyja's flat. It yielded with a low squeak, and Elma stepped in warily, as if not wanting to be heard. Of course, it was possible that Andrea was in there, so perhaps she should have knocked first.

A shiver ran down Elma's spine. She was unarmed, and alone.

'Hello,' she called. At that moment the automatic light on the landing went out and she was plunged into darkness, hardly able to see a thing as she groped for a light switch. The creaking of the building in the wind sent her heartbeat racing, and it didn't slow until she found the switch.

A yellowish glow lit up the flat. There didn't seem to be anyone home, and the silence was broken only by the muffled roar of traffic outside, which sounded like the sea.

Elma took a deep breath and, as a precaution, sent Sævar a text to tell him where she was.

She began by opening the doors to the rooms one after another, to reassure herself that she was truly alone. When the two bedrooms and single bathroom turned out to be empty, she breathed easier, though she wasn't satisfied as she'd been half hoping to find Andrea here. She wondered what to do next, not even sure what she was hoping to find. Some clue about where Andrea might be hiding, perhaps, or some indication that she had visited the flat at some point in the last few days. It occurred to her that there was no sign of the cat. Its food bowl was empty and its litter tray appeared unused. Freyja must have taken it with her to her friend's.

Elma went into Andrea's room first but found little of interest there. She'd examined it before and nothing appeared to have changed in the interim. There was no obvious sign that anything had been touched.

Freyja's room was on the other side of the hall and proved to be both smaller and very different from Andrea's. It was painted white and there were almost no personal belongings on display. No more than a few books and a wardrobe containing a strangely small number of garments. Freyja had apparently taken most of her stuff with her to her friend's place.

Elma came back out and went into the kitchen. She opened the fridge, only to close it immediately when she was met by an unpleasant odour of rotting food. No one had been here since Friday at least. Apart from that the kitchen was tidy; no cups or plates left out, and the surfaces were clean.

But there was something on the kitchen table, left there as if for her. A tape, she saw as she got closer. A small cassette. She picked it up and examined it, unsure for a moment or two what it was. Then she remembered having seen similar tapes long ago. This one was unlabelled, but it looked as though it came from an old video camera, of the kind Elma's family used to own when she was a child.

Wednesday 16 December

'I'll see what I can do,' Hafþór said, taking the cassette from her. 'I haven't seen a tape like this since before the millennium.'

Hafþór had started work at the police station while Elma was on leave so she didn't know him that well. He had come from the IT sector and now assisted the police with the kind of technical matters they had previously had to refer to Reykjavík.

'Yes, I expect it dates back to the nineties,' Elma said.

'Do you want it on a USB stick?'

'That would be great.'

'I'll bring it round to your office once I'm done.'

Elma sat down at her desk, and waited impatiently to see what was on the cassette. It had been left on the otherwise bare kitchen table where it couldn't be missed. All Elma could think was that Andrea must have slipped back to the flat in Freyja's absence and put it there for the police to find. Elma had got back from Reykjavík so late yesterday evening that she had decided to wait until this morning before trying to access the contents. She had come into the office at the crack of dawn, and luckily it seemed Hafþór was an early riser too as he had answered his phone almost immediately.

If this was the tape from Heiðar's video camera, it would probably only contain his attempts to make short films, as described by Máni in his diary. Not that interesting in itself and yet … they had been Heiðar's last days alive. Perhaps something of significance would emerge.

Of the kids Máni had written about in his diary, three were now dead, including Máni himself. Elma opened the report on his death and skimmed the text. Once again it occurred to her that clues had been left at the scenes of Thorgeir and Hafdís's murders that almost certainly pointed to the motive for the crimes.

With this in mind she clicked on the photos that had been taken at the scene of Máni's death and peered at the background. She tried to see if there were any words or numbers written on the wall but couldn't spot anything. Máni was lying back in the middle of the sofa, the coffee table in front of him with a collection of items like a still life she'd seen so often before: a card, a rolled-up banknote and traces of white powder.

Judging from the photos, Máni's flat had been unusually clean in comparison to others Elma had seen. The sofa didn't look grubby and it was flanked by side tables with ornaments on them. On the left-hand side was a dove made of glass, like the one she thought she remembered her mother owning, and, on the right, a statuette of a horse.

Strange, now that she stopped to think about it. From what she could see in these photos there were no other ornaments in the flat; nothing on the shelves but books. Máni was sitting in the middle of the sofa too, where the cushions met. Who would choose to sit precisely on the join like that?

His arms were spread out almost like the statue of Christ on the altar in the chapel at Vatnaskógur, which showed Jesus holding out his arms, as if inviting the children to come to him.

Elma unlocked her phone and looked through the photos she had taken during her visit to Vatnaskógur with Sævar. There was the chapel and the altar. In the middle, the white statue of Christ. When she peered more closely, she saw that on either side of Jesus were two pictures engraved in the wall panelling above the quotations from the psalm.

On the right was a horse and, on the left, a dove in flight.

❖

The pathologist picked up at the first ring.

'Máni Friðriksson?' he said, once she had explained why she was calling. 'Hang on, I'll see if I can find it in my records.'

'I just wanted to check what method he'd used to take the drug,' Elma explained.

After a brief silence at the other end, she heard the pathologist clear his throat. 'Ah, yes, that's right. I wrote here in the report that traces of the drug had been found in his airways and throat.'

'Meaning what? That he inhaled it?'

'I considered the question of how he'd taken the substance at the time. There are examples abroad of people overdosing via their nose, by the use of nasal sprays, as you may be aware.'

'Like the kind you use to clear a blocked nose?'

'Exactly. That way, the drug is transported quickly and efficiently into the bloodstream.'

'Are there any examples of this happening in Iceland?'

'I haven't personally seen a death from that cause yet, but no doubt it happens. You should know that better than me.'

'How long would it take the drug to work if it had been administered using a nasal spray?'

'In a large quantity? A few seconds until the subject lost consciousness, and a couple of minutes until he suffered respiratory failure.'

Elma thanked him and hung up. No nasal spray had been found at the scene, nor had any traces of Fentanyl. And there was no chance Máni could have disposed of the drug before he died. A few seconds wouldn't have given him time. If he'd taken the drug of his own free will, the packaging should have been lying beside him, or at least somewhere in the flat.

It was looking increasingly likely that the killer's first victim had been not Thorgeir, but Máni.

There was a knock at the door and Hafþór appeared.

'Here you go,' he said, handing Elma a USB stick.

❋

At first the screen was black. Then a line appeared, followed by a picture. Feet on a wooden floor. The sound of laughter. A door was reached. Beside the door was a number. Room four.

Inside lay Heiðar, the boy in room four, sound asleep, completely unsuspecting about what was about to happen.

The recording ended in the chapel. The last frame was tipped at an angle, but showed the boy lying on the floor, apparently unable to move.

'So the main perpetrators were Thorgeir and Hafdís,' Elma told Hörður, who was sitting beside her.

When Hörður had got back to the office after seeing the doctor the previous day, he'd announced, almost with pride, that he had fractured his pelvis, and he was now using a crutch and dosed up on strong painkillers. To Elma's relief, his temper seemed to have improved after getting his diagnosis. Or perhaps the painkillers were responsible for this positive side effect.

'And you believe that Máni was the first victim?'

'Naturally, I don't have any proof, but there are various details that point that way. And, if we work on that assumption, Máni would probably be as guilty as the rest of them in the murderer's eyes. He was Heiðar's friend. The one who should have come to his aid but betrayed him.'

'But who filmed it? And why?'

'I don't know. Matthías, I'd guess. But … maybe it was never intended to end like that,' Elma said. 'Never intended to go that far.'

Elma had spent a long time trying in vain to understand how a bunch of teenagers could have banded together to commit such an unspeakably brutal deed. Her conclusion was that they probably hadn't. It was an incident that had got out of hand; one had started it and the rest had followed suit. The video ended just as the beating had begun in earnest, as if the person holding the camera had belatedly woken up to what was happening.

While waiting for Hafþór to convert the tape, Elma had dived into a deep, dark world online, reading article after article describing murders committed by teenagers. In the US, initiation ceremonies into university fraternities could be so extreme that every now and then the victims died, either from being forced to consume vast quantities of alcohol and drugs or from the violence they were subjected to.

There had been a similar incident in Belgium two years previously in which a student had died after being made to drink an excessive amount of alcohol, then left to stand outside in freezing temperatures.

'No, I find it unlikely it was premeditated,' Hörður said. 'And his sister was there too. Do you think she could have witnessed something?'

'Possibly,' Elma said. 'Or perhaps seen the video later.'

'Then why didn't she tell anyone?'

Elma shrugged. That was impossible to answer. Perhaps the girl had been scared or perhaps she hadn't seen anything. Besides, what hope would a teenage girl have had against a policeman like Ottó? Especially bearing in mind that she lived with adoptive parents who treated her badly, and the only person she loved was dead.

'She must at least have seen the video tape. Perhaps she's been sitting on it all these years,' Elma said. 'But I find it more likely that she got hold of it recently. That the kids who killed Heiðar stole his camera and she only recently got her hands on the tape.'

'So, in other words, one of them must have kept it.'

'Yes, that's my guess.'

As far as Elma was concerned, the details of the case were coming into focus, but at the same time every fresh discovery raised new questions. The fact was that three of the people in the video were dead: Máni, Thorgeir and Hafdís. Four, if you included Heiðar.

The most urgent step was obvious: Elma would have to see to it that Matthías was given police protection because, if the murders really were connected to this incident and the killer was avenging

Heiðar's death, Elma suspected that Matthías would be next on the hit list.

After all, there was no one else left.

❁

The last few days had passed like a nightmare. Matthías had been walking around in a daze, unable to tell what was real and what was in his mind. He found some consolation now, though, in the bright gaze of the horses standing peacefully in their stalls. He sat down on a stool in front of them, shivering a little, and zipped his down jacket up to the neck. Despite the warm smells of horse and hay, it was chilly in the stables.

His feelings were in turmoil, torn between conflicting emotions. He'd known Hafdís for most of his life. How well he remembered the first day he saw her; everyone excited that a new girl was joining their class; the silence in which you could have heard a pin drop when she walked in and smiled, not shyly as you might have expected, but as if she were surveying her new domain. A new territory she was about to occupy.

He had been smitten then and there. Fallen head over heels. Couldn't think about anything but her.

No doubt that was why he had been blind to Hafdís's faults for so long. Her quick temper, her tendency to make impetuous decisions based on malice. Or perhaps on a carefully concealed insecurity.

The realisation had first hit Matthías at Vatnaskógur, but he'd ignored it. Besides, he'd been mixed up in the business himself. Hadn't he stood by and done nothing? Just watched as if paralysed. For years he had convinced himself that it had been an accident. A practical joke that had gone too far.

He had absolved himself of responsibility, and Hafdís too.

Matthías was far from perfect. He talked a lot of hot air and had big plans but seldom had the guts to put any of them into practice. When it came down to it, he had to face the fact that he was a coward.

As soon as he was confronted by anything difficult, he closed his eyes, like a small child that doesn't want to see anything bad.

His mind had been churning away relentlessly for the last few days and he longed for some respite, a moment when he wasn't being suffocated, drowned by his thoughts. But it was hard. It was all such a confused, incomprehensible mess, and his feelings were so snarled up that he couldn't unravel them.

How was it possible to love Hafdís and grieve for her, while simultaneously being repelled by aspects of her character? Love was such a complex phenomenon. He and Ólöf had a long and difficult period of recuperation in front of them before they eventually got a grip on their lives and their feelings again.

Matthías stood up and, fetching an armful of hay from the heap at the other end of the stable, put a generous helping in every manger.

The wind was roaring so loudly that the building protested. Yet in spite of the noise his ears caught the sound of a vehicle pulling up on the gravel outside and parking in the space on the other side of the wall. When he heard a car door slam, he was quite sure: there was somebody there. He sent up a fervent prayer that it was the owner of one of the other stables in the area and not his father.

❂

Elma drove up to Matthías's house and was relieved to see a light in the window and a car in the drive. She and Hörður, who had stayed in the car while she went to the door, because of his hip, had decided to explain to Matthías that they were going to have to put a temporary watch on his home until the killer was caught.

'Where's your father?' Elma asked when Ólöf opened the door. 'We tried to call but we couldn't get hold of him.'

'He went over to the stables,' Ólöf said. 'Is everything OK?'

'Yes,' Elma said, forcing herself to smile. 'Yes, we just need to talk to him. Do you know how he got there, because his car…?'

'Oh, yes. He must have gone on his bike. He sometimes cycles if he's planning to have a—' Ólöf broke off but Elma could have finished the sentence herself.

'I see,' she said.

'Actually, he left quite a long time ago and he's not answering his phone…'

'Oh, really?' Elma said. 'Look, I'm sure everything's fine, but I'll pop over there myself and let you know as soon as I find him.'

Ólöf nodded and closed the door. Elma decided to ring the station and ask them to send officers to guard the house anyway. She didn't want to take any risks.

'He's not home,' Elma told Hörður as she got back in the car, adding that he was probably at the stables out at Æðaroddi.

On their way there Elma tried Matthías's phone again but no one answered. When her own phone started ringing shortly afterwards, she expected to see his number appear but instead her colleague Kári's name flashed up on screen.

'I've been looking up Íris Kjartansdóttir, like you asked,' he began.

'Yes, and have you found anything?'

'Not much,' Kári replied. 'But I contacted the tax office and got a copy of her tax return. I'm looking at it now and see that she bought a house last year.'

'Where?'

'Here,' Kári said. 'In Akranes.'

'Are you serious?' Elma found it unbelievable that Íris should turn out to be in Akranes after everything that had happened. She couldn't have been living here for long without bumping into her adoptive parents. Unless she'd radically altered her appearance. 'Could you check out the house?'

Elma would have liked to go herself but it was more urgent to ensure Matthías's safety first. Kári agreed to check if Íris was home while Elma and Hörður drove out of town, making for the stables at Æðaroddi. The wind that buffeted and tore at the car on the way had scoured most of the snow from the ground, revealing withered grass between the patches of white. As they drew closer to the stable complex, they could see the rough, dark sea beyond it and somewhere the sun was setting, though the clouds were doing their best to block its blood-red rays.

❁

Kári parked in the street outside the house at the end of Vesturgata, not far from the cinema. The area was given over to factory premises and the buildings were more spread out than those further up the street. The perfect location, in fact, if you wanted to keep secrets from your neighbours. The house stood alone, with grassy fields on either side.

Next to it was a parking area containing a few vehicles, though it was impossible to tell whether any of them belonged to the occupant of the house. Or if there was anybody home.

There certainly didn't appear to be, though Kári couldn't immediately tell if the lights were on as the setting sun was reflected in the windows.

'There's nobody here,' said Begga, who had accompanied him.

'Don't be so sure.'

Kári knocked on the door. While they waited the silence was absolute. He tried the doorhandle but it was locked. Of course.

'We'll have to get inside,' Begga said. 'This is no time to worry about a warrant. It could be a matter of life or death.'

Kári scanned the building, considering the problem. Then he descended the steps again and picked up the largest stone he could find in the gravel by the car park.

The pane of glass in the front door broke easily and he reached gingerly through to undo the latch.

Inside, the place was sparsely furnished and didn't look as if it had seen any upkeep for decades. There was linoleum on the floor and the walls smelt of mildew, yet the air was thick with the odour of cooking, as if someone had recently been preparing a meal.

'I'm going upstairs,' Begga said, not even bothering to check out the rest of the ground floor.

Kári took a quick glance around. There was a kitchen and sitting room on this level but no bedrooms. As all was quiet, he assumed there was nobody else there and followed Begga upstairs.

'Here.' Her voice carried from one of the rooms.

Kári entered a bedroom containing nothing but a bed with a small table beside it and thick curtains over the windows. It took him a moment before his eyes adjusted to the gloom and he could make out the figure of the girl lying in the bed.

There she was, covered by a duvet, her skin so white she almost blended in with the sheets. The only thing that stood out was the flood of long, reddish hair on the pillow.

'Is she breathing?' he asked.

Begga bent down and for a moment or two there was a deathly hush.

❂

After feeding the horses, Matthías had taken a seat in the little coffee room that led off the stable area and opened a beer. His conscience was gnawing at him, aware that Ólöf was alone at home, but he just had to have a break. Just a brief moment to himself. Two more beers, then he would cycle home again. He closed his eyes and listened to the building. The wind stole in through the chinks in the planking, making the wood creak and rattle. There was something curiously soothing about the sounds.

He sat bolt upright when he heard the door of the stable opening. Unsure, he strained his ears and thought the horses seemed unusually restless, moving about in their stalls and snorting. Wild weather like this sometimes got to them.

'Hello,' he called into the corridor. Could it be his father? The old man often came here to tend to the horses, though that was mostly Matthías's job.

No one answered. No, it couldn't be his father. Thank God. He couldn't face meeting him just now.

Inspector Ottó.

That's how people always talked about him. His former title always preceding his name to leave it in no doubt who they were referring to.

Matthías had both feared and admired his father in his youth. His home life had been governed by the old man's moods and whims, and sometimes Matthías had scarcely dared to breathe.

Yet his father only wanted what was best for him. That's what he always said afterwards, when he explained why he had reacted the way he had to his son's words or deeds.

I only want to make a man of you. You need to toughen up.

Matthías had never been tough, though he pretended to be when his father was watching, but he knew his dad saw through him. Saw what a coward he was. Just like the day he had come home from Vatnaskógur, broken down in tears and confessed to his father what had happened.

It was never supposed to end like that, he had gasped through his sobs. *Never supposed to go that far.*

VATNASKÓGUR 1995

If Matthías could have had his way, the stay in Vatnaskógur would have lasted much longer. A whole month, the entire summer even. He was sixteen now but that didn't make any difference. He felt at home there and the thought that this was possibly his last year filled him with sadness. He wasn't ready to say goodbye to Vatnaskógur and had even thought of applying to be a leader next summer.

There was something about the tranquillity here. The surrounding forest, the lake and mountains. No one expected anything of him and there was nothing to worry about. No one to fear.

'What are you thinking about?' Hafdís asked.

They were sitting in the canteen, having just finished the homemade pizza that was the traditional meal on their last day.

'What?' Matthías asked absent-mindedly.

'You seem so thoughtful,' Hafdís said.

'Aren't I allowed to think?'

'Well, if you like, but I'm not sure it'll achieve much.'

'Ha ha.'

Hafdís grinned and stuck the tip of her tongue between her front teeth. Matthías felt as if someone was stroking his insides with a feather.

The friendly banter between them had intensified every day in Vatnaskógur. In fact, that entire year at school had been characterised by glances and gossip about them. Earlier that summer they had kissed at a party, but there'd been nothing more since then. Now, though, there was definitely something in the air.

'Hey.' Hafdís leant closer to him, lowering her voice. 'Come with me a minute.'

They left the canteen. It had been raining while they ate and there was a fresh smell of greenery outside. Matthías accompanied Hafdís up the path past the boathouse and over the bridge in the direction of the chapel. Before they got there, Hafdís took his hand and led him off the path, in among the trees until they were more or less out of sight of any passers-by.

'We've got something planned for this evening,' she said.

'What?' Matthías was so short of breath he could hardly think straight.

'We're going to sneak out. Hold a little party.' She stepped closer, gazing up at him. Her hair was curling in the damp air. All around them, birds were singing.

'I'm in,' Matthías whispered, holding his breath and leaning towards her until their lips met and he felt as if he were floating on air.

❁

That evening Matthías lay fully dressed under his duvet, staring at the ceiling in the grey light of the late-summer night. Thorgeir was in the bunk underneath him, and Máni and Heiðar in the bunks opposite. The rooms in Laufskáli were small, only four beds in each, which was one of the reasons why they had wanted to sleep there. There were far more bunks per room in the Old Hut, making it impossible to move without being overheard by the leaders next door. Admittedly, the walls were thin in Laufskáli too, as they were in all the huts that had been erected to plug a temporary accommodation gap but which were getting pretty dilapidated nowadays. According to Hafdís, though, it should be possible to climb out of the window without anyone hearing them.

Outside the birdsong had fallen silent and shortly afterwards it started to rain again. The drops pattered on the glass in time to the rapid pattering of Matthías's heart.

'He's asleep,' Thorgeir whispered.

'Are you sure?' Matthías wasn't convinced this was a good idea.

He'd only recently got to know Heiðar better and thought he was all right. When he first joined their class he had come across as shy and retiring, but over the last week Matthías had discovered that he was not only extremely bright but inventive too. He had a serious interest in film-making and knew all about cameras, angles and special effects. In fact, he was a mine of information about the industry, familiar with all the Hollywood directors and others besides.

'I'm sure.'

Thorgeir was the only one who hadn't taken part in the film they made. He kept finding fault with Heiðar and trying to provoke him, though he pretended it was all a joke, always treading on his toes or jabbing an elbow into him. Matthías, who'd known Thorgeir since they were kids, was aware that he was simmering with an inner anger that sometimes erupted into rage, like a pot boiling over.

'So, what's the plan?' Matthías asked, turning over on his side. He saw that Thorgeir was fully dressed too.

'Didn't Hafdís talk to you?'

'Yes, she did.'

Matthías resented the fact that Thorgeir and Hafdís had planned this together. They were always going off, just the two of them, and Thorgeir talked about her nonstop. Started all his sentences with 'Me and Hafdís', like they were an item.

'Guys.' Máni was sitting up in his bunk against the opposite wall. 'We're just going to carry him outside, aren't we? That's all?'

'Yes, of course. Chill out, we're only having a laugh,' Thorgeir whispered back. 'A little initiation ceremony.'

'Initiation into what? It's not like we've got a secret society anymore like when we were twelve.'

Matthías sensed in the silence that greeted Máni's remark that Thorgeir was offended. He always made out like they were a gang and sulked if they hung out with anyone else.

Since Thorgeir's dad had died the year before, he'd become even more fixated on the idea. He was always saying they had to stick together, that they were brothers. Matthías played along because he felt sorry for Thorgeir, who now lived alone with his weirdo of a mother. And perhaps because he understood him too. Because Matthías himself lived with a father he feared.

He could see that underneath his bravado Thorgeir was a sensitive soul. He'd never had many friends at school, and some people even dared to call him a porker to his face. The more cowardly called him a porker behind his back. The nickname no doubt referred to his appearance, his big head and snub nose. He was big all over. Tall, with large feet and thick fingers.

'I know we're not a secret society,' Thorgeir whispered back, stung. 'You never want to do anything fun.'

'Fun? I just don't want—'

Before Máni could say any more there was a light tap on the window. A glimpse of dark, curly hair and brown eyes. Hafdís.

'Here you go,' Thorgeir said in a low voice, handing Máni a bottle that Matthías hadn't noticed he'd been hiding in his bed. 'We're brothers, aren't we?'

Máni didn't answer but took a swig from the bottle.

Meanwhile, Matthías opened the window so Hafdís could crawl inside. It was a bit of a scramble and she had to lean on him, not that he had any problem with that. Far from it.

'Ready?' she whispered, once she was finally inside. The rain had tousled her hair and there was a drip hanging from the end of her nose that he yearned to wipe away.

He nodded.

'Right. We're going to have a quick drink,' Thorgeir said. 'And take his video,' he added, positioning himself beside Hafdís.

'His camera?' Matthías asked.

'Yes, the video. He wanted to make a film, didn't he? Well, this is going to be awesome material.'

Matthías picked up the camera and took a minute or two to locate the on button. Raising it to his face, he peered at the small screen, trying to remember what Heiðar had said about angles and brightness.

Tomorrow they would watch it and laugh. Next week they would make a longer film. Matthías already had several ideas. Maybe Hafdís could be persuaded to act in it too. He moved the camera and saw her face appear in the frame.

She smiled and he knew that the smile was intended solely for him.

'Start outside the door and come in,' Thorgeir whispered. 'It'll be cooler like that.'

'Who's developed an interest in film all of a sudden?' Máni asked mockingly.

'Shut up.' Red blotches appeared on Thorgeir's cheeks and his eyes were unusually dark. They always got like that when Thorgeir drank. The three of them – Máni, Thorgeir and Matthías – had taken up boozing that summer, though Matthías had limited himself to the odd swig since he knew that if his father caught so much as a whiff of alcohol from him, he was in deep shit. A sudden sense of trepidation assailed him, but he did as he was told nevertheless, taking the camera outside into the corridor to start the filming there.

Hafdís and Thorgeir picked Heiðar up by the arms and legs. He stirred immediately and, after a moment's bewilderment, began to struggle.

'Stop it. What are you doing?'

Máni reassured him: 'It's only a bit of fun. Relax.'

Heiðar relaxed and they manhandled him out of the window with the help of Máni, who had climbed out ahead of them. Thorgeir was still holding the bottle that he passed round from time to time, but only Hafdís really drank much.

'Where are we going?' Matthías whispered.

'To the chapel,' Thorgeir replied.

Matthías followed along in the rear, filming the whole thing. At one point he thought he heard someone behind them. As if the branches had swished or a twig had snapped. He paused, scanning the dim woods flanking the path but couldn't see anything.

'Come on,' Thorgeir called in a low voice. 'Hurry up.'

'Can't you let me go?' Heiðar asked. 'This is ridiculous.'

'In a minute,' Máni said.

'Yes, let's stop for a moment,' Thorgeir said. 'Heiðar needs a drink.'

'I don't drink.'

'If you want to be with us, you will.'

'I don't want—'

'Don't be such a pathetic loser,' Thorgeir said.

Heiðar snorted. 'I don't want to. Does that make me a loser?'

'Fine, your choice. Then we'll carry on.'

They carted Heiðar along the path until they reached the chapel.

'*Voilà*,' Hafdís said, holding the door open so the boys could get in. They were greeted by stuffy air permeated with a strong smell of wood. They had been there earlier that week, sitting in the pews, listening to Magnús telling a story.

Heiðar, who had been fairly calm up to now, suddenly began to struggle wildly. He was breathing in short, hoarse gasps, tears pouring from his eyes.

'I … I can't breathe. I've got asthma. Exercise-induced asthma. I … I can't catch my breath. Let me go. For fuck's sake.' This was followed by more swearing and they stared at him, momentarily at a loss. Heiðar's reactions were so violent, as if he couldn't control himself.

'Let him go,' Máni ordered. 'What's wrong with you, Thorgeir? Just let him go. You said it was only a bit of fun. But the fun's over, OK?'

Thorgeir loosened his hold, and Heiðar tore himself free. But he was still lashing out and inadvertently landed a blow on Thorgeir, who reacted by shoving him, sending him toppling over backwards so that he hit his head on the front row of pews.

He was calmer now and his breathing had slowed, but he didn't look up. 'You fucking pig. You disgusting—'

'What did you say?' Thorgeir rubbed his chin where Heiðar had struck him. 'What did you call me?'

Matthías knew Heiðar had found a weak spot.

'I said you were a fucking pig,' Heiðar repeated, only now looking up.

'Don't say…' Matthías groaned but his warning was in vain.

Thorgeir closed in on Heiðar and for a moment it was as if time were standing still while simultaneously hurtling forwards.

NOW

Wednesday 16 December

Matthías opened another beer and sat down at the table again. One more small one wouldn't hurt. Cycling home afterwards wouldn't be a problem. The cold drink flowed down his throat into his stomach and he leant back on the bench in the coffee room until his head touched the wall, giving a great yawn.

After Christmas, he ought to take Ólöf away somewhere. They could go on a fun trip together and try to forget all their troubles. In the next few days there would be the funeral, followed by Christmas. It would be a tough time and, if he was honest, he didn't know how he was going to survive it. The pain inside him wasn't fake. He missed Hafdís.

Matthías hunched over, rubbing his eyes until they were red.

'Don't cry.'

Matthías jumped. When he looked up, there was somebody standing in front of him.

'What … Who are you? What are you doing here?'

'Me? I just came to say hi.' The woman smiled.

Matthías was silent. He wasn't afraid. She was only a woman, younger and smaller than him.

'You must have come to the wrong place,' he said, taking another sip of beer. 'Who were you looking for? Palli's next door, if it was him you were after.'

The woman shook her head. 'It's you I'm after.'

Matthías had the vague feeling he recognised her. As if he'd seen her face before, though he couldn't place it. Her features were somehow familiar.

'Oh, what about?'

'Because we've got things to talk about, don't you think? I mean, we've never managed to have a proper chat. Last time we met I was only, what, fourteen. At least I think I was fourteen at the funeral.' The woman furrowed her brow, then shook her head as if giving up. 'Oh, it's all so hazy.'

'I don't know what you're talking about,' Matthías said.

'No? Not yet? OK, let's see. The time before that, we saw each other at the summer camp at Vatnaskógur. Or maybe you didn't see me because you were busy with something else: with carrying my brother to the boat. That must have been a hassle? It looked like a real hassle. Oh, yes, and throwing him overboard. I remember hearing the splash as he sank. Hardly more than a little plop. For a long time afterwards I used to hear that noise every time I was about to fall asleep. And I'd picture him sinking under the water.'

Matthías gulped. He had completely forgotten that Heiðar had been at Vatnaskógur with his sister. A small, shy girl. Even more self-effacing than Heiðar, although she was always hanging around him.

'But I remember you and your mates, Matthías. I saw what you did.' The woman was still smiling and only now did he notice that she had something under her coat. At least, she was keeping one hand tucked inside it, as if concealing something.

'What did you see?'

'I saw you carry my brother out. I followed you to the chapel. I saw you going to the boat.'

Matthías swallowed. 'What ... what did you see?' he asked again.

'Everything.'

Matthías closed his eyes, experiencing a mixture of relief and guilt. It felt as though it was time the whole thing was exposed. 'Why didn't you tell?' he asked.

'I...' The smile disappeared. 'I tried. I didn't dare talk to the couple

I lived with as they'd never have listened. But I tried to talk to your dad. I thought the police would help me. Listen to me.'

'You talked to my dad?'

'But he said…' The woman gave a harsh laugh. 'He told me that if I breathed one word about this again he would make sure that I went to a much worse place than the one I was living in. I was only fourteen and I believed him. I was scared. But I'm not scared anymore.'

'It was an accident,' Matthías said. 'We didn't mean to…'

'Oh, you poor things.' The woman wrinkled her nose, as if in sympathy.

'I'm sorry, it wasn't meant to end like that.'

His words were pathetic. Weak. Matthías felt as if all the wind had been knocked out of his body. All he wanted now was to lie down on the floor and give up. He deserved all this. He deserved all the bad things that had happened to him in his life, and more.

'Wasn't it?'

'No, I … It wasn't me,' he said, then faltered because in reality it was him. He was the one who had cleaned up after Thorgeir. He was the one who had suggested the boat and rowed out onto the lake with Heiðar's body. He hadn't even checked that he was definitely dead. The only thing he'd been able to think about was his father and what the old man would do if he found out what his son had been involved in.

'No, I understand,' the woman said. 'Of course I understand. Your dad is a horrible man. And things are never meant to go wrong, only sometimes they do. Sometimes things end up in the worst way possible.'

She withdrew her hand from inside her coat and Matthías found himself staring at a large kitchen knife. Yet she went on talking. 'Take me, for example. I thought nothing would go wrong when we were sent to live with the couple who were supposed to be my parents. I was only five. Heiðar and I used to live with our grandparents, who stank like rotten cabbage and were about as much fun. I didn't realise how lucky I was, though, because they were at least kind to us. But we were so excited, you know? I was told that we'd have a new home and that the couple were nice. That was the word they used: "nice".

Matthías didn't answer. He wasn't exactly afraid – he was fairly confident that he would be able to overpower this woman. But the knife looked sharp and he didn't want to cut himself. Didn't want to cut her by accident.

'But they weren't nice.' The woman shook her head sorrowfully. 'Oh no, they weren't nice at all. But that didn't matter, because Heiðar was my family. He was all I needed, and as long as he was there, he made sure nothing bad happened to me. He protected me. But once he was gone…' She closed her eyes, her face twisting with pain.

Matthías saw his chance to grab the knife and prevent an accident. He leapt to his feet but in that instant the woman opened her eyes and shot out her arm, so fast that Matthías had no time to defend himself. He felt a sharp pain in his belly and fell back onto the bench.

The last thing he saw was her triumphant smile.

❂

Elma and Hörður drove slowly along the row of stables, looking out for Matthías's bike.

'There.' Elma pointed to a bicycle lying in front of one of the blocks. It had probably been propped against the wall before being knocked over by a gust of wind and was now lying on the gravel.

'Right, let's see if he's OK,' Hörður said, easing himself out of the car with extreme care.

They made their way along the block, Hörður lurching along on his crutch, then through a metal gate that wouldn't keep anyone out except the horses. The gravel crunched underfoot and from inside the stables Elma heard a whinny.

Hörður was right behind her, though moving more slowly than usual.

She opened the door with a loud squeak of hinges and was met by a powerful smell of earth, hay and urine.

Elma called inside but there was no answer. She turned to Hörður. 'I don't think there's anyone here.'

'There must be.'

Elma stepped inside and noticed that there was a light on in the little room at the back. Was it possible that Matthías had nodded off and that was why he wasn't answering his phone or reacting to her shouts? As she hurried past the stalls, the horses threw their heads up in alarm, showing the whites of their eyes, and one snorted so loud that she jumped. She opened the door of the room.

There was no one inside, just a beer can on the table and an open biscuit tin.

Then her gaze fell on the statue. A statue of Jesus with his arms stretched wide, not unlike the one she had seen on the altar at Vatnaskógur, only much smaller.

She moved closer and almost tripped over the legs on the floor.

'Matthías,' she exclaimed, stooping over him.

He lay half under the table and wasn't moving. As she bent closer she saw that his jumper was sodden with blood. Then, to her relief, he opened his eyes and tried to raise his head.

'Ólöf,' he murmured. 'Someone needs to look after ...'

❁

Matthías had lost consciousness by the time the ambulance finally arrived at the stables, but he was still alive. Elma just hoped the blood loss hadn't been as bad as she feared, though judging by the pool on the floor, it had to be pretty serious.

The only information she had been able to extract from him consisted of two words: 'his sister'.

Hörður was on the phone, telling the officers on guard duty to keep their eyes open. In addition to putting Íris Kjartansdóttir's house in Akranes under surveillance, they had police watching the flat Andrea and Freyja shared in Reykjavík.

The problem was, they didn't know what sort of car Íris was

driving or how long it was since she had left the stables. For all they knew they might have passed her on their way out of town.

Elma squatted on her heels, trying to think logically.

Íris had, in all likelihood, murdered two, if not three, of the people who had been involved in her brother's killing. Matthías was wounded and there was nothing they could do but hope for the best in his case. Elma couldn't bear to think of Ólöf losing both her parents. That mustn't happen.

Hörður came back, holding up his phone.

'No sign of her?' Elma asked.

He shook his head. 'No, but I've just been talking to Kári. They've found Andrea. She was at Íris's house here in Akranes.'

'Alive?'

Hörður nodded. 'But it was a near thing. It seems likely she's been drugged, but we can't say anything for certain yet. At least she's in good hands now. We'll just have to wait and see what happens.'

Elma closed her eyes, heaving a deep breath, and sent up a silent prayer that Andrea would survive. She'd been half hoping that the girl had gone into hiding because she'd been mixed up in events that were out of her control rather than being yet another victim of the killer.

Had Íris achieved everything she'd set out to do? Had she finally satisfied her thirst for revenge?

Now that Elma reckoned she had a pretty good handle on what lay behind the murders, she could understand Íris's desire for vengeance. On the other hand, the woman had clearly lost her grip. She was so eaten up by vindictive hatred that there was no way of predicting what she would do next. Who else she might want to get even with.

Elma shot to her feet so fast she made herself dizzy. 'I know where she's gone.'

❂

There was a dim, flickering light in one of the windows of the green house on Presthúsabraut. Elma pulled into the kerb and switched off the engine, all the while keeping her eyes fixed on the car parked next to the house. Telling Hörður to wait, she went over to the vehicle and peered in at the figure in the driver's seat.

Elma recognised her instantly. Recognised the cropped, white hair. It dawned on her simultaneously that the person Aron had seen outside the swimming pool after his lesson wasn't an old man, or an old woman, but a young woman with dyed hair. In the dark it was hard to distinguish grey hair from hair that was bleached white.

Íris Kjartansdóttir was none other than Freyja, the woman who shared Andrea's flat in Reykjavík. It was Íris who had received them at the flat when they first went there in search of Andrea. She must have adopted the name Freyja in memory of the family Labrador she and Heiðar had loved so much when they were children.

Now Íris was sitting in her car outside her childhood home but didn't appear to be on her way in.

❁

Íris couldn't bring herself to enter the house. Even after all she had done, she couldn't face the couple who were once her adoptive parents. She was too frightened. Despite all the years that had passed nothing had changed, and the mere sight of the house was enough to release a flood of memories.

Her eyes filled with tears but she wouldn't let herself look away. She forced herself to look at the house she had once called her home.

The last time she was here she had promised herself never to come back. She'd thought that by running away she could bury the memories. Forget everything.

It hadn't worked.

In the immediate aftermath of Heiðar's death she had meant to report what she had seen. When those kids had carried Heiðar to the boat, she had sat by the lake, waiting for them to go back to their rooms so she could call for help. But Thorgeir had spotted her and paused, telling the others to go on ahead. Then he had turned to the bush where she was hiding and said that if she told anyone, he would kill her, just as he had killed Heiðar.

But his words hadn't stopped her. When the police came, Íris had gone to the officer in charge and told him what she'd seen. But the man had turned out to be the father of one of the boys, so her pleas had fallen on deaf ears. Then she had remembered Heiðar's video camera, but when she went through his belongings, it wasn't there.

Back then, a fourteen-year-old confronted by an impossible situation, she had given up. She'd been exhausted. Devastated. Life had been hard enough already and she hadn't been able to cope with this new blow. She'd had no idea then that her life was about to get even worse and that for the next two years she would bear the brunt of all the terrible things that Heiðar had previously shielded her from.

At sixteen she had run away and never looked back.

The years had passed and she had got a job as a taxi driver, working nights because she couldn't sleep. Too haunted by memories. Then, one evening nearly a year ago, a vaguely familiar-looking man had got into her taxi. It was Máni. He had been drunk and doped up, and obviously hadn't recognised her. She had driven him home, helped him inside and shared a beer with him. Once he had fallen asleep, she had searched his flat but failed to find the tape. She hadn't killed him then, but the following weekend.

They had met in town and gone home together, and she had hung around until he had fallen asleep again. Earlier that week she had got hold of some Fentanyl from the dealer who usually supplied her with grass, and, once he was safely out for the count, she had squirted it up his nose using a nasal spray. She had read online that two millilitres would be fatal, so she had given him four, just to be certain. Then she had watched his ribcage rising and falling spasmodically as the drug took effect. Right up until he stopped breathing. Since Máni was obviously an addict, she was sure no one would suspect anything.

Then there was nothing left but to arrange the two statues she had brought along, paying at least that much respect to her brother's memory, before she made her exit.

As if she had never been there.

The next steps weren't as simple. The other three lived the kind of lives that made them harder to approach. She couldn't simply go up to them, introduce herself and expect them to befriend her. She wasn't the type they would admit to their social circle.

Thorgeir, at least, was single, which made him the most straightforward.

Íris had tried to attract his attention on social media but failed. It seemed she wasn't his type. After that, she had parked outside his block, pondering how to break in. She had gone as far as entering the staircase and trying his doorhandle, but of course it was locked.

She'd need a new plan.

It was then that she'd had a stroke of luck. She'd come across an advert posted by Máni's sister, who was looking for someone to rent a room in her flat.

The evening Íris killed Máni, he had blurted out the whole family sob story while he was drinking, lamenting that his father had left them, whining about the people who had told lies about him, and talking of his sister's bitter resentment. So Íris had been aware that Andrea had a reason to want revenge too. Not only that but she could see that Andrea was the type who might well catch Thorgeir's eye.

When Íris met Andrea at the café, she had introduced herself as Freyja and lied that she'd been a friend of her brother, Máni. Andrea had immediately offered her the room and a few weeks later, over a bottle of champagne and two joints, Freyja had cunningly steered the conversation in the direction she had planned.

Persuading Andrea to open up about her brother and the injustice he had suffered had been the easiest thing in the world. Before the night was over, Freyja had successfully planted the idea in Andrea's head that the best course of action would be to put pressure on

Thorgeir. Not directly, but to gain his trust first, then gradually coax him to reveal what had really happened.

Íris pretended to have discussed this with Máni, and brought up the subject of the video tape that she doubted anyone knew existed apart from her and her brother's killers. Andrea, full of enthusiasm for the idea, had declared that the video could restore Máni's reputation. She was determined to find the cassette and show it to the world. Or perhaps just to her father.

A long shot, but possible. Quite endearing, really, when Íris thought about it. Like the moment in a Hollywood movie when everyone realises that they had got it wrong and that the bad guy was on the side of the angels all along.

Andrea didn't suspect for a minute that Íris had her own plans.

Plans that had nothing in common with the happy endings in movies. She couldn't give a shit about other people's opinions, about what they thought or said. Once Íris got hold of the video, she had realised that it wouldn't be enough to show the world what had really happened. It wouldn't change anything: Heiðar could never be brought back to life.

All Íris wanted was revenge, and now at last she felt that justice existed in this cruel world. She had no regrets. She'd actively enjoyed watching the people who had ruined her life getting their comeuppance.

She pictured her brother and sensed that he was smiling at her. Her big brother. The only family she had ever had. She missed him more than words could express.

Thursday 17 December

Hörður was in a much better mood, free at last of the mental fog in which he had passed the last week. He called Elma into his office after a long day of interviews that had proved gruelling at times, especially when listening to Íris describe the violence she and her brother had been subjected to by their adoptive parents, Kjartan and Sigrún.

These were people he thought he knew. People he'd been acquainted with for years and always greeted when he met them in the shops or out and about.

But he wasn't going to let himself dwell on that now. He needed a respite from grief and trauma, from anything difficult. He had been invited to supper with his son that evening. His kids were well meaning, but, busy as they were with their own lives, they tended to forget about him at times.

Elma was regarding him warily, as if expecting to have her head bitten off. Had he really been that foul-tempered recently?

'What's up?' she asked.

He turned his screen towards her. 'Oh, it's just that I don't know how this works.'

'Facebook?' Elma asked.

Maybe he was imagining it, but he thought he saw her lips twitching.

'I want to create a … a…'

'A profile?'

'Yes, one of those.' Hörður cleared his throat. 'Do you know how to do it?'

Elma smiled. 'Sort of.'

'Oh, never mind. I'll work it out for myself.' He waved a hand dismissively.

'No, come on. I'll help you,' Elma said, coming round to his side of the desk. 'We just need to start by entering your email address here…'

A few minutes later Hörður had a profile and two friends. Both his kids. Next, he clicked on the search window, as Elma had taught him, and typed in Fríða's name.

❂

When Ottó entered the stables, the traces of his son's blood were still visible. An irregular dark stain on the floorboards under the table in the coffee room. He wet a cloth in the sink, then knelt down and began to scrub at it. As the wood grew damp, it released an iron smell.

Matthías's fate hung in the balance. He had lost a great deal of blood and was still in hospital. Meanwhile, Ottó's granddaughter, Ólöf, was staying with him and Jónína, but said little and mostly kept to her room. Her grandmother had given up inviting her to join them downstairs.

Ottó scrubbed until the sweat was pouring off his forehead, then went back to the sink to rinse out the cloth. It had turned the colour of rust and the water that dripped from it was red. His hands shook as he wrung out the cloth, and for a while he stood there, rigid, staring down the plughole.

They said it was the sister who had done this. Íris, she was called. Ottó remembered her vaguely. When the report had come in at the time that a boy had gone missing overnight in Vatnaskógur, he had gone straight to the scene. After seeing the empty boat adrift on the water, they had immediately feared the worst and called out divers to drag the lake. The boy's body had been found the very next day, contrary to all expectations. Lake Eyrarvatn was nearly thirty metres deep at its deepest point, but from what he could remember the boy had been found in the shallows.

The previous evening Matthías had come to him in tears and told him the whole story – or rather shown it to him. Ottó had watched the video Matthías had stolen from Heiðar's camera and seen the whole thing. His wife, too spineless to watch the recording all the way through, had walked out before the end.

They were alike, his son and his wife. Weak, relying on him to do the dirty work. To solve any problems that came up.

Was he supposed to have destroyed those kids' future because of a single mistake?

Perhaps he'd been unduly influenced by the fact that his son was involved, and also by the fact Thorgeir was one of the perpetrators. Neither he nor his sister could afford to have Thorgeir's mother's business go bust. Regardless of the truth, when the chips were down the answer was easy. He had done a lot of people favours over the years, and now it was vital to be guided by the interests of the many, not the few.

What difference did it make how Heiðar had died? Whether he had killed himself or been murdered, the result was the same. The boy was dead and, as far as Ottó was concerned, there had never been any question about how to react, about the right thing to do.

Once a few loose ends had been tied up, the matter had been simple. The pathologist's report had been delayed and Ottó had made it disappear as soon as it arrived. Besides, the findings were ambiguous and no one had asked any very difficult questions. The injuries could have been sustained earlier, and the water in the boy's lungs meant he could conceivably have drowned. But water could also end up in the lungs of those who were already dead when they were submerged, though usually in smaller amounts.

Magnús had kept quiet about the signs of a fight in the chapel, and Matthías had taken the video tape and promised to make it disappear.

But the boy's sister, that girl Íris, had been a problem. She had come to see him the day after the body was found, looking much younger than you'd expect for a fourteen-year-old, a flash of fear in her eyes when she spoke to him.

'I saw something the night he died,' she had whispered. 'I followed them.'

The words had been like a blow. Cold sweat had sprung out on his back and Ottó had had a momentary vision of his whole world collapsing.

He had pulled her aside, pretending he was willing to listen…

The wet cloth had grown cold in his hands. He dropped it into the sink and noticed that his palms had turned red. He had his son's blood on his hands. And not only his son's.

It hadn't been his proudest day. Afterwards, he had been ashamed of himself. Felt he had gone too far. He recalled the fear in the little girl's eyes, her chin trembling with despair.

It wasn't his custom to threaten children but as he had driven home later, he hadn't regretted anything. And when everything had gone according to plan, he knew he had acted in the only right way in the circumstances.

Sometime later, one of the boys, Máni, had wanted to come clean. But Ottó had taken steps to silence him. If he wanted to take the blame, fine, but not at the expense of Ottó or his family. When the rumours started circulating, Ottó had summoned Thorgeir, Hafdís and Matthías and ordered them to stick together. If Máni wanted to implicate himself in a crime, that was his affair. But he would face the music alone, with no evidence to back up his story.

Ottó had only done what was necessary to protect those close to him. To protect himself. When threatened, he would go on the war path and stop at nothing. Now he had been threatened again – and by his colleagues, of all people. In spite of his warning, she had charged ahead, that police woman, who thought she could get away with blackening his reputation. Blackening his family's reputation.

Ottó picked up the cloth again and squeezed it. Red liquid dripped into the sink and left its mark on the stainless steel.

'She's so sweet, Elma. Such a cutie-pie.' Alexander was lying on his front, cheek in hand, waving a rattle at Adda, who was far more interested in grabbing her cousin's nose than in the toy he was holding out to her.

'Yes, she's a cutie-pie, all right, just like you,' Elma said, ruffling his blond hair.

'I'm not a cutie-pie.' Alexander scowled.

'No, sorry, you're cute. Good-looking.'

'Oh, stop it.'

Alexander was eight now and the baby softness was disappearing from his features. He was in the third year at school, and his main preoccupation these days was with whether the thirteen Icelandic Yule Lads were real. He had told Elma confidentially that he didn't believe they were responsible for putting the presents in his shoe but thought they might still live in the mountains and occasionally come down to visit the towns and villages over Christmas.

'What were you thinking of doing with the kitchen?' Dagný asked, placing her empty coffee cup in the sink. She had come round with a pile of her boys' hand-me-down babygros and other clothes for Adda.

'Doing with it? Is there something wrong with the kitchen?' Elma looked at her sister doubtfully. 'I mean, I was maybe thinking of changing the units later or painting the cupboard doors, but I think it's quite cosy the way it is.'

'Well, I mean, don't you want to open it out into the sitting room? Put in an island and so on?'

'You mean, make it exactly like your house?'

Dagný's modern tastes had never appealed to Elma.

'No, just create more space. Let in some light.'

'I can't stand light.' Elma shuddered.

'Sorry, Dracula.' Dagný took a biscuit Sævar had baked earlier and popped it in her mouth. 'How could I forget that you'd rather live in a castle and stay awake at night?'

Elma shrugged. 'I've never understood this obsession with having everything open plan. I want to be able to retreat into the kitchen for a bit of peace. Not to have to put up with the noise of the TV everywhere I go.'

'Good point. I can't get the *Paw Patrol* theme tune out of my head. I've had it on the brain for years now.'

'"*Marshall, Skye*—"' Elma began to sing.

'Don't,' Dagný interrupted, in the tone Elma remembered so well from their childhood. *Don't touch my things. Don't go in my room.* Luckily, the sisters' relationship had improved over the years.

Elma laughed. 'Adda will never be allowed to watch programmes like that. We're going to raise her on quality French children's TV dramas and documentaries about animals.'

'And only let her listen to Mozart?'

'Yes, and let her eat nothing but organic spinach and bulgur wheat.'

'Good thing you've got it all sorted out.' Dagný stood up. 'But don't forget that every time Adda comes round to be babysat at my place, we'll stuff her with chocolate biscuits and ice cream.'

'Karma coming back to bite me?' Elma had been guilty of stuffing her two nephews with enough sweets over the years.

'You said it. Right, lovie, we need to get going.'

Alexander stroked Adda's head in parting, and the little girl rewarded him with a broad, gap-toothed grin, her face radiant.

'Don't overdo it, Dagný,' Elma said. 'Christmas will still happen, even if you don't get round to baking six different kinds of biscuits.'

'You know, I'm not so sure about that.'

Dagný was joking, but Elma was beginning to realise that her sister's perfectionism was not something to be envied.

'You've had more than enough to do yourself,' Dagný said. 'I hope things are quieter now?'

'Yes, they're winding up.' Elma had been attending interviews for the last two days and the facts of the case were more or less clear at last. She was confident that charges would be brought shortly.

'So you can relax?' Dagný asked.

Elma surveyed the chaotic state of the flat. Sævar had unpacked the moving boxes but also bought a load of Christmas decorations and lights, which he was in the middle of putting up.

She didn't mind.

They had agreed to celebrate Christmas at Elma's parents' house this year. Nevertheless, Sævar was preparing some ambitious dessert and had purchased what looked like a blow torch that he claimed was for caramelising sugar. Elma wasn't going to get drawn into anything apart from playing with Adda, eating, and bingeing on TV. She might even fit a book or two into this packed programme of idleness.

'I can relax,' she confirmed, smiling.

'Good.' Dagný crouched down to tie her younger son Jökull's shoelaces.

Elma said goodbye to Dagný and waved to the boys until they were in the car. Adda started waving just as Elma shut the door. Typical.

Sævar had gone out to do the food shopping, so she and Adda had the house to themselves for a little while. That hadn't happened in ages.

Elma sat down with Adda beside the toy box and watched as the little girl grabbed her cuddly unicorn and gave it a big hug.

Although the sequence of events was clear now, there were still various elements that required further attention. For example, it might prove necessary to disinter Heiðar's body in light of what emerged in the video, then reopen the case and question anyone still alive who was implicated in the murder. In practice, that applied only to Matthías, who was still in hospital but no longer in a critical condition.

It looked almost certain that his father, ex-police inspector Ottó, had covered up for his son and his friends, and Elma sincerely hoped he would be forced to answer for his actions.

Similarly, she hoped Kjartan and Sigrún would receive their just deserts after listening to Íris's account of her life with them. Prosecution would probably prove more difficult in their case, though. The abuse hadn't been sexual in nature, but the punishments Íris described had involved such a criminal level of brutality that Elma had found it hard to listen at times. As long as Heiðar had been alive, he had shielded his sister and borne the brunt of it himself, but after he died, there had been no one there to protect her anymore.

Íris had described how the idea of exacting revenge had crystallised in her mind after a chance meeting with Máni one night while driving her taxi. Elma realised she had never asked Freyja what she did for a living, only recalled that she'd said she worked nights. An oversight that Elma was ashamed of.

But now her role in the case was mostly complete and she could breathe again. Allow herself to look forward to Christmas. It helped that Andrea was out of danger too. Elma was eager to speak to her once she was well enough, but Andrea was still too weak after being kept drugged and unconscious for twelve days.

She supposed Íris hadn't been entirely lacking in mercy. She had only murdered the people she felt deserved it.

Adda reached out her arms to Elma. She was tired, but at least she'd been good about playing, despite having become very clingy recently. Constantly wanting to be with Elma or to be carried around by her.

'I missed you too,' Elma said, kissing the plump cheek.

As she did so, she heard the snap of the letterbox in the hall. It was a strange time of day to receive post. It was nearly suppertime and the postman was rarely out this late. Perhaps it was a Christmas card, though they received fewer of those every year.

Elma went into the hall and saw an A4-sized envelope on the floor. Unmarked.

She opened the door and peered out but couldn't see anyone. Only traffic and some pedestrians in the distance.

The envelope contained two pieces of paper, and Elma saw at once that they were part of a police report. After reading the names, she realised it was a report about the car accident in which Sævar's parents had died. Why on earth would someone send them this?

She sat down with Adda in her arms and began to read.

Several sentences had been underlined. The first was: 'There was a man in the front seat and a woman in the back seat.'

The next was: 'It is unclear who was driving the vehicle.'

Five people had died in the collision. A man and a woman in one car – Sævar's parents, in other words. A young couple and a baby in the other car. A little girl of not even one year old. The only person to survive was the young couple's eight-year-old son.

Elma felt a knot in her stomach when she thought about the little boy who had lost his whole family in one fell swoop. But the knot also had another cause. This was something Sævar had never told her. He had always been so tight-lipped about the accident, saying as little as he could get away with. In fact, he hardly ever spoke about his parents.

'It is unclear who was driving the vehicle.'

Had anyone else been in the car apart from Sævar's parents?

Elma was suddenly in no doubt about who had sent her the report and why. She had been given a warning but hadn't realised who it was directed at. She hadn't realised that by exposing Ottó, she would also be exposing various other things.

Elma heard a car pull up in the space outside.

Sævar was home. She hastily stuffed the papers into the back of one of the kitchen cupboards before opening the door to greet him.

Wednesday 23 December

Kristjana had finally been given permission to go back to her summer house. She drove there on St Thorlákur's Mass, having bought herself a carton of grapefruit juice and some dried fish to chew on while she listened to golden oldies on Classic FM.

Halfway there, she feared the jeep was about to give up the ghost, but somehow it limped on. The old wreck had one year left before it would classify as a vintage vehicle, but as long as it did its job, Kristjana saw no reason to invest in a new one.

Money had never been important to her for its own sake, but for what it symbolised. Although only she had been aware of the fortune in her bank account, the knowledge had put heart into her, making her feel she was worth something.

Of course, she knew that money was intrinsically worthless: 'Blessed are the poor in spirit, for theirs is the kingdom of heaven.' But she wasn't perfect, and Reynir had valued money above all else, even above God's word, and she had wanted to impress him. Even if he was only able to watch from beyond the grave.

She hadn't chosen this path to riches herself, merely continued what Reynir had started when Guðrún and Bárður invited him to join in their scheme. Put the extra money in the till every day to make the turnover look as if it was bigger than it really was. So things had gone on for years, and naturally Kristjana had been rewarded for her part, paying the money into a Swiss bank account, as a reminder of what she had achieved.

If only Reynir could see her now.

By the time she parked at the cabin, it was pitch-dark among the trees. The summer house loomed large and menacing in the gloom, but Kristjana resolutely pushed away any feeling of dread. She had never been able to bear this place. It was where Reynir had given full rein to his temper. No nosy neighbours to hear when he beat the living daylights out of his wife and son. He could drink and be himself – the violent thug he really was.

An alien smell greeted Kristjana when she opened the door. She hadn't been here in a long time. As she went inside, she kept her eyes averted from the bedroom where she and Reynir had slept, and Thorgeir had died. She had no intention of sleeping in there.

Instead, she went straight to the kitchen, where she opened one of the bottom cupboards and groped around for the bottle that should be right at the back. It was still there. While she was taking a long swig from the neck, she thought the house had a different atmosphere now from before. As if a tiny part of Thorgeir had remained behind. The good part.

Her son had had to put up with so much.

After a few more hefty swigs, Kristjana opened a drawer and found a torch. Then she went back outside and down the steps until she reached the hatch cut into the deck. She could just about stand upright in the crawl space under the house.

Kristjana located the spot in the right-hand corner at the back, picked up a spade and began to dig.

The grave was shallow but the frozen ground made the job much harder, and she was soon in a muck sweat. It wasn't long, though, before the first bone appeared, then the next.

Bending down with an effort, she picked one up. It was an odd feeling to think that this was all that was left of him – the man who had terrorised her for so many years.

It was in September twenty-six years ago that she had killed Reynir. That day her husband had been drinking from the moment they arrived at the cabin. After supper, Thorgeir had failed to clear away his plate and Reynir had gone berserk. Kristjana had watched him grab a broomstick and start belabouring their son. Calling him a fucking pig and bringing the stick down on his back over and over again.

Until she had seized the kitchen knife and put an end to it.

Kristjana knew it wasn't in the spirit of Christianity to repay evil with evil, but she had waited so long. Waited and hoped that the Lord would deal with Reynir, that He would free her and Thorgeir from that terrible man, but in the end she hadn't been able to wait any longer. Afterwards, she had prayed to God for forgiveness for her sins and felt in her heart that He understood and that He had indeed forgiven her.

Kristjana gathered up the bones and put them in a plastic sack she had brought along. She hadn't yet decided what she was going to do with them but couldn't face the thought of having Reynir there a moment longer.

It was time to get rid of him once and for all.

ACKNOWLEDGEMENTS

Every summer when I was a kid, I used to go to a Christian summer camp called Ölver. I still know all the lyrics to the songs we used to sing and I have very fond memories of my time there. In *Boys Who Hurt* the idea was to explore how far people are willing to go when they are part of a group, and I wanted to do this by writing about something that happened in a summer camp for boys that still haunts those involved in adulthood. So I did my research and went to a summer camp in Iceland called Vatnaskógur, and there I was shown around by a very helpful staff member who I'm very thankful to. I did, however, receive a phone call when the book was already at the printer, informing me that other members of staff at Vatnaskógur were worried about having the summer camp in a crime book. I do hope I have managed to show Vatnaskógur in a good light, and would like to emphasise that the book is, of course, fiction, and also that nothing like that ever happened when I was staying at Ölver.

As always, the book turned out to be about a lot of other things too, and I think the English name, *Boys Who Hurt*, describes the theme of the book very well. And I like the ambiguity of the title, because boys who hurt, hurt.

I'm always thanking the same people, but there is a reason for it. I owe them all a lot. The book might exist without them, but it sure as hell wouldn't reach readers without the help of the amazing people behind me.

I am very lucky to be published by the awesome team at Orenda. Karen, West and all the people that work hard on each book: I am so grateful for everything you do. Thank you to my translator, Vicky

Cribb. She's the reason that my books are much better in English than in Icelandic.

I want to thank David Headley, my agent, for getting my books out into the world. Never in a million years did I think that my books would be translated into more than twenty languages, and that's all because of him. We always have so much to celebrate!

Thank you to my Icelandic publishers, Veröld, who have to go through the most difficult stage of publishing a book: the first few weeks, waiting for the reviews. That never gets any easier, so it's valuable to have a good support and words of encouragement when I need them.

Thank you to Gunnar, my husband – my first reader and the person who has gone through all the ups and downs of the last years with me. Everything is so much better with you!

And finally thank you to my readers and all those who have posted, shared and enjoyed my books. Because of you I've got this amazing job where I get to make up stories all day. I hope those stories will be worthy of your time.